Beyond the Pale

ELANA DYKEWOMON

Published in 2000 by Onlywomen Press, Limited, *Radical Feminist Lesbian publishers*, 40 St Lawrence Terrace, London W10 5ST, England.

ISBN 0-906500-63-X

British Library/Cataloguing-in-Publication Data.
A Catalogue record for this book is available from the British Library.

Published by arrangement with Press Gang Publishers, Vancouver, B.C., Canada

Cover design © Tyra Till

Typeset by Chris Fayers Associates, Lower Soldon, Holsworthy, Devon.
Printed and bound in Great Britain by Mackays of Chatham plc.

Historical note: The public figures (politicians, organizers, writers) named throughout *Beyond the Pale* are based on historical record. The women mentioned in connection with the Women's Trade Union League, with the exception of the character Lena Reznikoff, all existed. Chava Meyer, Gutke Gurvich, Dovid Greenbaum, Rose Petrovsky, their friends and extended families, and all "bosses" with the exceptions of Harris and Blanck, are entirely fictional. Any resemblance to persons living or dead is coincidental.

Parts of this novel were first published in *Sinister Wisdom* and *Bridges*.

For my mother, Rachel

Acknowledgments

It's been ten years between the time Chava's voice first spoke to me and the publication of *Beyond the Pale*. During that time I worked on the novel in fits and starts, researched continuously and spent months concentrating at various writers' retreats. Although I have worked with words all my life, nothing prepared me for the time and dedication *Beyond the Pale* required. Many people made the work possible, either through their direct help with research and revision or through their forbearance and support along the way:

Dolphin Waletzky, Evelyn Averbuck, Irena Klepfisz, Jo Keroes, Judith Katz, Maxine Chernoff, Myung Mi Kim, Susan Jill Kahn and Susan Levinkind read and commented on various versions of the manuscript. Their thoughtful work contributes to every page, and their time, patience and generosity were true gifts. Working with Barbara Kuhne, Press Gang's co-publisher, and my talented editor, Nancy Pollak, has been a real pleasure. And many thanks to my dedicated publisher in England, Lilian Mohin.

The transliteration of Yiddish words generally follows the guidelines of the YIVO Institute for Jewish Research, and was provided by Irena Klepfisz, whose help with the glossary and pronunciation guide, which come after the text, was also invaluable. Any inconsistency or the persistence of old forms of transliteration are entirely my responsibility.

Adrienne Rich, Alice Malloy, Annelise Orleck, Beth Davidson, Betty Dudley, Brighde Mullins, Casey Fisher, Claire Kinberg, Dan Nachman, Ellen Rifkin, Eva Schocken, Frieda Feen, Gloria Anzaldúa, Hadas Weiss, Harvey Nachman, Hilde Waletzky, Jan Hoffman, Jasmine Marah, Joan Drury, Joan Nestle, Judith Masur, Judy Freespirit, Judy Moore, Laura Munter, Lilian Mohin, Linda Shear, Linnea Almgren, Lisa

Edwards, Louise Turcotte, Margaret Sloan Hunter, Melanie Kaye/Kantrowitz, Michal Brody, Michelle Cliff, Miriam Inanna Bat Dharma, Nancy Nordhoff, Nina Wouk, Rachel Nachman, Red She Bear, Rose Weisberg, Ruth Rischin, Sabena Stark, Sally Koplin, Sally Savitz, Samara, Sandy Polishuk, Susan Goldberg, Susan Shulman, Susan Stinson, Terre Hill, Teya Schaffer, Toby Finkelstein, Tova, Tracy Moore, Tryna Hope and Windflower provided me with a variety of resources, research, support, shelter, inspiration and conversation without which I could never have completed this work.

Caryatis Cardea took over the complete operation of *Sinister Wisdom* three times during the period we were co-editors, enabling me to write and do crucial research. Her work on *Sinister Wisdom*, along with Jamie Lee Evans and Sauda Burch and a host of volunteers, helped make mine possible. One of the effects of Akiba Onáda-Sikwoia's becoming the new editor of *Sinister Wisdom* was to free me to concentrate on this book, for which I am deeply grateful.

Helen Mintz has performed a scene from the first half of *Beyond the Pale* since 1993 – the first time I saw her bring the characters to life, I cried. I am thankful for the opportunity she gave me to be a member of the audience.

Cottages at Hedgebrook, The Helene Wurlitzer Foundation and Norcroft Writing Retreat for Women granted me residencies at pivotal moments in the process. My thanks to those who make these writing retreats possible. I hope every lesbian writer can have the privilege of experiencing the demanding solitudes these places offer.

My appreciation to librarians and archivists everywhere, and particularly those who maintain the collections at The Lesbian Herstory Archives, YIVO Institute for Jewish Research, The Tamiment Archives at New York University, the Jewish Library of San Francisco and The New York Historical Society Library, where much of the research for *Beyond the Pale* was done.

And to my intimate friends, Dolphin Waletzky and Susan Jill Kahn, and my research assistant and beloved partner, Susan Levinkind, who saw me through every step of the way, my heart.

Part One

A Tiny Shofar

I am original alphabet.
Letters unfurl
from my spine
cutting ciphers in
my mother's cells.
I scan my fate
on the wrinkled walls
of that first room
clenching
in my red fist
scraps of prophecy.

In Kishinev the river Byk is frozen. The oven is stuffed with coal, yet Miriam lies shivering on a small bed in one of the few stone houses on Gostinaya Street, cursing the walls: "Everything is ripped out. Stone – why did you let yourself be cut off the mountain, for what? I can't, I can not go through this again. Stone – "

Gutke pulls Miriam's dark, damp hair back, ties and tucks it behind her neck. Her fingertips push into the soft furrows of Miriam's forehead, as if she could smooth the strain away. One of Gutke's eyes is as black as Miriam's, the other flecked gold. Miriam stares into one eye and then the other, working out a puzzle, letting the midwife's gaze travel inside her, all the way to the second heartbeat. Her breathing calms.

Gutke pours wine from a jar onto a rag and runs it over Miriam's lips. "Go on, say what you like. It's just me here, listening. Women bring

forth in sadness. We fulfill the word, God's judgment on Eve."

"I'm not Eve. I don't deserve this pain." She clutches at Gutke's stained skirt.

Gutke shrugs. "You know yourself pain is never a matter of deserving. We'll get through this together. Watch my eyes."

"What are you giving her?" Rabbi Isaac stops pacing, grabbing hold of the doorposts and pushing his chest into the room, bending his head to avoid the beam.

"Just wine."

"She's raving already. Only give her water."

"Rabbi, no offense, I do this all week long. Perhaps a psalm would calm the house. You could find just the right one, nu? Come and read to us, or else I'll call you if I need your help."

Isaac thumps into the other room, kicking up dust from the packed dirt floor. Why Gutke again? There are other midwives, even his mother Malka volunteered, but Miriam has to have the half-Jew. Stubborn. That's how they always argue, back and forth: *You have to be so stubborn. – Me, stubborn? It's you – .*

He should be in shul now, close to the stove, discussing the week's midrash. He could go anyway. No one would fault him. The other men would say he was every inch a rabbi – his wife is home giving birth, but does that stop him from honoring God?

The boys are at their lessons, baby Esther with his sister Shendl. Still, what if Miriam should need him? Leaving her alone with Gutke, that wouldn't be wise. Of course you cannot blame the woman for her mother's sins. No one ever complains about Gutke as a midwife, but she could be working enchantments. It's up to a rabbi to make sure there's no opening for Lilith. All right, all right, maybe Gutke is right, a psalm. He sighs, noticing how the Book of Job precedes the Book of Psalms. Everything is infused with meaning, certainly the word of God. Here is his message to bend his spirit to the event.

Gutke hears mumbling from the other room and is relieved. Miriam presses her eyelids shut, rolls her head away from the wall, opens them again. While Isaac stood in the doorway, Miriam could hear every word he thought. Everything is clearer, magnified when you give birth – or maybe when Gutke comes. A mixed blessing. Miriam gave in to Isaac when she had her second child. The Jewish midwife, he insisted. Gutke's a good Jew, she said to him. But he had just received his appointment at the guild congregation; he was so nervous. She wanted to tell him it was vanity, but she didn't dare.

Sweet, I thought it was sweet, how proud and vain he was about me, Miriam thinks. Then Chaim died a week later. Always you learn to hold your own in suffering. How else? Some of the women won't have Gutke in their house; they're afraid. So she sees things when the baby comes. Not much really, or maybe she sees more than she says and just gives a clue. I like clues. I like to know what I can. But maybe she only makes things up – Esther, she said, would be kasha and lace. Kasha, that's easy enough to predict for a girl. My Abraham, he'll be an olive branch in Zion. I could have told her that. But Daniel, what did she say about Daniel? He will cover himself in ink as a drunkard flings himself into the wine barrel. What a thing to tell a mother – *oh no* –

Suddenly Miriam's eyes are very wide, her breathing hard as a blacksmith's hammer. She sits straight up.

"Better to sit up. It hasn't been so long. You see, your body remembers," Gutke says. "Just follow your body. For me you shouldn't be modest. Sitting up will make it easier. Turn sideways on the bed, and I'll put a pillow against the wall for you. It's just a little while longer." Miriam's contractions are coming quickly. Gutke wedges two chairs against the bed. Miriam, pressing her bare feet against the wood, is grateful for the resistance. Her legs are wrapped in cotton cloth; the featherbed drapes around her like a shawl. But still she shivers, the cold reaching for her through the walls.

Gutke frowns.

"What? Is something wrong with my baby?"

"It's too soon to tell. We know it's coming feet first." The opening is three fingers wide now. Miriam always stretched well, no need for cutting. But the shape of the mound is wrong, not round as a fist pounding on the door of the world, the way it should be. And the smell is slightly off. Gutke knows the entire catalog of scent. She likes this smell, the condensation of woman – urine, sweat, blood, secretions that ease the baby's way. She can remember how Miriam smelled with Esther, strong, simple. Now this is just a little wrong, smoky, almost. Because the baby is coming backwards or something else? Gutke puts a knotted, dry rag in Miriam's hand.

"You have to trust me; keep your legs open just as they are. The baby is going to need a little more help than usual."

Miriam sweats and then gets clammy. She gives a shriek. "My kishkes – it's scraping them out!"

The opening seems to wink at Gutke, giving her hope. Yes, the baby is upside down, but exactly, which is better than sideways. Here's a

11

tiny foot, like a flag, surrendering, and here's the other. She puts her hands on the feet. The head you must not yank, yet everything depends on getting the head through fast.

"Breathe and push. You call that a push? Your baby Esther could push harder. Okay, take a deep breath. I'm going to pull and you're going to push." It hurts much more this way. Head first, the opening is widest in the beginning. Then it's easy and the mother can rest a little as the baby makes its way towards the light. But this – Gutke can feel the pain in her own pelvis.

"Give a little yell, that's good. Good, yell again. The baby just doesn't want to let go of you, coming into this world, and why not?" One hand wraps around the infant's thighs and as Miriam pushes, she drags, supporting the baby's back with her other hand, angling the shoulders slightly. Miriam's skin begins to tear and Gutke has no time to take care of it.

"Almighty God I can't stand this I can't – ." Miriam's lips are swollen, blood suffusing their brownness, turning almost pink. Coming out, the baby is like a noodle, stretching, long, thin and then – yoke and bulb, shoulders and head sticking.

"Push, Miriam, push. You're strong, you want your baby to live." Gutke, still calm, moves her hand to hold the cord tight against the body, so it doesn't tangle. She gives a good twisting pull. The baby's chin is coming out now, face down towards the floor. "Once more," and the baby is out. Gutke gives it a first somersault, keeping the cord away from the neck.

"Thank God." Miriam is gulping, moaning. Isaac's prayers are louder, frightened and sharp. But in this moment Gutke hears nothing. This is the best, this absolute silence before the baby cries. And then the cry itself, a new voice, a tiny shofar announcing its own first year. Gutke and Miriam breathe out together as soon as the baby wails. Miriam is ragged and bleeding at the base of the birth opening, but for only half an inch.

"It's all right?"

Gutke smoothes the baby's face, spreading the buttery secretion over legs, belly, shoulders.

"It's all right. You have a baby girl, born on the twenty-second of Shevat, 5649, a Tuesday, so ugly that if you show her to the river, it will stay frozen and spring won't come this year." That should keep the evil eye off this long, good-looking child, Gutke thinks.

Miriam laughs, dry, flat, grateful. The baby's all right! She can feel it

on her belly; her hands find her daughters' hands; she circles them in her fist, learning her daughter by the shape, feel, hunger of her. Miriam shudders, sweat covers the sheets, the shivering stops. Gutke clamps the cord now, the way she has hundreds of times, when the blood is quiet, not rushing between mother and newborn. She makes the cut clean, ties up the end close to the baby's navel, leans over Miriam, wipes her forehead, puts a little more wine on her lips.

Then she threads a needle with thick, special thread she makes herself for this purpose. She waits. Miriam's arm tightens around her daughter as she grunts out the afterbirth. Quickly Gutke sews the tear.

"It hurts."

"This is my fault. I hope you will forgive me – I didn't think I needed to open the skin. Now it hurts a little more. You will have to stay in bed at least a few days so it heals well and doesn't tear again. Your mother-in-law, maybe you'll have her in to watch the children? You'll do this so I can redeem my conscience?"

"For your conscience. It will be a mitsve for me." Miriam is stroking her tiny daughter's head, patting the circle of black hair.

Gutke smiles as she wipes Miriam clean, her thighs, her lips, the stitches, the underside of her cheeks. With her palm pressed against Miriam's vagina, she closes her eyes and sees water as big as the Black Sea. Bigger. Not unusual, she sees this ocean often. But now the water is bright, as if lit from underneath, sharp and steaming, too hot to touch. For a moment she is dizzy. Enough, she says to the water, enough. Then she pulls the sheets up and rinses her hands in the basin. Miriam holds her baby and watches Gutke. When Gutke turns back to her, she grabs her hand, pressing almost as hard as when she was bearing down.

"What did you see for my daughter?"

"A long, difficult journey. But she will be loyal and have courage."

"Courage?" Miriam runs her tongue over dry lips. A little more wine, why not? "Is that some kind of curse? Every Jew has courage."

" 'Some will go wandering; some will stay home.' I don't write the Book of Life, I only read it and, anyway, from a great distance. It may mean nothing."

"I'm very tired," Miriam says, moving her fingers in Gutke's palm as if she were trying to decipher some code imprinted there.

"It's time for you to rest now." She runs her hands through Miriam's hair. They breathe together, slow, intimate. "Rabbi Meyer," she calls as she straightens up. "There is a new girl in your house!"

Isaac hunches through the doorway in an instant. He reaches for the hand that isn't cradling the baby, but Miriam twines her fingers in his wiry beard instead. He shouldn't touch her now; she's still unclean from giving birth. Later he'll take a purifying bath and pray.

"I want to call her Chava, after my grandmother's sister," Miriam says. "She will be a friend to us. She came out backwards, Isaac, can you imagine? But she's all right, she's fine. My little Chavele."

"Backwards? So that's what all that yelling was about. I thought you were dying, kayn ayen-hore." He laughs and pulls her hand out of his beard. "So, Chava. Chava is fine. She's your daughter, very good looking in an ugly sort of way." Two boys, two girls. He accepts. He is good at accepting but he also worries that maybe he is not as powerful as before, not as favored by God.

"Yes, yes she is. I am going to fall asleep soon. Remember to pay Gutke."

His hand moves shyly across his daughter's black hair as if he were afraid of being burned, then he rests his palm around her skull. Quickly he pulls back and slaps the knuckles of his fist. It will be all right. There's plenty. Miriam could have another ten children. God would provide. Girls, girls are all right – it's good for Esther to have a sister now; she'll like that.

Gutke clears her throat.

"Well," he considers the solid, serious woman in front of him. Certainly his mother could not have delivered a baby that came into the world backwards. "Everything is good then?"

"Yes, and the charge is three rubles."

"Three? For a girl? It was only two for Daniel."

"Now it is 1889, Rabbi Meyer, and Daniel was easy. I'm not even charging you extra for the scare your daughter gave us."

"Chavele," Miriam is singing, "little Chavele, you don't know, your mother brought you into the world beside a wall of stone. Little Chavele, little Chavele, wine is sweet and stone is hard, the world is cold and the river frozen, may you live to walk among the plum trees blooming."

"What's that she's singing to the baby?" Isaac asks.

"Just nonsense, a comforting song," Gutke answers, putting the rubles in her skirt pocket.

"Chavele, my baby Chavele, drink now, the world is changing."

The words for it

The Christians say we are coming into the twentieth century, the beginning of a new age for humanity. May it please God that it be a better age than the last. I, Gutke Gurvich, have had the great good fortune to live these forty-one years. I want to hold my memories, bind them up as individual stalks of wheat are gathered in the field, that they may be part of the harvest of my life. I am a simple woman who has seen the very center of creation repeatedly as I have tended women in birth. Never having given a child of my own, I choose to create in Yiddish for myself and my few dear friends. Like Glükel of Hamlin, it may be that my words will be found by later generations, and help them understand how it was for us in Bessarabia. But if future generations think it perverse for a poor woman to have the chutzpe to write down her own life – well, much of my life would seem perverse, depending on the judge. I spend my days taking care of others. On these pages I do as I please.

What I like to write about best is Pesah Kohn, my great benefactor, may she be singing in heaven at this very minute. But like every woman, I must begin with my own mother.

My mother, of blessed memory, Feygele Gurvich, of Kamenka on the Dniestr, a mottled reed of a woman, was given in marriage when she was just thirteen years old and the boy fourteen. Think of it! As if the family couldn't wait to get rid of her. But it was a common thing in those times, only a minute after the death of the Tsar Nicholas.

The boy was the son of an innkeeper who had good relations with all the local police, so his family managed to keep him from the draft. Sometimes kidnappers – soldiers or vagabonds who'd get a ruble for their trouble – took boys as young as eight and shut them up with

priests, doing who knows what to them so they would forget they were Jews. If you said for one moment, just to make them stop yammering, "All right, I'll go by your church," that was it. No turning back, ever. A terrible thing, the family had to mourn for you as if you had died.

My mother's family was poor but very pious, somewhere a rabbi among the distant relatives, though my grandfather was just a man who sold a little this, a little that, a peddler. All my mother ever said was that he smelled like fish. Feygele was the oldest daughter and there was a younger one, by a year, who was a beauty. They wanted to make sure my mother was all set so they could get an even better catch for my aunt.

Of course Feygele didn't know her husband before the marriage, how could she? She was always working from the time she was nine. It was a very good match for her. The boy was a scholarly type and everyone said she was very lucky, since her family couldn't make a dowry for her except for two goats, a sack of potatoes and a few rubles. They agreed to give the boy the traditional food and lodging while he was studying. So they married. He moved in and she went on as before, taking in washing to help the family.

For six months they lived this way. I could never find out if they even knew each other as husband and wife. By the time I was old enough to ask, my mother had made a complete legend of him: good, kind, smart, shy, the prophets would drink honey from his lips. They were children, only, walking in adult clothes. Sometimes it just goes that way. You start walking around in your mother's big shoes and the next time you look down, your feet are all swollen and sore, the shoes barely fit. Then it's too late to say you were just pretending, am I right?

Since before the time of Catherine, Jews have lived the same way in Russia. We bend under one tsar, straighten up a little under another. So Tsar Nicholas died, my mother married the innkeeper's son and the innkeeper, maybe he thought he didn't have to bribe the police anymore for protection. Of course anytime you think you're safe from the authorities is an illusion. Seeing how much suffering a Jew can take is a game to them. And Jews – they turn away. I've heard the Gentile women talk about their Christ. "Turn the other cheek," he said. If he said that, then it must be true he was a Jew.

In Kamenka some soldiers came by, made a joke about the Jews. Feygele's young husband defended his faith. They laughed. "We need to show this Jew what it means to be a man, a Christian man! He looks eighteen. What is he doing, carrying books, when he should be

defending the motherland!" And they took him away. Maybe they hadn't heard Nicholas was dead and the draft had changed, maybe they just wanted a Jew to polish their boots. So into the army he went. His innkeeper father tried to buy him out, spent I don't know how many rubles, but the rubles went into the pocket of the provincial governor and my mother's husband stayed in the army.

By then she was maybe fifteen. Feygele did everything a pious, faithful wife should do. She embroidered beautiful lace for her sister's dowry. One day by the river, while she did the washing – hours this took, she had washing not just for her family but for maybe two or three others – a man forced her. When I was young I often tried to imagine that man, my father. Was he a Jew, a Gypsy, a Russian, a tramp, a magistrate? My mother never even whispered it in her sleep. It's an odd gift I have, to see bits of the future but never any part of the past. I remember well, though, what I've been told.

She came back late from the river. All the laundry was clean; that's how my mother was. But her own clothes were torn and she was wringing her hands. My poor little mother, Feygele. Of course, her mother, Bathsheba, found out what was what. It was close to the time for the sister's marriage and no one wanted to spoil the occasion. Feygele was sent to her father's grandparents' home in Orgeyev, where I was born. She told them she never saw her attacker's face. They had sympathy for her, a little, despite the shame, because she was so pious and sweet. But they were very poor and as soon as I was born, my mother shleped back to Kamenka, thinking now that her sister was married, everything would be all right. And still she thought her husband would come back and be my father. You can imagine what happened. It was only a poor shtetl of tormented Jews, and torment is like a river forced underground. Up it comes like a fountain somewhere else. The slightest breach of rules, Jews jump on each other like dogs on a piece of rotten meat. That's what happened to my mother.

I don't think she ever had much more use for men than I do. Her husband was only a hope, a little flame on a candle far away, the one who would save her. Maybe five years went by; if her husband had escaped the army, someone perhaps told him what happened to Feygele and he didn't come back. She was without divorce papers and all the town knew she had a bastard daughter, a mamzer. Worse yet, when they looked at my different eyes, one black, one gold, it was like a curse to them. They wouldn't let their children play with me and if,

God forbid, a hailstorm should break their windows, they blamed my mother for bringing in the evil eye. The village was too small. Not even the women who had sympathy could befriend her. Feygele was alone, swept into a corner by her family.

Around the time I was five, she finally understood this was no life for us. She had nothing. Bathsheba, her mother, gave her a pair of brass candlesticks, some black bread and dried apples, a featherbed. My bobe made me little bags of salt for my pockets and to wear around my neck. Bobe was always singing and talking, but on the day we left, she couldn't bring herself to open her mouth, not even to say goodbye. Feygele made up a roll like a wanderer, put a kitchen knife in her skirts and waved goodbye. My mother never saw her own mother again.

So we set out walking for Kishinev. Sometimes we got rides from peasants and I remember how my mother pressed me to her breast, as if I was a shield. This was just after the Tsar freed the serfs and many peasants were on the road. Throughout the journey she held me close and mumbled prayers in Hebrew. I think it took years, well, weeks to get to Kishinev. My mother would sing and tell me stories. She would call me her brave little walker, her soldier. There must have been other Jews walking too, luftsmentshn without homes or occupations, because after the serfs were freed times got harder for the Jews. Who can remember when they haven't been hard? I remember barns and once a Jewish family let us sleep on the floor and fed us borscht. That soup comes back to me, steaming sweet, thick with onions, potatoes and beets, the extravagant color alive and clinging to the sides of the bowl. Beets are proud vegetables; they love to show off in your nose and on your clothes. They take over in the bowl, claiming everything with their purple-red. Even though I was only five, when I think of that soup now I have the sharp sensation of hunger and pleasant fullness all at once.

We arrived in Kishinev. I had never seen such balconies, iron porches. I thought we had come to a land of castles until we came to the poor section, which looked almost the same as Kamenka, long ditches beside the roads, all the houses made of mud and straw. But so many! Even then, before most of the factories were built. My mother offered to do washing and chores. The women laughed at her. What would poor women pay with? When they saw my bright eye, they got nervous and sent her away.

On we went. My mother certainly couldn't have known where she was going. The city was vast, first a wooden section, then stone, one

side by the river and the other on the cliffs, looking down. We came to a busy place, and saw a sign for the public baths swinging on a chain. Now we were lucky – some spirit opened its heart to lead us there. I felt it like a soft kiss on my eyelids. Pesah Kohn, who ran the baths, was just that minute in her doorway, surveying the street. Yes, she had work – one of the bathhouse attendants had quit only that week. I suppose she was moved by my mother's pitiful story about her husband the dead soldier, her little fatherless girl, who walked all the way from Kamenka.

Pesah Kohn had room in her house for a boarder and she offered to trade my mother board for labor, a few rubles in a couple of years if it worked out. This was the best offer my mother ever had in her life, so you can see how small her life was even when she had good fortune.

Kishinev was already such a big city there were separate bathhouses for men and women, open every day except, of course, Friday afternoon and Saturday. The baths were on two sides of a big building in a fairly well-off part of the old city by the river, where most buildings were built of stone and streets were wide. Many Russian merchants and factory foremen lived in that district then, as well as some Jews who were doing all right for themselves. But all kinds of Jews came to the baths, anyone who could scratch up a few kopecks. The goyim say Jews are dirty – they should only know how religiously we bathe. All the grown men came at least once a week, for the steam and to gossip more than to be clean, but there they were. If they put on the same dirty coats when they left, that was all they had.

The women and children, it depended. Usually in the warmer weather they came every week and got a good scrub. So maybe the mikve water stood a little – it was still rainwater, ritually pure. In the winter things were harder but still they came as often as they could. Why not? In the baths the women took off their wigs and shook their hair down; they got to talk and complain with their heads uncovered. Women are supposed to be modest but everyone looked at each other, compared how much hair, what kind of hips, if the children were healthy. As they say, all are equal in the baths. On Monday afternoons no married women came, only prostitutes. Prostitutes could travel anywhere in Russia if they had a yellow identity card. Usually on Mondays Pesah would send me all over town on errands – it wasn't until I was eleven or twelve I figured it out. Now I'm ahead of my story!

Pesah Kohn never had a child of her own. Reb Kohn had three boys from his first wife, who died in childbirth, but he was already old when

Pesah married him. He wanted her to raise his sons. She had a reputation for being good with figures; she would be an asset to the business. By the time we arrived, the boys were married and gone. The Kohns had their own stone house behind the baths. They owned the property in the name of a White Russian living in Kiev whom Reb Kohn had helped somehow when they were young. Reb Kohn liked to spend his time talking in the men's baths and of course he had his religious duties. So Pesah really managed everything, even sometimes hiring the boys who were attendants to the men.

Pesah Kohn – I love to think about her. She was the most wonderful woman I ever saw. She was twice, maybe three times as wide as my mother, and at least a head taller, her hips filling the whole doorway. She smelled of sweet bathwater and roasted chicken all the time. I believe she was the first Jew I ever saw with green eyes. She was never frightened of my one bright eye, or if she was, she never showed it. I think she terrified my mother but Feygele couldn't resist Pesah's offer that first day in Kishinev. Pesah gave us a little room behind the kitchen that had been for the boys.

The first night we had finished eating (and that food tasted good – salty herring, fresh sweet onions, black bread and plums) when Reb Kohn came in. "What is this?" He asked, peering at us.

"Our new bath attendant." Pesah introduced my mother and me by our full names.

"And the husband?"

"Dead in the Tsar's Army."

"Ahah. And this husband – the girl's father – what was his name?" My mother turned red. I tugged at a loose button. Pesah watched us.

"Gutke's father was Shmuel Gurvich, of blessed memory, who died in the Tsar's army," my mother said, exactly as I'd heard her rehearse on the road. As far as I know, this was the only lie she ever told. Even at five I knew at least part of the truth about what happened in Kamenka.

"No Jew is the father of that girl!" Reb Kohn said, not to my mother but to Pesah.

"The mother is a good Jewish woman who has walked more than a hundred versts and recited psalms the whole journey. You know what could happen to them in the streets of Kishinev. What could bring more honor on us than to make another's honor possible?"

"It's they who bring dishonor, and you will spread it to my whole family with your foolishness, Pesah."

"No, Reb Kohn, we will be doing the work of angels by making it possible for them to live an honest Jewish life. It's a mitsve. The child, only the breath of Lilith when she was born."

"Lilith! A Gypsy or a Turk touched her face. That child's a Gypsy." He fumed.

"Gutke is a shayne maidele, the daughter of a Jewish woman," Pesah said. She moved to where I sat, still as a fish looking up from under ice, and pulled me against her huge breasts. "Shayne maidele," she said. All the fear I ever had in me thawed in her arms.

"You have your way, as usual. But you – " he said, pointing a finger at my mother, "you must behave as if you were the pious daughter of Rabbi Hershel himself. The minute I find you breaking the sabbath or sneaking off with bathhouse boys, back on the street!"

All the time walking from Kamenka my mother never cried, she would just sing and tell stories. Now she sat in the Kohns' kitchen with tears coming down her face. "Thank you for your great kindness," she said. "I swear on my life you will never be disappointed in me."

"We'll see," he said. Pesah put me down. Feygele and I moved like feathers into our new room while Pesah gave Reb Kohn dinner. That was the longest conversation we ever heard them have.

Whenever you tell the story of one woman, inside is another. Tending the enormous wood cooking stove with its three blazing chambers, Pesah would confide in me those early weeks, her voice low, crooning, while my mother went about her chores. They say children don't remember, but I remember Pesah's song.

"I always start with an onion. What Jew doesn't? Garlic is nice. With an onion and garlic, a little shmalts, you cook a smell that koshers the house." She dipped her finger in the hot chicken fat, blew on it and held it out for me to suck. "That's a good baby. You can taste how I keep a kosher house. My mother never needed to say such a thing. It was understood. My mother – " here Pesah stopped to sigh and wipe her forehead with a rag, "my mother was a farmer and a farmer's wife. What did they grow? With fourteen children, it was their joke that they grew me. Here I am, tall and round as a potato." She held up one of the potatoes she was cutting so I could see the similarity in shape. I laughed.

"That's good, Shayne, laugh," Pesah said. "Laughing is one way to fool your appetite when times are hard. I could never get enough of

anything. My family used to laugh at my appetite. Not just for food, which I can eat my share, but for work and knowing what's going on in the world. Outside the farm there were wanderers who could capture your face in a box and put it on paper, a frozen mirror. I heard about them, and about the great new machines, from the traveling magidim, our storytellers. I loved the feel in my mouth of foreign words. Russian, Greek. I always talked to strangers. I'm too big to be afraid. Always there is a road, just like the road you traveled to get to me. From the road comes news."

She kept slicing the potatoes, throwing them in the onion, garlic and fat mixture. The smell was like perfume. "My whole family murmured, 'What to do with such a girl?' " She made a clicking noise with her tongue. "As quick as they could, they sold me – believe me, I know what a dowry's for, every odd-shaped girl knows – sold as an ox, along with a team of mules, some boy could plow his field with me. What do you think: Am I worth a pair of mules?"

"Are mules like horses?"

"Yes, darling," she laughed.

"You're much more fun than a horse," I said.

"Flatterer. What a child. I only hope you will be spared being sold to fools. That fool they tethered me to was Benjamin, my first husband. The farm wasn't good enough for him, and I was restless enough to agree to anything. These potatoes are coming along nicely. Salt, rosemary – maybe I'll add some of last year's olives. Where was I?" She rubbed her big hands on a corner of her apron.

"Benjamin."

"Oh, Benjamin. We packed up and came to a big shtetl. He carried bricks. I learned to trade in the market. From two eggs, I got a fish. From a fish, five kopecks." She took deep breaths, turning and cooking, humming between the sentences. "For five kopecks, some plain cloth. I knew plants from my childhood. A certain herb makes wonderful red. Would you like me to show you sometime?"

I nodded, my mouth full of the fried potatoes she'd just given me. "If you and your mother work out, I'll show you everything. Red shawls I wrung from the cloth, three of them. The women admired my work. At the end of a week I had six rubles, my husband, only two. This you may not believe, but it's God's truth. So angry he got, he fell down dead. Would you cry for a shlemil like that?"

I shook my head no. She pinched my cheek. "Well, then I had eight rubles and it took four to bury him. I saved up every kopeck and finally

traveled to the big city. To me, the sidewalks in Kishinev were an event – oh, and the balloons. Have you ever seen a balloon?"

"A balloon?"

"You and your mother really did come from the shtetl, didn't you? Well, I remember how that feels. I got work in a tavern. People think a fat woman will know how to cook and give good portions. You're lucky it's true of me, though there are plenty of days I never want to see a chopping board again. And all that time, working, I still wanted – oh, who knows what? Want, what is it? The moon would fit in my hand if I could reach it. I always believed there was no great thing I could not do if I had a chance."

She sighed and added logs to the fire, then filled up a kettle bigger than me with water. "How did I end up here, you want to know? There was a widower. He liked how I cooked and organized. He had boys who needed a mother. I told him, I am not a mother. I had enough of children on my parents' farm. 'But it's commanded,' he said, as if that would convince me. They have their books, they can tell you anything is written. They think they're very important because they know the secret language of God. If you ask me, God speaks in onions. But who asks? Now don't tell Reb Kohn I said that. Turned out he owned the baths. A prosperous, respectable man, even if too pious for my taste."

Pesah lifted a basket of peaches onto the work table as if it were empty and started cutting up the fruit. Every once in a while she'd pop a sweet sliver in my mouth. I swung my legs back and forth and smiled at her.

"We made a deal," she said, adding some peaches to the boiling water. "I agreed to farm his sons. It was, after all, easier than plowing a field. And I managed the business. Plainly I'm a woman who can get things done. We arranged to live as man and wife – oh, what should a child know about these things? You know marriage allows the man to come into your bed, don't you? But I made Reb Kohn agree that we could have separate rooms. I get satisfaction enough by working, cooking, taking care of the baths and the garden. He was always a little, fussy man; even you can see that, can't you? My conditions suited him fine. It was really a business deal. The matchmaker says all the best marriages are. After we had the ceremony, I had my photograph taken on the steps of the baths. Wouldn't my mother have been surprised! Of course she's gone and there are no more Jewish farms. We all scattered. If hunger didn't send us off, the decrees did. The less you ever know about that, the better." She stopped for a moment, staring at the back of the stove.

"I like the baths, though. I've learned how to read people and how to keep what I know to myself. For instance, I can see you think I'm just going to spoil you, that I have a weak spot for little girls. But I'm not all that good-natured. You'll have work of your own, shayne, any minute now, you'll see. I just want you to get strong again, after your long walk. Everyone thinks I'm a soft touch and you can't stop what they think about big women any more than you can stop the Jew-haters, but when you know me, you'll learn how tough I can be. Oh, don't be scared. I'd never hurt a child like you!"

I gulped down the fruit in my mouth. When I looked at Pesah, an orange-red light seemed to fringe her body, as if she were an autumn leaf. "I'm not scared," I said. "I'd like to work."

"You would, would you? Plenty of time for that. Do you like peach jam? This is going to be a very good batch. You're lucky to be living now. When I was a girl there wasn't so much as a train. I comfort myself with the wonders of steam and engines. And my work. I have garlic, I have onions. This year both the potatoes and the peaches are good. I feed whoever comes."

I had never been in a bathhouse before. We always washed in the river, and in winter wiped ourselves clean from well-water heated on the stove. The bathhouse was a fairy tale, full of steam and pipes, faucets and pumps, with a hallway of rooms with doors and, of course, the mikve pool at one side of the main room, where women immersed for purification after they bled or gave birth.

In the courtyard between the Kohns' house and the baths, a horse moved ceaselessly around a treadmill, pumping water from the river into the bathhouse. There was a little stable on one side of the courtyard and two plum trees shading a garden on the other, with grape vines all around and olive trees beside the rear entrance. Behind the Kohns' house were another eight fruit trees – peaches and a different kind of plum. This was a whole world to me, and quite enough of a world after the ordeal of walking.

Pesah had convinced Reb Kohn they should have two horses that could each work a half day, so they might last longer and give more value. When my mother and I arrived, one of the horses was very old and one fairly young. The young one was spotted gray and white and was harnessed for seven hours a day, the old one for six. I could pet the unharnessed one, feed him oats and a little dried fruit, but the one going round and round had to be left alone.

My mother worked like those horses, though at least she had a

bigger circle. She was up before dawn lighting the kitchen fire and pumping water for the house. Then she was cleaning the bathhouse, scrubbing the floors, stoking the fires for steam. Then she was helping the mothers with children undress and washing their towels.

Pesah was a magician in her own way. She never spoke harshly to anyone, never let anyone whip her horses. She just told my mother how to scrape the benches in the steam room or let her know that the windows needed washing, and my mother understood it was her job. She would work and sweat without stop until Pesah would notice her and say, "Enough for a little bit. Come have some cold soup and bread, a plum maybe you'd like?" And then it would seem as if Pesah was the fountain of relief instead of work.

And often enough I think she was. I was kept busy from the week after we arrived, cleaning the dirt off potatoes, and later filling buckets in the bathhouse. My mother worked harder than Pesah ever asked, to show her gratitude and ensure our safety. Pesah was usually up before my mother, checking to see if there were enough towels and wood in the baths, checking the cleanliness of the men's side before the men appeared. She was the last to turn down the lamps at night, after she finished her evening's sewing.

She also had a little wine-making concern, plum and grape wines, which both she and Reb Kohn sold to their bathhouse customers. They were always very careful and secretive – God forbid the authorities should know, though I am sure the rabbi blessed it for kosher. Making wine was only supposed to be for rich Russians, but many Jews still kept taverns and had licenses to deal in liquor. Pesah was always giving a bribe to someone, even though she told the police it was part of the business of the bath, something about Jewish ritual she made up to confuse them.

"You see how they are," she was instructing me how to be in the world. "They are always suspicious, always wanting an excuse to take what we have away. But they know nothing about us, except what their priests tell them. So you can tell them anything, twist their ignorance in your hand like the braids of a challah loaf, make something from it for yourself. But don't make a mistake or ever show you're laughing at them. They don't want to ever see you smile. Their stupidity has no innocence in it. Ignorance is not like a child – you are a child, my sweet sugar lump, my shayne, and you are curious about everything. Ignorance is the opposite, closed, frightened, spiteful. Russians!"

Pesah hired Russians sometimes. Usually only the stablehand, who would be the Shabbes goy as well, and sometimes others for outside repairs or heavy digging, but never for inside the baths. I never saw a woman – or a man, even – stronger than her. Proverbs says, "She girds her loins with strength, she strengthens her arms," and that's how Pesah was. She ordered flour by the sack and would lift the sacks off the cart as if they were featherbeds, while the men strained with their burdens.

Pesah fed all the workers a midday meal: the yardhand, four boys from the men's bath, the barber who did cupping with leeches for the men, three women who came every day for the women's side and to help with the children, her friend Sadie who did the cupping for women and helped her with cooking, my mother and me. For everyone it was a feast compared to what they had at home. Always black bread and onions and cucumbers, radishes, cold or fried potatoes with salt and oil, olives, fresh fruit, watermelons in season or plum preserves in winter. If it was very cold, maybe a barley soup, and on Tuesdays Pesah usually added herring, sometimes a stew with a little chicken or beef tongue when times were very good. Because on Tuesday, she would say, it was easiest to forget the promise of the Sabbath and think that we were nothing more than horses turning around endlessly in our tracks. And besides, it's written that on a Tuesday, God looked at creation and was pleased. So Tuesday is a lucky day.

Everyone worked hard and ate as much as they could hold. Reb Kohn hardly ever ate this meal with us. He thought it was both extravagant and demeaning how Pesah fed the workers and ate with them herself. "And isn't it said that after the destruction of the Temple, the table became the altar of the Jewish people?" was her reasoning. She listened to everything people said at the baths, the women's arguments, the men's disputations on the steps, the students Reb Kohn brought home for dinner – and she never forgot anything. He couldn't make any arguments against anything she did. She was a giant and he was just an ordinary, little man.

The workers got paid two rubles on Thursdays so they could get what they needed for Shabbes, but I don't remember Pesah ever paying my mother. To her, we became like her own family. We needed something, she would get it. She would give me a few kopecks every week so I could buy myself sweets or little toys, and she would sew all our clothes herself. This made my mother particularly love her. Pesah

would ask her opinion about the cloth and the patterns, and when everything was agreed, we would get measured.

"Come, undress now, I'll see how big we have to make the waist and bust," Pesah would say. Every time my mother would blush. "All day long we see women naked in the baths. You should blush here in front of me, Feygele? You could fit inside me three times already and still there would be room. Come, we'll see."

And Feygele would undress in front of Pesah, a pink running under her skin, which was almost as dark as plums. Pesah had a long cord that she marked with ink for the measurements. Two lines for the breast, one for the waist, a circle for the hips, a triangle for the upper arms. She would wrap the cord around my mother's upper arm, then wrap another cord around her own, and compare them, laughing. "Don't worry, it's nothing to make a little dress for you, hardly anything to it!"

My mother would frown and Pesah would lean over and kiss her on the forehead. After all, the bee knows its strength and touches the flower just enough to get what it needs. "It's the heart that counts in us, isn't it, Feygele? Our hearts are the same size and that's what matters."

Once my mother told me that this was the biggest reproach she ever felt. No one had a heart bigger than Pesah Kohn, she thought. Pesah's heart was as big as her belly, while my mother thought her own heart was no bigger than my one gold eye. I wanted to tell her she was wrong but I couldn't lie. Instead I held her hand and told her she was the best mother I could ever want, which was truth enough for both of us. Feygele was like a horse with blinders on. You think the horse doesn't know? Yet the horse has no way to shake them off. That's how it was with my mother. She was set in her course and she was loyal to everyone who ever spoke a kind word to her. She knew there was a world full of miracles outside her, as if flies carried the news to her ears. But see it for herself? She couldn't; there was no way to shake off her restraints.

My mother never asked Pesah for a ruble for herself, but she made her promise that I would get some education. To do this was a mitsve to Pesah, a way to work a blessing. Of course Pesah made as if it were her own idea, which pleased my mother just as well. I don't remember Reb Kohn protesting, probably he never knew. Pesah could read Yiddish and knew how to keep the books with a counting frame. She knew a few prayers in Hebrew and I think she could actually speak Russian quite well. She had the idea that I should be able to read

Russian as well as Yiddish, and maybe German too.

"The world is big outside the bathhouse, but it all comes here to be laid out," Pesah said one day in the kitchen. "The men draw maps in steam explaining things to each other; sometimes I find their outlines on the walls. They argue about Mendelssohn, Chernyshevksy, religion all day long. I want you to be able to read the Haskole newspapers from Germany that explain about this 'enlightenment.' It won't be enough for you just to make a nice seam. When you get married, I want you to have a choice. I want you to have someone you can talk to, who will be interested in what you have to say."

"I don't want to be married. I want to stay and work for you forever."

"Hear what she says! First you will know a little bit about the world and then we'll see." She rubbed the top of my head as if it were the round top of a walking stick.

So she sent me to a school that a rabbi's wife had for girls. This I loved, even if the other girls called me the Gypsy, just like Reb Kohn. After I had gone for a year Pesah bought me a book for my very own, a little Yiddish fable about an angel disguised as a beggar who tested the hearts of men. First she read it to me, then I learned all the words and I would read it to her and my mother every night. Neither of them ever failed in their attention.

I wanted to be just like them, Pesah and my mother both. At night sometimes I dreamed of pleasing Pesah by becoming the fattest girl in the bathhouse, of Pesah washing me herself, admiring how big my shoulders and thighs were. Once or twice I ate until I made myself sick. Pesah sat me on her legs and rubbed my little belly with warm oil. "Now what is this about? Why keep eating when you're no longer hungry?" And I confessed I wanted to be just like her, so she would always keep me.

"Oy, gotenyu. First, I will keep you here as long as you and your mother like – you shouldn't worry with such terrible thoughts. No one is going to send you away anymore. Second, it's not always so wonderful to be as big as me. I have to have chairs made special, and people don't like to accept what falls outside their expectations – you understand? No one trusts a woman who's more beautiful than all the rest. People are afraid of me or make fun. Anyway, you will end up the size you were meant to be, just as you are a Jew with two different color eyes. Did you ever hear the story of the leper boy and Elijah? No? Well, it happened a long time ago, maybe yesterday, in Kiev – "

I learned from her to let myself be. My mother accepted bad and

good luck on faith; it was all part of what God had laid out, the road she was meant to walk. Pesah's understanding was more complicated. By her, you needed more than faith, you needed to admire yourself, just as you came. God was in you, of course, and loving God did honor to yourself, but your own self was also something you moved on your own. You decided to act, not just God – or, God forbid, the Tsar – decided for you. She had a way of understanding that let her do whatever she wanted, if it was good to her and caused no pot to spill. She called it honoring God because it honored her own desire. If she didn't use the mikve because she thought it was a superstition, she didn't bother to tell Reb Kohn about her decision. Why was it his business? There were altogether too many laws to control women.

"If I am clean or not clean, it is because of my actions, not because I bleed, – and it is between me and God," she would say to Sadie while they were cutting cabbages.

"But Pesah, maybe you put him in danger, if you touch him during your time."

"I don't ever touch him, except by accident." Pesah's cheeks moved up to her eyes with her grin. Sadie shook her head, as if this was just too much, but I could see she was smiling too.

Truth be told, what I learned from Pesah and the bathhouse was to love women. I grew to be a good-sized woman but no giant, certainly. Strong enough for what I do. And I am happy with what I do.

After I had studied with the rabbi's wife for several years, Pesah and my mother concluded I was not going to be one of the ten percent of Jews admitted to Russian schools and that I should have a trade. I was ten years old, old enough to apprentice with the midwife Milcah the Thorny.

"A midwife, she can travel even outside the Pale," Pesah said when she told my mother her idea.

"Why should she ever want to go out of the Pale? Unless she has a husband who wants to travel, God forbid." To Feygele, Odessa was as far as Berlin, even after the railroad came and you could get there in just one day.

"Being a midwife will be like having the dowry in her own person, she will always have work – there will never be factories to replace midwives." This argument convinced my mother. No one asked me, but it turned out just as well.

Milcah was called Thorny because of her tremendous knowledge of wild herbs and plants. She thought nettles were good for many things,

and she would sometimes apply the sharp leaves to a particular ache, especially in the back or legs. "At least," she would laugh, "it will make you forget your other pain for a minute." Sometimes it was a very good cure itself.

I was just ten but I was healthy and eager to please. Milcah was a weekly visitor at the baths; often Pesah invited her to take lunch with us. They would discuss everything – if eating horseradish made a woman have easy labor, if it was true that they were hiring young girls at the new candle and soap factories. It was not hard for Pesah to convince her to take me on, though at first Milcah had reservations about my eyes.

"Not by me," Milcah said, "but so much can go wrong in birth, so many babies die. You know they say nine out of ten people die because of the evil eye. She'll be too open to blame."

"We'll start a rumor that she has special power to ward off the evil eye, then," Pesah said. "We'll say women should see her early in pregnancy, and you'll teach her the herbs that help. Unless, God forbid, she isn't meant to be a midwife, it will be the same with her as with you – most live, yes? And what do you tell them when their babies die?"

"It depends on the mother. A pious woman, I repeat the story, how children are jewels that God only lends. When he calls them back, we must return them with an open heart. A superstitious woman, I tell her it must be her husband's fault. Maybe he was thinking impure thoughts when the baby was conceived, or maybe they have enemies. A stingy woman, I tell her who knows, it could be a judgment from God if, by accident, she forgot to tithe her challah loaves. A few I can tell the truth: it happens, we don't know why."

"So Gutke, she'll learn to say the same. 'Even a well-trained midwife is no match for Lilith when Lilith is determined.' " Finally Milcah agreed.

Usually apprentices go and live with their teachers. Boys do, anyway, but my mother and I would not be separated, and besides, Pesah was not ready to see me go. I started rising every morning with my mother, often when it was still dark, and as soon as light came I would run through town to where Milcah lived alone in a small house in the poor quarter.

Milcah was old to me, older than Pesah, though maybe she was only forty, younger than I am now. She had carried nine children of her own. One died in the womb, two in childbirth. A Russian, claiming he

was cheated in a business deal, whipped her husband to death when Milcah was carrying the last. She was certain this had caused her baby to die inside her rather than to come fatherless into the world.

She was already a midwife when her husband was killed. I think she took up her trade after her second baby died in childbirth. She wanted to make sure the midwife was doing nothing wrong. Later I heard people say Milcah was bitter, but I prefer to think she wasn't the kind of woman who would leave things to fate.

When I went to work for Milcah, her daughters were married and lived nearby. Two of her sons had gone off on the road to seek their fortunes, like so many. Her other son was a grain dealer doing well in Odessa and she was very proud of him.

"like God in Odessa he lives," Milcah would say. "Odessa makes Kishinev look like a shtetl – some day you'll see. They have opera in Italian, every race in the world comes to trade, and they pay more attention to business than to religion. If all of Russia were like Odessa, I think the messiah would come."

"So why don't you go live by your son?" Pesah would ask her.

"Kishinev is where people know me and I like to be here near my girls."

The first time I crossed her threshold, the mixture of scents went right up my nose and I sneezed for ten minutes while Milchah watched, patiently amused. Every inch of wall and rafter was hung with bunches of herbs and what I used to think of as weeds. Green, ochre and lavender bits drifted in the shafts of light that penetrated the twine wrapped stems. Milcah had to constantly dust the falling pollen and wind-crushed petals, a task that soon became mine. I thought her house smelled like secrets. I was afraid of spirits in the herbs, and because I was a stranger, I had the idea they would play tricks on me. Every day I went there, for at least a year, I would stand in the doorway and shout: "It is I, Gutke, the apprentice to Milcah!" so they would know I was under her protection.

"Oh, is it? Come in, apprentice to Milcah!" Milcah always treated me very seriously. Milcah was a wise woman, very strict. Since her husband was dead and she lived by herself, people were a little afraid of her, imagining her a witch. Often she was almost silent, showing me what to do by pointing or mumbling a few words, but once in a while she would make us both a cup of chamomile tea and hold forth, proverbs lacing her monologues.

"You might as well know, people will always think midwives are

witches, Gutke. You have two different color eyes, I'm a solitary widow – but that's not the reason. We deal in the inside organs of women; we concern ourselves with the details of sickness and health. To most women you shouldn't even mention such things." She drank her tea with a loud, slurping sound. Accustomed to being alone, she didn't make any pretense of manners with me.

"Men will be afraid because you are involved in matters of the blood," she continued. "The Torah instructs that bleeding women are unclean and we must not even drink the blood of animals. Women will be afraid because they will think you know them better than they know themselves – and if you are a good student, it will be true." She paused, sucking her teeth, and then pointed at me, her fingers swollen at the knuckles. "With men you must carry yourself as righteously as the matriarch Sarah, so they may never have reason to cast a stone at you. With women you will be firm. You must never quiver against their fear. After they know you are set in your course, then be gentle and patient with them. Do you understand? No, not yet, but you will."

I got used to the herbs and stopped sneezing, fortunately. At first I swept, washed and dusted, but after a few months she let me grind dried leaves with a pestle in a brass mortar and tie up fresh bundles to hang. We made all kinds of concoctions: comfrey and nettles dissolved in oil, a black green, for bruises inside and out; wine and honey mixed with clawroot for vitality after misfortune; tincture of clove for toothache, which I already knew from Pesah; a potion of lavender and an herb she called flaming heart that you were supposed to sneak into the food of the person whose love you wanted; and all the preparations for easy birth – raspberry, spikenard root, lobelia. There were shelves of green, amber, blue and clear bottles, as small as my thumb and as big as a milk jug, that constantly needed replenishing.

After the first year Milcah said that I was still not ready to attend a birth. She laid out seven freshly picked plants and seven piles of crushed herbs. When I could identify each one, tell what it did and explain when to administer it, then I could come with her. It was hard work being an apprentice – it made going to school seem like a distant holiday.

I was right, of course – there *were* spirits in the herbs. The herbs became my companions and when I was alone I started to talk to them. One day, for instance, I would tell them about the pig I saw running down the street beside the baths, three drunk Moldavians who kept bumping into each other while chasing her. Eventually one fell down,

the others tripped over him and the pig escaped. The herbs would rustle – I could tell they appreciated the attention. Then they'd tell me a story about foxes licking each other in the forest.

Milcah was always walking. We walked all over Kishinev, into the fields and a little bit even into the Tsar's forests outside of town. She knew Gentile women, and sometimes they gave her plants from their gardens, crossing themselves as they talked to us. Milcah pointed out the houses of Gentiles who spat and threw stones so I could avoid them.

"But," she said, "even the spitters come by after dark to ask for a potion that will make them have a boy, maybe, or increase their husbands' desire. They stand in the doorway with their shawls wrapped around them, God forbid anyone should know they talked to a Jew."

"Why do you let them come here?"

"This you should know already. They can go where they want. Not us, we go where they tell us. But I charge them double, don't worry."

I lay awake worrying about the circle that hatred makes. They say we cheat them, so we do, for spite. When I grew up, I would be more honorable than that, and then the Gentiles would see there was no reason to hate us. And I wouldn't take money in the dark from people who spat on me in the daylight. When you're eleven you think every idea is born with you, that no one ever tried it the right way before. Your example, your own honesty, will make you a hero to everyone who knows you – and better, it will make people come to their senses and stop telling vicious lies about each other.

Another year went by and I could distinguish between the whitish powders of yarrow and dried eyebright bloom, and knew that shepherd's purse stanched hemorrhage, anise increased and sweetened a mother's milk, blue vervain brought on sleep, particularly during the waning moon. Finally I passed my tests on herbs and was allowed to attend my first birth. Milcah was a short woman. Already, at twelve, I was taller. ("Because, kayn ayen-hore, you always had enough to eat, not like me, when I was growing up." I remembered how hungry Feygele and I were walking to Kishinev, but I never argued with Milcah.) She had very large hands, though, with wide palms, and each finger was like a fence post, square and knotted at the knuckle. Her hands were a sign from God that she was meant to be a midwife, I could tell. I wanted my own sign. Just having a gold eye wasn't good for anything.

"I was twenty-seven before I knew what my hands were good for, you'll know when you know."

She chose for my initiation a woman who had already had two girls, very easy, quick births, a woman with wide hips. The woman, Rivka Solomon, lived in the wood part of town. Her husband had good steady work in a flour mill. The daughters were with their grandmother, the father at work, Rivka's older sister was with her. "The best is not to have men in the house; they're too much trouble," Milcah said. "If they insist, make them go in the other room to pray."

When we entered the house, Milcah showed me the amulets the family had hung. " 'Adam and Eve excluding Lilith' – you remember what I told you about Lilith?" Of course. Lilith fascinated me, partly because they said it was Lilith who had tried to steal my eyes, and an angel had stopped her because of my mother's prayers. Milcah didn't believe in Lilith, well, maybe just a little. "So she was in the Garden of Eden, but she probably isn't in Russia. Not even Lilith would come to Russia if she could go anywhere. We have plenty of our own local demons and not all of them are invisible. Many people still believe, though. See here," Milcah pointed, "these are the names of the angels Sanvi, Sansanvi and Samangelaf written on the door, to protect the baby, in case the amulets aren't enough. Maybe half the families still do that, maybe less."

The featherbed was covered with rags. It was August and still very hot, just midday. Rivka wasn't more than nineteen years old. Milcah said she had her first child when she was fifteen.

"She very much wants a boy." Milcah's eyes wandered and she sighed. "Well, it's our work to help women have what they want; it's not so much to ask. I told her she must eat beef then, once a week, but no eggs, from a month after her last pregnancy until she conceived. Fortunately, she can afford to do such a thing. Then I gave her this, milkweed in shnaps, three drops only, every other day, as soon as she knew she'd conceived. So now we'll find out – maybe it works, maybe it doesn't."

Rivka was very dark, with many freckles and moles. She had long legs, I thought, but then I was just twelve and, though used to women naked in the bathhouse, not from this position. The sister, Tsipora, was by her side. Milcah asked many questions: how long since they saw the blood, how many minutes between the pains.

The sister said it was six or seven minutes between each pain. Rivka's belly was tight, in the shape of a balalaika. Milcah made her sit

up and rolled towels for her back. Tsipora stood behind, rubbing her shoulders. Rivka breathed deep into her belly. Milcah made her put her knees up, not too far apart. She spread the woman's legs.

"Later, when the baby is coming," Milcah said, "you and Tsipora will each hold one of her feet so she can push against you. There, now, you can see." She showed me the lips and the hole where urine comes from. "Here, where the baby is coming, is not normally so wide, only at birth. You can feel in yourself how the opening is usually just big enough for a few fingers. The man puts his member here and drops his seed in, like I explained. For him, just a minute. For her, well, now you'll see. And this one is coming quickly."

It seemed like hours but even a minute would have been too long to stare up a stranger's legs. None of my old classmates had ever seen anything like this, I was sure. I got a queasy sensation, from the strong odor of salted fish and excretions the woman had, and from being proud to finally witness this part of my trade. Two hours went by.

Milcah turned to look at me. "You are breathing like the mother. Why?"

"I don't know," I said.

"That's all right then. Both of you, relax, keep taking deep breaths. How long did that one last?" she asked Rivka.

"Too long – oy, here it comes again!" Tsipora wiped her sister's head with a cloth.

"Come down here now." Tsipora and I each held a foot with one hand, and rubbed a leg with the other, so the mother shouldn't get cramps, Milcah said. It seemed like so much to do – what would happen if Milcah were all alone? She would manage, I was sure, but if it were me? Then the woman started crying, puffing, shouting.

"Stop rubbing now, just let her push," Milcah instructed. "You always watch to make sure she isn't squeezing too hard. It shouldn't be desperate; you want it to move like a winter's current. Have you ever seen the Black Sea? No? In the river, then. Like a wave, you can't stop it. She shouldn't wear out too soon or force the baby too hard. 'No good comes from hurrying.' See – you can see in? In the back it's two fingers wide and see how it's all swollen, like the heel of a loaf of bread? That's the head, coming down, pushing against the opening. See, here it is – just perfect – but here – you have to watch this skin, how it's stretching."

I could see how tight and pale the skin was in the furrow going down to the woman's behind. When I was little I would sometimes

play with the hot wax from Shabbes candles when my mother or Pesah weren't around. I would mold and stretch it and sometimes the wax would snap. That's how the woman's skin looked now.

"Sometimes you have to make a cut, right there," Milcah said, tracing a line below the opening, "to give the baby more room. Otherwise the skin tears and it's very hard to heal. This time I think – " she had a little knife by her hand, she was massaging and looking, " – I think this time not. The first one of hers we had to do it for, but not the second. You're fine, Rivka, just keep pushing."

I caught glimpses of the opening from where I stood, holding Rivka's callused, curled toes. Below her dark hair was the place of mystery, shifting, enlarging. Milcah was busy then, almost forgetting me. The head was coming through.

"This is the hardest part," she said. "Yell, go ahead," and the woman gave such an oy-vey I almost dropped her foot. Milcah put her hands on the baby's head and the head turned sideways.

"This is the way it's curled up in the womb. You put your hand right away to hold the head, but don't squeeze or pull by it, you hear ?" she said without looking at me. "Even if it seems like it's taking too long, which, thank God, this is not. You just support and guide it." One shoulder was out and the baby opened its mouth, gulping, starting to cry.

Then the rest of the tiny body glided out like music, if you didn't mind the screaming. Fantastic music coming out of a woman's thighs! The baby was crying, the mother panting and oy-veying, the sister sobbing. If Milcah hadn't kept talking, I would have started weeping myself.

"Now is when you work fast. Hand me a clean rag." Milcah wiped the baby's head, around its eyes and mouth, cleaning away all the mucus. "See? Oy. Well, she'll have to wait until next time for a little yeshive bokher. Three girls is not so bad, she has plenty of time to make boys, we'll try tansy next maybe. All right, you see this? Like watery cheese on the baby? Spread it all over, nice and even. It keeps the skin from getting a rash, a present from the mother." Milcah massaged the tiny body all over. I was thrilled with its littleness, like baby snails I sometimes found, faithful miniatures that gave me a sensation I can only call awe. But then there was no time for awe. The cord was hanging, throbbing, and I had to remember every word Milcah said.

"You make sure the cord hangs free, not wrapped anywhere around

the baby. God forbid, the cord should come first, it can be a real problem. Sometimes you can still save the child, but it's not easy. Now you wait for the cord to lie still before you cut it."

Milcah handed the infant to me, and I was holding someone entirely new, red, wrinkled, covered with yellowy wax, her face bunched up from pressing against the window of life, the big red and purple cord twined at her belly. I felt dizzy, not because of the intimacy of it – but something else, like a voice coming over my eyes. I saw a room full of animal hides. On one hide, in a circle, nine Shabbes candlesticks, all lit except one, in which the candle had gone out.

"Gutke? Gutke! Here, give me the baby! What are you staring at?"

"I told you that girl is not right," the sister said in a kind of hiss.

"Of course she is. She's never seen a birth before, that's all. Are you all right, child?"

"Oh yes, please forgive me, I – "

"You did nothing wrong. You held the girl fine, as if you were born to hold babies. Now just breathe and watch what I do."

The cord had stopped pulsing. She made two clamps and cut between them, just so, near the baby's belly, not too close. The baby was lying on the mother's rounded stomach, the mother crying and laughing, running her hands over the baby's fingers and toes.

"Every mother does that," Milcah whispered to me, "even the ones who've never heard of a baby with missing toes."

"Oh, Chaim will be so disappointed."

"And you?"

"My sweet baby, my precious flower. Flora, that's a nice name for a girl, isn't it? I had a great-grandmother Flora. Maybe it's too nice, kayn ayen-hore?"

"Flora is a fine name. Don't worry. It's a mitsve to honor the dead." Milcah smiled; everything was good. But not finished. "She has one more birth to give." The woman moaned a little, tired, holding her baby against her breast. Then there was another wet sound and the cord wiggled and slid down the mother's leg. Milcah showed me everything that comes out, the sack the baby was in, the different liquids. She made me smell them, even though I gagged because it was so strong, like putting my whole head into a rotting carcass.

Milcah patted my back. "You'll get used to it, don't worry. A strong smell is good. If there's very little odor, or if you smell something different, like charcoal or anything that smells like metal, watch the mother carefully. In an hour, she should be washed with a tea made

from comfrey and shepherd's purse, especially over the lower parts. The gates of heaven are very close to women when they give birth, and who knows, maybe Lilith too, after all. I will teach you how to read all these things and save the mothers and children whenever you can. Sometimes of course – well, thank God, this is a strong woman and a beautiful girl."

"Flora will marry a tanner and have nine children, eight of them will live," a voice spoke. Then I realized it was my own.

"Sha," Milcah said, as if I had made some terrible mistake.

"You see, what did I tell you? Now it's predictions." Tsipora glared.

"My little Flora?" Rivka said. She seemed pleased. "A tanner is respectable. Very good. She can see my grandchildren? A midwife who can see the future, what a thing!"

"She just had a premonition, that's all. She's very excited – it's her first time."

"Yes," I said, "I'm sorry, I don't know what I was saying. I must have been thinking about the new tannery on the cliffs. It doesn't mean anything." Milcah nodded at me.

The sister, who wouldn't look at me any more, gave Milcah a loaf of bread and a cheese. "I'm sorry, it's all there is to pay you with." Milcah nodded graciously.

Finally, when we were on our way home, Milcah wanted to know. "When did you see? As soon as I put the baby in your hands?"

"Yes," I said, "then. Is there something wrong with me?"

"Oy, Gutke. Maybe you are part Gypsy, like they say. Or," she considered, "you could be able to hear the bat kol. You know what that is? No, Pesah doesn't teach you anything but the bathhouse and the table, am I right? The bat kol is a voice of God. Rabbis say they can hear whispers from God, sometimes talking, sometimes lamenting. But the bat kol doesn't just speak to rabbis. Often it talks about the future, about birth. When I was a girl – " she stopped and looked at me. "Well, bat kol or Gypsy, you are who you are. The sister is a gossip. If you don't want people to say you're a fortune teller, you must be very careful. It's a thin line we walk. I heard that once all over Europe women were killed if anyone even suspected they were witches – and the Russians always like an excuse to kill a Jew. And Jews – it will be very hard for you to get a husband if this happens to you again and you tell anyone." She pulled her shawl tight around her shoulders.

"I don't care about a husband," I said. "But why *does* it happen to me? Doesn't everyone sometimes see things that aren't – that seem – "

I felt cold on the back of my neck, though the day was warm. I didn't understand why everyone thought it was so unusual to know things about people by looking into them. It wasn't like I heard the voice of an angel, even if Milcah said that's what it was. I didn't know that when most people tried to do what I called 'looking in' they saw only a brick wall, and if they happened to see more, they immediately turned away.

"Don't trouble yourself so much, child. 'The truth has many faces.' You are good and honest, I know. What makes one hilltop green and another barren? Next time it happens, only tell me."

After I saw my first birth, I felt that I was a grown woman, separated from other children even more than I had been by having no father. I was allowed to go to the most private, important things that happened in Kishinev. Even Pesah treated me differently, not so much like a little girl. When I was home in the evenings, I still helped at the baths. On the weekday nights the baths were for old women and women who had no children to look after, the youngest wives and unmarried aunts, a few students from the very wealthiest families. Once I figured out that only prostitutes came on Mondays, I wondered how the other women knew to stay away. Sometimes I thought there was a secret meeting place where girls were told all the things women needed to know, or maybe the rabbi's wife explained these matters to her pupils when they were old enough and I had missed that lesson. Pesah insisted that both Feygele and I should work some other place than the bathhouse on Mondays. I would peek around the side of the building at the women who came, but they didn't seem so dangerous. They just wore brighter cloaks and more rouge.

The new factories were beginning to hire and working girls started coming to the baths too, fourteen, fifteen years old. They were from the poorest families, the ones who had to let their daughters go out to work where they might be with men and goyim all day, and although nearly every kopeck went to their families, still, they had a little money of their own for the first time.

"The factories might be good for the baths, but they're bad for Jews," Pesah told her friend Sadie.

"Isn't what's good for you good for a Jew?" Sadie asked, poking Pesah in her ribs.

"You know very well what I mean," Pesah answered, turning away, playing at being annoyed. But I didn't know what Pesah meant. Like so many of the bits of conversation I recall, the meanings hidden in

childhood only become clear now that I write them down. Most were just small lessons, people trying to prove their virtue to each other, but because I wasn't supposed to be listening, I made things out to be more important than they were. Maybe that's why our childhoods seem so big, so resonant, while our adult years slip by like fish in the river Byk.

Pesah discussed all the changes in her clientele with Sadie, and I watched my mother listening, trying to understand. It seemed to me my mother cleaved stubbornly to the innocence she had the day before she was raped. Nothing she saw in the bathhouse left a mark on her. She could listen to women and men arguing all day about socialism and nihilism and have no opinion. Well, she did have an opinion: "Someone will always be rich, someone will always be poor. Do you think the Narodniks will give the government to washerwomen?"

She was happy to see me growing and delighted to get good reports from Milcah. While Pesah thought of her as a little sister, Feygele never for a moment thought of Pesah as anything more than our kind benefactor. From a benefactor, goodwill must always be bought. I was much freer. In fact, my mother bought my freedom, day after day, chore after chore. Something I only now see. Not all understanding comes in visions!

So I was twelve, and Pesah let me help in the evenings. I would be tired but the steam in the bathhouse was invigorating, and the women who came at night were more interesting than the married women who shleped along their babies during the day. There was a group of unmarried women, "old maids" in their twenties, who would come on Wednesdays and take the four private rooms, with their own little bathtubs, twenty kopecks for each room extra. Yetta, Reyzl, Naomi, Golde – I remember their names still.

After a few months I was particularly aware of Golde. She was maybe twenty-two, one of the first women in Kishinev to have her own Singer sewing machine. She had opened a little tailoring business – beautiful work, everyone said. Golde was very much in demand as a seamstress, and three girls worked for her in the front room of her house. (The women in the bath always gossiped about each other, especially the old maids, so it was easy to learn whatever I cared to know.) Her mama died when Golde was still young. She was the only daughter, her father a traveling merchant. She kept the house for her papa when he was home and ran her shop. She had seven brothers, if you can imagine, and they had all married and gone.

Golde had eyes so dark they made the new moon seem like an oil lamp. Milcah was teaching me to pay attention to smell and I realized Golde smelled like an infant, the way healthy babies smell, like cherry trees fruiting during a summer rain. Already she had a small bump on her back, from bending all day at the sewing, but seeing how hard she must work made her spirit seem sweet to me.

It was my job to make sure everything in the private rooms was clean and the stove hot. Each room had its own long bench, tub, stove and a faucet. The old maids would arrange it so that one room wouldn't be steamy, and they would sit there after they were done bathing, playing cards. I could hear them laughing and singing. They liked to be left alone and they gave me five kopecks if I made sure no one bothered them.

One night the women came in, laughing. Their cheeks were red so it must have been winter, before Pesach. I don't know why, but I thought I had forgotten to bring enough towels for them. Some feeling pushed me. I got fresh towels, extra ones even, and headed toward their rooms. My hands were full so I pushed the door a little with my elbow, to knock. The door swung open without making a noise. Golde was lying on the hot bench and Yetta was sitting between her legs, like a midwife, yet not like a midwife – her hands were pushing, rubbing Golde's breasts. Golde turned and saw me. She grabbed Yetta's hand, and then both of them were looking at me. I stared at them. Tears were in Golde's eyes, and I didn't know what to do.

Yetta was mad. "You don't knock? Why do you sneak around, spying on us? For this we pay you?" She stood up, folding her arms across her chest.

"The door just came open – "

Golde leaned up on one elbow. "Gutke didn't mean to spy on us, did you?"

"No, I would never spy on you. I'm sorry. Please forgive me."

"Yes, I forgive you. But you must keep this a secret. Do you know how?"

When Golde looked at me, I felt a fog come over my body. Not from the steam in the room, but from a feeling that started in my belly. I knew, because they were frightened, that they were doing something forbidden, but I didn't know more than that. If there were words for it – women putting their hands on each other – I had never heard them. So I swore I knew how to keep a secret and they latched the door carefully behind me.

For weeks, when I went to sleep at night, I would see Golde's black eyes watching me. My own breasts were just beginning to fill out. I held them the way Yetta had held Golde's and rocked myself to sleep, imagining resting my cheek along Golde's breasts or pressing my lips to hers.

I became a very attentive student at the births. I wanted to know everything about anatomy, the way nipples pucker and how the different colors of a woman's underlips all have meanings that change in every phase of labor. "But isn't every woman different?" I asked.

"Yes," Milcah agreed, "but you can already see for yourself there are only so many types – small and phlegmatic, large and stoic, for instance."

I understood what she meant but it seemed to me that when you thought about type deeply, each woman became her own type. Golde, the dark-eyed seamstress who liked to lie on the rough planks in a steamy bathhouse while another woman swayed on top of her – is that a type or a particular?

"But even if we can't decide what type a woman is," I said, focusing on a shape I couldn't quite make out somewhere beyond Milcah's left ear, "we can still know the woman, can't we? If we pay attention to her body and her countenance while she's carrying the child, the changes she goes through in labor will be clearer, won't they?" Milcah put her hand on my shoulder, nodding vigorously, pleased with me.

One day after Pesach I went to Milcah's, as usual. A stranger, a man, was sitting at her table, his head and arm bandaged, his clothes filthy and torn.

"This is my son, Gershon. From Odessa, I spit on its name, *feh!* Gershon, this is my apprentice, Gutke, who lives with Pesah, the bathhouse manager. After you get a little strength, maybe she'll take you back there. You can clean yourself up a bit, maybe talk to some business-people here in Kishinev."

He started to cry, and she gave him a cup of hot tea, chamomile with valerian, to calm him.

"Stop crying already, tell us everything, how it happened," Milcah said. He must have told her the story already, but repeating helps people get over sorrow. Otherwise the words build up in you, a lamentation, and you can't stop grieving.

"I used to think Odessa was the whole of civilization," Gershon

mumbled into his tea cup. "Where else do Greeks and Rumanians argue in French about German theater? The whole world should know such civilization!" Bitterness was like a shawl around his shoulders. He pulled it tight to give himself a little comfort. "Of course there was anti-Semitism, where not? Every Easter the Greek sailors shoot guns by the synagogue and gangs of hoodlums, boys, eighteen, nineteen-years old, you know what kind – it happens, everyone looks the other way. Well, this is what their looking away gets them!" He waved his arm about. Then he winced and the tears started up again, pure pain tears. "Only a fool or some child longing for a fight goes into the street on Easter Sunday. We don't start this. I have friends, even, who put an Easter loaf in their windows just in case. This year, they were the lucky ones. Now there are thousands homeless – "

"Thousands homeless?" I had heard of pogroms, who hadn't? They happened years ago, in shtetls without defenses. But a pogrom in Odessa? In 1871? How could that be?

"Thousands. I don't exaggerate. Three days they sacked and looted our houses, and when they could find nothing more, they burned them. Burned up whole streets if there were only Jewish houses on them."

"How can they tell the Jewish houses?"

Gershon laughed as if the evil in the world were stuck in his throat like a fishbone. " 'And you shall put it on your doorposts for a sign' – look!" He ran wildly to the door, pointing at Milcah's mezuze. "This, our holy protection!" With his good hand he tried to pull it off the wood but Milcah stopped him.

"This is my house. Gershon, stop – sit down!" She was at least a head shorter yet she got her palms on his shoulders and pushed him back as if he were a boy. "The Christians put their saints and crosses on the outside, so it happens. We have a duty to honor our faith. It is bitter and bad when the public is wrong, but it doesn't mean we stop being Jews."

I was trying to see what had happened. Heavy clouds drew over my eyes and a buzzing started in my ears. After a moment the sound of flies cleared, becoming human voices, low, rumbling voices like carts rolling over cobblestones. Gershon's high-pitched complaint seemed miles away.

"Mama, it wasn't just the burning. You shouldn't know from what I saw. I broke my arm fighting to keep a woman from being violated. One of the boys, he, he cut off her ear – he was holding it up like a trophy."

"That's enough. Gutke's just a child."

It didn't matter. I could see the streets, the broken glass, the drifts of ransacked papers, legs of people poking up through the debris along with legs of furniture. I sat on my hands and started rocking, breathing the way women do when they're ready for birth. Gershon and Milcah were talking to me from the other side of clouds. I knew they were there, and I had to get myself back to them so Milcah wouldn't think blood scared me, or death. A midwife has to know death. Already I understood that. But this kind of death – where does it come from?

"Drink. Just cold tea. You can hear me now? So."

Her voice was faint, but I forced myself to nod and let the liquid run down my throat. The fog began to take form, wrapping itself around those deep voices. One by one the dead filled up the room, a few beardless merchants, like Gershon; women with their hands on their heads searching for the wigs their attackers tore off them; an old Chasid stroking his long coat, ripped up and down the sides. The old ones started to move around, lifting the lids on Milcah's herb jars, inhaling the smell. I inhaled the scents of lemon verbena and dust with them.

More and more phantoms were walking around, rubbing the mirrors. When Milcah pulled a pair of candlesticks out of the hands of a bobe, who was saying, "These look just like mine," I realized the ghosts were real, not just some private dream I was having.

Milcah pressed her fist against her upper lip, concentrating. As if it were a puppy, she brushed aside a crawling child whose entrails dragged along the floor. "Come, Gershon, you'll say kadish."

"Mama, I don't go to shul any more." A woman floating overhead, her bloody apron flapping beside Gershon's face, looked down at the floor, rubbing her hands, disapproving.

"Did I say go to shul? You don't remember the mourners' kadish? How do you think we're going to get these dead out of here?"

Milcah went to a drawer and retrieved a little yarmulke. Like a boy, Gershon put it on. When Milcah lit the candles, a group of women gathered around her.

"So, go ahead. The kadish," Milcah whispered.

Gershon started to choke again. One of the dead, a young yeshive scholar whose beard was still growing in awkward tufts, clapped him on the back. Startled, Gershon coughed once and stood up. The first words of the kadish came out in a strangled squeak, and the yeshive boy shook his head, mocking. A girl in the corner hid a giggle behind the stump of her arm. Gershon turned red, his voice cracked once and

then settled seriously in his chest. A real voice emerged, not the whine of someone beaten who has come home to cry in his mama's lap. The ghosts stopped prying into Milcah's things and closed their eyes.

"Go now, rest, we will remember you," I heard my own voice singing, as soft as Milcah's prayer. The ghosts were starting to float up to the ceiling, some with their heads upside down so they could hear the very last words of the kadish – *va'al kol Yisrael, v'al kol yosh'vay tayvel, vi'imru amen.* By the time Gershon was done, all had disappeared.

I walked with Gershon to the baths and asked our yardworker to find Reb Kohn. Reb Kohn was delighted to see Gershon, who was, after all, news. He pumped his arm without thinking or noticing how it hurt and led him off. Milcah said I had to come right back to her, not stop to see my mother or Pesah, no matter how much I wanted. To tell the truth, I was frightened and wanted to go to them, but I liked how seriously Milcah treated me.

"Oy, Gutke," she said when I got back. The house was full of burning herbs and Milcah was on her knees, scrubbing the floor. All the mirrors were covered. She got up, smoothing her skirts. "You must learn how to control yourself."

"Me?"

"You. You have in yourself a very powerful window between the worlds."

"What worlds?"

She laughed for the first time that day. "What worlds? How should I know? You think I can move back and forth like you do? You don't know how you move?"

"No." I didn't think I had moved at all. I just became still and the ghosts arrived. It was one thing to hear murmurs, an occasional word in the well-water, to feel, sometimes, that it was more than the wind brushing my arm. But to be the cause of ghosts? I looked at my shoes. "I'm sorry."

"Apologies have nothing to do with this. First you will have to accept that this happens to you. But inside you, you move – now I've seen it at least three or four times. It doesn't only happen around me, does it?"

Maybe we were a bad combination, she was thinking, like mixing the wrong herbs together. But I remembered how I felt seeing the bathhouse sign when I was just a baby, and how I had been drawn to Golde's room that night.

"No, I see and hear things other times, usually it just lasts for a minute," I said. "But it's when I'm with you that big things happen – the babies, the pogrom." Maybe it wasn't all my fault. I couldn't look at Milcah, so I concentrated on a bunch of lavender hanging on the wall.

"Yes, that's very wise, very true. The gates open in birth and death – and sex, but you're too young for that. Yes, and you're young. This may get weaker as you grow up. God forbid it should get stronger. So, now we know you have this talent, you can direct it."

"Talent?" A talent was to know how to save a baby's life or manage a business like the bathhouse. What happened to me seemed more like a curse than a talent, like being born with six fingers.

"Sometimes, Gutke, you're as thick as cold kasha. No one chooses her talents. We're lucky if we find out early what they are." She must have heard herself scolding, because her voice softened. "Think of this as a form of spiritual talent. If you were a man, you'd become one of those wonder rabbis who strive with spirits."

If I hadn't just seen the ghosts, I would have thought Milcah was teasing me. A wonder rabbi – she might as well have said I could have been the tsar. "I thought they were just in stories."

"Stories come from life. We don't rely on them the way we did when I was a girl but that doesn't mean they don't hold truths. So, what should we do with you?" She rubbed her hands together, thinking.

I had a knot in the bottom of my stomach. I was used to being different from other girls, that's not what bothered me. It was the spirits themselves. I never thought the wall that separated us from angels and demons was so thin that ghosts could actually use me as a place to enter the world. I felt transparent, as if I were a branch of leaves and a cold night wind was blowing through me, tearing off bits. I was silent, but Milcah must have heard my fear.

"Come, sit down beside me. It's not so bad, child. You will gain control of yourself, learn how to keep the window shut and open it when you want. You will have to learn how to say kadish like a boy, for the stillbirths and miscarriages – otherwise you'll start carrying around the dybuks of infants, what a mess that would be! It's a good thing Pesah sent you to me, she has her moments of insight. I myself will make you a talis – "

"A talis?" Only boys wore talesim. It's one thing to be different inside, another to wear your difference so anyone can see. The knot in my stomach grew by inches.

"For under your clothes, not exactly like a man's, but a fringed vest.

You'll wear it when you deliver women. You're almost thirteen now, right? For boys it's thirteen, for girls twelve, when they make the passage. That's what this is, your passage. Do you bleed yet?"

"Just last month, a few drops. My mother showed me how to make the cloths. She slapped me and said I would start to know what pain means."

"Your mother, may her life be long and sweet, is not the most enlightened of women. You know this?"

Of course I knew this. Even the yardboy knew this.

"Tell me when you bleed. It may influence the bat kol or whatever makes you prophesy at birth. We will experiment." She rose as though she had been stuck with a pin. "I have just the thing to help you. Here – " Milcah rummaged through some old embroidered bags in a bottom drawer, "this stone. You will carry it in your pocket whenever we go to attend a birth. If the birth is going well, you just need to think about it. If death comes into the room, hold on to it."

It seemed like an ordinary stone, with shiny flecks, but when she put it in my hand, I saw a little farm and could feel the black dirt of the Ukraine in my palm. My stomach relaxed. I put the stone in my pocket. Today, even, I have it still.

Much was revealed in those years with Milcah. I have come to believe that life is a long corridor hung with veils. Every time we get past one veil, we feel that now we understand, we have the true, clear picture. Then we move a little bit, see the next veil and are frightened – both because we were boastful in our ignorance, and because we must go on to find out what's behind it. When you're young, you run through this corridor, shivering with fear and excitement. Every day you're reborn a wise woman, every night you're a humble wretch, begging God's forgiveness. Then you come to the wonderful nights when you forget about God altogether. Now I find such a long distance between the veils that I sometimes think I'm at the end of the corridor. But it was not so long ago that I became the age Milcah was when I first came to her, and the veil separating us lifted. Then I could see what she meant and thought in everything she taught me. When I remember this, I know there are many veils still separating me from my end. Who knows what will be behind the last one?

When I think of the last veil, I believe behind it will be the splendor of the palace of God. And then I realize God's palace looks, in my mind, like the bathhouse. It could be worse.

Every day, every year, I was learning new things. At night I would tell Feygele and Pesah all about the women – who screamed loudest, who had the biggest babies. Pesah knew everyone, and she would cluck and hum: "Yes, I knew it!" or "Who would've thought?" I didn't tell them about the spirits.

I wanted to tell. Sometimes I thought of Golde, how dark her eyes were, how she would understand. But she was a grown woman and besides, Yetta was always with her. I made sure to be working the nights they came. Now they gave me ten kopecks. Yetta would frown and Golde would wink. That's all. I would make sure the girls who took the private tubs would get what they paid for, which was privacy.

A couple, maybe three years passed this way. Sometimes I myself guided the baby into this life, and Milcah helped me. I earned fifty kopecks from every birth, and made a few more selling concoctions from the herbs I gathered on my own. I felt I was truly blessed; this I never forgot for a minute.

One night Golde arrived at the baths alone. Her eyes were puffy from crying.

"Good evening, how are you? It's just me tonight," she said as if everything was fine. So I gave her towels. I waited a few minutes, considering. It didn't take a spirit to tell me I should go in to see her.

I knocked. "It's only me, Gutke. I thought maybe you would like a drink of cold water." When I went in, she was sitting on the bench with her hands folded neatly in her lap, a towel across her shoulders, draping her breasts. She was staring at the floor. I looked at her hair, which got so curly in the steam I didn't think you could run a brush over it.

"I'm sorry," she said, looking up at me, her eyes spilling tears.

"For what should you be sorry to me? Tell me what's wrong."

She laughed a little. "You're always so nice to me, Gutke. But this you wouldn't understand."

"I understand something bad has happened between you and Yetta – is she all right?"

"Oh, she's fine, just perfect!" Golde ground her teeth in rage. "The shadkhn's been pestering her for years. But she was her mother's youngest, the baby. For her, they could wait for just the right match. Yetta said, she said – "

"Yes?" I asked. I sat on the bench next to her. Of course, I had my clothes on, so I was very hot. Just a light skirt and a blouse with the sleeves rolled up, but even so.

"She said I was the right match for her."

Golde hung her head, and I could tell she was ashamed to reveal this to me. I wasn't sure exactly how to reassure her. "Yes, it seems to me she loves you very much."

"You could see it? Did other people see it?"

What an opportunity! "I don't think so. I can see things other people don't."

"What?"

"I see spirits, or visions, when women are giving birth. Sometimes I can see a little bit of what will happen to their children. Milcah says sometimes I hear a bat kol. She told me not to tell anyone about this, but I – " Golde looked at me so sharply it made the sweat burn and prickle where my skin was exposed.

"You can see the future?"

"Only a little bit, when babies are born. Other times I just get a feeling." I shrugged. I didn't want her to think I was too strange to confide in.

"Yes?"

"Just a feeling. Here – ," I pressed my chest, "or sometimes in my arms or legs. Not like something is taking over me but like something is giving me a direction. It's not such a big thing. I think if people paid more attention, more would admit to having ordinary visions." I decided not to tell her about my little talis or about the time the dead came to Milcah's.

"You mean you think there are spirits around us all the time but only a few people admit they feel them?"

"Not exactly." It was so hot, I was shvitsing up all my clothes. "It's more that everyone is so busy getting food on the table. Most people don't have time for spirits. So they feel a tug at their elbow – they think it's the wind."

Golde gave me a small sad smile. "Yes. I think you're right. So smart for a girl."

"I'm not a girl," I protested. "I bleed, I've seen 172 births and three women die."

"Really?" She patted my hand, almost forgetting I was there. "I apologize then."

"So. Yetta's getting married?" I didn't want her to drift away from me, even if I had to make her cry again.

And she did. The tears balled up, fell down her face and nose quietly. "Yes. She's marrying Leybl, who works for the railroad. The

shadkhn says he's very handsome and has a good steady job. I can't bear it."

"But Golde, what could she do? If it's a good match and the parents want it, how could she refuse?"

"She could have just refused. She doesn't care about him."

"So, she gets married. You can still see her."

"She doesn't want to make a scandal."

"What scandal? You still have your shop, nu? So she comes in to have you make clothes or to help you with something. Pesah's friend Sadie is here every day to help with the midday meal."

"Yes, but they're old. And both married. And besides, they don't feel about each other like I feel about Yetta."

"How do you know?"

Again Golde stared at me. "Pesah Kohn touches Sadie Rabinovitch?"

I blushed. "I don't know for a fact. Only after I saw you and Yetta, I thought, maybe – "

"Maybe. No, it can't be." She held my hand tightly, staring at something a long way off. "And you?"

"Me?" The breath tangled in my lungs like an umbilical cord coming out before a baby. I took my hands away and folded them in my lap. Sweat was staining my blouse and back, dripping down the curve of my ears.

"I'm sorry. I shouldn't ask such things. Even if I am doomed to gehene for my sin. This room – it was a world apart for me. Please forgive me."

"Where is it written that love is a sin?" My breath came back to me.

She sighed. "Among women, sins don't have to be written. You should know that. Not marrying is a scandal, not having twelve children a sin. Reading Mendele is a sin. Not lighting the Shabbes candles is a sin, not baking bread for the poor is a sin – "

"You don't light the Shabbes candles?"

"Of course I light the Shabbes candles. I'm just saying."

I was relieved somehow. I realized I had a picture in my mind of Golde bentshing likht, waving her hands over the flames, her dark eyes closed, her eyelids a delicate purple. My blush came back. "I don't know the answer to your question," I said, pushing the words out of me before I choked on them.

"My question? Oh." She looked all the way through me. Even in the steam, I could feel a coolness. "I don't mean to insult you, but you are young still to know this. And maybe you have seen too many things.

Too many intimate parts of a woman." She considered me a little differently. "I myself only saw Yetta, and the women in the bathhouse, but just passing by."

"So how did you know?"

"I don't know, really. I grew up with all boys. So I was curious about girls. And, well, some of my brothers were nice, but my brother Moishe, the second oldest, a rotten fish. Always making a disturbance in the kheder, always with his hands on me. I had to take care of all of them while Mama was sick and then after she died. I knew I didn't want to let myself be married to a villain like Moishe, and then, when I thought about it, I didn't want to keep taking care of boys at all. I looked around. I'm not a fool."

You couldn't be less of a fool than Golde, I thought.

"Most of the women are out in the marketplace or sewing a little this or that or keeping the store and the books. So I decided to be an old maid. Isn't that a funny thing for a Jewish girl!"

"There are worse things."

"Not according to the bathhouse women."

"Still."

"Yes, still. But how did I know? Swimming in the river, taking measurements for a skirt, when Yetta made a joke about a psalm. In little bits, I suppose. And – "

"Yes?"

"When I kissed Yetta, then I knew."

"Oh." This would have been a good time to excuse myself. I had a lot of work to see about. But instead I pulled together my courage. "Maybe, maybe you should kiss me, so I will know."

Golde laughed. I felt like I was burning up. I struggled to my feet, but she grabbed hold of my hand.

"Little Gutke, I'm sorry. Please. I'm not laughing at you. It's just, I can't. It wouldn't be right. I am mourning for my Yetta, and I don't have a feeling like that for you. Don't misunderstand me. I think you are a very comely young woman, very interesting. But I'm already twenty-three and you're only what, fifteen?"

"Sixteen in a month. Women get married younger."

"Yes, but we're not talking about marriage, are we?" So sad, she looked. "We will be friends, yes? We'll talk. I'll help you if I can."

I stood up as tall as I could. "Please forgive me for being so forward."

"You forgive me, I forgive you. All right? Friends?"

"Friends."

• • • • •

A year went by, maybe two. Business kept getting better at the bathhouse. Reb Kohn said Kishinev was the crown jewel of the southwest, with more traveling businessmen every day, Romanians and Turks. The increase in trade brought foreign Jews to the baths, even Arabic Jews from Turkey.

"The Turks are spies," Pesah said without looking up from her mending.

"Nonsense. What makes you think that?" Reb Kohn asked.

"There are too many Russian soldiers in town."

"This is the capital of Bessarabia and more important than ever. That's why the soldiers are here."

"And that's why I think the Turks are spies," she said, cutting the thread to repair Feygele's old apron.

"Everyone knows that our Kishinev wool is finer than Odessa's, and cheaper too. The Turks are just here for wool for their rugs."

"All right, Reb Kohn," Pesah said, "whether they're spies or traders makes no difference to me. We still need to hire another boy for the men's side. Our guests expect the kind of service they get in Kiev and Constantinople, and we have to keep them content. We don't want any trouble from the authorities – on either side. Now you'll excuse us. Gutke and I have towels to wash."

"You see how she is," Reb Kohn said. It seemed like he was talking to me, though he didn't look my way. He would probably rather talk to a ghost. "She may see conspiracies everywhere, but she knows what's good for the business."

Pesah rolled her eyes as we went into the courtyard.

Business was good not only because of so many foreigners in town, but because of an outbreak of illness. Smaller than a plague, the disease gave people fevers, chills, terrible pains and congestion. Some were dying. People thought sweating was healthy, that it drew the sickness out of you. Milcah said this was pure superstition, that people who were sick should stay home and not risk spreading it. When she told this to Pesah, Pesah got so mad her voice trembled.

"Who made you a doctor? And tell me, did you enjoy your classes at the university in Saint Petersburg? I have been running this bathhouse for twenty years. Nothing cures a person of sickness like a good sweat and maybe a little cupping, if it's serious."

"Maybe the cupping helps remove bad blood, but coughing and dripping in each other's faces spreads disease. 'Don't lie down with a healthy head in a sick bed,' " Milcah replied. She was one of the few

women in town who wasn't cowed by Pesah's size and self-possession.

"Are you telling me my bathhouse spreads disease?"

"Pesah, calm yourself, please. This is not about you personally. You and I, we both have a trust for the health of Jews. You can't take that lightly."

"I'm up from sunrise to the middle of the night, scrubbing, cleaning, because I take my duty lightly? Maybe I've had enough of you this week, Mrs.-Speaks-With-Angels. Go. Go home, crush a few herbs."

Two weeks later my mother, Feygele, started coughing. I was busy tending to births and sickbeds with Milcah, so I didn't notice how badly off she was until her groans woke me one night. She had thrown her covers off, her face was hot, almost burning to the touch. I ran to get Milcah through the unpaved streets, my shadow jumping sideways in front and behind the oil lamps.

"Please, I know you're angry at Pesah but my mother – "

Milcah followed me home. Pesah was already sitting by the bed, holding my mother's hand, rocking back and forth.

"You want to help?" Milcah said to Pesah, "here, heat these." She handed her folded rags full of clay and nettles. They didn't say another word to each other the entire week Feygele lay there, growing sicker and smaller.

My mother and I shared a room behind the stable, with a narrow iron bed and a straw pallet beside the stove. She insisted I take the bed after I started apprenticing because, she said, I had two jobs and she only had one. But while she was sick I went back to sleeping on the pallet, as I had when I was a child. And I felt like a child again, in everyone's way, unsure of what I should do.

"A midwife has to learn to bear trouble even when it comes close," Milcah said as gently as she could.

"But what good is everything I learned, and your bat kol, when I didn't even notice my mother getting sick right in front of me? Why couldn't I see it?"

Milcah opened her mouth as if to say a proverb but thought better of it. "Sometimes we do better by strangers than our own. No one knows why. I won't expect you this week. You stay by your mother."

Pesah avoided Milcah when she came to change the poultices or administer a tincture. On the third night she muttered, "That woman has no idea what she's doing."

"Pesah, we have to do something."

"Oh, shayne," she said, wrapping her big arms around me, "I'm

sorry. Of course, we have to do something."

But Feygele pushed the poultices off and spit out Milcah's potions. A smell like wet burning leaves lingered in the room, and then a smell of sulfur. On the eighth night, my mother gestured for me to come close.

"Gutke," she whispered. My name seemed torn out of her throat, and I waited for the important thing I knew she wanted to tell me.

She asked for a little of Pesah's plum jam.

"Anything, Mama," I said. The corners of her mouth turned up slightly.

I ran to get the jam and Pesah followed me back. When we got there, she was dead.

They say blood drops from the sword of the Angel of Death into water where someone dies. Pesah emptied all the water from every bucket, every tub, even the mikve, although Feygele died in her own bed. Pesah kept turning around in circles: first the water, then covering the mirrors, then hammering together boxes for us to sit on and cry. At least she could move. I felt as if every muscle in my body had turned to stone.

I never thought so many people would come. All day, morning and afternoon, the house was full of visitors. Many, I know, came because of Pesah and Reb Kohn, who knew almost every Jew in town. But I saw how my mother's hardworking spirit had touched people – she was always kind, never gossiped. She only let Pesah and me close to her, but her gentleness and singing voice were a sweet spirit in the bathhouse. The other workers and the women she attended appreciated her, even the ones who suspected her story was not entirely the truth, the ones who called me a mamzer behind Feygele's back. Reb Kohn finally admitted that it was a mitsve for everyone that Pesah had taken my mother in, and he paid for all the funeral expenses without a touch of bitterness.

I had never been to a funeral of someone I loved. A few times I went with grieving mothers to the burials of their dead; twice I stood behind the family when a woman had expired while giving birth, so I knew how the ritual went. Yet I never anticipated my mother's death. She rarely complained of so much as an ache, though I would sometimes rub her back and legs with olive oil in the evenings. My little dark-eyed mother.

It was early spring. Standing among the group beside the open grave, I noticed the first leaves had just rolled open. The rabbi

motioned to me. I picked up the shovel and threw a mound of dirt into my mother's grave. As the dirt thudded against her coffin, a wail I didn't expect shook my body. Pesah took the shovel from my hands, her own face streaked from weeping. She threw a shovelful in and we stepped back.

"Who will say kadish for this woman?" the rabbi asked.

I cleared my throat to speak and felt the full weight of Pesah's hand on my shoulder. "In private, at home, not here," she hissed in my ear. Milcah was on the other side of me, squeezing my hand.

Reb Kohn stepped forward and recited, *"Yis'gadal v'yiskadash sh'may rabah..."*

I was so angry I had a fresh burst of tears. Everyone thought it was my gratitude to the man who had treated me like a father, or perhaps my grief over my mother. But I was furious at the way Jews clot around a wound, a death, making such a hard scab. It was always appearances that counted. I loved my mother – I was the one who should be mourning and praying for her, the one whose kadish God should have heard first. I was the one she gave up her life for, the one who walked to Kishinev with her. I had the right and the obligation. I wanted to scream at them. Pesah's hand tightened. I kept crying and everyone thought I was a wonderful daughter.

I stood between Pesah and Milcah. They glared at each other. I could hear them, though they didn't speak a word.

– *Your fault for not listening to me.*

– *And what was I supposed to do? Close the baths? Your fault for putting the evil eye on me.*

And both of them believed, yes, they could have prevented this. They should have known. A few herbs. A week of rest.

I left them staring at each other and walked alone to the edge of the cemetery. I was looking up at the patterns the leaves made, wondering where my mother had gone, when I felt someone standing beside me. I turned, expecting to look into my mother's face. Golde's dark eyes startled me.

"I'm sorry."

"My mother – " I intended to give some easy epigram. Instead I started to weep, not in anger any more but because my poor mother – what did she ever have? "My mother had no pleasure," I was surprised to hear myself say. What a thing for a Jew to even think: Pleasure!

Golde quickly put her arms around me. Her sweet smell mixed with the smell of death that was still strong in my nostrils.

"Sha, of course she did. Of course she did, Gutke." Golde, who had nothing to prove, was such a relief after Pesah and Milcah's stubborn guilts. Although I was a little bigger than her, I felt at home when she held me. This time there was no fog, only relief.

She stroked my hair and kept talking softly. "All you ever saw was that your mother worked and sang. But I saw how she loved you, how she relied on you and Pesah. Every day that you were all together and safe was a miracle to her. She was a woman who had faith in little miracles and they sustained her. Faith is a kind of pleasure, Gutke. But it's right to feel terrible now. I remember when my mother died – " I moved out of her embrace but held on to her hand. "I felt something like what you just said, that my mother never had enough in life, my father and brothers stole all her time."

"I'm sorry, Golde. I didn't realize."

"No need to apologize. Time makes it easier, even if we never forget. Today it's your turn for a little comfort, Gutke. Come, walk with me. Cry as much as you want for your mother."

When the proscribed seven days of mourning were over and Pesah uncovered the mirrors, I told her I thought I had finished my apprenticeships.

"Yes," she agreed, hardly looking at me, "You always learned quickly. You probably know more than Milcah by now."

"I don't know if I ever will know as much as Milcah. She's a very learned woman."

"Even the wisest women can be fools."

"Pesah, you're not listening to me. Enough between you and Milcah – it wasn't either of your faults that Feygele died. God gives with one hand and takes away with the other, you know that."

"Oy, I'm sorry, Gutke, shayne, I should be the one saying that to you."

"Pesah, this isn't easy for me."

"No, of course not." She misunderstood me and pressed my hand against her breast, to soothe me. I waited a second before pulling it away.

"No, I mean leaving."

"Leaving Milcah?"

"Yes. And leaving here."

"Leaving here? But why? Where would you go?" She was startled and

as soon as the startle left her, she was full as a steam engine ready to explode. I immediately wanted to take it back. "You can't leave. It's my duty to your mother, of blessed memory, to make a dowry for you and see you married."

"Pesah, I appreciate your goodwill and generosity. But I can make my own way in the world now. I have a trade and I'm healthy and young. I have no interest in being married yet. You have been as much a mother to me as Feygele and I have no intention of deserting you – only of testing my own strength."

"Testing your own strength! And where will you go?"

"Golde Zelkin has a little room behind her shop where I can live."

"For this you leave me? To live behind an old maid's pitiful store? This is your big adventure in life? What makes this more appealing than living here with me?"

"I grew up in the baths, Pesah. Now I have to be a working woman on my own."

She drummed her fingers on the table. She got up, paced the room and looked out the window. I looked over her shoulder as a couple men ran through the courtyard but Pesah was oblivious. She sighed and turned around.

"You really mean to leave me all alone?"

"Alone? Pesah, you're not alone. Every day people crowd around to tell you the latest gossip, to eat at your table. Your friend Sadie doesn't miss a weekday meal here. And Reb Kohn – "

"Please."

"But anyway, you're hardly alone." I heard a sound like thunder a long way off.

"What's that? Not rain?" Pesah was momentarily distracted.

The sun streamed through the window panes. "I think your laundry is safe for at least a few more hours," I said. I had an uneasy sensation but let it go as Pesah resumed her complaint.

"Your mother, now you. You have no pity on an old woman."

I put my hands on her shoulders. I was only a head shorter than her, which made me among the tallest Jewish women in Kishinev, but she was still twice as wide, if not quite as big as she used to be. "Of course you will miss me. I'll miss you. It's sad but no reason for pity. You're not some helpless incompetent. You're a tower of strength, a beacon of Israel." I quoted what the rabbi recited at my mother's funeral: " 'Many daughters have done virtuously, but thou excellest them all.' "

"You! You could talk the snake into giving up its poison."

"I had a good teacher."

"Enough with the flattery. Go on, if you're going to go. Get your things."

What did I have? The talis vest Milcah made, my clothes, a few books on medicine, the storybook Pesah gave me when I was a child and a Yiddish translation of *David Copperfield*. My mother's candlesticks, my knife and tools for birth, an assortment of herbs and potions. When I was ready, Pesah handed me a heavy bag. It was crammed with rubles.

"What's this?" I said, amazed.

"It's your mother's wages. You think she was a slave here? Not in my house. She saved almost every kopeck. For your dowry. You should marry a yeshive bokher, someone from a good family. You're eighteen, off on your own. I give it to you."

"But the cost of the funeral – "

"Don't insult. This was an honor to me, and to Reb Kohn even, to bury Feygele Gurvich. And this – ." From her cabinet, Pesah handed me an old Chanukah menorah, an oil one, not like the ones for candles they make now. "This was my own grandmother's. I'm not giving it to any of Reb Kohn's daughters-in-law, I can tell you that. You take good care of it."

We stood there sighing, looking at each other. I'm not sure how long men were yelling in the background before we heard them. What now?

Pesah turned back to the window. The courtyard had filled with Russian cavalry.

"Quick, hide all your things. Get in the root cellar." Her reaction was instant, instinctual.

"I'm not leaving you alone up here."

"Do what I tell you! Go on."

I hid the money and my bag, staying on the stairs to the root cellar, listening. Pesah was talking with a man, but I couldn't make out what they were saying. No screams, no "hep! hep!" I came out again.

"Didn't I tell you to go to the root cellar?"

"What are the soldiers doing here?"

"Nu, it never ends. There's a new war. They didn't think to inform us until now. The Tsar is fighting the Sultan for Bessarabia again. I told Reb Kohn all those Turks couldn't be wool traders. Now the soldiers are taking over the bathhouse."

"What's wrong with their barracks?"

"Too small. Another plague, I tell you. What will we do?"

"Take back the money – "

"No, this is yours, and besides, you think I don't save my own? It's best you have somewhere to go. God forbid, we might have to go live with one of Reb Kohn's sons. The soldiers will need someone to cook for them, I expect. Maybe I'll get to stay put. Pray this war is over soon and that those Cossacks don't destroy my garden."

I retrieved my things, hid the money in my skirts as best I could and walked out through a street full of soldiers on horses. They made every kind of insult. I just looked forward and prayed, holding my skirt up. I remembered how I thought less of my mother for looking straight ahead in life, never turning to the left or right. I wondered if she could see me, swallowing my arrogance.

The whole town was in a state of excitement. The gunfire which we'd mistaken for a storm was still far off, so people were out on the streets, in the marketplace, buying up whatever they could. As I made my way to Golde's, I overheard the fruit peddler ask Yosl the cobbler if the Turks would really attack Kishinev.

Yosl had three sons over twelve at home and I could see memories of forced conscription cross his face. "Maybe they will, maybe they won't. Myself, I don't think they'll get that far. But the real question is, will this be an excuse to drag more Jewish boys into the army?"

Hannah, who sold eggs, stopped me to ask if I thought the Governor would maintain order among the troops, or would they just take what they wanted? Would the government pay cash for its extra provisions, demand credit or have everything brought by convoy from Saint Petersburg?

I started to laugh before I realized how serious she was. "Hannah, sell every egg you can today and hide the rest until we can tell better which way the wind is blowing. Here, give me a half dozen now."

Holding my eggs carefully in a kerchief, I slipped in and out of the confusion and made it to Golde's shop unharmed.

The Russian-Turkish war was over in less than two years but not before the troops left their mark on local women. Jewish women were particular favorites of the Cossacks. Milcah sent many who did not want to bear Russian babies to me. There is knowledge people hope never to need, and they entrust the knowing to a handful who become strong enough to bear it. We don't advertise, but midwives know what to do when a child is unwanted, and women know that we know. I gave those who came, usually in the dark, cloaked and stammering,

strong doses of pennyroyal oil and tea. Every night I remember those souls in my prayers. Many women chose to have the babies, the married ones pretending it was their husband's, the unmarried leaving Kishinev, even as my own mother had done.

The year before I stopped working with Milcah, she gave me a tattered piece of paper. "Something else to consider," was all she said. I never found out if she composed it herself or had gotten it from the midwife who taught her. After the war I memorized it.

The Midwife's Prayer

Lord of the universe, blessed be thy name,
I am among thy faithful, hear my prayer!
I have watched the bowels
torn out of women and girls
babies come sideways and stick
killing mother and child.
I have seen too many women without bread
birth their sixth, seventh, ninth.
We increase the carriers of your covenant
in blood and pain.
Creator of all things
who makes the summer days long and
the vineyards bear grapes, hear my prayer!
Give the women relief
from your commandment of fruitfulness.
Send us seven barren years
that each may simply breathe and make peace
with her fate and her faith or
give your humble servants some consolation,
some sign beyond the starving new mouth.
We are the daughters of Sarah, we have
served you well all these generations, hardly
do you hear a mother complain.
For them I beseech you.
The lot of women
is too hard and they are too worthy
to endure so much with so little reward.
Lord of the universe, bestower of light and life,

I pray that you may find in your vast treasure
a time to love your creature woman
even as I do, and give her rest.
Amen.

Even through those terrible times, I often blessed Pesah Kohn in my prayers for deciding I should be a midwife, and my mother for agreeing. Women always need potions for something. And even in the worst of circumstances, a midwife was given something, at least a meal, maybe a chicken.

I paid Golde five rubles a month and we took most of our dinners together, unless I was attending a birth. Her father had died not more than six months before my mother, from old age. I don't think she missed him and she had the extra room. As much as I hated to leave Pesah, Golde had the knowledge I needed next: how to be an unmarried Jewish woman, a rare thing. I was happy living with Golde, as happy as I could be in that time. Golde never changed her mind about me. Often I thought of kissing her but I was ashamed to ask again. Besides, she had become more like an older sister to me, familiar and dear. We were loyal to each other the way women can be when they share a secret they never talk about. I replaced Golde's image in my daydreams with the figure of a stranger, covered in a black cloak, who would come to our door looking for an elixir for some minor ailment.

Golde made up with Yetta but it wasn't between them like before. Her business expanded and she hired four more girls. She was busy with the shop and I was busy with my patients. A few years after I moved in, Golde started to see a teacher from the gardening school, Vera, a German. Vera had heard there were beautiful lace trimmed skirts in Golde's shop and she came to see.

Vera was a modern woman, handsome and tall. I never really took to her but Golde was smitten the minute the shop bell tinkled and she looked up. Who can afford such feelings in this world? Of course, Vera couldn't live with us. What would people think, a wealthy goy moving into a Jew's pitiful house? So they would take a walk in the evenings by the river or maybe go to a concert. Sometimes Golde would suffer a fit of longing during the workday. If Vera wasn't teaching, Golde would make up a bundle from the shop, like a delivery, and go by Vera's apartment. Saturday nights Golde spent there, after Shabbes. Sunday,

Golde's workers didn't come to work until eight. She was always home in plenty of time to prepare their work.

There were new clothing factories that could make a dress much cheaper than Golde's little shop, but many people, Jews and others, continued to buy from her. Her work was good and made to order. Some bought from pity, I think, because it was a house of old maids and poor working girls, yet there was no need to pity us. Golde was good to the girls. They worked usually only twelve hours a day. She paid a few kopecks a week better than the factory and did her best to make the light good for sewing. She encouraged the girls to know about the Russky Zyuse workers' union and the seamstresses' self-help society, and they in turn told the girls who were going to work in the factories.

Her goodwill kept the girls from gossiping too much. To them Golde was more like a patron or a teacher than a boss. And Golde kept the sabbath, contributed to all the Jewish funds for orphans and burials, always went out with a babushka wrapped around her hair even though, as an unmarried woman, she didn't have to. She was a good businesswoman, an honest Jew and, to most of her customers, an unfortunate. The marriage brokers pestered both of us but we always managed to put them off.

If Golde liked to touch the bodies of women, and I liked to think of her touching them, what difference could it possibly make? I knew there were a few other women like us. Some of the married women even – I could tell, after a while, how it was between them and their best friend who assisted at a birth. Bits of daydream came to me while I gathered herbs or before I fell asleep. I was young and hungry for touch, but I couldn't see how it was going to come to me.

Besides, so much else was happening. Tsar Alexander II was assassinated, and suffering was the air in our lungs. The uprooted filled the streets of Kishinev for more than ten years. Many families even had to borrow coal in winter in order to boil water for the newborn. Pogroms raged throughout the Pale – one year of misery, then maybe a little break; families moving from one town to another; then a famine in the north and more homeless. Tsar Alexander III enforced the May Laws; more Jews got thrown off their land, out of their shtetls. We got used to so many poor in the streets, living on less and less. There was a little calm, then a depression, and the Tsar took it into his mind to expel all the Jews from Saint Petersburg and Moscow. They arrived here chained together like criminals, doctors and businessmen.

When we consider our youth, we see only ourselves and the way

the world unfolds in front of us. We are full figures walking among cut-outs of buildings and people, never knowing exactly what's behind them – and we don't care. But gradually we grow smaller and smaller, until we are part of the landscape in which we move, and then we find others all around us, moving, becoming part of time. For seven years the whole catalog of human misery paraded before me and my own life began to seem like a blade of grass that escaped the scythe – fortunate and insignificant. I tended closely to women and I saw most of their lives only getting harder. Gradually the misery around me supplanted my daydreams and I became serious, almost bitter. There were no potions that could cure Jewish poverty or my own loneliness. Golde worried about me. One spring day when I was pounding herbs so hard that the old brass pestle clanged, she took my hand, turned my gaze away.

"You must find a little joy where you can, Gutkelle." She was the only one who called me that.

"And where does this joy live?"

"Saturday night you'll come by Vera's. She has guests from Odessa and Kiev. It's a party."

"I don't want to go to a party with goyim."

"Not just goyim, Jews too. Only women will be there."

I stared at her. Of course. If men have secret societies, then there must be some for women too. Only so secret no one knows until they're invited.

"You'll come then?"

Saturday afternoon a Mrs. Simkhovitch on Asia Street decided to deliver at least a week early, a protracted, difficult birth. Thank God the mother and daughter were fine. Only midwives work on Shabbes! Golde had gone to Vera's ahead of me. She left a note, so sweet, that I shouldn't forget to come.

To tell the truth, I was worn out. I needed some Shabbes rest. Then I thought again about Golde and Vera, how their hands found each other whenever Vera came to the shop. I liked to watch their hands, how they try to keep them still, behind their backs, in their pockets. Suddenly a finger is pushing a curl back from the temple, a palm is against a cheek that blushes, turning to see if anyone's looking.

I put on a clean skirt and the multicolored shawl that Pesah herself had knit for me. It reminded me of Joseph's coat of many colors, though I had no one to be jealous when I wore it. There were four shades of red, one pale gold, a light blue and purple. I stood by the

doorway playing with the fringe, for a minute unable to move beyond the threshold of my home – but I did.

It was a long walk to Vera's and dark already. I knew the spirits looked out for me, yet even so, I didn't like to walk alone at night. I reached Vera's apartment without anyone noticing me.

Suddenly my skin felt dry and hot, my palms wet. Nervous – this was what nervous was. Me! Brave enough to talk to demons and too afraid to go to a party. But from Odessa and Kiev, goyim and the daughters of wealthy Jews – I was only a midwife, Feygele of Kamenka's mamzer daughter. What would I talk about with such women? Pacing up and down in front of the building, I didn't notice that a man in a carriage was watching me.

"Is something wrong?" I heard a voice as he stepped to the sidewalk. There were only street lamps and shadows, but for a second I had the image of a flame. Just for a moment, the crackle of fire in branches.

"No, I'm just catching my breath."

"Are you going up to Vera Lessing's party?"

I nodded. He was just slightly taller than me, very dark, a neat little mustache, no sidelocks, probably a Jewish merchant from Europe. His Yiddish was formal – he didn't come from Kishinev, that was certain. He smelled of cologne and cities. Then I understood. We looked at each other closely. The gas lights flickered. Her eyes were a light golden brown that shone from the olive of her face.

"Dovida Greenbaum," she said, "though mostly I am called Dovid."

"Gutke Gurvich." I didn't know what else to say. I kept staring at her face, the little mustache. How did she make it seem so real? Maybe it was real. Many women I knew had hair they plucked. If they tended and shaped it instead, I could imagine some might have a mustache as handsome as Dovida's.

"Are you shocked by me?"

"Oh. No. Not shocked, surprised."

"Surprised. Well, that's honest. May I have the pleasure of escorting you upstairs?"

Such manners. Then I really felt like a peasant although I could see that Dovida meant to charm, not shame, me.

Vera's three rooms were stuffed like kishkes with women. I assumed they were all women, though if you saw them on the street at least six or seven you would think were men. And I thought I had seen every possible kind of woman in the bathhouse! I had never spent more than a minute thinking about what it would be like to move in the world as

a man. Long ago I divided men up into patriarchs, demons and ghosts. Patriarchs were worse than demons, because they made the rules. Demons just tormented you. Ghosts mouthed rules but had no spirit in them. Reb Kohn was like a ghost to me.

Now here was Dovida and other women who looked like Turks and Gypsies. Women who could walk where they wanted at night, who could attend any university, if they had the money. Most of the women looked as if they had rubles enough for anything, though plenty appeared to be ordinary working women.

"What are you tisking about?" Dovida came up behind me.

I sighed. Well, I was what I was. I wasn't going to pretend. "I have never been at a party like this."

Dovida examined me closely. "How did you get invited?"

"I board with Golde – over there – who is with Vera five years now."

"And you?"

And me what? Oh. I wanted to look at the floor but I looked in her eyes instead. Then I wanted to look in her eyes for a long time and not speak. But I did. "I – I am just a midwife."

"A midwife. Well, well. That's a very important trade. But – ." She took my hand. She was wearing white gloves, what a thing! " – That's not exactly what I was asking."

"I know. I just have never talked about such things with anyone. Just a little with Golde."

"Ah." She let go of my hand and I felt ashamed for not having words. It was with words God made the world, and now I couldn't find the words to make my life. "Then you're just here as a friend, an observer?" Her tone was arch and her voice deepened.

"No." I didn't want her to misunderstand me. "No, not that at all. I just – " What words could a person possibly use? "I just am innocent of my own desires." Oy, I thought, now she's going to laugh at me.

And she did. Then she took my hand again. "That's charming. You mean, you have never had the opportunity to act on your imagination?"

She said something in French, which of course I didn't understand though I had heard it in the bathhouse. Heat was spreading through my face and legs. Embarrassment, shame, anger, longing. Was that what desire was?

"I'm not a joke." The anger won. Anger was cool and relieving.

"Please forgive me. I didn't mean to laugh at your expense. I have seen many women with desire and no opportunity, and that seems like a sin to me."

A sin? I looked around. For a moment I was glad my mother was not alive to see such a party. Then I was ashamed for thinking any bad thoughts about these women – how amazing for them to have found their way here, how difficult.

"I suppose you have taken it upon yourself to right this sin?" I looked at her directly.

She laughed. "You know the Talmud says that we will have to account to God for the pleasures we did not take."

"The Talmud says that?"

"I don't suppose they intended us," she gestured across the room, "but every generation of Jews has to make its own interpretations, no?"

Golde came up behind me, put both her hands on my shoulders.

"Already you've made a friend! Introduce me." She shook Dovida's hand, moving beside me, putting her arm around my shoulder. I couldn't remember when she had been so affectionate or happy. Who could have known she'd come alive at a party? "Now don't take advantage of my roommate, she's an orphan." That she had to say! I was furious but before I could even give her a look she was off to another part of the room.

"An orphan. I'm sorry."

"Please don't be sorry for me. I loved my mother, may she be blessed by God, but she is dead seven years now. I have my own life."

"Yes. I apologize. I seem to just be blundering here. Perhaps you'd like to meet some of Vera's other guests?"

"No. I mean, if you like." But instead we just stared at each other.

"Perhaps some wine?" We went to a table that was full of pastries and cheeses, very nice. Kosher even, it looked. Well, the plates couldn't have been kosher but it was all dairy and I thought that was very respectful of Vera. In fact, suddenly I liked Vera much better.

"So, now you know I'm a midwife, an orphan and Golde's roommate. But all I know about you is that you dress like a man."

"Is that any way to ask me about myself?" We got a little wine and cheese and made our way over to the corner. I noticed the innkeeper's wife in the middle of the room with Golde's second cousin. Who would have guessed?

"I'm sorry if I'm rude but I am curious. How did you – ?" I asked.

"I ran away from my home in Krakow when I was sixteen. My father got me engaged to marry a furrier, ten years older than me. Oy, how disgusted I was."

"He was ugly?"

"Really, I don't know. He was ugly to me. My parents were Orthodox. It was against my father's wishes that my brothers taught me Hebrew, and I used to sit in the back of lectures at the gymnasium to learn German. I couldn't imagine being stuck at home with a man who stank of animal skins and petty ambitions. I left." Dovida wiped a crumb of cheese off her lip with an embroidered handkerchief.

"You just ran away, a sixteen-year-old girl?"

"No, not a girl. I stole one of my brothers' pants and jacket, his hat, everything. I took every penny I could find in the house. It would have been my dowry, am I right? And I got on the train to Warsaw. I wanted to go to Berlin but I didn't think I spoke German well enough yet. I never meant to pass for a yeshive bokher, like my brother, so I went into a tailor's shop and got a nice, modern suit. My breasts were still very small and if the tailor thought something was odd, he didn't let on. This is what I've learned, though I hate to say it – money is freedom."

"Why do you hate to say it?"

"Because it means so many are slaves. Do you read Marx?"

I was embarrassed. I didn't read much, medical texts and once in a while pamphlets that the socialist mothers gave me. I'd read *The Travels of Benjamin the Third* the year before but I didn't really care for the shlemils of Yiddish fiction. "I don't have much time to read." Then I was mad at myself for lying. "Besides, I'm not an intellectual. I read biology, for my work."

"I read for my work too."

"For what kind of work do you have to read Marx?" At least I knew who Marx was.

"I'm a banker. Not a banker, exactly, but I work drawing up and transferring negotiable instruments, especially between banks and companies in different countries."

I was almost frightened. What did that mean? How could a Jewish woman do such a thing? And I was confused. "What kind of banker reads revolutionaries?"

"Bankers who want to understand what they do. The more I know, the easier it is for me to move around in the world. And that's what I really want, the freedom to travel and do what I please. Even I myself don't exactly approve of what I do for a living." Dovida hid her grin by stroking the edge of her mustache.

This was the most interesting person I had ever met. All over Europe she went, speaking German, Polish, French, Yiddish, who knew what? She knew intellectuals, revolutionaries, the daughters of barons and

now a midwife. I was afraid she would find my little life – just that, little. You could take my life like a pinch of snuff to clear your nose and never think about it again.

I may have talked to other women that night, Dovida may have left me and come back at least once. I don't remember. She offered to give me a ride home in her carriage. On the stairs she stopped and looked at me.

"But perhaps you might like instead to come to my hotel?"

Almost everyone else had been afraid to hold my gaze. But for her, my eyes were a doorway, a scene where there was a mountain and lake, and she could never decide whether she wanted to rest staring at the mountain or the water. Back and forth her eyes went, into mine, so far I could feel her walking inside my breastbone. She had strong legs but each step was gentle.

"I am afraid to make a scandal." Of course what I really wanted was to make such a big scandal that I would have to leave Kishinev in the morning and never come back.

"Gutke, in 1884 it is not such a big scandal for a woman to go to a gentleman's hotel room. Besides, I have a feeling not too many of your patients live by the hotels on Alexander Street."

So I went.

Even now, sixteen years later, going with Dovida was the best decision I ever made.

Sixteen years is a long time but we had plenty of natural separations when she traveled.

"You could give up being a midwife and come with me," she'd say. "I make enough money to support you in style."

Then we fought. Why should I give up my independence, my trade? Could she really have believed style would be important to me? "You shouldn't confuse dressing like a man with being a man," I said.

"And what is that supposed to mean?"

"I love you for your courage, for deciding to make your life on your own, for not letting what other people think women can and can't do stop you."

She paced around the room with her hands in her pockets. "And?"

"And I want the right to live my life the same way. If I became dependent on you, you would tire of me in a year, like one of those spoiled bankers' daughters you used to romance."

"Tire of you?" The coppery tinge in her eyes caught the light behind her wire spectacles. I loved looking at her eyes. While she worked on documents at the table late at night I sometimes played with the bristly hair of her mustache, just to get her to look at me. "A week in Venice would only give me new inspiration in loving you – and taking a vacation, how could that possibly spoil you?"

Jews taking vacations! Well, those were the circles Dovida moved in, and she liked the adventure. I couldn't see myself floating around in a gondola. "Maybe, sometime, if it would really make you so happy, I'll go to Venice or Vienna with you," I said. "But this month I have three women due. I'm not going anywhere."

She peered over her glasses at me and gave an exasperated sigh. "You won't even consider pleasing me?"

"Yes, I'll consider it," I said smiling. This was the way she usually got us out of the argument. If money and traveling were sore spots, we knew how to rub the ache out of them. Dovida was such a pleasure to me that even when other opportunities presented themselves – an unhappily married woman reaching for my hand, a friend of Dovida's from Berlin trying to sweet-talk me – I was never tempted. The way it was between Dovida and me was what I wanted, not because it was the only possibility but because Dovida absorbed my attention, even when I wasn't sure I liked her. The flame I saw the night I met her never left, though it often changed shape, intensity or color.

But the words for what we were to each other? Every part of the body has a name. Sometimes I lay in bed with Dovida – she slept sound and late – and I would name each knuckle on her hand. I named the crease behind her knee, I traced the big muscles of her forearms, I called the left one Simkhe and the right one Latke, it was good enough to eat.

"What are you doing?"

"Just talking to Simkhele here."

"Should I be jealous of my forearm?"

"Well, you, you've known so many women, I have to make it up somehow. If I find twenty women in your body, will that even the score?"

She was sleepy, chuckling, pulling her arm around me. "Are we keeping score? You're the one who gets to look between other women's legs. You can't fault me for what I did before I met you."

Once something comes into being, shouldn't there be a name for it? I could call this love, like young girls dreaming about who they'll

marry, but to call it love would be like to call it God, no offense to the Creator. Everything is God's, isn't it? And all pleasure in life is love. What is between me and Dovida must be very close to God, because even if there were a word for it you could not say it out loud. Just like the name of God, you must not speak it. You can look at it, written out, but not even a whisper should cross your lips.

"So serious, my Gutke, always wanting to understand what makes us love. Maybe it's not such a serious thing. Don't your medical books tell you human beings are mostly water? We are just water, moving towards each other. Like this – ." She rolled towards me and took my lips in her mouth. Her lips were soft and expanding, until I thought my entire body was inside her. So much sensation – I had to pull back, to look at her.

I have to pull back a little, so often she's away on business. Now we rent an apartment together in Odessa, as if we are man and wife. But I keep my room at Golde's in Kishinev, so I can still bring new lives into the world among the people who know me. Once in a long time when a girl is born, I see that flare I saw when I first looked at Dovida. This one, I think, will be like us.

Even if I have no words for it.

A tall, serious girl

Mama was having a little trouble carrying the baby, nothing we should worry about, they said. It happens. That's what they always said, "It happens." Then they pinched my cheek. Aunt Shendl came to help Mama clean for Shabbes. I was helping too. I had a little broom and I was sweeping out the storeroom. All of a sudden Mama yelled, "Gevalt, it's early!" Aunt Shendl got so nervous she knocked over the samovar and the water made a little puddle of mud by the table. They sent Esther for the midwife but they should have sent me. I was already faster than Esther. I wouldn't have wasted a minute.

The midwife put up amulets by Mama's door, circles and hands with letters on them. When I tried to touch them Aunt Shendl gasped, slapped my hand away lightly. I could tell I scared her but I just wanted to get a closer look. Aunt Shendl got scared easily. She was already gray, even though she wasn't much older than Mama. The midwife brushed me and Esther into the kitchen. I knew Mama wanted me to be with her, but Shendl said I was too little and Esther should look after me. Esther was always trying to show me how to sew. I hated sewing. I wanted to read. Mama said next year if I was quiet I could sit with the classes she taught. Mama taught all the carpenters' and cobblers' girls. She was the best teacher in Kishinev, Aunt Shendl told me. Already I knew the letters of the alphabet. I said them to myself and tried to remember how they looked.

Mama screamed. Was the midwife hurting her? Esther said no, it was what happened when a baby came. It had to hurt. God punished women. Why would God have wanted to punish Mama? Esther must not have known. She never knew what she was talking about anyway. Mama will tell me, I thought. After the baby comes she'll explain

everything. I swung my feet in the air, making my skirt swish. The gimmel letter looked like a person with very short legs. I would have long legs, Daniel said.

Mama yelled louder. Then I heard a baby crying. Esther couldn't stop me, sitting there with her needle going in and out. I ran through the door past the amulets. I waited for a second in case a spell was going to grab me. Shendl was wiping Mama's face and the midwife was holding the baby. It was so big. How did it get out? I ran to Mama and took her hand. She held me tight. I was right – she wanted me there. The midwife put the baby on Mama's chest. The midwife was full of quiet. What was wrong? Mama asked. "Her left eye – " everyone looked. The eyeball was pushed over a little bit, like it was trying to swim out of the socket. The other one was right where it was supposed to be. Everyone shook their heads.

"Sometimes this fixes itself. You can pray for that," the midwife said.

Shendl and Mama started to mutter something, prayers probably, and Mama let go of me. The midwife covered her own eyes with her hand, then turned and started washing things up.

"This is the last one," Mama said in a scratchy voice, the kind she used when she played the parts of trolls and elves in stories.

"Yes, just as you say," the midwife said. "This daughter will always need friends. She will draw circles to include outsiders."

"Chava, this is your new sister Sarah. You'll be her friend, won't you?" Mama turned her head and smiled at me. "It's what your name means, you know. Little friend."

"Always Mama, I promise." My Mama knew how good I was. She asked me to get her purse and pay the midwife. I was old enough to count already. I liked to. One, two, three rubles. Mama said to also give the midwife a havdale candle.

I ran past Esther who shook her head at me. I loved the storeroom. I wanted to make candles when I got older – I helped already. I found the prettiest havdale candle, white and blue twisted together, the blue light like the wildflowers at the end of Gostinaya Street. The midwife patted me on the head and smiled. Mama was propped up a little, rocking and singing to the baby.

"Go tell your sister to tell your father he has a new baby girl," Aunt Shendl said.

"I can go."

"You stay here in case we need you."

Esther wanted to see if the baby was pretty. "Just go tell Papa," I said.

If Esther knew about Sarah's eye she would make a big fuss and Papa would be mad. She could know later. I knew how to keep a secret. I wasn't the baby any more.

When Papa saw the baby's eyes he got so pale I thought he was going to turn into a cloud and fly away. Even his beard started to be white. "Lilith," he said. Sometimes he shouted and pushed things around but this time he was silent. He went into the storeroom with his books and shut us out. Abraham and Daniel came home all excited about the baby but Abe got just as upset and went to be with Papa.

Mama started singing. Her curly hair was still wet with sweat and stuck to the sides of her cheeks.

"She's just a baby. Little Sarah, blessed of Israel, difference is not a tragedy," Mama sang. "Look how healthy she is." Daniel snuck outside to be with his friends because no one was making him study. Mostly Abe and Daniel had to sit at the table reading until we put dinner under their noses. Abe was serious but Daniel was always kicking the table and making faces at me.

Poor little Sarah. Lilith put her hand on her eye. Was it my fault Lilith came, because I wanted to touch the amulets? Mama said Lilith had to pull her hand away because we are a strong and good family, every one of us. We would take care of Sarah and everything would turn out for the best.

Papa ate his soup quietly for a change. He paid so much attention he didn't even get any in his beard. "Whatever is God's will," he said. I knew I shouldn't have been, but I was almost glad Lilith touched Sarah because for weeks Papa didn't bring home those smelly students to eat dinner with us.

I wondered what it felt like to be touched by Lilith. I put my hands over my eyes because if she touched them it would hurt. Nobody ever explained anything to me. What if she put her hand on your shoulder and took you away? Where would you go?

We were all around the table. My Papa Rabbi Isaac, my Mama Miriam, Abraham, Daniel, three students, Esther, baby Sarah and me. After havdale, Saturday evening. The morning's Torah portion had been on the Pharaoh's dreams, the ones that Joseph interpreted and so was made an overseer in Egypt.

Papa wiped his mouth. "Pincus." He nodded to the oldest student. Papa had a long face and when he nodded it was like he was pointing

a finger at you. "Where it is written, 'God shall give Pharaoh an answer of peace,' how do you interpret that?"

The student cleared his throat. He had probably been thinking about whether Mama would let him have the last piece of kugl. Before he could speak Abraham interrupted.

"It's only a figure of speech. It's what Joseph says because he wants the Pharaoh to bring him out of prison."

"Oh, so. My son the learned. But do you honestly believe God's servants would speak in their own self-interest? Ever?"

One of the other students put the kugl on his own plate quickly. "The servants of God, even the Patriarchs, were men as we are," he said as if to divert attention. "God filled them with his gifts but might they not have used those gifts for their own benefit if it served God's plan?"

"It cannot be that a man uses the revelations of the Lord for his own gain. But he might use them for the gain of his people, couldn't he?" Pincus asked.

Papa considered the question, stroking his beard, moving on beyond my brothers and the students. "It is of a piece. Joseph is moved from one place to another always by dreams," he said. "Don't you see how it is? First he dreams his brothers do obeisance to him, even as the stars, sun and moon bow to the earth in his dreams, and he is rebuked but innocent. Yet because of his dreams he is sold into bondage and because of the Pharaoh's dreams, he is lifted up from prison – "

"I wish the Tsar would have a dream and ask me to interpret it. I'd tell him something!" Daniel was restless, balancing his chair on two legs.

"Pay attention to your father and sit still," Mama said, mussing Daniel's hair, which he hated. He had hair like hers, curly. Abe had hair more like Papa's, stringy and greasy looking.

"Mama!" Daniel ducked below her hand.

" 'Behold, this dreamer cometh!' Not even bar mitsve and now you're ready to take on the Tsar. Is it the Tsar or you who's dreaming?" Papa pointed at Daniel.

"Don't laugh at me."

"I'm not laughing. 'A child's wisdom is also wisdom.' You want to interpret the signs of God. What could be better, eh?" Papa made a big wave with the back of his hand and the students nodded.

"Mama, I had a dream last night – ." With all the talk about dreams, I suddenly remembered it.

"Sha. Come, Esther, Chava, let's clear this mess away and put Sarah

to sleep so your father can continue in peace." Mama carried the baby into the bedroom. I cleared the plates and put them in the wash bucket for Esther, who had the job of taking them out to the pump.

"Did I ever tell you the story about the snake who interprets dreams?" Mama asked me. I didn't remember. Mama had a thousand wonderful stories, though sometimes she didn't get to finish them. She tucked Sarah into the crib I'd outgrown and sat down on the stool beside it. Sarah was quiet, fastening her good eye on Mama's face. I sat on the floor, playing with the hem of Mama's brown skirt. "No? Well, this was a long time ago, maybe in Rumania. A peasant is walking along the road, when he almost steps on a snake. 'Don't crush me,' the snake says, 'and I will tell you anything you want to know.' 'Anything?' the peasant asks. 'All wisdom will be yours,' says the snake – "

"Miriam!" Papa stood in the doorway looking at us, Mama rocking the cradle with one hand, rubbing my head with the other. I never minded it when she touched my head. "Why do you fill their heads with Russian fables?"

"They can only learn Jewish fables? Everyone dreams. Isn't that right, Chava? See, she knows. How could Joseph understand a pharaoh's dreams if he hadn't lived among the Egyptians?"

"His understanding came from God." Papa was tall and skinny, his beard went down to the third button of his shirt. I wondered if God looked like him, except much older. Older, with a longer beard.

"Yes, God, but my children must also learn to look with their own hearts in case God is busy."

"This is too close to disrespect for the Lord. God is with them also."

"I mean no disrespect, Isaac, you know that. It's only practical. God doesn't speak to women. We are excused from the study of Torah, so my girls must learn another way. You teach at the table, I teach in the kitchen. I have to pass on to my daughters what I know."

"You know too much superstition."

"Is that any way to talk to the rebitsin? Aren't your students waiting for you?"

He turned to talk directly to me, something he did only rarely. "Don't believe every story your mother tells you, just believe her heart. A good woman has a good heart, and your mother is a good woman. So, she likes to tell stories. You know a story is just a story, eh?"

"Yes, Papa."

"Good. Miriam, Abraham will walk back to the beys medrish with me. Don't let Daniel stay out in the street too long."

• • • • •

It was Sunday. I got sent to bed early because I was fighting with Sarah and Papa was mad at me. He was studying, as usual, and we had disturbed him.

It wasn't a big fight. I had a little goose carved in wood on a platform, and under the platform a ball dropped down on strings and if you swung the ball around, the string pulled the goose's mouth and it squawked. What I loved especially was the way I could put my finger on the goose's back – so smooth I almost thought it was feathers, wooden feathers. I had finished my chores and was just sitting by the stove playing with my goose when Sarah came up and tore it out of my hand and when I went to pull it back from her she held onto the ball and the string broke.

I knew she was little and hardly ever did anything wrong, but she broke it. Bobe Malka gave it to me and it was my favorite. I was only yelling at her – I didn't even hit her and I wanted to – and all of a sudden Papa appeared and told me to go lie down. Without supper. It wasn't fair. I was crying and trying to show him my goose and he said it didn't matter, I was old enough now, I had to learn responsibility.

"When you know better, that's what it means," he said, "you know better. I want you to think about it. You want to study like your brothers? Then you must not behave like a child. Go to your bed." His eyes were as black as his beard, almost as black as the long coat he always wore. When I tried to look at him for pity, he stared at me until I had to turn away.

In the winter, my bed was behind the curtain behind the stove. Sometimes I slept on the big tile oven to keep warm. The curtain was all covered with ash and I hated it. It wasn't too bad in the dark but it looked so ugly when I had to lie there in the light, looking at the stains from the smoke. If I pretended to see letters in the stains it was more interesting. Up where I could hardly make it out, there was a smudge that looked like a lamed, and very faint, beneath it, almost a vov. Maybe it meant I was one of the secret lamed vovniks – one of the thirty-six most holy Jews in the world – that would teach them! No one ever said the lamed vovniks couldn't be girls. Maybe I really was one and one day I would be revealed to them. They would be having supper or something, and a voice would fill the room, "Behold, my blessed Chava, one of the most holy, my righteous lamed vov." Papa would be sorry then. He'd be sorry he didn't send me to school in town and just let me learn from Mama and Daniel. He'd be sorry for every time he yelled at me. And Mama too, and Esther would be sorry for

putting on such airs and pretending she was so much better than I was just because she was pretty and liked to crochet.

I could hear Mama making dinner. I was hungry and my stomach hurt again. My stomach hurt a lot. I wanted to cry but I wasn't supposed to. Everyone was moving around. That was the worst. Suppose I died back here and they didn't even notice. That would have been a sin, to let a lamed vovnik die. It was daytime and the world was moving without me. I knew that it turned around and around, Mama told me. She showed me with an apple what it meant for the earth to go around the sun. I hoped Mama would bring me dinner. She was making potato kugl, one of my favorites. I could smell the fresh grated potatoes and onions. Would she forget about me? If I could make myself cry a little, very softly, she would come and see me and I wouldn't be so lonely. But then I would have been a coward. Papa said I had to know better. I didn't want to know better. I wanted my goose fixed and I wanted Mama to come tell me it was going to be all right, to bring me kugl. Mama was nicer. She would have helped me fix my goose and not have made me stay in bed in the daylight.

I found myself in a thick wood all alone. Suddenly there was a clearing, and then an orchard. Plum and pear and apple trees, with flowers and fruit at the same time. I started to pick the fruits, heaping them in my skirt. The plums were huge and ripe, the apples bright red and sweet smelling. Esther came. I could see the freckles on her cheeks. "You must not eat these," she said. All the trees started to burn and the fruit flamed in my skirt. I had to drop everything. I wanted to run but I couldn't. I couldn't move my legs. Esther disappeared.

"Chava! Chavele!" My mama shook my shoulder. "You're just having a bad dream. Sha, stop crying." I sat up and embraced her.

"Esther wouldn't let me eat the apples, Mama."

"It's just a dream, little beanpole. I know you're hungry. See, I brought you some kugl. You eat now. When you're done you'll help me with the washing and we'll see about your toy."

Mama had a special storeroom in our house. She sold everything that Jews needed to be Jews: Shabbes, yortsayt and havdale candles, talesim, tfilin, wine cups, everything. She even had a few books of prayers for women, techinot, because she led the women's section in shul on Shabbes. Mama said only rabbis' wives could have this special store. Good fortune smiled on us, she said, because she didn't have to

go to the marketplace or take in washing like other mothers, and she was usually home except when she took baskets around to the poor. Sometimes she let me go with her. What made someone poor and someone rich? When I asked Mama if we were rich, she laughed. She said the wheel of fortune was always turning and the only riches we could hold onto were our good feelings for each other.

I tried to count the good feelings I had but they weren't that many. When I saw my cousins Rebkah and Aviva wearing Esther's and my old dresses I didn't feel good about having new clothes at Pesach. Esther always made a big fuss about getting a new dress but I didn't see what was so great about it. They were scratchy and stiff and you had to try hard to keep them clean and you weren't supposed to run because you might tear them. Mama said I should be more grateful. When she was a girl she never got new dresses of her own, only second hand. I tried to be grateful for Mama's sake, but was it right to be grateful just because someone else wanted you to be? When I told Mama I didn't care about the new dress, she should put it in her basket for another girl who really wanted it, she got angry. Papa was angry at me a lot but it hurt more when Mama was.

Most of the time she was too busy to stay angry long. There were always strangers in our house, her students and women dropping by to talk to Mama. When Papa was home, men came to see him – almost every meal some boy with a few whiskers was eating with us, getting embarrassed while Papa questioned him about Hillel or Rashi. They wanted the right answers so much. Sometimes they held their breath, waiting for a heavenly voice to guide them. Then they choked on their cucumbers.

"Let the boy eat," Mama would say. "Really, Isaac, after dinner, when I clear the plates, then you talk Torah."

"You see, even an educated woman like my Miriam, she doesn't know Talmud from Torah," he was compelled to say to the student. She glared at him.

"The soup is excellent, Mrs. Meyer. Even my own mother never made such a vegetable soup!" the student said.

I made a face at Esther, who of course just shrugged. Like a donkey, a donkey with a pretty saddle. She thought everything Papa did was wonderful, to her he was a god. Sometimes I teased her, reminding her we were taught "you shall have no other Gods before me" and that talking about Papa like he was God broke the law. This confused her. She told Mama I was mocking the Commandments. Esther was always

so nice at the table it made me itch. At least when I made faces at Sarah she giggled and dropped her spoon.

When Papa was at shul, different strangers sometimes came to see Mama, not just for Shabbes things. Hatmakers, storytellers, beggars, sometimes even Moldavians. I thought she lent money to people as well as running the store. Papa didn't have to worry about such things. Only God was above him and he always looked up. Naturally he never saw how filthy the street was, how hard it was to live there.

Papa said we were lucky to have such a wonderful mother who made us such a good Jewish home. Yet he didn't really know where the money came from. He thought we managed to feed all the people he brought home on the couple of rubles and chickens the congregation paid him.

"Now you can try."

Mama made one loaf out of two long tubes of dough. The loaf tapered at the ends and swelled in the middle. I loved to watch Mama's hands, kneading, sewing, turning the pages of a book, always moving. She said my hands would look like hers when I grew up if I could stop biting my fingernails. At least my hands were finally big enough to pull all the dough for the second loaf onto the table.

"And what do you think you're doing, hmm?"

"What you did, Mama."

"Don't you remember what we must do with the dough?"

"Take out a portion for the priests and throw it in the oven when the bread goes in," I sighed.

"Then do it."

Mama laughed at my handful of dough. "Our 'priest' is not that hungry, little one. This much will feed him." She broke off a piece the size of a walnut. "You sin by wasting almost as much as by not doing at all."

Abraham, who was reading at the little table beside the window where the light was best, turned his shaggy face towards us.

"Don't look at me like that, Mister Scholar," Mama said. " 'To each according to their ability to understand.' We aren't disturbing you, are we?"

Mama was only half-serious. Abraham lifted one eyebrow, the way he practiced for hours – he could almost do it like the old men in shul. He had big, thick eyebrows that ran together above his nose. "No, Mama, I just got distracted for a minute."

"Then reapply yourself. You know we have work to do here." He bobbed his head over the book and Mama put the priest's portion aside. As I rolled and braided, she placed her hand over mine from time to time, directing, showing how to make the shape. Then she kissed the top of my head, which made me taste hot bread in my mouth. "Good, now rinse off your hands in the basin and bring me the bowl."

She put the covered challah on top of the oven and the bowl beside it. "When the bread is ready to bake, I'll call you and we'll go over the prayers together, all right? I have special work to do before I make Shabbes dinner. Remind me we have to plan your costumes for the Purim play. Esther will measure you."

"Mama – ." I knew I was supposed to let her finish her work, especially before Shabbes, but I couldn't stop myself.

"What is it, Chavele?"

"Mama – ." Why was it so hard to ask? I bounced from foot to foot. Mama looked like she was going to laugh. I hated that look. "It's not fair."

"And exactly what is not fair this time?"

"Just because her name is Esther doesn't mean she should get to play Queen Esther every year. I don't want to be Vashti again. I don't like her song."

"And which song don't you like?" Mama was already concentrating on threading her needle. Embroidering the edge of a talis was more important to her than me.

"You know, Mama," I said as dramatically as I could, shouting and clutching my dress, so she'd look at me. "That pitiful one, 'Help me, fields and help, stones. Help me, every feeling soul. Help me, help me, help me, every feeling soul!' "

"If you sing like that," Mama said, laughing, "you'll turn the whole play into a farce. But you miss the point, little one. Without her refusal to dance for the drunkard king, there'd be no play."

"I don't care. I'm old enough for a better part." I scratched a line in the hard dirt floor with my shoe.

"You're eight years old and you want to play Queen Esther this year? What will your sister do?"

"I don't want to be Queen Esther either. I want to be Mordecai." There, I said it. I didn't care if she didn't like it, if she swept me out of the room as if I were a pebble littering the floor.

"Mordecai! Your brother Abraham is always Mordecai."

Abraham looked up again. "Let Chava be Mordecai if she wants to

be. Maybe I won't be in the play. I heard there was going to be a meeting – "

"A meeting? Every year your father has you put on the play for his students and the cousins. You know how he depends on you. He wants a dignified play, not like the purimshpil that goes on in the streets. Some other night you can go off to a meeting. And what kind of Jews have a meeting on Purim?"

"Purim isn't the most holy day, Mama. It's not my fault it comes Saturday night this year, after Shabbes, when everyone likes to have meetings. It's only students, to talk about what's happening in the north."

"In the north?"

"You know, about the Zionist conference Theodore Herzl organized last year."

"You want to go to this meeting?" She studied him.

"There'll be other meetings," he shrugged and pretended to go back to his reading.

"That's right, there'll be other meetings. On Purim, you'll be here with your family. Before the play you have to go with your sisters and brother and distribute the food baskets. You can't just shake off your duties and run off with your student friends whenever it suits you."

"All right, all right. But I don't care about the play. I'll be Haman, even."

"Daniel wants to be Haman, God in heaven knows why." Mama frowned, but I couldn't tell if it was about Daniel or because she had to pull out a stitch. Almost always her embroidery was perfect, even though the light by the stove wasn't very good.

"He says he wants to understand how the evil one feels, so he can know how to fight him. He may be no scholar but he's always thinking," Abraham said, as if Daniel's ideas were silly to him. "It doesn't matter, Mama. So I'll be the king. It's part of Purim for Chava to be able to play Mordecai if she wants."

Abe hardly ever paid any attention to what I did. Usually it seemed his idea of our family stopped at Daniel. It was about time he stuck up for me. "See, Abe thinks it's all right. I never get a chance to be the hero."

"A hero you want to be! You and Daniel, you're cut from the same cloth, think you know everything there is to know. But you don't know that Mordecai's not the hero. We just tell that to your brothers." She looked at Abraham and he tilted his head, half closing his eyes, smiling. "For Purim, it's Queen Esther who's the hero."

I banged my hands against my legs. "But Mama, Esther will never let me play the Queen and I want to be Mordecai."

Abraham stood up, stretching. He would sit reading for so many hours that it amazed me he could move anything besides his hand to turn the pages. "You know, Chava, they say on Purim you're supposed to get so drunk you can't tell Haman from Mordecai anyway, or boys from girls."

"Drunk!" Mama said. "Just because you're not getting to go to your meeting, you're not getting drunk. And I don't like you putting all these ideas into Chava's head." She turned to me, "Abraham will play Mordecai."

"Oh, please Mama! Abe said he didn't care and I want a real part this year. I'm old enough. Sarah can be Vashti and Abe would make a great Akhashverus. I'll do extra work – I'll make up all the food baskets."

"You will, will you?"

"I'll do whatever you tell me. I know I'll be a great Mordecai. I already know his lines – ." I found my deepest voice by pushing my chin into my chest, " 'Think not that thou shalt escape in the king's house, more than any Jew.' "

"You remember that?" She looked over my head, out the window where there was nothing to see. "Well, maybe it will be all right. It's true what your brother says. Once I even had to play Haman myself."

"You?"

"Why not? You think your mother never had any fun in her life, she was just put on this earth to take care of all you children and teach little girls their grammar? My mother had three girls first and then four boys – I was just the opposite. So anyway, when we were young, my mother, blessed be her name, made us the most wonderful costumes. It was a good time for the Jews then, not like now." She stopped and bit off the end of the thread. "We could afford to spare golden thread like this for the sleeves of our costumes. Can you imagine?"

"What kind of costume will you make me?" Once Mama started to talk about the old days, I knew she'd give in. I hopped around the table to her side so I could examine the embroidery.

"For you, sackcloth and ashes."

"Mama!"

Mama laughed and ran her palm over my head. She went beneath the hair, checking for lice. "Well, doesn't Mordecai wear sackcloth and ashes at the king's gate after Haman decides to kill the Jews?" She looked to Abraham for verification. He closed his eyes again and

nodded, to show how weary of us he was.

"Abraham never had to wear sackcloth and ashes."

"Because he could read the whole story. Can you do that?"

"If you'd teach me, I could."

"Oy, an answer for everything. You think you could learn the whole Megile in two weeks?"

"Mordecai is very brave. Mordecai can do anything!" I stood as straight as I could so she'd know how serious I was. If she let me be Mordecai, I'd show her how smart I could be, too.

"Enough of this nonsense. Go find your sister Esther. I want her to start doing this embroidery herself. You can watch Sarah until it's time to put the bread in the oven and make dinner. Go on."

Papa and Daniel fought so long about Daniel going to apprentice with the printer Simeon Wolowitz I thought God himself would have to intervene. Who was right? Daniel tried to plead his case at dinner, pressing and clenching his fists against the table top, as if only that motion would keep him from flying out of the room. Papa's face got dark red splotches under his beard. Mama would make them stop, saying they'd ruin our digestion. Daniel took it up again on the way to shul, following six inches behind Papa, but Papa would cut him short and Daniel knew better than to show disrespect in front of others. But when he and Papa returned home they would start again.

They didn't know I listened, maybe they didn't care. I was in the kitchen dipping Shabbes candles. Their words bounced off the stone walls of Mama and Papa's room. I could hear each one.

"All day long you read books," Daniel argued. I imagined his fists so tight they were white, hidden behind his back or punched in his pockets. "You honor and revere them. Someone has to print them – you should be happy it's going to be me, someone who also loves books."

"You are only one step removed from an idolater, Daniel. It's not the books but the words within them. If they were written by hand on mud tablets, our love for them would not be lessened." Papa pronounced each word slowly, separately, as if they were barbed and hurt him when they left his lips. Daniel jumped into Papa's pauses.

"But think, Papa, how many more can study because books aren't written on mud tablets. It's an honorable trade – "

"A rabbi's son should be studying, not apprenticing. You know what

happens when you go to apprentice? You spend years cleaning, fetching, carrying, all the things no one else wants to do. You have too good a mind to throw away in some miserable shop." Papa was pacing back and forth.

"You mean I have too good a pedigree to waste – what kind of wife can I get as a simple printer? Whereas if I went on to yeshive I could expect my wife's family to support me for years." The thought of Daniel marrying startled me and hot wax dripped on my finger.

"It's not a question of living off of others, Daniel, the way you make it out. It is the duty of women to make the home, as it is our duty to study and praise God. All things work together to make a life. If you break with this, what kind of life can you have?"

"You mean to say the tradespeople in your congregation have no life – the tailors, the bristle-makers, the carpenters, the weavers – all of them, no life? Where is it written only scholars and the sons of scholars get this precious gift, this meaningful life?"

Even I knew that this was the wrong argument, though I was glad Daniel knew how easy the scholars had it, someone always making a fuss and taking care of them. Papa was furious.

"You mock me, Daniel, and that is a sin." I could hear his voice trembling.

"Please forgive me, Papa. I mean no disrespect. I just don't have the temperament to be a scholar." Daniel must have wanted to be a printer very badly.

"You think you have the temperament to be a worker? What do you know about work? You have no idea how long the hours of a worker are." From the sad, heavy way Papa was talking, I could tell he was going to give in. The anger had leaked out of his words. I was glad. I thought being a printer was more interesting than bending all day over the very same books your father and your grandfather had bent over. What new thing did they keep discovering to talk about, anyway?

"Then let me find out. If I'm wrong, I won't be ashamed to say I'm wrong."

"I should live so long to hear you admit you were wrong about anything, meshuginer." Papa knew what he was talking about. All the men in our family – Esther too – always thought they were right about everything. Even when they did apologize, you could tell they still believed they were right. They were only apologizing because the other person needed the apology and they were generous enough to give it.

"You'll let me go by Simeon?"

"If he agrees for you to sleep here and take at least Shabbes dinner with us. I'll talk to him. But mark my words, this is a mistake for us both."

"You won't be sorry, Papa. You'll see."

Daniel sprang out of the room, eyes glittering. I always liked Daniel's eyes, a soft brown like a well-baked challah, just a little darker than Mama's. He stopped when he saw me.

"You heard?" I nodded. "Just like from the lions' den, I am delivered," he whispered. Papa was already praying.

"Mazel tov," I said. So he's going to work. What does he think I do all day long? Now maybe he'll appreciate us more.

"Nice candles," Daniel said as he ran out the door.

Men must have a factory where they make disagreements. Ordinary ones sold for a couple of kopecks, big ones for a ruble. My family kept this factory in business, the men especially. Women worked so men could argue. Argument seemed to be all that they lived for. I was ten and the Christian century was turning. We weren't supposed to pay attention to this, but of course we did. Everywhere people were gripped with the idea that they could take time apart and change it, like playing with the gears of an old pocket watch, and this made them argue about every thing. Even Mama said that in the new century me and Esther and Sarah would have more choices in life than she'd had. I wasn't sure what she meant unless we might be able to choose our own husbands, which didn't seem like such a big improvement to me.

My brother Abe, on the other hand, thought he could choose to go to Palestine. He was obsessed with the idea. Settlements had been made in Palestine when he was barely a year old, he said, and he didn't want to be late for history.

"This is where history is and it's being made now," Daniel taunted Abe. "You want to till the soil? Till the soil of change. That's what's exciting." He had learned about socialism at the print shop and had become like a rabbi himself, making speeches when he was home and we had time to listen, which wasn't often. I actually liked Daniel's speeches. They were more interesting than when Abe talked about Zion. It was as if Abe had fallen in love with a Bible story.

Which one would Papa yell at first? "This is the age of false messiahs, no?" Papa would say. "Everywhere there's a champion rising up to say

we will remake the world. You boys should know better. You think you can remake the world? In your own image? It's an age of false messiahs. What do you know, what have you seen? You, Abraham, you think you can teach me now that you've been to the university? We sacrificed everything for you. It's time you were married and raising your own family. Here. Here in Kishinev!"

"Sha, Isaac," Mama interrupted, "you'll upset the girls." Sarah was outside feeding the chickens, I was carrying water in from the well and Esther was sewing. I think Mama used us an excuse because she was tired of listening to the same arguments.

"The girls. At least the girls behave themselves. But I'm not going to walk around a hostage in my own home. Everywhere in Kishinev Jews respect me. They want my opinion, my judgments are called equal to Solomon's. In my own home I shouldn't be able to speak my mind?"

"Speak, speak, then. Just a little quieter, not everyone on the street has to know our business. Chava, will you make some tea in the samovar and bring me a cup?" Mama was working on her business accounts. She could do sums on paper, without a counting frame.

Being busy with the tea let me sneak looks at Papa and my brothers. Abe looked like a smaller version of Papa, who was so tall he had to stoop in most doorways. The last couple of years Papa had gained weight and now was a very imposing, dark man.

"Nu, Abraham?" Papa said. "You're a smart boy. Five in a hundred boys get to go to the university – and you want to throw away everything and go farm in Palestine? What do they teach you there? You I thought I could trust. Your brother Daniel – our little tradesman – he wants immediate results, never satisfied. You can be anything you want."

Abe paced to the window, looked out, turned back to face Papa.

"Pa, it's not 1865 any more. You can't see what's going on in Russia?" He gestured to the street outside. "They won't even let a Jew be a dogcatcher. What am I going to do with my degree? I want the chance to farm like an honest man."

Papa stroked his beard and snorted, which was as close as he ever got to a laugh. When I heard Mama sigh, I realized she'd been holding her breath. Esther didn't know enough to be worried or maybe she just didn't care. She was always more concerned with what the local boys thought of her than with our brothers and their big ideas. Abe was waiting for Papa's reply like a boy eager for Chanukah gelt.

Papa peered over his glasses at his eldest son. "What makes a scholar dishonest, tell me that?"

"Oh Papa, you know I don't think that. I've studied until my veins are full of words. But there are hundreds of young men ready to commit themselves to Zion like bridegrooms. I want to be in the heart of where it happens."

"Revolution is happening in Russia!" Daniel said, biting into a plum and spilling juice all over his little beard.

"Stay out of this, nudnik." Papa shot Daniel a hard look but Daniel just shrugged, leaning against the wall, watching. "Abraham, you can stay in school. You can be a lawyer if you don't want to be a rabbi. Or a university professor." Papa had decided on the gentle approach. I brought him a cup of tea after I brought Mama hers. He nodded but I don't think he really saw me.

Abe rolled his eyes. He stared at the ceiling. "You don't know there's a quota on Jewish lawyers? Even you don't have the connections to get me past the quota."

"I got you into school. We'll worry about the quota when the time comes."

"Papa, if only you would read Herzl – "

"Herzl Shmerzl. He thinks he discovered anti-Semitism. You don't think Jews have been talking about this for the last 1,800 years? I listen to you. You think I don't, but I do. I've gone back to Jeremiah."

"I know what it says in Jeremiah – 'I will take you one of a city, and two of a family, and I will bring you to Zion.' " Abe was pleased with himself.

"Mama, I'm going outside to weed the vegetables," Esther said. When Papa and Abe got to trading quotes from the prophets, they could go on for hours. Mama looked up and smiled as she flounced out.

"So now you're an expert? It is understood, when the true messiah appears, the Jews will be gathered from everywhere we are in exile. Is that what you see happening? No. Dreamers like you float off to Palestine. People who want to get rich go to America. Nudniks like your brother think they can make an alliance with the Russian peasants."

"I'm not a nudnik!" Daniel stopped smirking. "A Jew like Martov is the co-founder of the League of Struggle for the Emancipation of the Working Class – "

Abe frowned. "We're not talking about the emancipation of the working class. There is no future for Jews in Russia, inside the working class or outside." No future for Jews in Russia, he said. But if people go

on living someplace, doesn't living give them a future? I couldn't picture all the Jews suddenly rushing out of Kishinev. Abe turned back to Papa and they traded more quotes from Jeremiah. I was heating up the iron on the stove and I didn't catch everything they said.

Finally Papa cleared his throat. "My son, it's written that the children's teeth are set on edge because of their fathers. My teeth are set on edge from my father, and you, now, tell me from your heart – you don't feel my iniquities on you? You don't do this to rebel against me?" Could Papa really mean to say he had sinned somehow and we were rebelling against him? Probably he didn't think about us girls, just the boys. Daniel looked stricken and was about to say something, but Papa continued to talk.

"Think, Abraham, think – this is not the time of the messiah. All my life I've longed to feel it was, and now you just go off to Palestine, bim-bam, that's that? I know you believe you are right, but it's written, 'I will gather them out of all countries, whither I have driven them in mine anger...' *I* will gather them – there is no mention of Theodore Herzl." He banged the table for emphasis. Mama looked up and grimaced but the men paid no attention. I filled her cup again and she patted my hand without a word.

"It's always the same problem with Jews," Abe said, softly at first. "We should sit around Russia for another thousand years waiting for the hand of God to point the way? Can't you understand that it's up to us to fulfill these prophecies?" His voice trembled. "We have to act."

"Leaving Russia isn't acting. It's running away," Daniel said. "There's plenty of things a Jew can do here."

"Didn't I tell you to stay out of this? Your brother may have grown a block between his ears but he's no coward."

"Thank you, Pa," Abe smiled and almost seemed to bow.

"I'm not agreeing. Not for a minute. I can understand and not agree. You're young. You think you can redeem yourself through sweat, prove you're not some money lender, a no-good who lives off others, by going to farm. I know what the Russians and Moldavians say about us and it's hard to bear. My grandfather dreamed the same thing – then the Tsar took his land, everything he had worked for his whole life, and sent him on his way with not one ruble in his pocket."

"In Palestine there is no tsar."

"No, you trade the tsar for a sultan. This is not the fulfillment of prophecy. This is just a romance, a longing you have. I'll tell you what. You stay here, you pass your exams, maybe I'll read your Herzl. Then

we'll talk about it again." Papa got up and put on his old coat.

"Isaac," Mama said, as if all the arguments were a game of chess. "That coat needs to be mended. Leave it here and wear your good one."

"You can mend it when I come back from shul. I don't want anyone to think I'm proud, wearing my good coat on a Tuesday. Boys, are you going to come with me for evening prayers?"

"I have to get back to the shop, Papa. We had a late job coming in," Daniel said, pushing his cap down and running out the door before Papa could argue.

"And I'm going to study so I can pass my exams like you want," Abe said.

"Prayer is also study, but all right. You're a grown man. You see I respect your choices." Papa almost whispered this and for the first time he seemed like any other Jewish man in a worn overcoat, shuffling off to the evening service through the April mud.

I lay awake long after the lamps had been turned down, a little moonlight making patterns on the blanket by my feet. What if I had wanted to go too? I'd never been farther than the railroad station. Abe wouldn't take me with him. Besides, I didn't care about Palestine like he did. Everyone said it was just a desert. It made more sense to stay and fight where you were – if I were a boy I'd be the best fighter you ever saw. And I wouldn't spend all my time arguing about it either.

Abe went before the exams were given. Maybe he was afraid he wouldn't pass. One day, while Papa was in shul and Mama and Esther were distributing charity baskets and I had taken Sarah down to the river, he packed a small suitcase and left a note on the table.

He wrote in 1901. Mama read his first letter out loud: "Finally I am at Rishon le-Zion. The Baron Rothschild by his great generosity has set up these vineyards. It is not yet truly self-sustaining, and we depend too much on his contributions to meet our expenses. I am in contact with other groups of settlers and may strike out towards Galilee. You cannot know the joy I have in writing these words 'Galilee' and 'tending vineyards in Zion.' Do not despair of me, I keep you in my thoughts and prayers. With all respect, I am proud to say that I am a son of Zion reborn. I will write again soon. Your loving son and brother."

Papa looked out the window, his hands clasped behind his back. Esther cried. Mama shook her head. "Every prophecy comes to pass," she said.

• • • • •

Daniel was pacing in front of the stove. Mama was rolling out dough for kreplekh, trying to ignore him. Finally she looked up.

"All right, Daniel, talk to me. Tell me what's eating away at you."

"Papa concerns himself with the souls of a handful of Jews, while I'm talking about the greater good of millions of workers."

"A handful of Jews! Do you know there are 50,000 Jews in Kishinev – almost half the whole city now? And even if we were ten, you should be ashamed to turn your back on your people." She wiped a smudge of flour off her face.

"I'm not turning my back on anyone. The synagogues do nothing for the people. It's the Bund that will lift Jews up. I'm opening the doors of unity instead of perpetuating oppression and ignorance."

"Daniel, God forbid your father should hear you talk like this."

"He's as bad as anyone, Mama. Papa has the power to make men see, but he throws God in their eyes like dust." Daniel called God dust. I was afraid a lightening bolt might come through the ceiling and strike him dead. But nothing happened and Mama seemed more concerned about Papa than God.

"I won't have you talk about your father like that in this house, do you hear me? You think you're a big maskil – "

"I'm not a maskil, Mama." Daniel was exasperated. "The so-called enlightenment was just a way for the bourgeoisie to consolidate their power. I'm an agitator, a revolutionary."

"All right, so a revolutionary. Chava, what do you think? Does your brother look like a revolutionary?"

Now I was even more surprised. Was she asking me to take sides? Daniel was exciting, his enthusiasm and ideas were wonderful to me. But I didn't want to get on Mama's bad side. "I don't know what a revolutionary looks like," I said, taking the safest course.

"No, why would you? Here, you take the rolling pin." She handed it to me, cleaned her hands on her apron and turned to Daniel. "When I was a girl, the maskilim were Jewish revolutionaries – your father still thinks so. Now you're a new kind of revolutionary. You think we haven't seen that before? Revolutionaries killed Tsar Alexander – you were born just after the pogroms that caused. A nice present from the revolutionaries, pogroms and the May Laws. We're not stupid, your father or me. I read your pamphlets. There are many good ideas, but –"

"But what?" Daniel cocked his head, as if he were engaging her in argument for fun.

"But you are always talking to the wrong people. The Moldavian

peasants hardly read, and the Russians here, half have government jobs. You won't convince them with your down-with-the-Tsar slogans. And you don't talk to Jews as if you ever lived with any. You tell us to give up our faith – "

"Faith keeps people from changing."

"Our faith gives us courage to keep going on." She got a bowl from the cupboard to make the filling. I knew Mama's store was doing well because she had bought fresh chopped meat from the butcher that morning. "You don't understand; you're too young. It's not simply faith in God, each of us making a little personal bargain – if it were just that, Jews would have been Russified generations ago."

"So?"

I could see Mama and Daniel, tiny and distorted, in the Shabbes candlesticks I left on the table after I shined them. I didn't like how he was talking to Mama, impatient and snarling. And I didn't know that Mama had thought anything about the revolution all the men talked about. Why didn't she ever talk about it with me and Esther?

"So it's each of our faiths in keeping faith with each other. That is a wonderful thing. Even in these times, you can count on Jews all over the Pale keeping the sabbath – "

"Right, keeping the sabbath keeps us out of the big factories because we won't work on Saturdays."

"You have a lot to learn about who your friends are." I could hear how angry Mama was getting. She was squeezing the filling so hard it oozed in little rivers between her red fingers.

"And you don't understand your enemies," Daniel stuck his hands in his pockets as if to keep from pounding on something.

"All right Daniel. This is getting nowhere. Now you get those pamphlets out of the house. If you want to stay for dinner, you promise me you won't start this with your father again."

"He starts it with me."

"I'm not asking you. I'm telling you."

"Oh Mama, you wouldn't kick me out."

"Don't try me. I love you but maybe it's time your 'comrades' knocked some sense into you. I can't tell you what life has to teach you."

"What do you mean by that?" Daniel looked at her for a minute as if she might know something. Then he returned to his regular superior look.

"Just what I said. Only living teaches you who you can trust. Tonight

I'm trusting you to let us have our meal in peace."

"All right, I promise I won't start any fights. But I don't promise I won't defend what I believe."

Mama should have known better. Papa asked why Daniel wasn't coming to shul on Shabbes. Daniel looked at Mama, then he looked at me, Esther and Sarah. Slowly he looked back at Papa and wiped his mouth.

"I don't go to shul because I hold workers' circle educational meetings on Saturday mornings."

That was the end of it. Papa threw his napkin on the table, stood up and pointed to the door. Daniel didn't look at us again.

"None of you girls are allowed to see him." Papa said after the door slammed. "Not unless I authorize it. Do you understand?" Then he picked up his books and walked to shul.

None of us, not even Sarah, said anything for the rest of dinner. When we were cleaning up, I noticed Mama wipe her eyes as if she'd been crying. Was she crying because Papa frightened her or because Daniel wasn't going to come back? Parents were always saying "everything changes" but when change actually happened, they didn't seem to like it very much. I could go see Daniel if I wanted to – I knew where Simeon's shop was. I knew almost every place in the Jewish parts of Kishinev. How would Papa find out? Daniel wouldn't tell him. But I was mad at Daniel for how he'd talked to Mama. So I obeyed Papa, even though I didn't want Daniel to think I was scared. Someday he might realize the revolutionaries needed someone like me, a girl no one noticed, who knew all the back streets.

We had three little baskets to distribute food. Usually we went around on Thursdays so the families who had no work would have something for Shabbes.

"If we give away our food, does that mean we're rich?" Now Sarah had the same questions I'd had. If questions didn't get answered, did they just get passed on, like handed-down clothes?

"We should live so long. Your father doesn't have a kopeck to his name, believe me, besides this house his great-uncle left him." Mama was making up a small basket, even though it was only Tuesday.

Sarah thought this over. Her bad eye ticked a little when she concentrated but it wasn't actually ugly. She would have been pretty, otherwise, if you gazed at her nose and chin, her light olive skin and

sweet, heart-shaped face. "How can we give things away if we don't have enough ourselves?"

"Did you ever go hungry, hmm?" Mama patted Sarah's head without taking her eyes off the basket.

"It's commanded for the rich and poor alike, to give as much as we can – right, Mama?" I said.

"See, your sister knows. Now, weren't you going to bring me some water from the pump, Sarah?"

It would take Sarah a long time to come back with the bucket. Mama lifted a little cake out of the oven and wrapped it up when she thought I wasn't looking. She pressed her lips together until they were pale pink. "I don't like to ask you to do this," she said quietly.

I finally realized what she was doing. I was surprised, a little frightened and pleased. Maybe Mama was secretly a revolutionary too.

"I would go myself but a married woman can't – "

"Don't worry Mama. I'll do it."

"I'm sorry to ask you to disobey your father." She sighed. "Did you ever hear anyone say that Jews are a stiff-necked people? No? Sometimes it's important we know how to bend. At least for our own, just a little. You're sure you feel all right doing this?" Mama looked at me so intently I could see the little amber flecks shine against the brown of her eyes.

"I want to see Daniel too."

"I know you do. Go, don't take too long and don't let anyone see you."

What a racket! All of Daniel's shop was a clank and clatter, with a chaos of pounding, repeating sounds underneath. There were fumes, rags, pieces of paper scattered on the ground. It was so dark I didn't recognize Daniel at first and could barely hear his voice.

"I said, what are you doing here?"

"It's your birthday, Daniel. Mama sent you supper. Here – ." I handed him the basket. He motioned for me to wait and went over to a tall, thin man wearing an apron of black splotches. Once my eyes got used to the dark, I could see the machines. Almost one whole wall was taken up by a huge contraption unlike anything I could have imagined. A man sat playing it as if it were an organ. Every few minutes something gray whizzed past him, a huge wheel groaned, a claw moved down from above and then there was a tinkling while a piece of metal fell down a chute onto a tray. All those dark dancing parts! I wanted to get closer but Daniel was back.

"The boss says I can take a break and have supper with you. Lucky we're not too busy today."

"What's that?" I motioned to the big machine.

"That? That's the lever that will help us move the world. It's the first big change in printing since Gutenberg."

"But what's it called?" To Daniel, everything was a political cause, even machines.

"It's a Linotype. It makes whole sentences in lead, zip-zip-zip, so we don't have to put every letter in every word together by hand. It was invented in America but this one comes from Germany. It's only the second one in Kishinev – the other's over at the Bessarabetz printing shop."

"Can you show me how it works?"

"I suppose it will be all right." We walked over to the man sitting in front of the Linotype.

"Zalman, this is my sister Chava. She wants to see what our Linotype can do."

Zalman grinned at me. He rested his fingers on little buttons with Yiddish letters. He pressed the aleph and something clinked down into the small container in front of him. "See," he pointed to the top of the machine, "all the letters are in their own rows up there, and when I press here, the one I type comes down." He pulled the piece of metal out and showed it to me. It looked like a small key, made of brass, with a mold of the aleph indented into its thin side. I'd never seen anything like it. While I was holding the beautiful aleph, Zalman's fingers flew over the alphabet buttons. Brass keys glided down into a straight row until the tray was full. Then he pushed a lever, pulled a handle and the wheel pressed against the tray.

"That's where the hot lead fills the letters on the sides of the brass molds and makes the line of type," he said. As the wheel moved back, the claw I had seen from across the room came down and picked up the letter keys. They dangled in the air over the gears and then moved up to the top of the machine. Soon I heard them plopping back into place.

"Wonderful, isn't it?" Zalman said. He grabbed the new metal bar and swiveled around to face me.

"Does it burn?" He was throwing the bar back and forth between his hands.

"Lead cools fast. Here." I caught it. The bar was warm but not hot. Little letters stood up from the background, hard to read, because they

were backwards. Slowly I made out *'Ven ale mentshn zoln tsien oyf eyn zayt, volt zikh di velt ibergekert'.*"

"That's right : 'If everyone pulled in one direction, the world would topple over.' I made it for your brother, our organization man."

"Hush, Zalman." Daniel frowned, took the line from me and threw it in a pot of liquid metal behind the machine. I could see the words melting. "So, Chava, what do you think?"

"I'd like to do this," I said.

"We'll talk to the boss. Maybe he'll hire you when we get a new contract."

I walked right into that. They thought I couldn't do it, but why not? I could press buttons as well as they could. "Very funny."

"We're just teasing, Chava. Come, we better get going before the boss thinks I'm organizing another strike."

I still had the aleph in my hand as we started towards the door. I tried to give it to Zalman but he waved me away. "There are a hundred of those; the boss won't miss one," he whispered as he turned back to his work.

By the entrance was a big case full of drawers. Daniel pulled one open. Inside were many compartments filled with small letters made of dull gray metal, each letter on a square stem.

"Before the Linotype, we had to make up every page letter by letter," my brother said. "Well, we still do that mostly – we only have one Linotype. But Zalman can make up a page in fifteen minutes that takes me an hour and a half to do by hand when I'm quick, and his pages are easier to print. Now almost everyone will be able to have books."

Outside the sun startled my eyes. I saw a little green patch behind the shop and led the way towards it. Daniel took gulps of fresh air. I put the bright brass aleph in my skirt pocket.

"You sound like a capitalist, all excited about machinery," I said. "Aren't you afraid that machine will put printers out of work?"

"I was, but now I understand that the more books and pamphlets there are, the more men will read." He dropped his voice. "And with this machine, we can make up our own pamphlets when the boss is out and melt the evidence before he comes back." He leaned back in the sunlight, very pleased with himself.

I opened the basket. Mama had sent cheese and bread she made herself, as well as herring and plums. The little round cake had the letter daled shaped in dough on top, daled for Daniel. This would have made Papa turn purple. As I unwrapped the food I could see Daniel

remembering home. In the daylight ink spots showed all over his shirt and pants, even on his suspenders.

"Everyone's well?" he asked as he broke off some bread and cheese. "Mama, Esther, Sarah?"

I nodded. He didn't ask about Papa, but I wasn't interested in talking about home. "What did you mean before, when you said you organized a strike?"

"Oh." Daniel puffed up again and talked with his mouth full. He was nineteen and clean shaven now like all the socialists. Even without a beard he looked like a grown, serious man. "You must not tell this, you promise?" He looked around. "I'm the representative from our shop to the workers' council in the city. I let them know what the other printers think, and they suggest tactics for agitation and authorize strikes. We had a strike last year – all eight of us just stood by our machines and did nothing until Simeon had to give in to our demands. That was something to see, I'll tell you!"

"And what did you demand?" I felt bad, almost ashamed, that I didn't know about this. Since Daniel left, Mama and Papa didn't talk about socialism or the unions. Papa brought home his students, the same as always, and they rehashed the ancient arguments about Torah and Talmud at dinner.

"We demanded a twelve-hour day – it was ours anyway by law – and now we have it."

"By law?"

"Can you believe it? Catherine, the same Tsar who herded all us Jews into the Pale like oxen, wrote a law that the workday should be twelve hours, with a half hour for breakfast, an hour-and-a-half for dinner. Of course the capitalists buried this law, but the Bund found out about it. There've been hundreds of strikes – maybe a thousand – all over the Pale. And I led the one here."

I wished Daniel wasn't so pleased with himself. He was interesting enough, but such bragging. "And does everyone win their strikes?"

"Well, not always, of course."

"What happens to the workers then?"

"Most of the time they just go back to work sixteen, seventeen hours a day. I myself worked eighteen hours when we had a special contract." He stopped and sighed. I had a little more sympathy for him. After all, as a student he never had to do anything much besides read. Work must have felt like falling into an icy river. He looked at his hands and I looked too. They were scraped and scabbed, ink running into red creases.

"Sometimes the capitalists bring in strike breakers from another town," Daniel said, "or Russians, who don't understand the meaning of unity. Then the workers get fired."

"And they still strike?" Having a trade seemed a wonderful thing to me – I couldn't understand why you would strike if it meant losing your work. There were so many who could find nothing, scraping from kopeck to kopeck.

"Of course. We're all poor workers, what have we to lose? The tailors can always sew from their houses if they have to, and printers – well, we can go to another town."

"Another town?" I never thought about Daniel moving away.

He took my hand. I couldn't remember him ever doing that before. "I may have to go soon anyway, strike or no. The central committee may send me north to organize and distribute propaganda."

I pulled my hand away. "Here – Mama made this special for you." I handed him the cake with the daled.

He smiled in a sorrowing way that reminded me a little of Abe. "Mama is a bourgeois sentimentalist. But tell her thank you for me."

"You won't go away without seeing her?"

"I honestly don't know, Chava. I can't come to the house and she can't come here. We could meet in the birzhe, the organizing street, near the New Bazaar. She could wander through on her way to market." He blinked, looking into the trees, picturing it. "Ask her if she'll come say goodbye to me a week from Wednesday. I'll be there at four o'clock if I'm being sent away. I'll try to wait an hour. You tell her and Esther and Sarah I do this for them as well as for the workers. A day will come when we won't have to depend on Russian masters for every crust of bread!"

"Meyer!" Simeon stood shouting from the doorway with his hands on his hips. "This isn't a resort on the Black Sea. Say goodbye to your sister already and get back to work!"

"I'm glad you came," Daniel said. "If I don't see you for awhile, remember that I'm working for your future too, comrade Chava." He brushed the dirt off his knees and held out his hand to pull me up.

Comrade, he called me. I was sorry I hadn't gone to see him before. I must have frowned.

"What's wrong?" Daniel asked "You're too good to be a comrade? I thought you had more spirit than Esther."

"I do. No one ever called me comrade before, that's all. Thank you."

"You're welcome."

"Meyer!" Simeon yelled.

Daniel held out his hand and I felt proud to shake it, to be his sister and comrade. I got a little smudge of ink inside my thumb and was careful not to rub it off for a long as I could.

But Daniel forgot, or never knew, that people don't fall into neat rows like letters. I told Mama his plan to meet. First she wanted to know how he looked, if he was taking care of himself. Then she wanted to know what he'd said about the cake.

"He said you were a bourgeois sentimentalist, and thank you."

"Sentimentalist?" She looked up from her sewing. Esther, who had been looking at me, stared back down at her stitches, pretending she didn't understand. I was preparing the wax for the candles. Mama pursed her lips and raised her eyes to the ceiling. Then she said it again. "A sentimentalist, am I?"

When the appointed Wednesday came, she didn't go.

At first I thought I had swallowed a nail and it was piercing me from inside. My stomach hurt often enough, but this was lower. Something terrible was wrong. Mama was over on Ismailovsk Street distributing clothes with Sarah. I had no choice but to go to Esther.

Esther took a minute to really look at me. The freckles spilled across her nose and I watched them instead of her watery green eyes. "Don't be so dramatic," she finally said. She was doing hand embroidery on a pile of yarmulkes that were special for boys' bar mitsves.

"Dramatic? What do you know?"

"This I know. Check and see."

"Check what?"

"In your underwear. For blood."

"Why would I bleed in my underwear?"

Esther sighed and put her needle down. "Just do what I say."

I went behind the curtain and checked. There was a little stain. How did Esther know? What was going to happen to me now?

"Well?" she called from the kitchen. Her voice had that "I told you so" sound. Now that Nathan, the tavern owner's son, has been courting her, she was more self-important than ever.

I came back. How could I be bleeding below when I could feel all the blood in me rushing up to my cheeks and upper arms? Maybe the blood was making circles like a whirlpool in my body and at the bottom of the whirlpool it was draining out. "What is it? How did you know?"

"It happens to every woman. It happens to me and Mama."

"To Mama? Why didn't she tell me?"

Esther shrugged her soft shoulders. I still didn't want to look in her eyes so I watched her mouth instead. I noticed how thin Esther's lips were for someone plump. "She didn't tell me until I started. Why worry about something before you have to? I'll show you what to do. Come with me."

We went into Mama and Papa's room. She opened the bottom drawer of Mama's chest, which had lions carved at the base of the legs. When it was cold and I couldn't sleep, sometimes I'd pretend I could hear the lions growling, and Mama would let me come sleep beside her. Of course I was beyond that for a long time already.

"Here, see these rags?" There was a stack of neatly folded cloth squares, leftover pieces of this and that, all with old stains. "When you start to bleed, you put these between your legs. Change them when they're uncomfortable and wash them out behind the pump. Mama dries them on a shelf behind the oven. Maybe she'll make you some new ones for your own. Don't let Papa or any boys see. And don't go running around while you bleed! It will just make it worse – you might get the blood all over you." This she said with some satisfaction. She was always trying to get me to hold still. "Take one now. Your undergarments will hold it in place enough if you don't squirm so."

"For how long?" How was I supposed to go around with rags stuffed between my legs?

"Oh, it lasts for three or four days and it comes almost once a month. Mama says every woman is a little different, how often, how long."

"Every month, all my life?" I was shocked, not just that this was happening to me, but if it happens to women everywhere, how do they all keep it secret?

Esther looked perplexed, as though she'd come to the end of her knowledge, which happened often enough. "I think so. Yes, I think all our lives. It's what it means to be women. When you're finished bleeding, you go to the mikve with Mama. She'll show you what to do." She paused. "Chava – I'm sorry it hurts you. If it gets bad, when Mama comes home, ask her for a hot-water bottle."

I went back to my bed behind the curtain and put the cloth in as Esther instructed. Was it the bleeding that made Esther so proper? No, she had always been that way, as long as I could remember. Maybe the blood made it worse. I wouldn't change, she'd see. She didn't want me to run only because she didn't, that was all. My legs were already as long as Daniel's. A little blood wouldn't stop me. But what if blood did

shake out of me when I ran? Esther said it would only be for a few days. I could run when it stopped.

I supposed this was a good opportunity to read for awhile. I had some of Daniel's old pamphlets underneath my mattress, even though he hadn't sneaked into town for over six months. I liked this one with the picture of Rosa Luxemburg, *Sozialreform oder Revolution*. Well, what I liked was her profile on the front – serious, she had a serious face. Sometimes I looked in the mirror to see if my face could be serious enough to be a revolutionary's. You can't be too pretty, otherwise no one pays any attention unless they want to marry you. Or so ugly no one would want to look at you. I was glad I had a long, dark face with a little mole on the left, towards the back of my jaw. You had to have a serious face, like Rosa Luxemburg. Mama had a serious face, not quite so stern, but then she wasn't writing pamphlets. Papa said Mama was a handsome woman and if I was lucky I'd look like her when I grew up. I could be handsome and serious too. Maybe being a revolutionary made you look more serious. I couldn't understand all the words the revolutionaries wrote, though I got most of the ideas. I liked to run my hand over the page and feel how the type cut into the paper, all the indentations it made on a page. I closed my eyes and pressed my fingertips against the pamphlet. Could words enter through your skin and change your mind without your knowing?

If I had gone to school I would have been able to understand Rosa Luxemburg perfectly, but Papa wouldn't send me after Daniel disappeared. He was afraid I'd get involved with the intellectuals or socialists. What if I did? "Esther, at least, is a jewel – see how she behaves," he liked to say. "A good match we'll make for her. But you – you need a firm hand and the only way you're going to get it is if you stay home. Besides, your mother is as educated as half the teachers in Kishinev. She'll teach you all you need to know."

Everything started to seem sour to me. I was never going to be bar mitsved like my brothers – no celebration, no one clapping me on the back and inviting me to read to the congregation. I sat beside my mother on Saturday mornings in the balcony while she led the women's praying. Some of the women liked to just sit up there and gossip, but Mama kept everything as orderly as she could. She made me keep Sarah from fidgeting, and that was the whole of my religious duties – besides lighting the candles and separating the dough.

I would never have gotten into the gymnasium anyway unless Papa had been rich and willing to spend his riches on me. It was miracle

enough that Abe went so far in Russian schools with the quotas, and Abe had gone to pick grapes in Zion. The longer he was away, the sillier his dream seemed. It wasn't like going to Vienna or Berlin, where there was opportunity. Palestine was like going backwards, from the city to a shack in the country, from the start of the twentieth century to the start of the sixteenth – or even back to the Second Temple. I could see Abe wearing a loincloth and carrying a staff, followed by a flock of sheep. If I could have gone to the university, I wouldn't have thrown it away by becoming a farmer in a desert. I would have been a doctor. Or someone who designed machinery, though I didn't think they let girls do that. That was the other thing: every time I turned around there were walls. What was I going to do, cooped up in the house with Mama, Esther and Sarah, bleeding and dripping candlewax? I suppose it was better than working at the candle factory, but at least there I could have joined the Bund and organized the other girls. Wouldn't that have been something? Daniel wasn't the only one in this family who was important. I would have made speeches. At home no one listened to me. Except Sarah and what could I say to her – Rise up, little sister, we must organize against Mama and Papa, who exploit our labor?

Now that I was twelve-years old and bleeding, my parents were probably going to marry me off the first chance they got. They were already making arrangements for Esther with Nathan's parents. Who would they find for me? One of those sickly students who came to dinner? Then I'd have to work to support him, and what did I know how to do besides make candles and run a shop?

Maybe I could support a household selling books instead of candles. Would people buy books from a girl? Women would – and women read. I would order all the Yiddish novels and translations from Poland, Germany and Saint Petersburg from the peddlers who came around. I would always know what was new, what the important people were reading in Europe. Women would come from all over Kishinev to buy or borrow books – I'd keep a few to lend out, for a few kopecks. Maybe Mama would tell the matchmaker I needed a husband who would let me run a business as I saw fit. If I asked her, she might agree. She'd have to have pity on me because I was bleeding now and it hurt. So I would marry some shlemil, have ten children and run a little bookstore.

Then I felt a stomach ache higher up than the first pain. I grabbed my belly and sighed. Who would want to marry a tall, serious girl with a bad stomach, anyway?

Sharp, but not sharp enough

In between the morning and evening Shabbes services, we walked home to eat the tsholnt Mama made on Fridays. Tsholnt was one of my favorite meals, even if we did eat it every Saturday afternoon. Barley agreed with me and I liked to look at it on my spoon, the little crease in the middle of the grain like the skin folding around my knuckle.

The men returned to the shul for the afternoon service and the rest of us stayed home. Mama would sit between me and Sarah with a book on her lap. She was supposed to read us Bible stories, which she did from time to time. Sarah liked the Bible stories for the pictures: Moses striking the rock in the desert, the Jews dancing around the golden calf, Miriam with her tambourine. I liked it better when she read us Pushkin or Gogol; I liked listening to the Russian, though I didn't catch every word. Even these books had pictures, fewer, but more dramatic: a man clutching his overcoat in an alley, with every shadow a menacing face etched in a thousand lines. Sarah would run her small fingers over the page delicately, closing her eyes. "I can feel the winter in my hands," she said once. Mama and I smiled at each other. She was small for nine and good natured. Sitting with her eyes closed, her hand moving over the engraving, she had the aspect of a delicate angel, not because she was especially well-behaved, but because all the worry of our lives, all the arguments, were still removed from her. Although she was aware that her wandering eye made people uneasy, she never seemed to take it to heart.

Esther was restless now that she was engaged to Nathan. And she was cranky because she couldn't sew on Shabbes or walk down to the river with him until after sundown since he was in shul. I never understood the big attraction. Nathan was a clumsy, red-headed mama's boy who never talked about anything besides the weather and

beer. But at least Esther got to choose him, which was more than most girls were allowed to do. Papa would have preferred a scholar, but Mama convinced him that a steady income from a tavern was nothing to sneeze at. That was exactly how she put it, and it amused me to think of Papa making a sneeze big enough to blow the tavern away.

"Why are the things I like to do forbidden?" Esther complained.

"And what would you like to do?" Mama asked.

"I want to go to the concert in the park."

"You know your father would never allow that on the sabbath."

"I know, Mama, but there's going to be another one tomorrow, in the afternoon." Esther looked pleadingly at Mama. She was standing in front of the window and the shaft of light made her hair look almost red. Wine-dark, I'd heard somewhere. Now that she was almost a bride, I sometimes saw her differently, as if she'd crossed a line I hadn't known was there. But it wasn't changing her personality much – she was even more convinced she was the center of civilization.

"We all have so much to do to get ready for Pesach," Mama said doubtfully, which meant that she was going to give in.

Sarah opened her eyes. "Mama, could we please go to the concert tomorrow?" And that, of course, decided it.

Papa sounded betrayed. "Going to the concert? Parading the girls through the streets when there's so much unrest in town? A week before Pesach? Do you really think this is a good idea?"

"Doesn't it say, 'Make a joyful noise unto the Lord?' The girls need a little exercise and I could use getting out of the house for more than my dutiful rebitsin visits. Don't worry so."

"A joyful noise is not interpreted to mean concerts in the Royal Gardens, mixing with the goyim."

"Isaac, this is not a court case. The girls are restless and so am I. All week we work and on Shabbes we keep the Commandments. After Esther is married, I won't have this opportunity to be with all three of my girls so often."

Papa scratched his ear. "But how do you think this will look?"

"It will look like the learned and progressive rabbi is tending to his studies, while the rebitsin and daughters open their spirits with a little music. What looks so bad? Not even a patch on the girls' coats, thank God. Come, Isaac, you know there's no harm."

"But the unrest – ." Papa had an odd expression, as if, for a second,

he was looking at us and not at God.

Mama pursed her lips. "It's better for us to show ourselves as dignified human beings, not afraid. As long as we all mingle respectfully in town, maybe the worst will be averted."

"With God's will." He slapped the table as if he was keeping the score on their arguments, looked away, looked back, sighed, raised his eyes to the ceiling, where God lives. "What can you do with a woman like this, I ask you? Go."

Mama was already buttoning Sarah's coat up to her chin.

Since Abraham was in Jaffa and Daniel who knows where, Papa was more critical of what we did, but he had less energy for argument. He was often like a ghost walking around in our house. If we asked him something, he stroked his beard and said "the Talmud this" or "the Talmud that" – for any question – even could we have a piece of candy, could we go and watch the glassblowers work, would he give us a few extra kopecks for the beggars?

Esther and I, we liked walking down Alexander Street with Mama. We imagined the street was as grand as any in Paris or Berlin. Mama showed us a book with engravings of society ladies walking in the latest fashions down the Champs Elysees. I knew Esther wanted to be a *grande dame*. Since the engagement was announced, she worked her wedding dress into every conversation, the one she ordered special from the spinster Golde Zelkin's shop. She walked with her nose in the air and said all four words she knew in French, which probably meant "my umbrella wants an outhouse," and then she giggled and skipped ahead. I ran after her, past her, turned around and stuck my tongue out. Sarah tried to catch us but her legs were too short. I still liked to run. Mama said it wasn't ladylike and I said, who wants to be a lady? Esther frowned but I could tell Mama was pleased by me, though she couldn't say, in case of the evil eye.

I could run so fast the evil eye couldn't catch me. I was running and skipping backwards, making faces at my sisters, when I bumped into a man on the sidewalk, a Rumanian.

"Damn zhids," he cursed, shaking his newspaper at me. "The day is coming when you'll get yours." The newspaper was in my face, and I saw the headline: Crusade Against the Hated Race!

"Thank you very much." I was cold as ice. "I'll be looking forward to that." Mama grabbed my arm.

"She's sorry if she caused you any trouble, sir. Just a high-spirited girl."

104

"Damn zhids," he said again and turned away from us to spit.

When he was out of earshot, I complained. "Mama, he was cursing us – why were you so nice to him?"

"It's a difficult time, you know that. Every one of us must do what she can to make peace with our neighbors. You have to behave like model citizens, each of you. That means you too, Chava. Do you understand me?"

"Yes, but I don't think curtseying to every moujik is going to change their hearts. You think they're going to wake up and say, 'By God, you know we were wrong about those Jews, let's invite them over for dinner'?"

"You are too much of a smartmouth for your own good. Now just do what I say and walk like young ladies or we're going home."

Esther gave me her "you're in trouble ha-ha" face. I pretended not to notice and took Sarah's hand. I looked up at the acacia trees, which were just beginning to bloom. It was a beautiful Sunday, one of the first really warm afternoons, and the air came into my chest like clear-cut crystal, bright and tinkling. I didn't really want to go to the concert and hoped that Mama would let me wander off to the botanical gardens. I liked to read the names of all the plants and feel the undersides of the fuzzy leaves. The winter had been hard, everyone said, but not as hard as in the nineties. That was what everybody always said, "Oy, it was hard, but not as hard as such-and-such a time, you should know how lucky you are to be living now." Sometimes I thought there must be a secret school where you went to learn how to be a grown-up and forget what it was like to be a child. I knew Esther snuck out to this school at night. She'd say she was going for a walk with Nathan but she couldn't fool me. She went someplace where they taught her it was no fun to jump across stones in the river, and whenever you were asked a question, you must reply, "You'll understand when you're as old as I am." Even Mama was more fun than Esther. But then, she didn't have to prove to anyone what a grown-up she was.

At the concert I looked at the faces of the people, trying to decide which of them went to the secret school for forgetting how to be a child and which of them went to the school for anti-Semites. It took time to learn things, I knew. It couldn't only be that someone's mother said, "You should hate the Jews," and then that person smacked her forehead and said, "What a good idea."

Three rows over sat a girl about my age, staring at me. I smiled and she scowled. So. They had her in their school too. They had actual

books. Uncle Elihu showed me one once, when I promised not to tell Mama and Papa. Russian books with long essays and diagrams of Jewish heads and noses. It made me want to throw up. And then I spent all day looking at my nose in the mirror. I knew it wasn't only my nose that made me a Jew, but I used to lie in bed holding it, trying to reshape it, so not everyone could tell just by looking at me. I was only eleven then.

We sat in a row of all Jews. Mama said hello to everyone. Some of the women elbowed their husbands and looked uncomfortable. Rabbis' wives always seemed to make a little stir when they showed up somewhere unexpected. My mother simply smiled and adjusted her wig. All around us there were Moldavians, Greeks, Armenians, a few moujiks. Did they have books about each other's noses or only about the Jews? I wondered if the girl who was frowning at me was trying to measure my face. I had a beautiful chin, everyone said so. It wasn't too pretty though. It was strong.

There was so much talk about pure Russian this and the great Russian spirit it made sense that the local orchestra performed Mussorgsky. I liked *Pictures at an Exhibition*, though. I'd heard it once before and the idea of music that showed how to walk through an art gallery in sound made the hair on my arms prickle. Sarah kept her eyes closed for most of the concert while her mouth stayed open in a little "o" and she sucked in every breath. When the concert was over, people were walking around making ordinary comments: "Wonderful violin, wasn't it," and "Nice weather. Good to see you, dear." Sarah and I went up by the concert platform, skipping, looking around. She found a Russian handbill on the ground and handed it to me.

> Citizens! Once again your mortal enemies, the Zhids, have perpetrated their heinous crime of murder for blood! In Dubossary, last month, Rubalenko, a twelve-year-old boy, was found stabbed thirty-seven times, with ritual marks on his neck and palms. All over Bessarabia the Zhids are baking their passover matzoh, and their bakers use the pure blood of our beloved Christian youth!
>
> The foreign scum takes our money and drinks our blood! Everyone is crushed by the filthy parasitic Zhids! Enough! Don't let them kill your children! Avenge the death of Rubalenko! Our father, the great

Tsar Nicholas II, urges us to inflict a just and bloody
punishment on the Zhids. Take up your cudgels, now
is the time brothers! Death to the Zhids!

"What does it say?" she asked.

It took me a long time to understand it. I was glad that I could read
some Russian, but it was hard to read this, standing in the Royal
Gardens on a pleasant Sunday afternoon. I kept looking up from the
page towards Mama.

"It says – lies about the Jews," I said to Sarah.

"Why?"

"I don't know. We should show it to Mama."

Mama read the handbill in a second. I was always proud when
Mama read in front of other people, even if they didn't notice how
good she was. She held the paper away from her face since she didn't
have her glasses and moved only her eyes quickly down the page.
Then she sat down hard on a bench and covered her mouth.

"What's wrong Mama?" Esther asked.

"There's going to be trouble."

"Just from a piece of paper?" I asked.

Mama almost laughed. "Trouble, Chavele, almost always starts with
a piece of paper. I think there's going to be a pogrom."

"What's a pogrom, Mama?" Sarah asked.

I sucked in my stomach and got taller. I remembered vaguely Mama
and Papa talking about the pogrom in Kantakuzen a long time ago,
when I was ten.

"A pogrom is something I hope you never see. It's like – a street full
of men like the one Chava bumped into this afternoon, yelling and
beating up the Jews."

Sarah looked down at her shoes. "Does the paper say they're going
to have one?"

"The paper says that Jews have killed a Christian boy to use his
blood for Passover matzohs."

"Ich. That's stupid!"

"Yes. Well. Stupidity is the most dangerous thing on earth. And we
live in very stupid times. So. Now we're going to go home and talk
about this with your father."

We passed the statue of Pushkin at the entrance to the park. I
remembered when it was put up, with bouquets of flowers arranged at
the base. I wondered if Pushkin would have told people how silly it is
to think Jews drink Christian blood. Who thought these things up? If

someone could made up a lie like this, maybe they drank blood themselves.

When Papa read the handbill, his skin turned the color of wax. I didn't think he could look any more pale.

"We'll talk about it after dinner."

Dinner was quiet and quick. Mama sent us to clean up, and she and Papa went into their room. Since the boys left, I didn't have to sleep behind the stove anymore, though sometimes I missed the private feeling I'd had behind my little blanket. Of course we could hear them anywhere in the house. When they whispered I listened harder or walked silently to the wall of their room.

"Isaac, I have a very bad feeling about this. Something terrible is going to happen."

"Always a feeling, never a fact. In the Talmud – "

"Isaac, please, please listen to me. You know what happened in Shpole and in Nikoleav."

"It's been four or five years. It was almost twenty before that. This is Kishinev, Miriam, not some little shtetl."

"Isaac, you know what this means." Papa got up and started pacing. I knew he knew she was right. "The men respect you. Talk to the Chief Rabbi. Maybe you can go to the Mayor or the police and find out what they know, if they're prepared for this."

"Yes, the police. I'll get together a distinguished citizens minyan, and we'll just stroll into the police station. And the police captain will say, 'Don't be afraid, little brother, everything will be fine.' "

"This is not a joke. Schmidt, he's always been friendly to the Jews, go to him."

"Our German mayor? If there's going to be pogrom, he won't be able to stop it. We have go to the Governor, General Von Raaben."

"Then go. We have to defend ourselves."

"I'll go. To please you. But God's will is God's will, who can change it?"

"This is not about God, this is about men."

"I said I would go, didn't I?" Papa patted Mama's hand. "You're a good Jew, Miriam. I appreciate how you take care of things, don't think I don't. But really, I wish you wouldn't go to the Royal Gardens for concerts."

I was hanging at the edge of the doorway, pretending to be polishing a candlestick. I could just make out Mama pulling Papa's beard a little. He laughed and a strange brightness came into him. "I

shouldn't forget to enjoy my wonderful wife, the modern woman!" It was a mystery to me why anyone would want that scratchy beard close to them. But I didn't have to think about that. I didn't have to think about anything if I didn't want to.

When I fell asleep I dreamed I was surrounded by men wearing shields, old-fashioned shields that hung around their shoulders and strapped around their waists. The shields were all made of newspapers.

On Thursday Papa went with the Chief Rabbi and the rabbi from the shul in the Bender Rugatka quarter and some very well-dressed men to see the Governor. He came back with his faraway ghost look again.

"So what did Von Raaben say?" Mama asked after he removed his overcoat. They didn't notice me standing by the stove.

"They are taking all necessary precautions. You know how it says in the May Laws the Jews are under the Tsar's protection. He is bound by law and by decency to protect us."

"So what does that mean he will do?" Mama had been reading and her reading glasses were pushed down on her nose.

"He has the troops. If there should be a pogrom, he'll stop it."

"What he should do is make them stop printing that anti-Semitic paper *Bessarabetz*."

"Should. Should. Rabbi Horowitz himself told me that when he went to the Greek Orthodox, the Bishop asked him if there were not, after all, a sect of Jews who used Christian blood for matzoh."

"I thought the Bishop – "

"Don't be so surprised, Miriam. None of this would happen without the church's complicity. Well, Sunday is their Easter. If we can get through that, this will all blow over."

"Do you think we should send the girls out of town?" She took her glasses off and folded them slowly.

"Railroad tickets grow on trees? And who knows where it's better. The girls should stay by us."

That weekend we made no plans to go to the Royal Gardens. In shul on Shabbes it was like usual. I didn't like the smell of perfume, sweat and garlic in the women's gallery. My stomach jumped like a slaughtered chicken and I didn't even want to eat the tsholnt Mama took out of the warm oven when we got home. Only Sarah was really hungry. Everyone else ate slowly and quietly.

"Chava, your mother works hard to make such good meals for us. You must eat your share," Papa said.

"You know her stomach isn't strong. Let her be. She'll eat when she wants." Mama took my plate away and left it on the shelf by the washtub.

"I'm going back to the shul, I'll be home before sundown."

"Isaac – "

"What, Miriam?"

"Suppose it happens?"

"I will go to shul in the morning and pray."

"All right, you pray. But what about us?"

He wet his lips as if we were a particularly difficult passage of the law. "If there is trouble, kayn ayen-hore, you take the girls by my sister Shendl. It's not far from the shul, and she has a secret room in her chicken shed. You'll be safe there. But I think the mood is calmer now, everything will be all right."

My mother didn't like to be in Shendl's house. They were so poor their furniture gave you splinters just looking at it. My Uncle Elihu was a capmaker, but there must have been a hundred Jewish capmakers in Kishinev and work for maybe twenty. Every Friday night after dinner Shendl would say, "Next week you'll come by us!" and my mother would answer, "Of course." Then the next Friday, there they were again, all eight of them, kicking up the dust in the road. Shendl had four boys and two girls, Rebkah and Aviva, twins a year younger than me. Papa liked to have all those boys in the house. I could have lived without it, though my cousins were very polite. Politeness that came from hunger didn't feel right. I didn't know if Papa even noticed – anyway he would think it was a sin to notice hunger because it made the appetite a source of shame. Sometimes he even let my cousin Reuben say kiddush since he was bar mitsve.

Sunday morning the air crackled around my head and I didn't want to get up.

"It's because you didn't eat supper last night. It's going to be a long day, Chava, at least you'll eat some bread and butter. There's tea. Come, get dressed." Mama's voice sounded different, not exasperated, but calm and insistent.

I could hear the morning church bells ringing. All the Christians went to celebrate Christ rising from his grave, which made no sense to me. Of course, it didn't make sense to me either when Papa explained how, when the messiah came, everyone would rise from their graves to join God in heaven. I knew what happened to people in a grave – why would God want a million skeletons dancing around? Wouldn't he

rather just have our minds there with him? We could hear the carriages rolling by, taking people to church. Papa was in his good Shabbes clothes. Mama was smoothing his collar.

"Everything will be fine, Miriam, don't worry."

"And if something happens, where will we meet again?"

"You stay with Shendl and I'll come there after dark."

"And if you can't?"

"Still, you'll wait for me. I'll come. Don't come to the shul. I expect if there's trouble, the shul won't be so safe."

"Why are you going, then?"

"Because I'm the Rabbi, it's where I belong."

"Oy, Isaac. Not everything is resolved by faith."

"But without faith, nothing is resolved. I'll see you again by tonight." He put on his best fur hat and kissed each of us girls on the forehead. I didn't want him to leave us but I said nothing.

Hours went by. Our neighborhood fell unnaturally silent. In the square near Alexander Street booths were usually set up for the Christians to have their festival after church. Was everyone in the city waiting? The Christians were waiting to get out of church and have a good meal and the Jews were waiting to see what the Christians would do. All the waiting, pulsing in the air. Then the church bells rang again. Noon.

We began to hear shouting. Mama looked like she had eaten a rotten fish.

"Mama, were you ever in a pogrom before?" I asked.

"Before?" She pulled her shawl around her shoulders, and an odd, perplexed look came over her. "No. But I was twenty and carrying your brother Abraham when Tsar Alexander was assassinated. There were pogroms everywhere. We had family whose houses were destroyed in Kiev. Here there was only rock throwing. We thought we were lucky to live in such an enlightened city. If we all live through today, you remember I said there is no enlightened city in the whole of Russia. Now we must hurry to your Aunt Shendl's." She had a little package of food prepared.

We followed my mother like baby chicks through backyards and alleys. Once she became disoriented but I knew a short cut behind Armenia Street. We could hear a mob very close, screaming about the Jews and Christian children, and then the noise of glass breaking. Sarah was crying without making any sounds and I whispered that she was very brave and smart to keep quiet. Esther turned around and gave me

a dirty look which changed to fear, and I forgave her.

We got to Shendl's before the mob was in her street. Already there was no one around. Mama took us to the courtyard by the chicken coop.

"Shendl, it's Miriam. Let us in," she whispered into a knot hole.

A door swung open that looked just like the wall of the coop. I had always admired how my Uncle Elihu could make a whistle from a scrap of wood and this was even better. The little room was already stuffed with my cousins and Shendl, who didn't hesitate.

"Come, you'll squeeze in." And we did. There were many holes in the boards so at least there was air, even though there was hardly room to turn around. The air was full of chicken feathers, chicken stink. It felt like a coffin.

"You get used to it," my cousin Aviva whispered. Sounds came from far away, then close and then far again. Horses and breaking glass and hurrahs! mixed with "Kill the Jews." I looked at my cousins' faces in the streaked light. For a minute I forgot my fear and anger. I felt the strangest sensation, like the top of my head was lifting off. Why were we all packed in there like beasts? What did we do? Ever since I had been old enough to think, I'd been trying to understand why everyone hated the Jews, and still it made no sense. I felt as if I had to make up for the rioters, and I wanted my cousins, my sisters, to know how much I loved them, how wonderful their lives were. My heart felt so big it hurt.

No one spoke. We stood like statues. There was enough room left for one person to rest on the floor at a time. When it was quiet we changed places. Eleven of us used one chamber pot, squatting only an inch away from someone else's leg.

Esther whispered to Mama about Nathan.

"It's up to God now," Mama shrugged.

We heard footsteps, crashing, then going away. "Where is Elihu?" Mama asked.

"He went with a group of Bundists to see where they could fight back. Not that they had even guns, just sticks and homemade alcohol bombs." Shendl sighed like her lungs would break.

"Sha," Mama said, "he'll be back. The Bundists know how to get in and out of bad situations. He'll be all right." I looked at her. This was the first good thing she'd ever said about the Bund. To comfort Shendl or because she actually believed in their cause? I didn't ask. The light left the shed like a sputtering candle and we stood in the dark for at

least an hour. Finally Shendl asked Mama if maybe we could go in the house to rest. The littlest boy had messed his pants and all of us were exhausted. Esther and Reuben were having spasms in their legs. Mama thought it would be all right – the only sound we'd heard for a long time came from the chickens. Shendl cracked the door and peeked out. It didn't look so bad from the courtyard. Some of the houses had their doors broken in, some had broken glass. I thought, if this is the pogrom, all right, we lived through it. We took turns standing guard for each other in front of the outhouse and washed up a little at the courtyard pump.

My cousins had only two rooms in their house besides the big kitchen. Mama, Shendl, Esther went to sleep in Shendl and Elihu's room. The boys slept around the stove. Sarah and I shared a little straw mat on the floor, the twins sleeping beside us.

I could hear Mama walking around, looking out the windows for Papa. I got up and went to her. She put her arms around me and pulled me close, stroking my hair. Even after a whole day sweating in the chicken coop, I loved the feeling of being close to her.

"Something's happened to your papa."

"No, he just can't come. He will, he'll come for us, Mama."

She remembered she was supposed to be comforting me. "Yes, that's right, he'll come for us soon."

My papa, Rabbi Isaac Meyer, lay in the new Alexander Street market. Face up, staring at God. The mob had found him in the temple, holding the Torah. They ripped the Torah into little ribbons in front of him, and he cried.

"What babies these Zhids are," a man taunted. "They're made of straw. Push them just a little, they cave right in!"

"Let's make an example of this Jew!" someone else yelled. They tied up his hands and forced him outside where the mob shouted for the rabbi's blood. "We'll show you what it means to kill Christian children!" They pushed him down the steps and kicked him until he was on the ground. Then they tied his feet. While he was lying on the steps of the synagogue tied up like a calf for the butcher, the Bishop rode down the street in his carriage, blessing the crowd. The crowd made a little wall around my father, so the Bishop didn't exactly see him.

When the Bishop had passed, the mob tied another rope around my papa's beard and connected the ropes around the hands and beard to

a rope on the saddle of one of their horses. The army was in the street, watching. A number of other Jews were tied or being held by the mob, students and old men who thought the house of God would either protect them or be a good place to die, two women who were found hiding behind a curtain in their shop.

"What do you think of your rabbi now?" the mob asked. "Huh, Jews? And your God, where is your God this afternoon? We'll teach you! You exploit, you crush us, you kill our children – now we'll show how we take care of our Jews!"

The Moldavian rider spurred his horse and dragged my father through the street. The crowd threw rocks and stones at him. He was praying, wasn't he? Reciting the shema while they dragged him through the dirt. They dragged him all the way to the market. No one knew when he died.

My father was dragged by his beard until he was dead. He was in the Alexander Street market, counting the number of stars. If he could get the number right, it would spell the secret name of God.

It was dawn when Elihu came back, exhausted, cut and bleeding. He kept looking at my mama, at all the children. Shendl washed him from the bucket, gave him a little shnaps and a piece of dry bread.

"This was just the beginning," he said. "They're going to be back as soon as they wake up from their drunken sleep."

"But what about the army?" Shendl asked.

"The army! Who do you think organized this? There are bands of strangers all through town. The seminarians lead them – you think the army is going to do anything? They just sit on their horses and nod. I guess they're supposed to make sure only Jews get hit. I'm going to meet the Bundists on the other side of the quarter. We will try to keep the mob out of here if we can."

"Stay here with us, Elihu," Shendl begged. We were all calculating how it would be, another whole day in the chicken coop.

"I can't. You'll be safe here. Don't worry, I'm just a shlemil, and you know it's impossible to kill a shlemil, especially one who's trying to get himself killed.

"Elihu—"

"You know I'm joking, my wonderful wife. I'll be careful, you'll be careful. We'll get through." Then he remembered and looked at my mother. He cleared his throat, looked out the window, looked back.

"Mrs. Meyer, I have to tell you."

Mama didn't say anything. We drew around her, Esther on one side, me on the other, Sarah in front. She looked straight at Elihu.

"I saw Rabbi Meyer." Still Mama didn't say anything. No one even sighed. My mother's knuckles got white as her hands dug into Sarah's shoulders. "The barbarians found him in the shul. They wanted to make an example of him. I'm sorry."

At first I didn't understand. When Mama asked, "Where is he?" I thought maybe he was at the police station or in the hospital.

"In the marketplace. We had to leave his body there until this is over." Elihu put his hand softly on Mama's arm. "He was a good Jew. You know what they say, 'If God lived on earth, all His windows would be broken.' This is that time."

Esther started to scream. Mama turned to her slowly, like a mechanical doll on a music box, and slapped her face.

"You have to pull yourself together," she said. "We must endure the bad with the good. This is a nightmare. Tomorrow we will find your father and do what has to be done. Now we have to stick together. You understand?"

Esther sucked her tears in. Mama turned to each of us. "You, Chavele? You, Sarah?" She turned back to Elihu. "I appreciate your honesty, Reb Rubin. I hope you will be safe today."

"With God's will."

"With God's will." Mama looked away as Shendl kissed Uncle Elihu goodbye. We might never have seen him again, either. The cousins couldn't look at us anymore because Papa was dead. Now no one protested about getting back in our tiny hideout. We took all the food there was, a pail of water, the cleaned-out chamber pot, and closed the door behind us. The Angel of Death had his cold hand squeezing around our hearts so tight that the closeness of the chicken coop was somehow a comfort. Last night we couldn't wait to get out of our prison. Today it felt like home and none of us wanted to be more than an inch away from the other. We were connected by blood, urine and feathers.

Only seven o'clock in the morning but already we could hear the yells starting in the street. Sometime near midday the screams and yells were closer, horrible. I forgot my father for a minute. All of the cousins looked at each other. The littlest boy, Yankl, started to cry. Shendl covered his mouth. Yankl took in a couple of deep sobbing breaths and then quieted. I kept my hands in fists in my skirt pockets. I couldn't

see anything from the crack in front of me. The screams came closer.

"What are they doing to her?" I asked in a whisper.

"I don't know," Shendl said. "Whatever they're doing, you don't want them to do it to you. Hush." There was a baby's wail. Then it stopped and a woman screamed, "Then kill me too!" Then high-pitched screaming that must have come from the mouths of demons, and men laughing and shouting. Something happened to Mama. Her eyes got glassy, as if she was going to faint. Shendl put a wet rag on the back of her neck. Mama coughed and blinked, then pressed the same rag against all our foreheads. Esther was squatting with her back against the wall, her hands over her ears. Cousin Aviva was holding Esther's arm. Rebkah was leaning on Aviva's shoulder. Reuben was bouncing up and down on the balls of his feet, as if he were an old man, davening. Then we heard footsteps and someone yelling "hep, hep!" almost next to our ears. The regular door of the chicken coop was opened. None of us breathed. The chickens screeched and clucked.

"Nothing in here but dinner!" some man yelled, and I could hear the chickens gurgle as they were strangled. Everywhere things were breaking, falling, crashing. I wanted to sneeze. I looked up, expecting to see my papa hovering above us in a band of light, but there was only the tar roof of the coop. There was a whoosh and some man shouted, "On to Asia Street!" As the sounds of their boots faded, there was a new smell. Smoke.

Shendl, who had been up against the door – they should kill her first before they touched her children – was out in an instant. Flames were beginning to consume the buildings and for a minute we were transported into stillness by our shock. The courtyard looked like the gate to gehene. Had we died in the chicken coop? Was this our punishment for the pride we had in our lives, to see life wrecked and burning before us? None of the houses had doors, one had a whole wall missing. In Shendl's house every window was broken, the doorway full of shattered furniture. Chamber pots and candlesticks poked out of the sea of feathers. Blood, mud and smoke were everywhere. Mama took the rag she had used on our foreheads and placed it over Sarah's mouth. On the far side of the courtyard I could see bodies lying in strange positions. Mama put her hand on my cheek and turned me away. Flames were sliding up and down the wooden houses like water.

"My candlesticks!" Shendl was already mourning the little bit she had.

"Candlesticks don't burn. Later you'll look for them. Come." Mama pushed Shendl forward softly, but Shendl turned and clung to her, unwilling to give up the closeness of the coop. For a second my mother lay her head on Shendl's shoulder, grief fighting with resolve. Then resolve pulled her back.

"All right – we'll go by the alleyways to my house – at least the stone won't have burned and the mobs should be past it. Chava, you know the alleys – you go up front with Shendl."

Reuben was insulted. He was the oldest boy after all. "I know the alleys too!"

"Okay, Reuben, you be the scout then." Mama pulled a long kitchen knife out of her skirt. I had never thought of Mama as fierce like that.

"Guarding the rear is important too," she said brushing the hair out of my eyes. Shendl nodded. She too had a knife hidden in her skirt and she moved up to join Reuben. Esther had Sarah by the hand in front of the twins.

"This way is blocked by fire!" Reuben called back. The only other route cut past the market. For a moment Mama's eyes clouded over and she paused, as if she'd seen a demon. I thought it could have been my papa's spirit. Terrible feelings were moving through Mama's body the way fire pulsed across a bed of coals. She drew a breath and called encouragement to the front of the line, motioning me to move ahead.

We made our way through the smoke and debris as if the Cossacks were at our backs. I was covered with a cold, stinking sweat. The older cousins helped the younger over metal bed frames and piles of broken dishes, and Esther did the same for Sarah. Way ahead of us Aviva stopped in front of a body, frozen, but Rebkah grabbed her arm and pulled her forward. I stayed just in front of Mama – we were going slower, watching out for the rest. There were little flames sputtering in piles of garbage. When I got to the corpse that had stopped Aviva I could see it was a dead woman, most of her body covered by fallen stones, but something was wrong with her face – I looked a little closer, not too close. Oh God, she had nails in her eyes. I turned away into a doorway and threw up. I felt Mama's hand on my back.

"Come Chavele, we can't get separated from the others."

I sucked air deep into my stomach, but that made me cough. Mama wiped her sleeve against my face and pushed me forward. The others were at least two blocks ahead. I could just make out one of the twins turning the corner that led into the market square. I heard men yelling. With my head tucked down I ran towards them like a bullet. As I came

into the square I heard two men scream, "Stop, zhids!"

"Who are you calling a zhid?" I screamed back. They turned around and chased me instead of Shendl and the children. They were wearing layers of stolen coats and I could run much faster. I ran out the other end of the market. On Alexander Street there was a mob going through the shops, dragging away anything of value that was still left. The men in overcoats joined them, forgetting me. I darted in and out of side streets, back to the market place.

Shendl and Mama should have been almost home. There was a circle of men beside one of the dead bodies and then I saw Mama, standing in the middle. Papa, she must have found Papa's body. Why did she have to stop? She could have gotten away with the rest of the family. Maybe she tried. Maybe she just looked down and there he was and then the men came.

I ran behind a row of carts. From between the spokes of a wheel I could make out my papa's torn face, and the men surrounding Mama. Mama didn't look at them. She was looking at Papa.

"What's the matter, zhid? Some old man you know?"

"Maybe she was his mistress!" One of the men poked another and they laughed. My stomach knocked against my ribs with a terrible pain.

"Now, zhid whore, you're going to know what real men feel like!"

Mama's jaw clenched. She pulled out her knife and struck the closest man across the cheek. His hand let go of her, rushed to his face. She used the moment to thrust the knife into another one's side. She looked like Judith leading her army, except there was no army. She was alone inside a circle of a dozen men. She pulled the knife out, aiming at the closest.

"Damn zhid!" one of them shouted, while another grabbed her from the rear and pinned her arms behind her back. The knife fell onto the cobblestones. A tall blond man passed a metal flask to the injured ones.

"Some spirit!" one said. "She must be part Cossack. Zhids don't fight back!" He laughed and she kicked at his legs. "All right, that's enough from you. We'll find out what kind of zhid you are!"

The men pushed Mama to the ground and tore off her wig. It landed in the dirt beside Papa's leg. She didn't scream. My stomach heaved but there was only bile now, and I swallowed to keep it down. I pressed my forehead against the wheel. My hand got a little splinter. I stared. A little splinter. Finally my mother yelled. I thought the sky should crack open and God himself should pull her up, away from those men. She yelled two, three times, and then all I heard was the sound of the men

grunting, "It's my turn!" "No, me!" I didn't know how long they kept doing this. It was starting to get dark. One of them yelled, "You fools are raping a dead Jew! C'mon, there's plenty more live ones!" The one on top of Mama jumped up, pulled up his trousers and ran off following the rest of the band.

I stayed behind the wagon. Maybe I would just stay there until I turned to vapor and disappeared. I pressed the splinter into my palm. Esther and Sarah needed Mama. I should have gotten them to chase me, to kill me instead. What good was it for me to stay alive? It was dark and cold and I was crying for my Mama and Papa. I wished I could remember a prayer for this. I wished I knew something to do besides cry but I couldn't stop.

From somewhere in the city came a gunshot, then the sound of horses in the street. Who knew how long it was? After awhile there was quiet, the kind of sick quiet when everyone was afraid of cholera. I wanted to go out to my parents yet I couldn't seem to move. I put my hands against my forehead. When I pulled them back, I saw a bubble of blood around the splinter. I hardly felt it. Maybe I was dead too. Maybe this was what it was like to be dead, in the in-between place where you wait for God to call. I slumped back against the wall and shivered. The dead didn't shiver, at least I didn't think they did.

I heard a kind of clucking noise and looked up. An old woman, a Jewish woman, with a babushka and a torn shawl tight around her shoulders, was leaning over my mother and sighing.

"Moyshe!" she yelled, and a man came over.

"It's Rabbi Meyer and his wife Miriam," the man said. I could see he was crying too, tears falling into his beard. "We'll get the cart over here as soon as we can."

"No, don't touch them, don't touch them!" Suddenly I was beating my fists against the man's chest. Too late, I was too late. The woman came over and put her hand on my head while the man held my fists.

"Little one, it's all right now. The murderers are gone – the pogrom is over."

"Don't touch my mama. Don't touch my mama!"

"Her mama!" The old woman started crying. The man released my wrists and the woman embraced me. My whole face and chest were soaking. "There are other children, little one?" My breathing was hard and ragged. I told her my sisters and cousins were at my house.

"I'll take her home," the woman said to Moyshe. "Don't worry," she said to me. "This man is a good Jew. He knew your parents. He will do

everything right for them. The righteous will be in heaven. Time brings us wounds, but time also heals them, you'll see. Don't look anymore. Come, I'm taking you home now."

She walked slowly, lifting up her skirts to keep them from the debris. I picked up Mama's knife and cut my finger on its edge. Sharp, but not sharp enough. I saw a drop of my blood fall on a cobblestone. The old woman glanced at me but said nothing. My arms hung by my sides, the flat edge of the knife slapping my calf through my skirt. It was dark. Only a few of the gas lamps were lit here and there. We made the long walk back to Mama and Papa's stone house. I felt exhaustion on the underside of my skin, pressing at me, pressing in and out at once.

A fiddle roughly bowed

Plums were falling into the river. Seven, eight, nine ... a hundred-and-one ... all the trees were bent over like old men bowing towards Jerusalem, their branches scraping the ground. Then I heard a Pesach song – *Eliyahu ha novee, Eliyahu ha tishbee, Eliyahu, Eliyahu Eliyaaaaahu ha* – there should have been a rabbi. Where was the rabbi? Mama?

The strangled sound of my voice woke me. From the other side of the river in my dream, the Angel of Death was flying towards me, a raven, his wings blocking out the sun. I sat up. Only snoring in the dark house. I counted the living snorers: Sarah beside me, Esther, Bobe Malke, Uncle Elihu, Aunt Shendl, Rebkah, Aviva, all the boys' snores mixing with the snores of Papa's students. The pogrom wasn't a dream. I knew it was a sin, wishing to die, but still I wished to wake in a different place. I rubbed my forehead with my thumb knuckle. Sarah stirred.

"Sha, go back to sleep little one. It's not morning yet," I said like Mama would have said – Mama would have – . I wrapped my arms around my ribs and waited for daylight.

When day came I went outside to sift the dirt for feathers, trying to get enough to remake our featherbeds. At first I was afraid – so much debris and blood. Two men lying in our street were covered with stones and broken glass, and cousin Reuben told me about a woman just three houses down, her stomach cut open and stuffed with feathers. I told him about the woman with the nails but I didn't say anything about Mama.

Sarah wanted to help and so I let her. Why not? She had already seen everything horrible there was to see. Almost everything. At least

finding clean feathers was something to do. Sarah and I spent hours in the streets and no one seemed to care, although we were supposed to be inside, sitting on boxes, mourning like proper Jews. But there were no boxes left and no more proper Jews. Only Uncle Elihu, mumbling in Hebrew and Yiddish with the fever from his broken leg, was really sitting shive.

Sarah made pictures with feathers and dirt. I squatted beside her, trying to make out what they were. Most were trees. One, she said, was Mama's baking apron. "See, here's the red embroidery," she said, pointing to a line of dried blood.

The house was too crowded, too full of broken furniture. Relief people, strangers, came and talked to Aunt Shendl. I didn't want to answer any questions. Instead I wandered, kicking every stone on the streets of Kishinev. It took me two days to find myself in front of Simeon's printing shop. The street was filled with scraps of paper, little bits of metal and letters scattered near the entrance. The oak door swayed on a single hinge, moaning like the survivors being carried to and from the hospital. It was dark inside. I forced myself past the entrance. When my eyes adjusted to the light I saw Zalman's magic Linotype pushed over on its side, all the parts splattered with melted lead. The printing presses were smashed, the type cases thrown around the room. Ink was smeared over the walls, black patches giving way to slogans: Kill all zhids. Smells of kerosene and ink made my nose itch. The metal case that held the Linotype letters was split like a fig, the brass keys spilling as if they were seeds. Seeds on paving, no place to root. The aleph Zalman gave me had disappeared in the wreckage of my house. I sifted the keys until I found another and put it in my pocket.

Daniel came to the funeral in disguise and slipped away before anyone besides me noticed him. He'd let his beard grow back – without one it was too easy to spot him for a socialist. I think he had been preparing to make peace with Papa. Daniel always had to hide somewhere. If a person believed in something, then he should fight for it, even if Papa said that I didn't know what I was talking about and that fighting only makes our enemies more intent on crushing us. How much more intent could they get? Fighters should come out in the open. Maybe Daniel didn't believe as strongly as he said. Maybe I was hard on him.

Mama fought but she – . I thought many Jews must have fought the pogrom but afterwards they said only a handful mounted any

resistance. That didn't make sense to me, yet it made it easier to bring Elihu his soup. At least he had been fighting.

Every day, after all the cousins were out scavenging, I swept and packed the dirt floor down as well as I could. I liked to walk around the house barefoot, feeling how smooth the dirt of the floor was, how Mama kept it. Esther said when Nathan came to live with us he'd put wood on the floor, planks of wood, as if that were something special. Maybe Mama would have liked it. I wanted to be fair. But I liked the dirt floor – I'd fixed it again so you wouldn't trip on a pebble anywhere.

You were supposed to wait a year after a parent died before you even went to a party. Since both Mama and Papa got killed I thought Esther and Nathan would have to wait at least two years. But Aunt Shendl said these were exceptional times and it would be a mitsve for all of us if there were a man in the house. It wouldn't look right for us three girls and Bobe Malka to have yeshive students here without Nathan. As soon as Elihu could walk a little, the relief committee was going to help resettle his family in the Jewish ghetto of Warsaw, where his brother had a little hat factory. I didn't think Elihu was going to be right in his mind again, but maybe working for his brother would help him.

We had one window unbroken in my parents' room, a little gift. The rest we covered with cloth, trying to keep the cold spring wind out of our pockets. The moon was half full. The wind smelled already of young wheat growing beyond the city. We hung rags for partitions which made shadows in the dark that reminded me of Cossacks with whips. Elihu wouldn't go into Papa's bedroom, so he and Shendl and the four boys slept in the big room. The twins had my old space behind the stove. Bobe Malka had what used to be the storeroom to herself. Papa's two students stayed in the room Papa had built for the boys. I made a featherbed from the street feathers big enough for me and Sarah, and lashed the wood of Mama and Papa's bed up as best I could, a few miserable planks. We took their room. Esther slept on a little cot that Nathan's father brought over, close to the door.

"How can you sleep over there?" Esther worried at me, as if it was some kind of holy place. But I knew it was just a room. If Mama and Papa were ghosts, they weren't there. I would have known. Mama used to sing to us. Remember, Sarah? But Sarah was already asleep beside me in the lopsided bed.

"Sarah's old enough to sleep by herself," Esther fussed.

"Where?" I said, annoyed. "Is it so exciting for you, sleeping alone?"

We whispered though I was sure everyone listened.

"I'm a woman now and I'm waiting for Nathan." As if Nathan were Elijah, all clean and pure, and his arrival would obliterate the horror. I didn't like how Nathan smelled. And that red beard – he always wore his soup in it. Waiting for that?

Then there was another sound. Near the window. Sarah was sleeping but Esther sat straight up in bed. I slept with Mama's knife under my pillow. If they came to get me, they'd be sorry. I pulled the knife out and drew my nightgown closed. Esther was so quiet she scared me. Would she have sat there and let anything happen? Not me. I stood up. There were pebbles against our one window. Daniel. Daniel's sign, the one we had arranged before he left Kishinev the first time. He had usually come when Papa was at shul, and even if Mama thought it was odd that I went outside to stare at the stars, she never objected. Now Esther started to cry. She didn't sob but I could see big tears running down her face. She was still sitting up in bed as if she were made from stone except for the tears.

I went to the window. A figure moved in the bushes. He pulled a red handkerchief from his pocket and then I knew for sure it was Daniel. I tapped the window from inside three times to let him know it was safe. The cousins thought Daniel was a hero because he was in the Bund, and they would never have betrayed him.

Esther lit a single candle. Sarah was still sleeping. I had told her stories about our brother who came in the night and she thought they were fairy tales. She remembered Daniel a little but Abraham not at all. Sometimes I wasn't sure either. Did I only dream my brother threw stones at the window? Then I remembered the weight in my hand of the pamphlets he would bring. I had kept them hidden behind a loose stone in the wall. "Cease your slumbering, sisters and brothers," one pamphlet said. "Awake! Unite! See to it that all are equal." There was a world beyond Kishinev, a world that even a girl could get to. I knew in the north, in Vilna, girls who went to the university joined the Bund.

Esther never wanted to look at the pamphlets. "Martov," she sniffed, "you think this Martov cares about you? That you go sneaking around in the night as if you were in love, bringing love poems to strangers?"

"That's good," Daniel said, "very good. I'll put it in my next tract. Don't you see, Esther, I am in love. I am in love with the Bund, with the cause of the people. It's for love of working people I do what I have to do."

"Aren't we people?" You could count on Esther for the predictable.

If there were pamphlets left after the pogrom, Shendl must have used them for kindling. We couldn't risk drawing attention now by starting a fire to boil water in the middle of the night, even if we'd had enough wood to waste like that. But there was cold tea and Esther brought Daniel a glass. We were whispering, sitting on Esther's bed with a salvaged table between us. We didn't want the cousins to hear, but of course everyone except Sarah was just pretending to be asleep.

"What is it, Daniel?" Esther could see he was agitated.

"Don't you have anything to eat?" he asked, which is not what Esther meant. She brought him a plate of cold beets and black bread with a little precious butter. Most of the cows Jews kept in town had been killed too – and the rabbis said no one could eat their meat, it wasn't kosher, so the goyim got even our cows. Papa probably would have said the same. It was hard to find butter. Butter meant Esther was really glad to see him.

Daniel ate as if he'd been hungry for weeks. I shouldn't have believed he didn't fight back. We just watched him. I wanted some bread and butter too. My stomach hurt. I was used to the ache but it made me remember how Mama would give me bread and honey, and I had to push her memory away.

I didn't like to watch Daniel chewing, all the hair on his cheeks squirming around, but he was almost done and I knew he had something exciting to say. We hadn't seen him since Mama and Papa were buried. Then police were all over. They acted like it was a big favor to us, that they let us come to bury our dead. The Vice-Governor showed up in his dress uniform. He said too many of us came and we should resign ourselves, that what happened was payment for our sins and our fathers' sins, God's will. He, the Vice-Governor, had compassion for us so he wouldn't send us away. Remembering, I wanted to beat the table with my fists and cry but I didn't like to cry anyway, not in front of Daniel.

"Do you remember our mother's half-sister, Bina Petrovsky?" he asked. This was not exciting. I swung my foot to keep it from falling asleep.

"She lives in Odessa now, with her husband, Isadore the watchmaker. They have a daughter, Rose, about your age, Chava."

Of course I knew this. They lived here until I was nine. Sometimes Rose would come for the reading lessons Mama gave. She was nice enough, I supposed. Right after the lesson she'd run home. She had four older brothers and had to clean up after them, even when we were six and

seven. To me, she seemed too meek and cheerful about all the work.

Daniel said that when Isadore's first wife died, he had four boys and Papa arranged for him to marry Mama's half-sister, Bina, in Odessa. After Rose was born, Bina couldn't have any more children. They moved back to Odessa when grandpa Yosl was sick. The old man died two years ago. Isadore did all right for himself in Odessa.

So what, I thought. I got very bored with those so-and-so begat so-and-so stories everyone liked to tell. I was afraid Daniel wanted me to marry one of Rose's brothers. That was how it always started, "The father did all right." I was just fourteen, I didn't have to get married yet. Daniel couldn't make me – even Esther got to choose.

"I heard they were going to America," Daniel said. America. They were going to America. I felt excited again. "I went to talk to them." He looked down at the red stain of beets on his plate and wiped his beard. I liked that about Daniel, that he remembered to wipe his beard.

"I don't know what's best to do," he said. He was trying to look as serious as Papa and I didn't like that so much.

"What's to do?" Esther asked. She never understood anything. Obviously Daniel was going to America, leaving us all to rot in Kishinev. Very exciting. I stood up and went to the window. Maybe my real brother was still outside and this man was an impostor.

"Chava, please, come sit down, I'm not done yet." Everyone was always telling me what to do, but I did what he said. "So, Chava, what do you think, would you like to go to America with the Petrovskys?"

Me? He was talking about me? I tried not to show my feelings. "What about Esther? And Sarah?" I asked.

"Esther has the house for her dowry. You want to stay here with Nathan, don't you?" Esther nodded. "And Sarah," he shook his head. "Sarah can't go to America because of her eye."

"You need a certain kind of eye to go to America?"

"Yes, don't be so smart. You do need a certain kind of eye to go to America. We don't even have to send Sarah to a doctor to know they won't let her in. Sarah must stay with Esther and Nathan and Bobe Malka."

I could see that Esther was finally listening. She realized that when she married Nathan, me and Sarah would have had to stay with them until they could find us husbands.

"I don't like to break up the family," Daniel said. "America is a long way. You don't have to go, Chava. But I thought, there's no place for you here." I understood what he was saying and actually thought

Daniel wanted to give me an opportunity.

"In America," he continued, "a girl can go to work herself, and can go to school too. They have free schools in America, even for girls." Of course I knew this already. What did he think, I didn't know about the letters all the yentes got? They used to come to Mama to read them, and I'd hear everything about America. But I didn't know about the eyes. I wished Sarah could come with me. Would Esther and Nathan be able to take better care of her than I could in America?

Esther turned to look at me for the first time in months. She was crying again. "Oh, Chava, it's so far!" As if she wouldn't mind if I went to Odessa and she only saw me at Pesach, then she could still think she was a good sister. "She can stay for my wedding?"

Daniel nodded, weary. Even Bobe Malka said it was important to pick life up again, to follow bad with good. Their wedding was in a few weeks, only two months after the pogrom. I was glad it would be soon now. Esther came over and hugged me. "If you want to go, little sister, I won't stop you."

I thought I didn't really like Esther. I thought she didn't really like me. I thought this while she was hugging me and it hurt so much that I couldn't help myself from crying a little too.

Daniel became alarmed. "Do you want to go? We could also try to find Abraham in Palestine, if you think you want to cast your lot with the Zionists."

I let go of Esther. I hadn't thought about Palestine in a long time. The life Abraham wrote about, when he wrote, sounded so dry and difficult. Farming! Not exactly my idea of paradise. Besides, Abraham was a grown man and at least if I went with the Petrovskys there would be another girl my own age.

"No," I said, wiping my face, "I want to go to America." Everyone sighed, even some of the sleepers in the shadows. Esther sat down again.

"I already talked to Nathan," Daniel said. I got mad again. To be so arranged about. "Nathan agreed he would help provide for Sarah's dowry when the time comes. And I managed to get a ticket for you from the relief agency. They don't want to pay for very many tickets to America, especially from Odessa – the Americans who are there now don't want to see more of us Russians come in. We're too dangerous!" He laughed, thinking of himself. "But because you are an orphan and the Petrovskys are as good as adopting you if you go, they made an exception. It's luck for you – don't frown at me like that. I know it's not

lucky to be an orphan. 'When an orphan suffers, no one notices' – but we're all orphans now. I am doing what I can with what I have. It's lucky for you you're able to leave Russia."

They all wanted to send me away. I was no use to them here. What shall we do about Chava, they said, and then they said, "Oh, send her to another part of the world so she won't bother us anymore." But I wasn't going to break down in front of them.

"Chava," Daniel said, pulling my chin up to look in my eyes in the candlelight. "You don't have to go. I don't really want for you to go but I can't be any kind of brother for you here. Esther is going to start a new life with Nathan soon. I know you, you wouldn't be happy. I'll write to you in America. I'll send you my pamphlets and you can see if they like them in the golden land."

Then I cried again.

The train station in Kishinev used to be one of my holy places. Sometimes, after Shabbes services, I would walk down there, sit on the benches and watch the people come and go. Hardly any Jews traveled on Shabbes but I always felt safe in the station, before the pogrom. I liked to study the train schedules and pick up newspapers the travelers left behind. *Bessarabetz*, the Kishinev paper, was just full of lies about Jews. I could make out Russian pretty well and I liked the newspapers from Moscow best, though they were rare in Kishinev. Once I found a copy of *Iskra*, Lenin's paper that Daniel was always talking about, but it gave me a headache to try and understand the arguments. Rumanian, I couldn't read a word, so the papers from Bucharest were useless.

Where should I go? Every Saturday afternoon this was the game in my mind. It would take more than three days to get to Moscow, five to Saint Petersburg. Jews couldn't go to Moscow or Saint Petersburg but I was so young, I thought they wouldn't pay any attention to me. I'd have enough money for a first-class ticket, and I would look out the window, answering everyone very politely in perfect Russian. I would have a fur hat to hide my hair and people would think I was the daughter of a great baron.

At last I was going on the train even if it wasn't what I had imagined. Sarah was crying, her nose running. Shendl gave me a piece of cheese wrapped up in clean paper. My cousins were waving and telling me to write to them in Warsaw. I had the address where they were going next week. The station was full of Jews leaving Kishinev and all the goyim

knew who we were. I thought they must be laughing at us – see how we've got them on the run again, scared as rabbits! For the first time I felt proud of Esther and Nathan for staying. Esther had sewn ten rubles up in my jacket. I complained it made me feel like a fugitive but she insisted. I let her take care of me. She sewed my steamer ticket under another patch. I had three rubles of my own in my pocket, one Daniel gave me and two I had I earned myself making candles.

Thirteen rubles did not make a baron's daughter. Anyway I spat on the barons of Russia and all the princes. When you grow up, you have to be proud of who you are. Finally I understood what that meant. I tried to stay proud, for Mama and Papa, but everyone was so sentimental at the station I pushed out a few sobs to comfort them.

"I'm just going to Odessa," I said.

"Oh, you're such a brave one!" Aunt Shendl pinched my cheeks and blew in her handkerchief. All the bravery she had shown in the chicken coop had melted in the fire. She did everything required of her but she had been soft and weepy the last couple of months. As I was going up the train stairs, Sarah pulled on my skirt. I bent down.

"I saved this for you." I didn't know how she did, what made her think to, or where she'd been hiding it, but there it was: the photograph of Mama and Papa taken after they were married fifteen years. I put it in my bag quickly, kissed the top of her head and wiped her nose with my sleeve.

"Good luck, Sarah, if I get rich in the goldene medine, I'll make it so you can come, no matter about the eyes."

"Write me, Chava. Tell me everything – ." The conductors were shouting and I grabbed the handrail to keep from falling back on the platform. Inside I could only find a seat on the aisle. I leaned over an old woman in a fancy peasant shawl to wave goodbye through the open window.

"Did I hear them call you Chava?" the woman asked.

"Yes," I said. "Chava Meyer." I felt startled by my openness, even though I was used to kindly strangers fussing over me.

The woman got up. "Gutke Gurvich. Come, we'll trade places – quick, so you can see them better before we pull out."

I put my little bag down on the inside and stood while the train jerked as it gathered speed. My family got smaller, until the whole crowd was one hand waving, waving goodbye to all the travelers. When I couldn't make out that one hand anymore, I sat down and leaned out the window.

"You've been on the train before?"

"No," I said curtly. I wanted to be alone with my thoughts.

"You might want to pull the window down. Things fly in."

I did what she asked and resettled myself on the wooden bench.

"You go to Odessa?"

"Yes, I have cousins there. We're going to America." It felt like a boast and I was embarrassed. I realized I scarcely knew my Odessa cousins, which made me feel small and exposed.

"To America. You're going too." She repeated the words as if they were exactly what she'd expected me to say.

"Yes, I got a ticket from the Alliance Israélite Universelle in Paris," I said before I could stop myself.

She smiled at me the way grown-ups do, which I don't like. "So you speak French?"

"No, just Russian and Yiddish, and I can read a little German. Now I have to learn English, I suppose."

"I'm sure you'll learn quickly." She fell quiet, studying me. I wanted to turn away but before I could she spoke again. "I'm sorry about your mother and father. You have my sympathy. I thought very highly of them."

She didn't pat my hand or shoulder, like so many of my parents' other acquaintances. I didn't want sympathy. Her head bobbed for a second and I knew she was looking back at the pogrom. I sucked my breath in.

"I knew almost all the dead," she sighed, straightening her shoulders.

"Almost all?" that puzzled me. My stomach lurched, perhaps from the motion of the train.

"I'm a midwife. I stayed and helped with the sick, but now I have to leave, at least for awhile. It's too painful to be in Kishinev. Everything ends in weeping. Yes?"

"Yes." I looked out the window. That, at least, was how I imagined it – sparks hitting the glass, something to see every second, the moving world pulling me to its breast. I knew Gutke was still looking at me but I couldn't look at her right away.

"You go to America from Odessa by boat?" she asked after a few minutes.

I nodded without turning away from the window. She made little tchish-tchish noises.

"What's wrong with that?"

"Oh, nothing, excuse me if I sounded rude. I was just remembering something."

"Remembering?" I asked, more out of politeness than interest.

"I was your mother's midwife."

I turned back to her. She shrugged. I looked at her more closely and realized she was familiar. "Were you there when my sister Sarah was born?"

She nodded yes, and I had a faint memory of Papa arguing with Mama about the midwife, Mama insisting on this Gutke. I remembered he called her a Gypsy mamzer, and no one would tell me what mamzer meant. I got a shiver.

"Were you there when I was born?"

"Yes." I noticed then that her eyes were different colors, one black and one a kind of mottled amber, something I didn't remember ever seeing before. I looked down at my lap.

"Your mother loved you very much," she said, this time laying her hand lightly over mine. And I didn't mind.

The train wheels turned another hundred times before Gutke drew a deep breath. "Sometimes, not always, when a baby is born, I can see a little bit of their future come out with them."

"Really? Did you see mine?"

"I saw that you would suffer very much, cross the ocean and have courage."

"That sounds like half of Kishinev. I'm surprised women let you deliver their babies if you told them that."

She pulled her hand back. "In my business, you learn to tell what a woman wants to hear."

"And me, are you telling me what I want to hear?"

"A little."

"Tell me the truth then."

She considered me for a minute. "All I know more is that you will not rest on the other side. Your sorrow will keep you moving, but you will have good years and you will have the great good fortune to feel another love you."

"How do you know this?"

"I see things. As if there were a room I could look at through a tiny hole, not up, not down, not to the side, just what is arranged in front of my looking. So you should take what I say with a grain of salt. It's just an old woman's imagination."

"That's what they say about me – just a child's imagination." For a

minute it seemed as if Gutke was someone I knew closely, an aunt or a teacher.

"We make good traveling companions to Odessa, then," she said.

"What are you going to do there?"

"I'm staying with an old friend, a woman who sells things to the rich. She thinks I help her business. And I might. Now I want to read for awhile. I don't think you'll mind the chance to look at the scenery." She had a kind of portfolio filled with loose handwritten pages.

"What book is that?"

"A book of days. I've been writing it for three years, not all the time, of course."

"Really? Like Sholom Aleichem, you wrote a book?"

"Not a real book, just my memories, for myself and my friends. It has nothing artistic about it, don't worry."

"I'm impressed."

"Go, go on, look at your own business," she brushed me off.

Gutke watched Chava for a few minutes and then turned to an empty page:

From the beginning, when I was just learning my trade, I would often see a great basin of water, stretching on forever. Sometimes that's all I would see. At first I thought it was the water of the womb – how it flows over everything, how it shapes our destinies. I would tell the mother the child would have a long, strong life.

When I was about fifteen or sixteen, Pesah took me on a trip to Odessa. She was going to look at new fixtures for the bathhouse. I was excited, of course, and only a little bit frightened. Odessa made Kishinev look like a little sister at a wedding, what a place! I begged Pesah to come with me to the port. I wanted to see the ships, the docks, the sea. Finally she indulged me.

We came to the great steps of Odessa. This you wouldn't believe without a picture. Wide marble steps, maybe a verst long, and two or three hundred of them, going down to the harbor. Pesah wiped her brow and raised her eyebrows at me.

"So, now you've seen it."

"I want to touch the water."

" 'Touch the water,' she says! God in heaven! I'm staying up here, on this bench. If you faint walking up those steps, don't expect me to rescue you."

I laughed, kissed her and flew down to the docks. I looked out over the expanse, the mountains of Rumania rising and then fading on one side, the water shivering at the horizon and nothing beyond except the promise of more water. The sight made me breathe deeply in my chest, until the air filled my belly and even my legs.

Suddenly I realized that what I had been seeing when I delivered babies was a sea, not the waters of the womb, but a sea. Oy, what a dolt I was. But all those children? Where were they going? The water I saw didn't look like the Odessa harbor and it made no sense that the children of Kishinev, so many, would be headed for Constantinople. I tucked this into my mind as a question. Maybe I was right to start with, the water was a symbol for life's journey, a difficult and strange passage. That would be no surprise.

It took me almost ten years to realize that the babies were going to America. Not just the babies, the mothers too, naturally. It takes at least sixteen years in my profession to see the prophecies visited on the next generation. I had been looking in the wrong directions – south and inward. That's my own nature, to move south. But the children were following their natures and the times. For almost a third of all babies, I would see this great body of water; sometimes, later, crowds and buildings.

I rarely told the mothers. They got too excited. Either it was "My baby will never leave the land of her mothers," or "'My baby is going to the goldene medine to make us all proud and rich." It doesn't pay to tell the mothers anything too specific. And it had taken me a long time to believe what I saw. How could it be that the rivers of Bessarabia would empty into the Atlantic? It hardly made sense but I had to admit, there it was: the children were going.

The six hours to Odessa seemed too short to me, even with stopping at every little town. I looked out the window at the peasants tending their fields, the houses of nobles set off in the distance, orchards full of ripening plums and cherries, flocks of sheep growing back their coats. At the beginning of the ride, the light flickering through the forests fascinated me. I held my hand up to double the blinking red patterns. Then we came out into the open steppe and the trees vanished. The noise of the train repeated and repeated, like people at prayer. Only once in awhile I saw my father being dragged by horses, or my mother –. Somehow, each time I did, Gutke took my hand. Since she'd seen my

birth, I figured it was all right to let her comfort me. Then I could see again a small grape cluster under leaves or catch a glimpse of a bird.

Gutke put the portfolio away and rummaged in her large cloth bag. She pulled out a round bundle not much bigger than a cherry and handed it to me.

"I want you to have this," she said. "Don't protest. I'm sure you were taught to respect your elders' wishes."

I unwrapped it quickly. Inside was a silver ring with a dark red stone, smaller than a cherry pit. "What is it?" I asked, holding it up to see the way the light played through.

"Only a common garnet. I want you to have it so you'll remember Russia in the New World."

I wasn't sure I'd want to remember Russia. On the other hand, this gift gave me a warm sensation in my stomach, like the sweet wine we drank at Pesach. "It's very generous. Thank you." For some reason I didn't feel like I should wear the ring, just that I should have it. I wrapped it back up and put it in my own bag.

"You're welcome," Gutke said, waving her hand in the air, dismissing the subject.

When I turned back to the window, it seemed as if we were going through a small village for a long time, without stopping. I looked at Gutke, confused.

"This is just the beginning of Odessa. You could fit Kishinev in it more than five times."

So big! How would my cousins find me? Now there were buildings three and four stories high. The train went between them and under bridges. I saw every stone, every column, every statue, poor women hanging out laundry in little backyards full of garbage, tradespeople, shopkeepers, pushcarts, wagons, soldiers on horseback. Maybe my brother Abe had come back to Odessa – did he know what had happened yet? Before I could wonder very long, Gutke was poking at me to get ready, and we were shoving with all the other shoving people, leaving the crowded car.

The station was fantastical. Track after track of trains, crowds of people, women hawking bagels from pushcarts and boys wanting to sell us newspapers competed for space under a great arched roof. "Hold on to your bag and keep your hands in your pockets if you have anything in them," Gutke warned me. Then she saw her friend, waved. I realized she was going to go on without me, and I felt like I was saying goodbye at the Kishinev station all over again. How would I find my cousins?

"Here, Dovida, over here!" I expected to see a woman but instead it was a short chubby man, dressed like a German merchant, clean shaven except for a mustache, his tie tight around his neck even though it was a very hot afternoon. They embraced each other like long-lost friends. Something about this embarrassed me.

"Who's this?" he asked.

"The daughter of an old friend of mine, going to America no less, with her cousins Petrovsky. I want to see she finds them before we go, all right?"

"Of course, Gutke. If the world had a heart like you, we would be in paradise. Here, let me take your bag. Look – over there I think could be your Petrovskys." The man gestured into the crowd and suddenly I saw my Uncle Isadore and a girl who must have been Rose, except she didn't look so much like she did when we were nine. It was hard to keep people's faces clear in your memory and for a minute I panicked about remembering Esther, Sarah, Daniel. I went over their faces quickly to make sure I had them in my mind. I put my hand on the photograph in my bag. I would never forget Mama's and Papa's faces. Then everyone was talking.

"Here she is! Give your cousin a kiss, Rosele!" I had forgotten she had blue eyes. Rose kissed me and I blushed. There was too much emotion in all this coming and going.

"You're in good hands now, Chava. Take care of yourself." Gutke made me look her in the eyes. "You hear me? You have a good head and a strong heart. Use them well and be good to your cousin here." I wanted her to go away then and she knew it. "I'm off now, don't you worry about me. Good luck in America! Come, Dovid."

I was sure she had said "Dovida" the first time. I looked at the man again. As they turned away I realized he was a woman dressed up to look like a man. Was that possible? I never imagined such a thing. Gutke turned her head and winked at me before they were lost in the crowd. I turned to see if the others had noticed, but my Uncle Isadore was trying to shepherd us through the mass of bodies. He put his arm around Rose's shoulder and Rose took my hand.

"Every time I come to this station it gets worse!" my Uncle said. "Good thing you don't have much luggage. I don't mean – oh, you know what I mean. Who was that old woman? Did you enjoy your trip? Your first on the great Russian railway, eh?"

My uncle asked his questions and didn't care if I answered them. Just as well, I didn't feel like talking. He turned for a second to smile at me.

"Speech is good but silence is better, is that it? Worn out from the ride? Need the conveniences?"

I looked confused. "The toilet, he means," Rose said.

"No, I'm all right, I went in one of the towns on the way."

"Good. You're tired, I know. We'll get a carriage to the house." A whole line of carriages was waiting in front of the station: beautiful ones with bells on the horses and broken-down carts like the kind farmers drove to Kishinev's market. By the entrance was a long row of beggars too. My uncle pretended not to see them.

"We go to Saint Catherine Street, past Nikolai Boulevard," he told the driver of a good-looking carriage and we all got in. I sat across from them. My relatives looked more prosperous than they had in Kishinev. Uncle Isadore's beard was trimmed in fashion and he wore a hat just like the goyim. He and Rose pointed out the sights as we rode past: the Richelieu monument in the central square, the beautiful opera house.

"Do you like opera?" Rose asked.

I frowned. There was an opera house in Kishinev but we were not allowed to attend. "Opera? All I've ever heard is the chazen sing *Kol Nidre*. Is opera like that?"

"Your small-town cousin, eh, Rose?" Isadore laughed at me but he was soft, not mean. I realized he was being so jovial because he didn't want me to be embarrassed by my "plight," as the relief boards called it. "Tomorrow you can show her around if you want, give her the tour. You'll be a city woman before you know it, Chava."

"You're going to make me a city woman?" I tried to joke with Rose but she got shy all of a sudden. I felt foolish. I had no business trying to joke.

"We're just girls still, Papa," Rose protested.

"Yes, indeed, good girls, aren't you?"

And then we were in front of a large, whitewashed house with a fence running all around the yard. In Kishinev you would have had to be a factory foreman to have a house like this. It was on a long street, with many houses almost the same. A cherry tree grew in the middle of the yard and flower bushes were planted in rows along the walk. Uncle Isadore gave the driver a whole ruble. My shining hoard of thirteen rubles tarnished under my patches.

Before I could feel too sorry for myself, Aunt Bina was in the doorway, drying her hands on a lace-trimmed apron, waving at us. When she called out, I heard my mother's voice. My throat closed up and my stomach tightened. Bina was six years younger than my

mother, and much more fair. She wore her own hair, light brown and reddish, in a modest bun and her face and arms freckled. I looked at Rose to see if Bina was in her the way my mother was in Bina. But Rose was plump and dark – except for her eyes. It was impossible to trace Bina in her with everyone so noisy, moving, wanting to know all about my trip, clucking, sighing.

I knew they meant well, that Bina had lost her half-sister when I lost my mother, but their flutterings made me feel like I was wearing wool underwear.

"Tchish, the child is tired," Bina said. "She needs to wash a little, maybe, and rest before dinner. Rosele, you take her to your room, show her the house. You need anything dear?"

"Don't worry," Rose whispered, "they'll get used to you soon – and if you're lucky, you'll get used to them."

I nodded, trying to be serious. I didn't want to act like a child when childhood was already behind me. When I looked at Rose, I remembered her saying "We're just girls still," and I felt for a minute that I was still just a girl, on an adventure. I had a strong sensation of anger at her for making me feel this, and then I was ashamed. Why was I mad at my cousin, who hadn't done anything?

Rose had a room all to herself. "Well, it wouldn't be right for me to sleep with the boys, and anyway they're just my stepbrothers," she said. "Aaron and Ephraim are at school – they go to public school, you know, not just kheder. Saul's at work."

"Wasn't there another one?"

"Jacob. He was killed two years ago trying to desert the army. Don't mention him in front of Papa, right?"

"No, of course not. Do you miss him?"

"Jacob? Hardly. I never liked him much. I suppose I shouldn't admit it. Do you think it's wrong?"

I shook my head. I didn't feel like giving reassurances. "I don't think not liking your stepbrother is a crime. I couldn't stand my sister's fiancé, Nathan. He always smelled rotten to me. Even at their wedding."

Rose giggled. "Here, Mama had me clear a space in my chest for you." She had dresses nicer than any girl I knew in Kishinev. "You can put your things in it, they won't begin to take up any room. Oh – I don't want to offend you."

"No, that's all right. I used to have more, you know. It's just they destroyed everything." Then we weren't girls anymore.

Rose looked at me deeply. "It was terrible?"

"Terrible. I don't want to talk about it."

"We're family now," Rose said after a long moment. "It's good to have another girl in the house. I'm glad you're here."

She was being too nice to me. I didn't like this "poor relation" business. What did she know about what I went through? I wanted to say something mean. Instead I bit my tongue, stared at my shoes. "Thank you. Now I do need to use a convenience." I meant to be very formal but Rose laughed.

"Come, I'll show you. It's behind the kitchen, right in the house. If you don't want to wash up in the kitchen, I keep a basin in the bedroom."

After dinner, we went back to Rose's room. I couldn't remember when I had felt so tired, not even after I spent all day digging feathers out of the dirt. Rose gave me a flowered nightgown. It was a little short but loose and comfortable. We turned our backs when we changed.

"Do you snore?" she asked.

What a question. At home you could always hear someone snoring. "I have no idea. Do you?"

"I don't think so. But sometimes Aaron snores so loud you can hear him all over the house. Don't worry. I won't make you sleep in the kitchen if you do."

"Thank you, missus. What side do you want me on?"

"Left is okay?"

"Left is fine." Rose turned down the lamps. I suspected she was disappointed. I wasn't grateful enough to be pitied properly and I was too serious to be a playmate. What was she expecting, anyway? A sister? I wasn't her sister – she hadn't seen what I'd seen. My face felt too full, as if there was a thin layer of hot tar under my cheeks. I realized I had to sleep with this girl, in the same bed, for a long time. I moved over a little closer to the edge.

Rose sighed. What did she have to worry about? The shadows did little somersaults on her white ceiling as the lamps died out. Life was easy in Odessa. Everything was so clean and big here. Except of course the bed, which seemed very small, the two of us lying like rolled-up newspapers, our own stories curled so tight within us no one could read them.

There was a bright sword with a long curved blade. Someone was beating it on a pump. There was no water. Many people were running, trying to get away—

"Wake up, wake up!"

"What is it, what's the matter?" I sat bolt upright, reaching under my pillow. Nothing there. Where was the knife? What bed was this?

"You were shouting in your sleep," Rose said. She put her hand on my shoulder. I turned away. Morning light was coming through the curtains. There were little red roosters running along the curtain hem. After a couple days I was already bored with the roosters. I wondered how Rose could stand them month after month. Plain was better, I decided.

"I'm sorry," I said, pushing Rose's hand off my shoulder. I got out of bed and went to the window. People were going to work and carts full of grain were thumping down the street. I dropped my chin to my chest and took a deep breath. This was too hard, to be seen like this, to have my insides fall out in front of a stranger, the way the letters fell out of the smashed Linotype. I was startled to hear Rose crying.

"What have you got to cry about?"

Rose swallowed and didn't say anything.

"I'm too mean?" I asked.

"I thought you would be different."

"Different! You thought I would be grateful my rich cousins were saving me from being an orphan, taking me to the great America? I'll tell you something – I'm still an orphan. And I didn't know how it would feel to take charity. You wouldn't like it either."

"Charity?" Rose considered it. "Half the Jews in Odessa beg the other half for food for Pesach. We're lucky, I know. But – ." She was confused, sleepy. "You're supposed to take what's given to you without shaming the giver, isn't that what they say?"

"Have I shamed you? I'm so sorry I haven't learned big city manners yet."

"Fine. Have it your way. I thought – "

"What? What did you think? That I would be content for you to take me for those walks around your lovely neighborhood? That I would be like a toy your father brought home from the market for you? Something clever from Bessarabia to show off to your friends?"

"Friends! What do you know about my life? You remember how I lived in Kishinev cleaning up for all those boys? It never stopped. When we first got here we lived in two rooms over by Meldavanka, in a neighborhood of gangsters. Now I have two friends and I have to leave them. I thought maybe – "

"I would be their replacement?"

"You have to make everything sound the worst."

"Everything is the worst. You still think you're a little girl and you don't have to know what happens in the world."

"Chava." Rose came up to me and looked in my eyes. "I didn't do anything to make you so mad at me. If you don't want to be friends, fine. But you could be—," she took a deep gulp of air, "kind to me. You could think of it as giving charity back. Because I don't want to have to live every day in the same room with someone who hates me."

"I don't hate you."

"That's a beginning." Rose smiled a little. "We might as well be up now. Are you hungry?"

"I forget to be hungry most of the time. I suppose I am."

"I'm the opposite – I always remember to be hungry."

I sighed, looked at my feet, my little toes all alone on the wood floor, and then I looked at Rose. "I'm sorry to be so rude. Sometimes I think there's a dybuk inside me." I balled up my fist and thumped my chest.

Rose laughed. "Come, then, and let's feed your dybuk some of the rolls Mama baked for breakfast." We rinsed at the washbasin stand and dressed.

At the top of the stairs we stopped. Isadore and Bina were arguing in the kitchen.

"Steerage from Marseilles!" We could hear Isadore shouting. "Don't I make a good living, isn't there enough for everything? What possessed you to get steerage tickets? Why did I leave this to a woman?"

"Is he often like that?" I whispered to Rose.

"Not often. Only sometimes about money," she paused, "and my brothers." She looked embarrassed. I shouldn't have been glad to find out her life wasn't perfect but I was.

Bina patiently explained how much more expensive it was to travel from Odessa than from Germany, even calculating what they saved in railroad tickets. There was something about bribing for legal passports.

"I thought passports were free," Rose whispered.

"Nothing's free if some Russian can make you bribe him to give it to you," I whispered back. "At least it was that way in Bessarabia – I assume it's the same in the Ukraine."

Bina told Isadore that Saul was still making up his mind whether to join the family, but she had purchased a ticket for him and he could sell it if he wanted to.

"You gave that Narodniki bum his ticket already?" Isadore was shouting. "Where was your head? He'll trade it for a bomb and get us all arrested."

140

"You like to think of yourself as enlightened," Bina said calmly. "So, your son hangs out with Narodnikis and anarchists. This does not a bum make. He's like you when you were nineteen."

"Don't talk to me about Saul," Isadore said, disgusted. "Chava has her own ticket?"

I rarely blushed but I could feel how hot my cheeks were. I slid my hand back and forth on the banister. Rose looked at the stairs.

"That's another thing – you think they'd give her anything better than steerage?" Bina asked. "And there will be more bribes so they won't turn us back at Constantinople – I have it on good authority. Altogether with the passports it was over two thousand rubles, Isadore."

"Two thousand!" He whistled.

"Your family has that much?" I asked.

Rose's eyes were wide and her shoulders went up to her ears. "I guess," she said but she seemed surprised too.

My aunt and uncle had moved on to arguing about bringing kosher food. It had never occurred to me how hard it would be for Jews to travel a long way. Isadore said it was as good a time as any to give kosher up.

"Give kosher up?" I whispered. In all those letters from America that Mama used to read for the neighbors, no one talked about giving up keeping kosher.

"Shh," Rose said, straining to hear.

"I heard in America only greenhorns keep kosher," Isadore said. "I don't intend for my family to be viewed as greenhorns – at least, not longer than a month."

"If being a greenhorn means we keep being Jews, then we'll be greenhorns. I happen to know there are many women who keep kosher houses. Mrs. Finklestein already gave me the name of a kosher butcher in New York."

"They've argued about this before," Rose whispered. "Papa thinks we should move into the twentieth century. Mama says she's all for the new inventions but it's important to remember our traditions."

"And you?" I was thinking about Daniel. Did he eat treyf when he was moving around, organizing? Maybe if you were going to starve otherwise, it would be all right.

"I can't imagine it," Rose said.

"Me either." Isadore was telling Bina they could keep kosher in New York, but he didn't sound sincere. He went back to complaining about the money.

141

"You're the one who insisted we go. 'If we stayed at home, we wouldn't wear out our shoes,' " Bina said.

"And you wanted to stay in Odessa after what happened? It's only a matter of time before we get the same here. They've done it before, they'll do it again. I suppose we're lucky we can afford to go. We should give thanks even if they are bleeding us dry."

In Rose's blue eyes there was some kind of sorrow I couldn't interpret. We were so quiet we could hear almost every word.

"So we have to go in steerage," Bina said. "At least we'll be in the company of more Jews that way."

"But what kind of Jews?"

"Jews like you, Isadore, working men and their wives."

"From Marseilles, they'll all be Italians and French." He sounded tired now, as if arguing were work and he'd finished his job.

"You know a little Italian. Ephraim reads Dumas in French, and he must be able to make conversation. Jews are Jews. They'll all know a little Yiddish. In America, you will make back the cost of the trip ten times, you'll see. I have faith in you. In all of us."

Rose smiled. I could tell she loved her mama, that she was proud of how Bina managed. I started to say something spiteful and then held my tongue. Wasn't she supposed to honor her mother? That didn't mean she was dishonoring mine. Their banister was so smooth. I wondered how they got it that way.

"Bina, I don't know what I would do without you." Now Isadore was trying to be charming.

"Is that an apology?"

"Apologize? To a rich woman who can spend two thousand rubles – not me!"

We could hear him in the hallway getting his coat. We waited to go down to the kitchen until we heard the front door close.

Aunt Bina had papers spread over the table. She pushed them into a single pile when she saw me and Rose. We had hot rolls with a little white cheese and glasses of milk with just a thin skin of cream floating on top, pure luxury.

"So what are you going to show Chava today, Rose? Mrs. Wishnefsky told me there's a new klezmer band in the park." She gave Rose a handful of coins for our outing. Every day I was still surprised that Aunt Bina was ready to send us off without a chaperone. Papa would never have allowed me to go where wandering minstrels played. Rose said everything was different in Odessa, even girls went to the university. It

was safe enough in the day if you knew where to go.

We walked for several blocks and then jumped onto a streetcar drawn by four matched gray horses. Rose pointed out the elevated railroad that brought grain from the steppes to the granaries. Would it be as modern in America as Odessa? We got off close to where the city formed a ledge high above the port. The sunlight was a bright track on the water and I imagined the wheat train whistling past the port, into the sun.

"That's the Black Sea – you've never seen it before?" Rose asked.

I shook my head. The water was endless. The streets were so wide, paved with blocks of granite. In Kishinev I knew miles of roads and alleys, not that knowing them helped, but the scale of everything here, streets and sea, made me dizzy. Rose watched me. She pretended not to but she did.

"Tired?"

"No. It's just very big, isn't it?"

"When we first came from Kishinev, I wouldn't go anywhere without Mama. I was little then. But I know how you feel. Maybe we'll wait to go down to the port, unless you want to see it now."

"No, I expect we'll have enough water soon."

Rose frowned and kicked some paper off the sidewalk. "You're glad to be going to America."

"Why not? I'm afraid I won't be able to see Sarah again. But I could never imagine what kind of life I was going to have in Kishinev. Maybe that's because my life wasn't supposed to be there. I've heard in America we can go to school for free."

"I heard that too."

"You don't want to go?"

She shrugged. "I don't believe that you just pick gold up off the streets there. I've seen people come back from America who say there's as much misery as here. Why trade one misery for another? We'll have to learn a new language, new ways of doing things, probably we'll have to get jobs – ."

"I want a job. I don't want to be stuck at home making candles. I want to learn a real trade. And besides, in America there are no pogroms."

Rose's mouth opened a little and closed. She shook her head. "No, I never heard about pogroms in America. Or catacombs either."

"Catacombs?"

"This you wouldn't believe. Under the streets of Odessa there are other streets – not streets – tunnels, a whole other city."

"They built the city on top of another city?"

"Mama told me people dug the limestone from underneath for the buildings. They left a maze below our feet. Now the poor live there."

"Live in them?" I tried to imagine. Were the tunnels smooth and white like the sides of shops, or pitted and full of rats and water? Could people make fires to keep themselves warm? Were they scared of the dark or did they get used to it? "Can we see?"

"It's too dangerous. Papa says times are hard in the grain business. Men come from the country to get work in the port, and there's no work. But I heard that even women and children live down there."

"How? How can they live?"

Rose shrugged. "By begging or stealing I suppose. I don't know. It must be awful."

Below the city there were women and children living in caves off of charity. The Petrovskys could have changed their minds, never met me at the station. The relief workers could have refused me a ticket. I could have been down there too. Who decided how charity was parceled out? Maybe everything was written in the Book of Life every new year, like Papa said. I shivered.

We walked along a street with fine stores, well-dressed people wearing hats, not just caps or babushkas. "Papa's shop is three blocks from here." Rose was boastful for a minute, then she looked at me again. "But maybe we won't go there. The park's in the other direction."

When we got to Aleksandrovskii Park we saw a small crowd, with music coming from the middle. Rose took my hand and we threaded our way to the front. There were the klezmorim: Jews with clarinet, violin, accordion, tuba, drum and something I hadn't seen before.

"What's that?" I pointed.

"It's a tsambal mik, a Rumanian kind of dulcimer. Not exactly opera," Rose said. I liked the music. They were playing waltzes, marches, wedding tunes that I remembered from Kishinev, a little different of course. I didn't miss Kishinev, how could I? But when I thought about Sarah and Bobe Malka staying there, my own breast felt like a fiddle roughly bowed. Rose moved easily through the crowd. She bought us hot bagels from a woman with a cloth-covered stick near the park entrance. She ate hers quickly and looked at my almost untouched one. "You're not going to finish it?"

"You take it." Something about this made me soften towards her. She had been plump when we were little and in Odessa she was just

the same. I used to think plump girls were all stuck up. Rose looked more like a Russian than a Jew in her roundness and blue eyes, except for the darkness of her skin and hair. Rose was like a havdale candle, the dark and light wax braided together.

We went by the Café Richelieu where her brothers Ephraim and Saul liked to argue politics. Saul was a Social Revolutionary. Rose said the Social Revolutionaries believed in assassination, though none of them had ever assassinated anyone.

"Brothers! My brother Daniel doesn't trust the Social Revolutionaries or even the Social Democrats now, since the pogrom. He says they all want Jews to cast their lot with the Russian masses, but the Russians will never tolerate the Jews."

"He's right, isn't he?"

I had to agree. He was right.

Hats were the last thing on Aunt Bina's list. All the women in the family had to have new hats so we wouldn't look like we just got off the boat when we landed in America. Rose and I looked at each other and rolled our eyes.

"You think I'm not making sense but believe me, I know what I'm talking about," Bina said. We almost believed her – she was the organizing force of our migration. She'd sold all the household furnishings except the menorah, candlesticks and featherbeds. She sold her and Isadore's seats in the Brody Synagogue – it was late August and people were already looking ahead to the High Holidays; she waited to sell them as long as she could and got her price, a hundred rubles. Then she took us to the milliners.

I'd never owned a hat, only a shawl I used on Shabbes to cover my head in shul. Ribbon, silk flowers, bright felts and strong perfume were everywhere. Aunt Bina and Rose tried on every hat in the shop. I chose a plain dark blue with the narrowest brim I could find, trimmed with ribbon, no flowers. I didn't think it was right for someone in mourning to even consider new hats.

"That's really what you want? It's too severe for you, darling. If it's the money, I'll pay the difference."

"This is what I like. It doesn't matter about the money." I never told her how little I had. Even if it meant this foolishness, I was determined to pay my way. In New York I'd get a job and make my own money. Rose chose dark and light purple velvets held stiff by wires, with a

small bouquet of white silk roses on the side. When she put it on I was startled. She changed from a thirteen-year-old girl to a young woman, just with a handful of ribbon! Aunt Bina bought a wide-brimmed affair that tied under the chin and fit easily over her wig. Carrying the hatbox she seemed completely satisfied until we passed the Café Richelieu.

She stopped, frowned and decided to have a glass of tea. Since Rose and I were with her, it would look all right, no one would mistake her purpose. We sat at an outdoor table, everyone unusually quiet.

"He was six years old when I married your father," Aunt Bina finally said.

"What's Saul going to do with the ticket money?" Rose asked since the subject was open.

"Go to Kiev. Imagine! He doesn't have a special passport – he'll have to sneak in. What can he do there?"

"He'll be all right, Mama." Rose laid her hand on her mother's sleeve.

"As long as he doesn't throw a bomb."

"He's not throwing any bombs, Mama. You know he talks about change, but I think really what he's interested in is becoming a party official himself."

"A party official?" I asked.

Aunt Bina made an exasperated gesture. "You know how men are – they make a committee, then they need a chairman, a secretary, a who-knows-what, then they want someone for their chairman to report to. Everything is a complication with them, nothing straightforward."

"Saul's the treasurer of his circle. He says it's more important who controls the money than who calls meetings to order," Rose added.

"Well, at least he has a little ambition, nu?" Aunt Bina pushed crumbs of powdered sugar around on her plate. "Not simply content to just be another talker."

Listening to them I realized how foolish it was to think all revolutionaries wanted the same thing or were driven by the same ideal of "the workers." Maybe some of them fought the authorities so they could have the authorities' jobs, only with different titles. Maybe many of them. I tried to imagine Daniel as a bureaucrat, moving papers around on a desk. That couldn't have been what he was fighting for, even if it seemed to be what attracted Rose's brother.

Aunt Bina stirred her tea vigorously, tapping the sides of the glass as if announcing the end of discussion. Saul was a grown man. How could a stepmother hope to influence him? "Well? What are you thinking about so intently, Chavele?"

146

"That after tomorrow, I'll never see Russia again."
We nodded our heads, taking deep sips of tea.

At the top of the great Odessa steps the world shifted. I dropped the hatbox. Rose and Ephraim stopped to look at me.

"You're all right?" Ephraim asked. He had bags under each arm and over his back.

"Fine," I said. Rose gave me an I-know-you're-lying look. Ephraim went on down the steps towards the rest of the family. "Fine," I said again to Rose, picking up the hatbox. I had little of my own so I was carrying the bag of zwieback and hard cheese and the hatbox, as well as my small satchel. "Just maybe nervous."

"You?"

"We have to catch up to your family."

I followed her down the two hundred long, flat steps, counting them. Every detail seemed important. Merchants, sailors, porters, travelers, immigrants, thieves, soldiers, peddlers, customs agents all kept their eyes on each other while appearing to be rushing about on their own business. During the last two months I had grown used to big city crowds but this was new. My fear swallowed my senses. Then I regained control and my fear seemed as small as everyone else's – pushing, shoving, trying to get in the right line, find the right people, avoid the wrong ones.

Finally Uncle Isadore located our freighter, which was also carrying wheat to Marseilles. He mumbled about setting off in a little tub, even though it looked huge to me. The porters took most of our luggage away while Aunt Bina fussed at them to make sure everything was handled properly and "don't crush the hats!" We walked up a long plank onto the deck. A man in a suit, with the sideburns of a Jew, smoked a pipe and studied us. Aunt Bina whispered, but so loud everyone could hear, that he was the captain. I never thought Jews could be ship captains. Isadore began to walk towards him but the captain turned and walked away. A crewman showed us to our bunk rooms. He said eight other families and some single men were passengers, thirty-six women and forty-seven men in all. Rose, Aunt Bina and I had to share one room and one bathroom with thirty-three other women. Aunt Bina said this was nothing, nothing at all, wait until we got to Marseilles. She must have known from the letters and the "returners," the ones who missed their homeland and came back. Her

warning didn't make this freighter seem any less dirty.

Aunt Bina took a bottom bunk while Rose and I headed for the top. The beds were so close together it was almost like sleeping in her old room, except there were no sheets, only a wool blanket and a thin mattress which smelled of strong disinfectant. The room became crowded with women, some of them little girls, younger than Sarah. I looked at their eyes as I sat on my bunk swinging my legs.

Rose walked around, talking to the other girls. She made it look so easy. Just – "How do you do? Are you from Odessa? What street? Oh, do you know so-and-so?" Maybe it would have been easier if I came from Odessa. If the women found out about me they'd drown me in sympathy. I hoped Rose wouldn't tell them. I jumped down just as the ship lurched and blew its horn and I fell on my knee. I got up quickly, hoping no one noticed but Rose was right away by my side.

"Does it hurt?"

"No," I lied to her again. I pulled up my skirt to make sure I hadn't cut myself. "Listen," I whispered as the boat started to move, "don't tell anyone I'm from Kishinev."

"What should I say then?"

"Just that I'm you're cousin from – from Berdichev, whose American uncle sent for me, so it's convenient to travel with you. Promise?"

She narrowed her eyes. "What about Mama?"

"Where is she?"

"Up on the deck I think."

"Let's go find her, quick, before she can tell anyone." We raced up the narrow metal stairs. My knee hurt, yet I was still faster than Rose.

Aunt Bina was watching the Ukraine diminish. It was a warm day on shore but moving across the water was a sharp cool wind. How small Odessa looked already, even those great steps seemed a miniature of themselves. Bina looked over at us.

"The wheel turns as it must, isn't that the truth?" she said. "What is it, children?" I wished she wouldn't call us children.

"Chava wants us to make up a story about her and not tell she's from Kishinev."

"Not from Kishinev? Is that right, Chava? You want to disown your origins?"

"I'm not ashamed," I said, realizing how bad it sounded, as if I was sneaking out of being myself. "It's only that I don't want anyone to pity me."

"Pity you!" She laughed. "Who would pity you? You're a strong,

handsome young lady on her way to America."

This embarrassed and pleased me. "You know what I mean."

She nodded. "So, where did you say you were from again?"

I heard a murmur in the pattern of sound the sea made. The murmur turned into words that surrounded and separated me from everyone else, words that floated in and out of my ears like foam.

> *Trains now steamers*
> *the brilliant new engines underneath the century*
> *take me away from the Ukraine*
> *away from Moldavia our family graves.*
> *The wave has a name it whispers as it slaps the ship:*
> diaspora.
> *Carried on the curve of faith*
> *with millennia of Jews*
> *I give myself up*
> *to the water*
> *to the route.*

"I'm going back downstairs," Rose said, shaking the words out of my head. "Want to come?"

"No. I feel sick to my stomach."

"Well, I don't like the smell of the ship's engine up here." She wrinkled her nose.

"It's better than the bunk room."

"I need another trip for an accurate comparison," Rose said. "I'll probably be back before you miss me."

Left alone, I squinted so I could keep looking into the wind. I thought being at sea would be boring, but I could make out the shores of Russia, Rumania, Bulgaria as we traveled south, sometimes just an outline at the horizon. Tracing the world gripped me, all the hills and rivers I would never pass again, and I worried something beautiful or important would go by. I would have fallen asleep on the railing, watching and listening to the wave's melodies, if Rose hadn't pulled me down to dinner.

"It's a Jewish ship so the food is kosher," she said. "Let's go see what they have." The idea of food reminded me of my queasiness but I followed her out of curiosity.

The dining room had five long tables. Since there were nine families, some of them had to split up, but we managed to all sit together. A bucket of plain kasha, some cold potatoes, some kind of fish I had never seen before and stale black bread were on each table. Nothing I wanted to attempt eating. Rose took some kasha but she found bug shells in it and made a face. Uncle Isadore tried to tell us that as long as they were cooked, bugs wouldn't hurt us – a special dispensation allowed Jews to eat bugs in grain if there was no dairy. How else could we have survived all these years? Not bad, not bad at all, he said, eating the kasha to prove his point. Aunt Bina shook her head.

"What can you do with a man like that, I ask you? There is no such thing as a kosher bug!"

Aaron raised his eyebrows and pushed his plate away. He was not going to risk breaking any of the laws of kosher, no matter how his father blasphemed, although if the Torah had said it was all right, he'd be just the type to religiously eat bugs. Aaron seemed out of place with the rest of us. Rose told me he was supposed to have gotten married last year but his fiancée had died of cholera two months before the wedding. At eighteen he had the beard and look of a Talmud scholar, even though Isadore made him buy modern clothes for the trip. He hardly spoke to me. Rose said he was afraid of being tempted by impure thoughts. This seemed ridiculous though it suited me fine.

Ephraim was only sixteen. The way he talked you'd have thought that he was hoping temptation would kidnap him. When Aunt Bina and Uncle Isadore weren't listening, he told us he wasn't going to settle for any arranged marriage, not him. Ephraim was going to find himself an American girl. What a pair! Ephraim avoided the kasha but ate the fish and potatoes greedily.

Rose said the potatoes weren't so bad and put some on my plate. I took a bite and spit it out in my hand. It didn't taste so bad, I just couldn't eat.

"It will be a few days before you get your sea legs," Isadore said. How would he know? The boat pitched from side to side, just enough to remind us that we'd put our lives in the hands of the water. "But you'll see, you'll get used to it," he continued. "It's good to start out on the Black Sea and the Mediterranean. They're smooth as glass next to the Atlantic, so we can adjust gradually. The little adjustments are always the best."

"Provided you don't have to make too many," Aunt Bina said. "Do you know the Darwinists say that man came out of the sea?" She put a little bit of fish on her bread.

"Mama!" Aaron said, as if Bina had struck him.

"I didn't say I thought so, did I? It's not sacrilegious to know what the scientists think. A person can hold the scientific and the religious, each in one hand, isn't that so Isadore?"

"Yes, quite so," he said, "but I didn't think you knew from Darwin."

"It's easy to find out a little this, a little that in a big city. I was only telling the girls what I heard. There's no harm in it."

Aaron started to quote scripture and I excused myself, saying I didn't feel so well, I needed the air on deck.

When we arrived in Constantinople there was a big commotion. A party of officials got on board and announced that Sultan Abdul Hamid II demanded 25 rubles from every passenger going on through the Sea of Marmara. For our group, that added up to 150 rubles. I remembered what Aunt Bina had said in her kitchen. I went to her but before I could speak she shushed me.

"It's done already. They gave me a receipt for my niece from Berdichev," she said.

"I'll pay you back."

"I'm sure you will. In America."

"In America." Some of the other women were crying. One whole family had to get off. What would happen to them? Aunt Bina said they'd probably beg at the Jewish relief agency. In Constantinople? Everywhere there was a Jewish relief agency, she said.

I wished we could get off the boat and look around. The word Constantinople sounded like a fable, a story that Mama forgot to tell me. Would she have liked this journey? We passed a beautiful clock tower and so many palaces! The buildings didn't look terribly different from Russia, though there were many more mosques than in Odessa – in Kishinev only one. When Uncle Isadore pointed out the "seat of the patriarch" to me I had to keep from asking him where the head was. I told this to Rose and she giggled every time she looked at me all the way through the Dardanelles. Maybe it wouldn't be so bad to take the place of one of Rose's lost friends, I thought for the first time.

Traveling through Turkey was almost like being on a river. We could watch the shore on both sides and sometimes the buildings were so close I believed I could make out the patterns on the arches. When we steamed into the Aegean, the air and the color of light changed. Everything was a little bluer. Our path passed a hundred little islands.

I wondered what kind of life you would have, living out here? Aunt Bina told us there were legends about these islands – of singing sirens who drove the Greeks mad and made them crash their ships.

"Our ship?"

"Do you hear any sirens?"

We listened. The wind pressed against my ear, the way it had since we sailed. I still heard soft voices, pieces of words. But I didn't think that was what Aunt Bina meant by sirens. I resolved to stay up in case they did sing, the captain lost control and girls weren't affected by their song. Could I have saved the ship in time? Suppose instead I went mad – well, maybe that would have been better. Sometimes I thought I was already mad and I just held myself in, my skin a wrapper for the madness. If the madness came out, would my skin split apart?

Rose found me asleep on the deck. She made me stay awake long enough to jump up into my bunk. Rose and Aunt Bina started to sing a folksong in a whisper: *Hof, hof, hof. Nit vayt iz shoyn der friling ...* (Have hope, hope, hope. Spring is not far off ...) The other women joined them and the bunk room swayed with song in rhythm to the freighter plowing through the waves.

The boat squealed against the dock. Officials of the steamship company herded those of us who were America-bound in a single file. Aunt Bina kept asking about our luggage but the men didn't speak Russian, only French and a very few words of Yiddish. We came into a long building where we showed our passports and tickets. They took them away. One woman who could understand French said, "Don't worry, they will be returned when we leave." Then we were marched into another room like the bunk room on the ship, only twenty times larger. Most of the beds were already taken and we had to split up. Aunt Bina traded some food so that she could sleep on the bottom again.

Someone laughed. "On the steamship you won't be so eager for the bottom, missus. You'll see!"

All these women – French and Italian, some Serbs, Albanians, Hungarians, Austrians, quite a few other Russians – were leaving their homelands. Were pogroms everywhere? Or was it only the idea of America, where the jobs would make us rich? Rose was as sociable as ever. She found Italian girls who spoke a kind of Yiddish, some who knew French and could translate back and forth with the French girls.

We found out that our steamship wouldn't leave for another three days and we were quarantined in the bunkhouse until then.

As soon as I heard we were locked in I felt a sudden fever of panic. I pulled all the doors and finally one set opened. I tried to run past the guard but another emerged from the shadows and grabbed me. As he threw me back in the room I bit him. He yelled and lifted his hand to strike, but a young woman stopped his arm, saying something I didn't understand.

"It's not a good idea to draw such attention to yourself. What made you do such a thing?" she said in Yiddish as the guard locked the door.

"I'm not sure myself," I said, shrugging. Rose came up and stared at me. Fortunately Aunt Bina had missed my attempted escape. The stranger introduced herself.

"Lena Reznikoff, of Vilna." She made a half-bow. I judged her to be eighteen or so.

"Where did you learn French?" Rose was more impressed with this than with my outburst.

"I picked it up," she shrugged. "You're going to America from Odessa?"

"How did you know?"

"The ship came from Odessa. The guards are all right – if you don't bite them." She raised an eyebrow at me. "They let us know what's going on. The local authorities are afraid of disease. They make the steamship company keep us here until we can leave."

"What right have they to hold us prisoner?" I demanded.

"A firebrand, huh? We could have used you in Vilna." Her head bobbed up and down.

"For what?"

"Never mind. Just be careful here and you'll manage." Lena turned and strode away.

Rose followed her across the room. I went back to my bunk and stared at the plaster peeling off the old walls, the high windows covered with wire to prevent escape. My chest felt like a stone was crushing it. The room was full of languages I couldn't understand. Would everything be like this from now on? Half-explained, uncertain, stinking, confined? They could see we didn't have any diseases. Why didn't they let us out? Ephraim said Alexander Dumas wrote a book that took place near here, that it was beautiful and interesting in France. I just wanted to see. I didn't like being locked up this way. At least if you were trapped on a ship you were going somewhere. Here

they could have done anything to us.

Aunt Bina could just reach my face and she wiped me with an old cloth. After a minute she passed the cloth to me. "Keep this. Don't worry, little one, we'll be all right. At least you're traveling with family." This made me cry harder, though I tried not to make any sounds.

After two days they led us into a room where they ordered us to take off our clothes. They had tubes of water that poured from above. A shower, one of the French Jews told us. This was supposed to make us clean. They took our clothes away and held them over huge pots of steam. Some women yelled for their clothing – they must have had money sewed up like I did – but yelling at the steamship guards didn't accomplish anything. We got our clothes back, hot and damp. Hurry, hurry, the guards were gesturing, pointing to the doors.

Dressed, we went out in a large courtyard. Our men stood there and everyone rushed to reunite while the guards shouted. An enormous cart drawn by four horses came into the yard and luggage was dumped out in a mountain. Women were everywhere wailing and oy-veying. The luggage had been steamed like our clothes. Most of the featherbeds were misshapen lumps. When Aunt Bina found the crushed hatbox she sat on the ground and couldn't move. Uncle Isadore knelt beside her, running his fingers along the brim of what had been Rose's hat. Rose and I stood awkwardly.

"Leave those alone," Bina said to Isadore.

"They're not so ruined, you'll see. The girls will help you fix them up. In New York you'll find a milliner who can make them look like new again."

For the first time, I saw Aunt Bina fade. She sat on the French cobblestones weeping and weeping. I'd heard people say that oceans were made from the tears of women and I'd thought the saying was silly. I looked around now and thought it was probably true. Rose put her arms around her mama.

"Maybe you should have this back," I offered the rag she gave me.

She dried her face, "What you must think of me! Crying over hats." She stood up, brushed the dirt off her skirts. "Boys! Ephraim, Aaron, come over and help us carry all these things – Lord knows if they'll be any good to us now, but they're what we've got. Come on, you don't want the ship to go without us."

Aaron and Ephraim seemed relieved to hear their mama ordering them around. We hurried our luggage out with the crowd of hurrying people, deposited it again on the dock. When no one was looking, I

opened my satchel to make sure my photograph of Mama and Papa hadn't been ruined. I had stuck it in a book I bought for a few kopecks in Odessa – Abramovich's *Verse*. The binding seemed loose and mushy, but the pages and photograph weren't harmed. "Thank you," I said under my breath.

Quickly I had to follow everyone up the planks into a boat bigger than a tsar's palace. Maybe a thousand of us – where did everyone come from? Pushing down narrow metal stairs into the hold, a moldy room with hundreds of three-level bunks. What a stench! Underneath, the ship was an abyss filled with the smell of vomit and urine, odor as thick as fog. You could have touched it except you were constantly repulsed, trying to escape the clawing fingers of this foulness. Two toilet stalls for more than seven hundred women.

Just past Gibraltar we approached a small island and thousands of flies swarmed aboard. The women on the upper bunks swatted them and struggled for breath. Anyone who could walk abandoned steerage and crowded the decks. There was a drenching storm and those who could, clung to the railings, glad to be rinsed off. Their relief never lasted long. The wind kept shifting and everything was covered with human spew. A few people had stomachs that stayed upright, some internal gyroscopic organ saved them – to eat what? We remembered the bug-shell-laced kasha from the Odessa freighter as simple, wholesome food. Flies, and probably rats, infested the steamship's kitchen.

Rose bribed and pleaded, boosted her mother onto a third-tier bunk and left her with a small can, all she could find. Now we both had to stand in the toilet line, covering our faces with a wet cloth – and for what? A second of privacy to lift our skirts as high as we were able and still our hems were rimmed with filth. It no longer mattered where in the tiny reeking chamber we squatted. Even the walls were splattered with urine, excrement and blood as if a child had flung mud in the rain. Near the toilet door the sharp assault of vinegar and rot caused most women to erupt from both ends at once, leaving as quickly as they could, still dripping, covered with sweat, gasping for what now seemed the better air of the sleeping shelves. Someone told me the corpse of an infant was found in a washbasin, covered by inches of filth. The crewman heaved it overboard – the only time they did anything to clean steerage.

● ● ● ● ●

Maybe ten days had passed, I could only remember fragments. Finally I was on deck again. Rose said it was a blessing if I didn't remember. She said the sea was calmer and the crew had hosed down the deck because the stench was beginning to nauseate even them. We were sitting with our backs against the steamer walls. Every inch was covered with people. The strong smell of unwashed bodies rippled around my face but the breeze wiped it away for a moment at a time, making it possible to swallow fresh ocean air. Rose had a very small orange, a little dried up and mottled green. She handed the fruit to me.

"Where'd you get this?"

"It's the only unspoiled thing to eat on the ship – they have to carry them against scurvy. Try to eat. You need to, Mama said."

My stomach contracted even though it was empty. Rose gave me a sideways glance. I tried to remember if I had vomited near her but I couldn't ask. Her smell was strong too. At least it was familiar. I realized her smell reminded me of Sarah when she would mess herself as a baby. I gulped at the air. Rose took the orange back from my hand and peeled it very slowly. This smell was good. I closed my eyes and breathed. She put an orange section close to my lips, under my nose.

"Try, Chava, just a little."

I reached for her hand with my eyes closed, going by the flavor of orange in my nose. Everything seemed so strong – the smell of bodies, the orange, the ocean slap, the engine smoke, the sounds of people coughing, talking, singing, the feel of Rose's smooth hand, her long fingers, the bumps of her knuckles, the wet, smooth feel of the orange section as I took it into my own hand, the cold sweet against my lips, which were cracked and painful, I realized as the fruit touched them. I bit the section. Juice hit my tongue, teeth, the roof of my mouth, the back of my throat. The juice swelled and filled me. I'd been beyond realizing how dry and hungry I'd become. Rose was still smiling as I opened my eyes and took the orange from her hands, eating it all quickly.

"Thank you," I said when there was nothing left.

"You're welcome." She stood, went to the railing and dumped the orange peel into the water.

Could I stand? I raised myself slowly and walked over to her. Looking down at the white wake of the ship made my stomach turn. I didn't want to lose the orange she had been so kind to bring me. I looked towards the horizon. This was nothing like the Sea of Marmara or the Mediterranean. Here there was only water coming towards us from

forever, going out beyond us in bright patterns.

I remembered how Mama showed me the round world in an apple. It had seemed clear then, the curve of the fruit, the curves of mountains. But now I understood why old-time sailors thought they'd fall off if they got too far from land.

A woman came up on my other side. Lena Reznikoff, who had saved me from a beating in Marseilles. I thought about how much help I'd been given and felt ashamed. I should have been able to take care of myself. I would have taken care of myself if they had left me alone. I pretended I didn't notice Lena.

She waited beside me, her arms on the railing, looking out. She seemed to ignore my ignoring her.

"You were in Kishinev, weren't you?"

"Who told you? Rose, did you tell her?" I turned to Rose but Rose was gone. I remembered how Lena seemed to know everything in the bunk room.

"Rose didn't tell me. Not with words, anyway. I just watched you with her family. And your accent – I'm good at telling people's accents."

"Kishinev has an accent?"

"Everywhere does. And in Kishinev of course there's a Moldavian accent and a Jewish accent – even if you're speaking Russian. Isn't that true?"

"True."

She was quiet for a long time. Maybe she wouldn't say anything else. "It wasn't until I was in Vienna that I found out all of what happened in Kishinev. It's hard to get news in Russia."

"Vienna?"

"I had to leave Vilna."

I looked at her.

"There are very few women in the Bund so it's easier to arrest us."

"You were in the Bund? What about your family – did they know?"

"They were in Warsaw. They encouraged me." She stretched her back against the railing. "Did you see the poem Bialik wrote?"

"About what?" I was amazed that a woman could be in the Bund, that her family would have allowed it. Encouraged her, she said. What kind of family was that? Intellectuals, Papa would have spat, as if the word burned his mouth.

"About the pogrom."

"Bialik wrote a poem about the pogrom?"

157

"That's how I found out. It was in the Vienna paper. I remember some pieces. Do you want to hear?"

"Yes." I felt a flush and turned away from her as she recited:

" 'My people is as grass plucked up, and how
Shall that which has no root revive and live? ...
Has none a fist?....
What are they praying for? ... Tell them to protest!
To shake their fists at Me and justice to demand!
Justice for all they've suffered throughout the generations,
So that My Heaven and Throne shall quake to their
foundations!' "

She looked at me quickly and looked away. I pressed my jaws tight. Why did she tell me this?

"Do you believe it?" I asked.

"What part?"

"What he says, that we didn't fight back or protest?"

"I just read the poem. It moved me."

"We did. We did fight." My knuckles were white against the railing. I realized I had the same hands as Mama. I didn't look at Lena but I could tell she was looking at me. "We did fight."

She put her hand on my shoulder. "I believe you did," she said. I watched the lines of water cross and recross. Maybe the ocean had a face like the moon and we couldn't see it because we were so close. Many faces? The faces of the dead.

"Perhaps Bialik was wrong to be so harsh," Lena reflected. "From what I can tell it's only a few in any oppressed group who are ready to risk everything – or know when to risk everything. How can we know? A pogrom happens, a war – everyone wants to make sure they're the ones who live. Everyone has their own escape route."

She made it sound so simple.

"What do you know, what could you possibly know about it?" I asked.

She squeezed my shoulder. Her hand was strong and I didn't resist. "Well, after all, here I am, escaping myself – I leave dead behind me too."

"You?"

She shrugged.

"I'm not escaping," I said. "I would rather have died with them. They could have killed me instead – ." I stopped. Why didn't I get there first? Why didn't I stop them? I could have distracted them. Mama didn't

have to – a few tears gathered in the corners of my eyes, spilling out. Lena made a little tchish in her throat but didn't say anything. We stared at the water for a long time.

"Well, here I am. It's my fate, I suppose," I said, drying my face on my sleeve.

"I don't know what fate is," Lena said. "But maybe in America we can learn to choose when to fight. Maybe we might even win once in awhile."

"I thought in America you don't have to fight."

"There is no such country," Lena said.

Part Two

The needle goes in, the needle goes out

Did we look ridiculous in our dried-out crushed hats with their frayed ribbons and limp flowers? Or like respectable bourgeoisie who had undergone indignity? Rose and I had pressed the precious hats back into their original shapes as best we could in the few minutes they gave us to clean up when we landed on Ellis Island. The other women stared. The immigration men whistled. Aunt Bina said it was because we were in style but I thought she didn't understand. Rose was unsure whether to be proud or embarrassed. What did I care about fashion? I was only relieved to be on the ground with a washed face.

Pushing and pulling us through metal gates – what was new about this world? It smelled. Not exactly as badly as the ship's hold, but worse than the steerage deck – all the sweat and sickness of Europe and Russia fused into the unmoving, hot September air. And the food smells: everything that people had no stomach for on the sea – garlic, pickles and rotting sausages that poked out of greasy wrappings and were now confiscated. Most of the clothes people wore were grayish black or brown, no matter what color they had started out. A few embroidered flowers on women's hair wraps had some resemblance to their original pinks and oranges. The white roses on Rose's hat were dingy though there was still a little shine in the purple velvet brim.

We were bunched together with the passengers of two ships that had just arrived from Germany, herded up a flight of stairs through a massive chamber and separated by iron bars into neat, compliant rows. They should have had klezmer bands welcoming us, to make us feel our terrible journey had been worthwhile. Instead they had only immigration police, shouting at us above the babble.

Everyone was busy with their shame and fear. It was pitiful to see

how worried we were, anxious to distance ourselves from the ones who could not rise above the terrors and filth of the ship, who turned in frantic circles, gesturing to the air. It was clear they'd be rejected, sent back. Sent back – to have to take this whole journey in reverse and show up in Kishinev so failed as to not even have been let in – I would have died first, thrown myself overboard and let sea monsters tear me in pieces. So I acted like everyone else, adjusted my plain, mashed blue hat, whispered to my relatives, looked straight ahead – though when no one was watching I turned to see what was happening around me in the vaulted room.

Hours moving through the lines. We studied those who got singled out, pushed aside, even if they weren't talking to themselves. There were corridors where the ones removed from the line were taken. Rose said at least none of those women were wearing hats like ours. The women pulled their shawls tight with bony fingers, though it was so humid you could see waves of air carrying off the human stink. Only because the room was as big as Odessa's whole train station could we breathe. I looked up at the ceiling, which was woven out of yellow tiles, resembling our straw trunks. I tried to point out how clever this was to Rose but she nudged me forward.

For us there were questions. We moved from questioner to questioner, trying to decipher what each one wanted. Uncle Isadore didn't joke or talk back to the immigration men. He looked unusually unsure of himself, taking on the half-stooped shuffle of so many in the line. Our Russian passports had been stamped "Jewish" when they were issued. An officer mumbled loudly, and I made out a word that sounded like "zhid."

"Please, sir," a woman asked another uniformed man with dark black hair and eyes, "what's he saying?"

The man narrowed his eyes. "Another shipload of dirty Jews," he replied in rough Yiddish. Maybe America wasn't going to be so different from Russia after all.

More people were pushed aside, held back. Officials were called from one line to another to interpret. Our dark officer spoke a broken German-Yiddish, just enough to read from his list and interpret curses. A woman in a white apron pulled up our eyelids looking for disease while another interrogator asked what day we were born.

What day was I born? A cold day, that's what Mama always said. That was not the right answer, I knew, but what answer could I give? They didn't know the Jewish months, and I remembered that Russian

dates were different than the rest of the Christian world's. Something about a fight between their churches. I knew I was born in February, 1889.

"February?" the American said. "All right, we'll put you smack in the middle. February 15th. Next." I repeated the English words to myself. "Smeck in de middle." What did it mean?

Aunt Bina only knew she was born in the month of Kislev. "What's that, Kislev?" our official yelled to another. "December," someone shouted. "Okay – another Jew for December 25th," our Yiddish-speaking officer wrote down, laughing. "Next!"

Uncle Isadore said the ferry to New York City would be nothing, nothing at all after what we'd been through. I could see Rose hated the idea of getting on another boat as much as I did, but she walked up the ramp lifting her frayed skirts, holding her back straight.

"Do you think they call us greenhorns because of the color we look after coming across the ocean?" she asked from the spot she squeezed into by the railing.

"You do look a little green – though not as green as her," I said, pointing to the Statue of Liberty as the ferry sounded its horn.

Uncle Isadore put his arms around us. Now that he had passed the entrance examination he was feeling expansive again. "Very good, Chava, very good. Yes, she's here in the harbor to let us know everyone lands green. There's no sin in that."

"But what about the horns, Papa? How come everyone says green *horn*?" Aaron asked, scratching his beard.

Ephraim laughed. "If you'd ever take your nose out of a book, you'd know what goes on in the world. The goyim think Jews actually have horns."

"But don't they call Germans and Italians greenhorns too?" Aaron asked. Now I was confused too.

"Wherever it comes from, they won't be calling us that for long. That's why your mother and the girls have those wonderful hats," Uncle Isadore said.

Aunt Bina pursed her lips and raised her eyes at him for a second. She turned back to look at the statue and the water towers rising over the receding spires of Ellis Island.

A thousand people must have been gathered in the park where we landed. At least as many peddlers as in Kishinev's entire market, selling

things I'd never seen before: long curved yellow fruits and strange fish, as well as familiar suspenders, tin cups, giant loaves of bread. Some men had ropes of sausages around their necks or dozens of hats balanced on their heads. People held up signs with family names or the names of towns: Bialystok, Kovno, Berdichev, Lodz, as well as many I couldn't read in Germanic lettering. Rose pointed to a small man holding a sign that said Kishinev but it wasn't anyone I recognized.

Under a tree near the peddlers, a man stood on a box making a speech in a language I didn't understand, pointing his finger at the sky. A little farther off, a man in worker's cap like the kind Uncle Elihu used to make was yelling in Yiddish. I could make out an occasional word – socialism, unite, bosses. I recognized Lena Reznikoff, whom I hadn't seen since we got to Ellis Island, walking towards him. She caught my eye and waved. Closer by, two ladies and a man with a top hat had a banner for the United Hebrew Charities written in Yiddish, Hebrew and what I supposed was English. Many people were gathering around them.

"We're not going to ask a charity for help the first minute we land," Aunt Bina said, staring at Uncle Isadore.

"No, no of course not. Let's just look around here and see what's what. We'll figure out what to do next, don't worry." He patted her shoulder, gazing wistfully at the elegantly dressed charity people.

An organ grinder near the dock had a small chained monkey that ran up to the crowd holding out a tin cup, just like a little boy. I wanted to get closer but Rose said it might bite if we didn't give it American money. "American money, that's what we need! Very smart, Rose," Isadore said.

On the other side of the park were a couple of clean shaven men with signs in Yiddish: Money Changed. "Take mine too," I said, pulling the rubles I had left out of my coat lining. Isadore and Aaron went over while the rest of us waited, staring at the new world. It was as if soap bubbles were forcing their way through my brain and bursting. Each burst was a picture, like a photograph, that filled the space, crowding out what I used to know.

New York. The energy was jumping up from the streets – I could feel it through my shoes. Right in front of the market a one-car train with no engine stopped. It was being pulled from above by a wire, like a toy. Was there a giant on the other end, controlling the string? Sparks leaped when the train started up again.

"Electric trolley cars. I heard they were going to get these in Odessa

next year," Aunt Bina said. "It's like Mrs. Finklestein said, New York is first in everything."

"A landsman! He gave us a special rate," Isadore returned, fanning a sheaf of American money. "Dollars! And for you, Chava, one dollar of your own." When he gave it to me I tried to pass it on to Aunt Bina but she said I would need it while I looked for a job. My stomach danced like the organ grinder's monkey as I folded the new dollar into a tiny square.

"And look," Isadore had a scrap of paper, "he gave me the name of a man from Olgopol, where my mother was born, who rents rooms. I tell you, Mrs. Petrovsky, everything is going to be great." He was beaming.

"Are you sure this landsman gave you a good rate?" Aunt Bina asked. Isadore paid no attention as he began to shepherd us through the streets, mumbling about how the money changer said to just go by the tall building and turn left. All the buildings were tall. Many of them had the dates they were built carved into their cornerstones, only a few over fifty years old. New York must have sprung out of the ground, quick and brown as a circle of mushrooms in the yard, overnight.

"How about one of those electric cars, pop?" Ephraim asked.

We all felt disappointed when Isadore said that we didn't know where they went, that on the streets we were more likely to run into Yiddish speakers who would help us find this Essex Street. Aunt Bina agreed we didn't have a penny to waste on getting lost.

As we headed into the maze of the great city I was surprised at how much trash there was in the streets, as if everyone in America had forgotten their manners.

After the second flight of stairs Rose put down her satchels and sat on them. The walls were covered in pressed tin, which I thought very elegant even though they were layered with grime. Sweat was plastering Rose's curly hair to her cheeks, twisted like a yeshive boy's sidelocks.

"You look like you have payes," I teased her.

Rose quickly brushed her hair back. "No one said it was going to be like a furnace in New York in September."

"This is just a warm day, girls, you should have been here in July when it was really hot!" The landlord called down from the landing above. The man from Olgopol had no rooms left, so he'd sent us on to Mr. Abrams,

a German, who, he'd assured us, would charge an honest price.

Bina rolled her eyes as she caught up. I rearranged my luggage so I could carry one of Rose's bags.

"You don't have to – ," she protested.

"It's nothing. Besides, I owe you at least one favor from the ship." We plodded up to the fourth floor. The stairwell smelled of urine and I could see bugs in the shadows on the third landing. Maybe not so elegant.

"Good air up here," the landlord said. "More light than on the ground floor, too. Seeing as how this is your first place in America, I'm not charging extra – $17 a month – that's all. And you don't have to go to the yard for the toilet, there's two by the stairwell. Good price for two bedrooms."

"How many families use the toilets?" Aunt Bina asked, unimpressed.

"Well, there's the Horowitzes, Libermans, Brodys and you – not too many. The Liebermans are only five of them. You got a basin here in the kitchen. Cold water in the apartment, any time of day."

Bina shook her head. He must have thought we all came from some backwoods shtetl. It was true that in Kishinev I got water from the pump in the yard, but it was our yard. Uncle Isadore and the boys were walking around the kitchen in a circle, opening the few cabinets. We stood in a plain, empty room, with a grease-spattered stove, washtub and old wallpaper peeling down to reveal an even older pattern of stained flowers. What little light there was came through the soot-blackened glass of the rear room, what the landlord called the "parlor." There was a small window in the kitchen that looked across to another small window in a brick wall. Aaron tried to open it.

"For two years that doesn't open, son, don't worry about it. The bedroom windows do open, though, onto the air shaft. And look how the parlor window looks over the street. That'll give you some cross ventilation. The little bedroom has a window right on the fire escape, a very nice feature."

Rose bit her lip. Ephraim stared at his shoes. I could see his toes wiggling impatiently.

"I see you have gas jets in here," Isadore said. "I heard in American buildings there was electric light now."

The landlord made a gurgling sound, by way of a laugh. He was a very thin man with big hands, and he kept fingering his watch chain, making sure we noticed. "Uptown. Matter of fact, I just built a new apartment building in Harlem, all modern. For that you'd pay $35,

168

maybe $40 a month. Big building boom in New York but you pay for luxury. Most folks off the boat want to stay here on the East Side anyway – no problem finding jobs or landslayt down here."

Isadore cleared his throat, put his hands in his pockets, jingled his change and squared his shoulders before he agreed, so the landlord wouldn't think he was a shlemil. "We'll take it."

"Of course you'll take it. Would I have shlepped you up those stairs for the view? Lookit – the last tenants even left a broom and a rag. Your girls can start right away making it nice." His Yiddish was rough, as if he only used it for tenants.

"Pa," Aaron said, rubbing his hairy cheek.

"Hush. This is America, isn't it? We'll be able to afford better soon, isn't that right, Mr. Abrams? How long since you've been here?"

"Fourteen, maybe fifteen years. From Germany," he said, as if that made all the difference.

Uncle Isadore ignored the implication. "See, just a little more than a newcomer himself and already a landlord. Am I right? We'll do fine, we have to start small but keep thinking big. Here it is, $17 for the month, in advance."

As Abrams was leaving, Aunt Bina stopped him. "And the Horowitzes, how long in this country?"

"Well, here, three years. I don't know before that." Abrams shrugged and left.

Bina looked at Isadore. In Odessa it was upstairs, downstairs, a cherry tree in the yard, the most prosperous time in their lives.

"Come, boys, we're going down to find some nice furniture for our new home," Isadore said cheerfully.

"How much we got left, Isadore?" Aunt Bina asked.

"Twenty-eight American dollars."

"You leave twenty here."

"Now Bina, I got to go down with the boys, start talking to people."

"Twenty."

"All right, $8 for the furnishings. But I'm taking $5 for myself. Now that we're in America you don't get to say what's what all the time. I got a few things to take care of on my own."

She laughed. "Well, Mr. New World, you go, but come back soon. There's plenty work to do here, to make this a place we can even sleep."

"Don't worry, Mama, we're going to get directions to the street where the gold is," Ephraim said, leaping back down the stairs.

Aunt Bina, Rose and I scrubbed every surface until our hands and knees were numb. Many of the walls looked worse for our scrubbing, dark blotches showing through the different layers of wallpaper, but at least we had the sense that we were removing strangers' dirt, leaving our own desire for cleanliness in the corners. By night we had furnished our little rooms. Isadore and the boys dragged up chairs, none matching, and two of what they called bedsprings, creaking, rusty metal squares. One went for Bina and Isadore, one for me and Rose. We put them on old wooden herring barrels and smoothed out our featherbeds – a little lumpy, not exactly clean, yet comforting, even if they smelled still of the ship. The boys grumbled about having to sleep on chairs pushed together. Aunt Bina flattered them about their strength and courage until they gave in.

It was too hot to sleep. Voices and hoofbeats kept waking us.

"Oh, God!" Rose mumbled.

"What?"

"Bugs are crawling on me."

I got up and lit the gas jet. I saw something move on the featherbed but it was gone quick. I turned the jet down. The room was still streaked with light coming off the fire escape. Rose was curled on her side, with just a plain white slip on. She looked like my sister Sarah, a little, in that position. I lay back down, put my arms around her shoulders. She backed into the curve of me.

"It'll be all right, don't worry. I'll protect you from the bugs."

"Not even you can save us from bugs," Rose said.

For some reason this struck us both funny and we started to giggle. I felt the giggle in her hips. From the other room we heard a sharp snore.

"Shhh," she said, "we should try to sleep. It's not too hot for you like this?"

"No." It surprised me to think about being too hot. I should have been. I rubbed her soft upper arm a little. I had been packed in with people all my life but I had never felt a naked arm like that. "No, I'm fine."

"Good," she said, snuggling.

I felt a blush move through me and I pulled my hand back. I closed my mind up so the bugs couldn't get in. I hated living with bugs at least as much as Rose did, being bitten in your sleep by things you couldn't see. "We live in the world with all its creatures," Mama used to say, but she still swept the ants out of the house and hardly anything ever bit us

in bed. Mama's house was clean. On Essex Street the bugs lived in the walls, under the loose, uneven floorboards, just waiting for their chance. I could feel their tiny insect eyes on us. I didn't cross a whole world just to cower before bugs – they weren't going to boss my sleep! I put my arm back around Rose and followed the rhythm of her ribs into the dark.

The next day we saw a woman and her children sitting on the street in the middle of a pile of furniture, pots and pans, bundles of clothes.

"What's this?" Aunt Bina asked her.

The woman gave a pitiful sigh. "Evicted – couldn't pay the rent. Lady, couldn't you use something? A table, a pot?"

Aunt Bina bought her old couch for two dollars. I was embarrassed that we were buying because of someone else's misfortune. The evictee, a short, square woman with four young children and apparently no husband, appeared grateful. But from behind a pushcart a yente called Bina a greenhorn for not making a bargain.

"From you, I'll make a bargain. You got cabbages?"

"The best, four cents only."

"Four cents! In Odessa this cabbage they wouldn't feed to the goyim's pigs. One penny."

"One penny – you want me to be put on the street like Beryl over there? You won't find a better cabbage. It could serve as the eye of an idol in India. Your children will bless you for the soup this makes."

"You think I'm just a greenhorn? Two pennies, that's the end of it." Aunt Bina turned as if she was going to walk away.

"May your hand spill the salt and ruin the soup for driving such a bargain. You don't know how this costs me but all right, two cents."

"You see, if you mix around, you learn," Aunt Bina said to Rose and me as the corners of her mouth went up and down with satisfaction. "Now go get those boys to move this couch." I admired how quickly Bina added up the parts of America. Her eyes were on everything: the laundry waving like a thousand flags between buildings, the signs in Yiddish, Russian, English, the pushcarts piled with bruised fruit and baby clothes, the shirtwaists the younger women wore. Already in Odessa she didn't wear a wig – Mama and Papa had been scandalized when they found out. Now she gave up even her light summer shawl.

"We may be greenhorns," she said, "but we're smart greenhorns, you'll see."

So we had a cabbage and a couch. Aaron and Ephraim were supposed to share the couch. They tried sleeping head to toe but you could hear them cursing each other all night long. Aaron was stocky with wide shoulders, and, as the oldest remaining son, was determined to get his way. Ephraim tossed in a state of constant agitation, as if he were trying to sleep quickly so he wouldn't miss a minute of the new world. Aaron complained that Ephraim's feet stank and Ephraim called Aaron a bearded biblical bully. By Sunday morning Uncle Isadore got a separate cot for Ephraim, plus a couple of fruit crates to use as tables.

On the second night of the cabbage soup, Bina added a tongue that was delicious with the rye bread we got from David's pushcart on Broome Street. In our neighborhood we had a choice of four Jewish bakers, just on two blocks. Mrs. Brody told Aunt Bina that David's was the best, even if he was her second cousin. My stomach acted like it was still in Kishinev – or on the boat – most of the time, but it seemed a little better when we didn't eat dairy. I even asked for a second bowl of the tongue soup.

Isadore leaned back in his chair, which gave a cracking sound. He sat up straight and wound his pocket watch. "Didn't I tell you this was going to be a great life? Tomorrow morning, the boys and I will get jobs. Soon I'll have enough for my own shop again and we'll get real furniture."

Aunt Bina looked unconvinced but smiled and nodded at him, stifling a yawn. Since we landed, she'd barely stopped moving long enough to eat and sleep.

"Can I get a job too, Papa?" Rose asked eagerly, though clearly aware of what Bina's answer would be.

"Isadore, she won't even be fourteen for three months. Mrs. Lieberman down the hall told me in America it's against the law to let a girl work before she's fourteen," Bina implored, reawakening. "Besides, why should I send her out on the street to find who knows what? She can go to school for free. Think what an opportunity that is."

I was already fourteen and Aunt Bina knew I was determined to work. I had a queasy feeling of being on the outside, the tag-along they had to bring with them, not figuring in discussions about either school or work. I got up and cleared the dishes.

"That's right, she's a child still. Me and the boys, we'll make so much money, next week you'll have pearls! Isn't that right, Aaron?"

"I thought I was going to go to university here," Aaron complained.

"Well, of course. Absolutely. But you've got to know English first

and how better to learn than to work? You'll come with me and Ephraim – we'll go by the watchmakers and see what's what. Then you'll go to night school for English right away. You'll have to pass entrance exams and you want to be ready. That's a plan, isn't it?"

"It's a plan," Aaron said with definite misery.

On the landing that night I overheard Mrs. Brody telling the Horowitz boy they were hiring down by Samuel's box factory, and I decided to find the place the next day. I let Rose in on my idea but made her promise not to tell Aunt Bina or Uncle Isadore. I wanted it to be a surprise, in case I actually got hired. Rose and I blocked and straightened my blue hat, and Rose said I looked so fine she'd hire me in an instant. I felt the job was already mine.

Early Monday morning, as it was beginning to be light, I put on my hat and went out. All the buildings tinged with gray shadow made me feel small, even frightened, that first time I was on the street alone. But by 6:00 A.M. the peddlers were wheeling their carts into place and people were rushing everywhere, spitting sunflower seeds into the gutters. At first no one knew where Samuel's was. Finally someone told me to go to East Broadway.

I had a little piece of charcoal and I made a circle on the buildings on the west sides of the streets, at the corners, so I could find my way back. I had to ask directions many times, but at last I stood outside the factory, a long, three-story place surrounded by a high fence. I took a deep breath, walked up and knocked at the first door I saw. A tall woman opened it and asked me something in English.

"I heard you were hiring – ." I started in Yiddish. She silently pointed around the rear of the building. Inside the next door a man chewing an unlit cigar looked me up and down.

"Greenhorn, huh?" he asked in Yiddish.

"Yes sir," I said. "But if you give me a job, then by next week I'll be an American."

The man didn't bother taking the cigar out of his mouth. His laughter created a trickle of brown spittle which he quickly wiped away. "I bet you will be! All right. I'll take you on. But work started thirty minutes ago, so today you're just a learner, no pay, all right?"

"Of course! And tomorrow?"

"Well, tomorrow, you'll be almost an American – you'll get one cent for your part on every 100 boxes. In this factory, you're lucky. We don't make you work on Shabbes, but you got to come in Sunday or else don't come in Monday, you understand? You be here tomorrow at 6:30

A.M. Go to Mrs. Schwartz, over there – she'll show you what to do." He made a show of lighting his cigar while waving me away.

It was a filthy place, this box factory. We stood three in a row on each side of a table: the first girl folded, the second glued, the third one collared, putting a band around the box. If you made a mistake, you threw it on the floor and the mistakes were charged against everyone at the table, even the workers on the other side. We waded among scraps of cardboard and paper, sometimes as deep as our ankles. If we whispered for longer than five seconds, Mrs. Schwartz or one of the bigger boys who distributed the box pieces would shush us. Even so, it was noisy. Machines in the back clamped and shuddered as they cut through the box materials, and when the machines stopped for a second I could hear hundreds of hands rustling cardboard. The windows were in a high row at the top of the wall, covered with cardboard dust. The boss had installed electricity to prevent dust fires. A single, bare bulb dangled over each table.

At my station we were putting together boxes for candy. The boxes had a picture on top of an American girl with blond curls and eyes bluer than Rose's, holding a red ball. At the other end of the room the boxes were for cigars. My co-workers whispered quickly, keeping an eye out for the bosses, even when they had to give necessary instructions. I got to glue. I didn't like how the glue smelled: a sweetish, nauseating odor. The whole factory reeked, but it was better than some smells I'd recently known. At first I made a lot of mistakes, put on too much glue or not enough, got the pieces crooked. The others at my table – no one was older than fifteen – glared at me. Most hadn't had a good bath in a long time. "Learners!" they said in disgust, "you don't even know you're losing money all day." But it didn't take me long to understand the job and I started to go faster.

"Not too bad for a beginner," the gluer girl opposite me said, when they blew a whistle for us to stop for lunch. "My name's Sadie."

"Chava," I said, glad she was talking to me. She had on a sailor shirt, which seemed to be popular for girls, though it was a size too small for her.

"You got something to eat?" I shook my head. "For a penny you can get an apple. For another two, a piece of bread and a cup of milk from the pushcart outside, but you got to be quick—." She gestured. Girls and boys were running through the entrance. By the time I got to the pushcart, there were only a few pieces of bread left. I handed the man my folded dollar.

"A whole dollar!" he said. I couldn't tell whether he was laughing at me. "I guess I can let you have a piece of bread for that."

"A piece of bread is one penny."

"I was testing to see how green you were. Here's your bread – and your change." He put a big pile of nickels in my hand. It felt so heavy and important I left it stretched in front of me, staring at it. "All right, all right," he said, "here's the rest." He put some bigger coins on top and I stuck the whole mass into my pocket. Had he cheated me anyway? The bread was almost stale. As I started to eat, the whistle blew again and I ran back in.

By the end of the day my eyes burned from the glue and my feet hurt from standing, though Sadie showed me how to dance up and down, standing in one spot, while keeping up my pace. When the quitting whistle blew, it was 6:00 P.M. What does a penny a hundred mean? I tried to count what I made but the line went too fast, the packers taking the boxes away every ten, fifteen minutes. I asked Sadie.

"If you're really fast, don't make mistakes, work every day – $3 a week," she said.

Three dollars a week. What a wonderful thing! The burning in my eyes stopped after a little while in the city air. Here I was, off the boat five days, and already I had a job. I could help with the rent and probably even save some. Mama, maybe even Papa, would have been proud of me.

Whether or not they would have been, Uncle Isadore certainly seemed pleased. "So that's where you were today. Your Aunt Bina thought you did something like that. Good for you. Fourteen years old and making $3 a week, what a great country!" For him, the day hadn't gone as well. Many watchmakers had come before us. Every street had a watch repair shop and no one needed help. They told him that uptown in the diamond district there were big jewelers and factories. Tomorrow he and Aaron would take the electric streetcar and see. Ephraim had been out on the street all weekend and today he somehow talked his way into a job in a tailoring shop, finishing men's pants, even though he had never sewed before.

"What's to it? The needle goes in, the needle goes out." He laughed, pulling on his suspenders. He was almost seventeen, but he still acted like a boy.

"You have no idea what you're talking about," Rose said.

Bina backed her up. "She's right, Ephraim. If you want to still have your

job tomorrow, you let Rose show you the stitches. Go on, Rose, take him into the other room. I've got to get dinner ready for my workers."

"You pay attention to your sister, Ephraim," Isadore added. "Tailoring is a good business here. I talked to some people, they told me – you can really get ahead if you have a talent for it. It's about time we found out what talent you got in that nebish head of yours."

"The needle goes in, the needle goes out," Ephraim repeated over his shoulder as Rose turned up the gas jet in our room.

"So – it's the American," the boss said. "Here's your pay." My first pay envelope contained $1.90. My first wages. I bounced up and down on the balls of my feet and asked Sadie how she did.

"Only $2.95 – Samuels took out a nickel for the learners." I offered her a nickel from my envelope but she refused. "You weren't the only learner we had this week and you were faster than the others." She looked me over, cocking her head to the side. "I live over on Broome by Ludlow. You?"

"Essex near Grand, not far. Want to walk home together? I could buy you a seltzer."

"Only a greenhorn would think she was rich with $1.90. I'll buy my own, at least until you start getting full pay."

I was a paid worker now and I knew someone else in the neighborhood, on my own. I ran all the way from the soda shop on Canal to Essex to give Aunt Bina the rest of my pay. Aunt Bina looked at it, looked at me.

"You worked hard for this, darling. You keep it."

"I want to pay my share. For the food and rent. Next week it will be more." Sometimes she treated me almost as if I was her own daughter. This hurt me in an entirely different part of my body than Rose's kindness. Rose, after all, wanted things back from me. What did Aunt Bina want? To fulfill her duty. Her affections drew me in but she was affectionate to everyone. Not sloppy affectionate like some women – she was almost as smart as Mama. If I wasn't there, though, I didn't think she would ever miss me. I appreciated her fairness but paid my share.

"All right. But a working girl needs money for herself. You've got your own expenses now. You keep fifty cents this week and I'll take the rest. Then we'll see."

Rose was jealous of my job, more so after I told her about having a soda with Sadie. She wanted to work too.

"I want you in school," Aunt Bina said.

"Chava and I can go to night school together. I don't like the day school. I'll learn faster if Chava comes with me at night than I could ever learn going by myself in the day. I'm a hundred times better than Ephraim – I could sew him into one of Chava's paper boxes. Let me try, please, Mama?"

"Rosele, what kind of life is that, to work all day and go to school at night? What's wrong with the day school?" When she wrinkled her forehead, her freckles made a smudge across her brow.

"It's all American-born and girls who already know English. They make fun of me and I can't even understand what the joke is, Mama."

Aunt Bina's head swayed from side to side and we could tell she was going to give in. Anyway, what was Rose asking? A chance to bring home money, improve our fortunes, have enough to buy a cloak for the High Holidays, maybe a new dress. If you worked, you were doing something, you had something to show for yourself. Night school was the place for immigrants. We would make money during the day and still have our pride at night.

On our second Tuesday in New York, Uncle Isadore and Aaron finally got jobs uptown, at a watch manufacturer. Isadore walked around discouraged, hardly speaking. We all knew he had been expecting something better, having his skill rewarded, his success in Odessa counting for something here. Now he was just a hired hand like everyone on the Lower East Side. Worse, his new co-workers called him Izzy, which he hated, and he and Aaron had to get up a half hour before the rest of us to catch the streetcar. They were giving Isadore $11 a week to start, and Aaron $7 because he was an apprentice. Rose's sewing lessons helped Ephraim hold on to his job. He was making $7 too and didn't have to pay for the streetcar, he liked to remind Aaron.

"I'm not doing this for long," Aaron said through gritted teeth. Uncle Isadore rattled the newspaper and grunted. We tiptoed around him for days.

Rose found a job in white goods – that's what they called it when you made ladies' underwear. White goods. As if saying the word "underwear" would invite demons to grab your soul. They started her tucking and hemming. She'd never used a machine before, but she took right to it the minute they gave her a chance. She could sew a straight line barely looking. Right around the time I had my fifteenth birthday, her forelady decided to teach Rose the fancy work. After five months in America she was making $5.10 a week; everyone said that was very

good for a girl. In the paperbox factory, I worked faster and faster, thinking about Rose sewing with the machine, but the most I could make was $3.25. When I worked that hard, by Shabbes I collapsed.

On my way home from the East Broadway factory I sometimes stopped in Seward Park. There were benches where you could rest your feet and listen to people gossiping. Usually I could find a copy of the *Jewish Daily Forward* someone had left behind – the newspaper's office building was right across the street. I liked to make up stories about the people who went in and out of their offices. Maybe the man in the long overcoat was a famous revolutionary in exile going for an interview, or the woman in the straw hat could be begging the editors to consider her latest poem.

From every corner of the park a constant stream of agitators interrupted my daydreams with their speeches. Anarchists, socialists, labor leaders exhorted us weary workers to stand up to our bosses. Almost daily I read about a strike in the paper and almost as often passed one by on the street. Striking in America seemed even more popular than in Russia. Now people wanted a ten-hour day, better conditions. Why not? I knew it was foolish to keep working at the box factory – it was just work for greenhorns. Now that Rose and I were going to English classes Tuesday, Wednesday and Thursday nights, I knew I could get a better paying job, but I didn't like to think about looking for something new. If I closed my eyes for a minute in the park, I could imagine I was back in Kishinev, listening to Daniel. Then I'd open my eyes and see it was beginning to get dark in New York City and if I didn't hurry I'd be late for school.

Rose saved out of her lunch money to get Aunt Bina a new cloak for shul. This was hard for Rose, I knew, because there were pushcarts on every corner with interesting, if not always fresh, things to eat: hot pretzels, ears of corn and roasted chestnuts. When I wasn't very hungry at lunch, I saved what I bought for myself and gave it to her, so she could have more money for clothes and treats. The stores were crammed with new styles, shirtwaists with fancy embroidery and skirts trimmed with lace. Back home we used to make almost everything ourselves but here we made only money, and there was never enough to buy what we needed in order to get better jobs so we could make more money. America wasn't just new hats: all our clothes had to be new. Going out in winter with a shawl made you look green, even if our wool shawls were warmer than New York coats. But I liked how we all looked in shirtwaists. I'd seen some women in cafés wearing ties

with them, almost like men, and they looked very crisp.

"Come to services with us, darling," Aunt Bina said every Shabbes, yet I couldn't make myself get ready in time. Maybe because I didn't like the idea of having to look at an American rabbi, his beard – . Nobody pushed me. I knew I should be honoring my parents' memory but I decided I had to honor them my own way, with my own thoughts. I could remember all the words of the service. I understood that going to shul wasn't just knowing the words, it was belonging among the Jews – that was how Mama used to put it.

But how could you stop belonging to the Jews if you were one? Not every Jew went to shul in New York – or could. In the new world, we each had to carry around a little shul inside ourselves. Anyway, I was mad at God. I didn't understand how someone who made the Garden of Eden would also make pogroms. I remembered Papa folding his hands under his beard and nodding while his students would argue about free will: how we have to have the choice to sin in order to not choose it, to choose God. Now I thought if this was God's reason, he must be very vain to think it was more important to be worshipped than to let people live in peace. Thinking about God gave me an uncomfortable feeling in my stomach. If I'd gone to shul with Bina and Rose, maybe I'd have gotten sick. It was better that I stayed home.

Besides, it was nice to have these hours on Saturday mornings. Most Saturdays, Isadore and Aaron had to work. Ephraim wouldn't go to shul if he wasn't working, instead he went somewhere men gathered to talk. Rose put on her fanciest waist – she had two for the week and one for Saturdays and holidays – and she and Aunt Bina would leave for shul. I only had two shirtwaists, but that wasn't why I didn't like to go. I could have had another if I wanted to, with more lace than Rose's, even.

Lying on top of the bed after breakfast with my clothes on was such a luxury. Even though my shirtwaist didn't have lace, I could follow the starched pleats down my chest. I pretended my fingers were revolutionaries going out for a walk in the hills at the north end of Kishinev. Over the hill, under the grass, the fold of cloth, my fingers walked, coming to the marker where the forbidden pamphlets were hidden. With my eyes closed I could remember how the wind rippled through wildflowers on a sunny afternoon. Stroking the cloth was making me dreamy, and I opened a button. My fingers curled beneath the edge of my undershirt and the green behind my eyes became dark, dark as the worn wood in the pews of shul. I touched my nipples. They wrinkled up into square knobs. "These are the handles to the ark of the

covenant," I heard myself murmuring. Then I worried if Mama would have thought I was being sacrilegious. Was it sacrilegious to touch yourself on Shabbes? Sometimes after Rose fell asleep I would lie on my side, cupping my breast, trying to measure it with my palm. It was still growing, round and smooth, not as big as Rose's, hardly, but my breast felt good. If you had bigger breasts, did they give you more pleasure? Maybe I could have asked Rose – or maybe not. I didn't like how men stared at women's chests. Mine were too small still to get much notice, thank God. Did having breasts make a woman so different from a man? If I didn't have them, would it have made it easier to get a better job?

Rose told me I could make more money if I sewed. But I didn't want to sew. She kept trying to show me anyway, just like Esther used to.

"No, I will not sew," I told her fifty times.

"Everyone sews. Look at Ephraim – he's already making $10 a week, tailoring. You think sewing is beneath you?"

"It's not that."

"What, then? It's so good being a gluer, you get drunk from the smell all day long and it addles your brains, what?" Rose was getting good at arching one eyebrow, just like her mama. I practiced with my reflection in window panes when no one was looking, but I couldn't get the hang of it.

"I just don't want to sew. I don't know how to tell you why. I want to do something else."

"Nu?"

"I want to be a bookbinder."

"A bookbinder? How did you come to this idea?"

"It seems more – I don't know. I would rather have my hands on books than dresses." I looked down at the floor, worrying that Rose would take my comment as an insult.

She stared with her blue eyes, as if she wanted to say something but changed her mind. "So how are you going to go about getting bookbinding work?"

"I saw a bindery over on Canal Street. I asked and they said they could only hire union."

"Union?"

"You know, like the Bund."

"I knew that," Rose said, exasperated. "What I heard was that they

sign up girls from inside the shop to be in the union, and then the unionists work with the non-unionists, try to get them to go over – "

"It's like that in the box factory, only if they find out you're union, they fire you. Last week they fired a boy who had one of those strike papers the unionists are always handing out on the street. That's how they keep the wages so low."

"So go somewhere else if you can't go by the bookbinders. In sewing, almost none of the girls are in the union and we still make almost twice as much as you do. You don't want to kill yourself for nothing."

"I should kill myself for something?"

"Stop, Chava, you know what I mean."

In May the boss, Samuels, said that it was slow season, everybody would get 10 per cent less. What did that mean? we asked. A penny for every 110 boxes, he said. It was too much. We stood at our tables with our hands at our sides, clenching and unclenching our fists. Probably none of us was older than sixteen – some had to stand on wooden crates to reach, they were so little. Sadie looked at me. I took a deep breath and whispered, "Strike?" and she nodded yes. The whisper filled the room until we were all saying it in a soft voice, "Strike." The boss's eyes got wide.

"Strike! You're just children, what can you know about strikes?" Samuels was snorting. It was a big joke; his cigar rolled around in his mouth. "Now get to work and I'll forget I ever heard you use that word, you miserable offspring of cockroach lice. You should be ashamed of yourselves, foul language like that in your innocent mouths!"

We stood still. I never told Rose this, but the rats liked the taste of paste, and the boss did nothing to keep them from making tunnels in the waste cardboard on the floor. When I heard a rustling under our table, I moved towards the door. It was warm already and no one had a coat – in the box factory it was hotter than outdoors because of the sealed windows. From every table a leader was heading out and the rest followed. No one stayed. We were all out in front of the factory, looking at each other. Now what?

As we were massing on the sidewalk, a woman walked by. She stopped, stared at our group and asked what was going on.

"We're on strike, lady," I said.

Molly from Norfolk Street added, "We gotta get better conditions" –

using English for the word "conditions." Sadie linked arms with me and Molly.

"We're not going back until the boss gives in," Sadie said.

The woman looked us over carefully, seriously. She was dressed very nicely, like a picture you see in a newspaper, with a shiny blue jacket and wide-brimmed hat. "And what are these conditions that make you want to strike?"

Someone told her about the wages. I found a voice to speak about the rats. Samuels was out on the steps yelling that God would curse our souls and make our mothers grow beards. When he spotted the lady he turned around and went back in.

"I have a friend who would be very interested in this," the woman said. "I'm going to telephone her." Telephone! This woman must have been a very rich American lady if she knew how to use a telephone, even if she did speak to us in Yiddish. "You children stay here but you must walk in a circle on the sidewalk. It's the law. Walk two by two. Can you do that?"

"Sure, you bet, lady, absolutely!" We all yelled.

"Good. I'm going to get you some help and maybe someone from a newspaper will come down. But remember to walk in a circle, stay on the sidewalk, don't block the doorways – stay inside the law, all right?"

We walked with our heads high, like it was a parade. Some of the younger children probably thought it was a holiday. We made faces at each other, pulling our shoulders up to our ears and swinging our arms around. "Be serious!" a boy in a torn yellow shirt barked, "We have to look strong, like the strikers over on Delancey Street."

Sadie pulled on her ear. "Do you really think this is going to work?" she asked me.

I threw my hands up in the air and made a silly grin. Even the serious boy chuckled before rearranging his mouth to look intent. All of us seemed glad, at least, for the break in routine.

In about an hour, I recognized Lena from the boat, Lena Reznikoff, with a couple of young women behind her, striding towards us. She looked taller than I remembered; maybe it was the change of background from sea to city. The other women had signs under their arms. She passed out the signs: "Strike!" "Fair Wages, Fair Hours" "We want the Union shop!" Some of the children didn't know what a union was. The organizers were everywhere explaining, moving us along like mother geese.

Finally Lena saw me. She pursed her lips, frowned.

"Bialik," I said and she nodded, remembering everything.

"So you've found a fight already?"

"You're the one who appears to be out looking for fights." I gestured to the sign she was carrying: "An Eight-Hour Day." What a luxury that would be.

A man with a card in his derby showed up, a reporter for the *Call*, he said. Lena pushed me towards him and he started asking me about the factory, the boss. But before I could say much, the police showed up, three wagons of them, jumping off, waving their batons in the air. Samuels came out to the sidewalk and lit his cigar.

Most of the children scattered like the rats did when I kicked at the cardboard waste. "You have the right to strike!" Lena called after them. Only a dozen stayed behind, including Sadie. I told her I came over on the same boat as Lena and she seemed impressed that I knew an organizer.

"Now what?" I whispered to Lena. She squeezed my hand, staring at the boss.

Samuels was all red with anger and triumph. The police glared at the remaining strikers.

"Those AFL mamzers are sending you women around to stir up trouble among children?" the boss yelled. "Who the hell do you think you are?" Drops of perspiration fell all over his face. "You tell those kids if they're not back at work 6:30 tomorrow, I'll replace them all with ones fresh from Ellis Island, and they'll be glad to work for a penny every 120!" He stalked away. The reporter tipped his hat and left. A few policemen stuck around, keeping their eyes on us.

"You – ," Lena motioned to those of us who walked out – only girls, I noticed, "you want to try and keep the strike going?" Some of them couldn't even look at her but everyone found some way to say yes. "Go find the others – tell them to be here tomorrow at 6:00 A.M. to picket."

"But we don't have to be at work until 6:30," Molly complained.

"The boss will bring the strikebreakers at 6, you'll see. Chava, you come with me." I looked at Sadie and made an effort to smile.

"Don't worry," Sadie yelled loud enough so anyone still listening could hear. "I'll be here at 6:00 A.M.!"

I walked up to Allen Street with the organizers. Lena paid for me to go on the El, because, she said, I was a striker now. A striker! I threw my shoulders back. I wished Mama could see me – maybe she wouldn't have thought it was right for a girl to strike. No, I thought, Mama would be proud of me for not giving in. This definitely would have made Daniel happy. But the Petrovskys? Uncle Isadore wouldn't like it. But

what could he do to me? I wasn't his daughter. He could make me leave though – no, not just for striking. He wouldn't, would he?

As we rode along the tracks at the top of the tenement buildings I could look right into windows at women like Aunt Bina, scrubbing clothes on washboards, bent over big tin sinks, old rags tied around their hair. I wasn't striking to prove anything to anybody, not Mama, not Uncle Isadore, not even Daniel, but for myself and for others like me. Is that what every person who went on strike learned? Still, I wished Daniel could know – maybe if I wrote Sarah and Esther, they would be able to pass the letter along. Sarah would have been proud of me, I knew.

We got off at First Street. "We work for the Women's Trade Union League. You've heard of it?" Lena asked. I shook my head no. "Well, we want to organize women and girls like you into unions, then you can join the AFL. You know what the AFL is?"

I felt like a greenhorn all over again, but I didn't want Lena to think I hadn't learned anything in America. "Like the Bund?"

"A little, but not just Jewish. The American Federation of Labor is an organization of trade unions, for all the workers." She knocked on a door. Inside there were four other women, some sitting at desks. She introduced me around, getting me to tell about Samuels' Paperbox Manufacturing Company. The others clucked over me like my Aunt Shendl used to, except in English. I could tell most of them didn't know from Yiddish. "Such a smart one!" one said, though I was beginning not to feel so smart if I was going to lose my job, and the other girls too. But when Lena asked me to sign a union pledge, I got my courage back. Belonging to a union meant to fight against tyranny – and wasn't that what Samuels was, a tyrant?

"Yes," Uncle Isadore said at dinner that night, "but a union also means there are many of you – how many others signed the pledges?" He wasn't angry like I had expected, only scornful. Scornful I could deal with.

"I was the only one there, but tomorrow – ."

"Tomorrow," Ephraim butted in, "the rest will go back to work and you can eat your pledge."

"Tchish," Aunt Bina gave them a sideways look, "don't pay any attention to them. You did what you thought was right. You have no idea how hard Chava works for only a fraction of what you get – ." She gestured to Isadore and the boys. "Three dollars – remember? Your wages went up,

not hers. And you can see she puts in as many hours as you."

"Chava's just a girl, what does she need?" Aaron forked another potato onto his plate.

"And what do you need? The wages of this family to send you to the City College in September – that's what you need. Why do you think I take in trousers to finish? It's not for the entertainment, I'll tell you that!"

"Two firebrands we've got!" Isadore said with his mouth full.

Bina arched her eyebrow. He looked away. A flush rose and subsided in her cheeks as she turned back to me. "You don't pay any attention to them, darling. You do what you think is right."

"But what if they fire you?" Rose asked.

I shrugged. "Maybe I'll have to learn how to sew after all."

"That I'd like to see," Rose slapped my shoulder lightly as she started to make ready Bina's evening workspace.

The headline in the *Call* read "The Children's Strike!"

"We'll show them how strong children can be!" Lena said. At 6:00 A.M., just as she predicted, carts full of new children showed up.

"Don't scab!" we called to them. "You're just going to be exploited in there! Watch out for the rats!" The police folded their arms and made a fence around the strikebreakers, so we couldn't even get close. We kept walking in our circle. I was glad that Sadie walked beside me. It made picketing familiar in an odd way, like we were still together at our work station.

At noon Samuels came out. "Well, I replaced a quarter of you this morning – and I got more learners on the way. How long does it take to teach somebody to put together a box? You, Fannia, how long did it take you?" The girl he singled out hung her head. "I'm giving you children one more chance. If you want your job, come back inside when the second whistle blows for the end of lunch."

"On what terms?" Lena called out.

"You're still here? I'm a fair man. They can come back when the whistle blows for what they were getting yesterday, a penny for every 110 boxes."

Lena's jaw was tight. "And the hours?"

"The same. You think I'm in business for charity? You go back uptown, give piano lessons at a settlement house, don't bother my workers no more!" He glanced over at me. "You, you think your socialist friend knows how to show you to be an American better than me? Let her show you what to do now. You're fired, just like an American!"

"You can't fire her for picketing!"

"I'm firing her because she's a disruptive worker and it's my factory!"

185

He spat and missed Lena's shoes by an inch. Then he stalked back in.

The girls were whispering together, even Molly and Sadie. Lena told them they had to be united but they shook their heads. Sadie turned to me. I saw there were dark circles under her brown eyes.

"I'm sorry," she said. "It's a rotten job but my mother – "

"Go on," I said. "It's all right. I wanted an excuse to look for another job anyway. Maybe I'll see you at the soda fountain." She clasped my hand. When the second whistle blew, she went back in with the rest of the girls. I stared at the gob of spit on the sidewalk.

"All right, so this one we didn't win." Lena put her knuckles under my chin and lifted my face. "You know there are better jobs you can do, don't you?"

"I don't sew."

"You don't sew! A Jewish girl who doesn't sew, will miracles never cease! And I was hoping you'd become another Vera Pavlovna."

I wanted Lena to take me seriously and now she was talking in riddles. She knew I didn't have her education. "Who's Vera Pavlovna?"

"The heroine in Chernyshevsky's *What Is to Be Done?* You never read it?"

"No, I heard of it, I think."

"Read it if you can. It was an inspiration to us in Vilna. Vera Pavlovna starts a sewing cooperative which the workers own. They look after each other."

"That sounds like what my brother Daniel used to talk about."

"Probably. The right book at the right time can change many minds – that's why we have study groups. But you, what work are we going to find for you?"

She took me into her dark green eyes, measuring me. I stood up a little straighter. I'd been growing lately; everyone remarked on how tall I was going to be. "I want to work in a bindery, but they say you have to belong to the binder's union to get in and I don't know how to join."

"A bindery. That's not so easy, but it can be done." Lena considered. "Come back by the League headquarters tomorrow and I'll see if I can find something for you. But don't tell anyone else – we're not an employment bureau!"

There was no bindery work but Lena got me a job stripping tobacco leaves for a cigar manufacturer, Polstein's, on Grand. A block shorter walk and $5 a week to start. At least in cigars a girl could move up, maybe get to be a buncher or even a roller. The good rollers got $12 a week.

If we were really free to choose

Dear Esther and Sarah,

In the American papers we read about the Saint Petersburg massacre – now the Tsar kills Russians as well as Jews. I worry about you all this Pesach. I hope you are continuing safe and well. It took me so long to write because I know you're waiting for me to tell what America is like but still I cannot say. Almost everyone in Kishinev would fit into Essex Street where we live, that's how crowded. The dust of the world comes to New York on the feet of immigrants, so it's a dirty place and no trees. I miss our yard, the water pump – what a funny thing to miss. Here the water is inside the house. We are on the fourth floor so it's good not to have to pump. There are carriages that move without horses – the new automobile. When I saw one myself for the first time, I ran down the block following it. Then the driver saw me and started to go so fast I couldn't keep up. Do you have them in Kishinev yet?

In New York so much is going on that every day the street is a carnival, like Purim. But I am always working and I don't see much. First I was making boxes in a factory, but we had a strike. If you see Daniel, tell him I was one of the organizers. There are many strikes here – you could be just walking in your neighborhood and bump into one. Now I am stripping tobacco, which makes my hands brown but I get $5.50 a week. Don't think this is so much. In America you pay for everything. I am saving to get Sarah a ticket, second class.

The Petrovskys are a fine family. We all contribute to send Aaron to school to be a lawyer maybe. Ephraim changed his name to Harry but only Rose and I call him that. Rose and I learn English at

night. We are the best students. It is very tiring to work and study, not enough hours left for sleep.

Please let me know you're staying safe in this troubled time. I send you many blessings.

Remember your sister across the water,

Chava

"Look at your hands," Rose said as we hurried to class. Every school night I met her in front of Fine's where she found a job sewing fancy undershirts after being laid off when white goods got slow. At Fine's they would usually let girls under sixteen leave by 6:30 if they had night school. When they didn't, the girls had to work until 10:00 or 11:00, in busy season, without extra pay – the older workers too.

We regularly ran up the stairs of Essex Street, washed our faces quickly and ate bread with boiled onions, kissed Aunt Bina, grabbed a piece of fruit and got to the high school by 7:30. Rose had been out of work from February until April and was ahead of me in her studies, but I was catching up.

"What's wrong with my hands?" I held my left hand up under the faint glow of the gas globes over the pawn shop.

"They're getting all stained and they stink from tobacco."

"Can you say that in English?" I was trying to joke, but I stuck both hands in my skirt pockets, squeezing my reader under my arm. "Your hands aren't so beautiful either anymore." I sucked my cheeks in, ashamed at criticizing her.

"At least I manage to keep mine clean," Rose came right back.

"Rose, how come we're fighting? Something bad happen at work?" I stopped to look at her. The smudges of last evening light were beginning to blend into the smudges of the tenements. The smudges reflected the circles under her eyes. "Nu?"

"We'll be late for class." She hurried up the steps. Usually I had to drag her up after me. She always wanted to skip "just this once" – to get an eggcream from Mrs. Bergman or hang around the doors of the Yiddish theaters, watching the people go in. Now I had to run to follow her. I didn't mind. English class revived me. Sometimes after pulling the stems out of the big tobacco leaves all day I just wanted to put a cold rag on my face and sleep, forget how my stomach hurt and my hands burned. But when we entered the high school I got a little thrill from the echoes of learning.

The girls who came in the day left their voices in the cool hallways, calling back and forth to each other, having their private jokes and important heartaches. I saw them the afternoon Lena took me to the League office, almost a year ago now. They wore clean new dresses, and you could tell they wore corsets to give them an American figure; maybe Rose had made their underwear.

"Just summer school," Lena had said. Just! Now I wished I could go to school all day like them, even for a summer. Aaron failed the first entrance exam for City College, so Isadore told him he had to quit his job to go study everything, not just English, in order to get in next term. I wouldn't have failed. But I gave Aunt Bina all of my pay except a dollar I kept for my own expenses, and every week I saved twenty-five cents for Sarah's ticket in a torn stocking stuffed in a hole in the mattress.

Rose managed to get a seat on the second row aisle. She turned and gave me her I'm-perfectly-happy-now smile and looked away before she could see that I was giving her my you're-going-to-tell-me-what's-going-on expression. I sat three seats away from her. The room was always full, sometimes there weren't chairs for all of us. It was mostly all Jewish girls in our class, a few Italians, two older women who always sat together up front. They owned a grocery store on Houston Street.

"Miss Meyer, would you spell 'appointment,' please?"

I wasn't paying attention and the girl beside me giggled when I stared at the teacher. "What?"

Mrs. Kaufman half-closed her eyelids. You wouldn't have thought a teacher could look as weary as somebody who worked in a factory. "Maybe next time you'll be awake for class," she said – sharp words from a patient voice. I hoped she remembered I usually paid good attention.

When class was out, Rose walked close beside me, quietly. It was dark and there were no gas lamps in the middle of the street, only at the intersections. We could usually pick our way easily from the lights in some shop windows, but tonight the shadows from the awnings and in the stairwells gave me a chill.

"Okay," I said, one of my favorite American expressions. "But I've got to know what's wrong by you." I took her hand so she couldn't run ahead. Of course, by nine o'clock we were too tired to run anywhere.

"The foreman called me into his office – ," she said.

"They don't like your work?"

"Oh, he likes my work just fine. And my hair, he likes, he wants to

make sure I have it tucked up good, it shouldn't get caught in a machine."

Even on the gray street I could see a bitterness in Rose I had never seen before. I looked at the dark, thick braids, circling her head, like a nest you could lay your heart in. "Did he touch you?"

"He tried. I ran to the bathroom and locked the door. It's a pit of filth in there, I can tell you. He's outside yelling he's going to dock me $1 for using the bathroom without authorization. We've got to pay for our needles and thread, now we've got to pay for his 'authorization.' " She kicked a wad of paper into the gutter.

"He's a bully and a lecher. You can't go back."

"I'm not losing almost a week's wages." Rose's jaw clenched.

I took her arm and could feel the clench in her whole body. "You think he's going to just forget about bothering you?"

"I don't know. There's lots of girls – maybe he'll pick on someone else."

"Oy, Rose, why wish that son of the devil on another girl?" She turned to look at me and I realized she was scared. Sorry for what she had just said, and scared. I was tall, my face was long, my breasts small, my hands smelled and I always had my guard up. But Rose – maybe this wasn't the first time it had happened to her, just the first I noticed enough to make her tell.

"What can I do?" She said, pulling her arm loose from mine.

"Don't go back. I'll go by Fine's in the morning and tell them you're sick and if you don't get better I'll be by to pick up your wages on Saturday. Monday you'll get another job. They say all the sewing shops are hiring now."

"You'll do that for me?"

"Of course, it's nothing. You can't let that bully treat you like a whore."

"Maybe it's my fault, I did something – "

"That sounds like Aaron's talk, 'A woman is the downfall of every man.' If that were true, why would they say 'fallen woman' but not 'fallen man'? You can see how the men are still on their feet, while it looks to me that it's women and girls who get knocked down."

Rose pulled one shoulder up to her ear and dropped it. "What will I tell Mama?"

"The truth."

"But maybe she won't let me work anymore."

"She'll let you. It's busy season and you can make more in the

factory than doing piecework at home. Besides, if you quit Fine's, she'll know you can stand up for yourself – she'll trust you more."

We shuffled up the four flights slowly, sighing at every cockroach that skittered out of our way. We were going to move to one of the new buildings where they had hot water and toilets in every apartment, but Isadore was out of work after the Christian New Year, and then Rose. For awhile it was just my wages, Bina's piecework and whatever Harry gave in. He said he couldn't just hand over his whole pay envelope like a girl; he had expenses. So instead of moving we got a boarder, Leon. He slept on a cot across the kitchen from Aaron and Harry, snoring worse than anyone. It was a busy season in tailoring too, and often Leon wasn't back until midnight.

Aunt Bina took her thimble off when we told her why Rose had to quit. She looked at her daughter. "You're all right?"

"Yes, Mama, I didn't let him touch me." Her voice was so quiet I wondered that Bina could hear.

"Overnight, rent and girls grow," she sighed. She looked at Rose and then me, then back at Rose, starting with her shoes and going up to her hair. "You promise me, Rosele, no matter what, if this happens anywhere, any time, you always quit. I should have both my arms cut off before I'll see my daughter reduced to the level of the prostitutes on Allen Street. You promise?"

Rose looked towards the greasy pane of glass in the window and promised.

Then Aunt Bina got up and made us both bowls of sour cream with a banana sliced in. She saw how we bolted dinner before school and didn't want us to go to bed hungry. Or she wanted an excuse to keep us close to her, as if her night-time indulgence would protect us during the day. I felt too tired to eat and pushed the slices around in my bowl. Two years ago I'd never seen a banana. Rose knew it had become one of my favorite foods.

"Finish it," she said. How she spoke gave me a flicker of warmth in my breast. I turned to show her how I was spooning the bananas into my mouth, but she was staring at the bottom of her dish.

Aunt Bina started up the treadle again. Rose had been lucky to get jobs in the bigger shops where they didn't make you bring your own machine. Maybe in the smaller shops the bosses wouldn't be so quick to make advances. Probably the size didn't matter. If I thought Rose was pretty, so would men, and they could always find a reason to keep her late, alone.

The needle seemed to roar through Bina's piecework. Harry had dipped into our savings to get her the sewing machine; before that she did hand finishing and fancy embroidery but there was more money in volume. Harry shleped her piecework up the stairs himself, acting as if he were the world's most thoughtful son. Yet he never said exactly where he was working anymore. Rose and I thought he was trying to become a contractor, starting with his own mother.

"How much does Harry give you for those children's trousers?" I asked, picking up Rose's dish to wash it.

"What, you're going to organize me in my own house?" Aunt Bina didn't bother to look up.

"I just want to know."

"Enough. I think of it as payment for the sewing machine and I want to help him out a little."

I wasn't sure how she managed to think that she – we – hadn't already paid for the sewing machine. "Help him out? What kind of help could he need? He lives here, eats here – "

"He wants to rent a little shop on Delancey, see if he can start his own business."

"He's going to be a sweatshop boss?" Rose said, coming out of the far place she'd gone while eating.

"So he wants to get ahead. Is that a crime? If he does well, we'll all do well."

"But in the meantime he gets ahead on your shoulders," Rose said. I translated this out of Yiddish in my mind and realized she had made an English joke. But it was too late to explain.

I dreamed I was outside our house in Kishinev. The street was empty. I walked inside. I could see every rock in the wall, every piece of furniture, the splinters in our long kitchen table, the stained sideboard that came from my Bobe Malka's mother. I was looking down at the floor and then I heard my mama humming. She sat at the end of the table, braiding challah loaves. I ran to embrace her but she put out her hand to stop me. "Remember, you must make the offering." When she opened the oven, smoke poured out. As I reached for her my hands disappeared into a cloud of smoke. No one was there.

"Mama!"

I was embarrassed to wake up like that. It was nothing that Rose did. If I roused her, she rolled towards me, her long braid flipping over her

shoulder, and stroked my cheek. I thought of the challahs. The bed only had the sharp, familiar smells of our sweat and the kerosene we used to kill bugs. Nothing was burning.

"It's all right, all right – " Rose never complained about how often I interrupted her sleep. I couldn't get mad at her anymore for being kind. But I wished sometimes I slept alone so I wouldn't have been indebted to her for that gentleness, or that I could have done something for her, besides protecting her from bedbugs. Something she would have liked. Since Uncle Isadore was working again I thought about saving up to buy her a new jacket. I saw how she was looking at the ones with lace collars in the fancy stores on Grand Street. She would be able to get a good job if she wore a jacket like that. If I ate dry cake and tea for lunch, I could save five cents every day, borrow a little from the ticket money, have enough to get it for her birthday. Yet if I had extra money, I shouldn't spend it on a fancy coat but on Sarah's ticket.

Lena told me we were mistaken about Sarah's eye, that the inspectors look for a disease, not a deformity. Although, she said, sometimes they'll turn someone back for a deformity as well, because they think they won't be able to earn a living. I didn't think of Sarah as deformed – what did that mean? We all had the forms we were born with. She had a wandering eye. In that case, Lena said, if she came second class and wore stylish clothes, especially with me to meet her, she would probably have no problem getting in. I felt for the small rip on my side of the mattress where I secreted my nickels and dimes, and poked my finger into the hole. I could feel the texture of the stocking they were in, the edges of my deposit book. Whenever I accumulated as much as a dollar, I put it in the Jarmulowsky Bank on Canal Street, not far from where I used to slap boxes together. I understood that interest came from the accumulated sweat of workers, but I was also a worker – why shouldn't I be getting 2 per cent on the $7 I had managed to save so far?

I never told the Petrovskys I was saving for Sarah. Maybe Aunt Bina and Uncle Isadore wouldn't have wanted her to come, maybe even Rose wouldn't. After all, Sarah would have had to share the bed with us, and that was too much to ask Rose, wasn't it? In a couple of years I'd be old enough. Then I could get a bindery job and be able to afford my own place. My own room, at least. Rose could come too, if she didn't get married. Aunt Bina said now that we were in America we didn't have to worry about getting married until after we were eighteen. We should take our time. It was a relief not to think about

anyone arranging marriages for us here. If we were really free to choose, maybe I'd choose no one.

Rose fell back asleep but thinking about the future always made me restless. The *Jewish Daily Forward* was full of news about Russia – they said the Japanese had beaten the Russian armies in the east. The tsars had turned back Napoleon and they'd done a good job crushing Jews, so it was hard to understand how the Japanese could beat them. Maybe it was different in eastern Russia; Vladivostok was almost as far from Kishinev as New York. At Pesach there were pogroms again, thank God none near home. Home, I still called it, even though I knew I'd probably never see Russia again.

It was often frightening to read the paper, yet I forced myself. I had a map of Russia, that I had bought for three cents from a pushcart book peddler, beneath my underwear in the bureau. When Rose didn't look, I circled the towns where pogroms happened. Since April I had made twenty-two new circles, and not every atrocity was reported over the telegraph. But now there was a big railroad strike, the *Forward* said. All over Russia strikes were breaking out in every industry, every city – was there going to be a revolution? For a moment I regretted leaving. Wouldn't that have been something, to be in Russia for the overthrow of the Tsar! But then what would happen? There'd be the Bund, the Social Democrats, Saul's Social Revolutionaries... . Sometimes I pictured a way to understand the whole world, stretching my mind across history and everyday events, like a puzzle in the shape of a snake. But every time I thought I'd worked out the puzzle, the snake shifted and I had to give up.

I went to sit on the fire escape in the last bit of dark. It was chilly with that warm October undercurrent, the last-minute dowry summer gives the fall. I should have been getting dressed since I had to go by Fine's for Rose and be at Polstein's by seven o'clock. On the fire escape I could fill my lungs for a minute, at least the landlord was right about that. Down in the street the first pushcarts were moving into place. I listened to their squeaky wheels, the cough of sick horses, the cotton softness of Rose's breath.

Sometimes I'd find myself scribbling down a few lines. I thought of them as pictures. From my entire childhood in Kishinev, what did I have? One photograph. But if I could make an outline of someone with words, I'd be able to hold them in my memory. I wouldn't always live

with the Petrovskys, I knew. From time to time I would be struck with the desire not to forget: a gesture, the way the circles of gas light reflected a small bit of red in Aunt Bina's hair.

> *In Russia, revolution.*
> *In New York, sewing machines*
> *on layaway.*
>
> > *Late, even my Aunt*
> *would sometimes stop stitching*
> *when she thought we were asleep*
> *looking around guilty, frowning,*
> *would sigh, pick up*
> *the* Jewish Daily Forward
> *and read.*

"Aunt Bina, did you see this headline?" I asked, pulling the paper from under a pile of her ribbons.

"No, Aaron or Ephraim left it here. I've been too busy with this trimming to look."

"That must be what had the streets in such a commotion," Rose said, looking over my shoulder.

"What is it?" Bina turned towards us for the first time since we'd come in, troubled.

I pointed to a column halfway down the page. "There was a pogrom in Odessa. The revolution is crushed."

"No! In Odessa? What else does it say?"

" 'The Tsar was only pretending to give in to the cry for reform... He unleashed the forces of the nether world... There were attacks everywhere as if by prearranged signal... Jews and the intelligentsia are the chief targets... In Odessa estimated losses in the millions of rubles, over two hundred dead, three thousand homeless' – two hundred dead!"

Aunt Bina put the trousers down. She looked around the tenement room, at the air shaft window where moldy dust clung like carpeting, the piles of sewing and rags, a rabble shouting for attention. She put a hand over her face.

Rose and I had come home for a quick dinner before night school. Now Rose put her arms around her mother, her head on Bina's shoulder. I could see them looking together at their friends, their relatives, their old streets, their synagogue, di alte heym. They got out.

When Mama and Papa were killed, Aunt Bina decided it was time. How can you know when to leave? Sometimes you know, but how? My sister Esther stayed, as if it were still possible to make an ordinary life in Russia. Everyone acts as if death happens to someone else. Even if it happened to your half-sister, was that enough to make you give up everything, flee the country where you were born? What made Aunt Bina know that bribes would be useless when the mobs came? Bina had said to Isadore, "I don't care about the shop, the garden, the house – we have to go." Out of Russia, away from Odessa with its great opportunities for Jews. Rose never saw a pogrom, she said, God willing she'll never have to.

Rose looked at her mother, then at me. I looked away. She never saw a pogrom, but I – suddenly I felt as if my heart was a pile of broken rock dropping through my stomach into my shoes. I could see my yellow-stained hands gripping the back of a chair, my knuckles turning white. Bina gestured Rose over to me. Rose took my hand. I could feel the calluses on her fingertips from sewing, the softness of her palm, but I couldn't respond. Rose pulled up a chair and sat down beside me, stroking the back of my hand, humming, very quietly, the folksong, "What a Beautiful Night."

An old love song seemed an odd choice. Then I heard the melody for the lyrics, *I swear I'll never forget you until death*. Did my mother still remember me? Was she humming like Rose, somewhere above us, while she stitched the evening onto clouds with her mother, and her mother before her? My mother was so sweet. When my stomach hurt she'd bring me a plate of hot soup. I sucked in my cheeks and closed my eyes. Tears came anyway but I held my breath so as to make no sound. Rose got another chair, pushed me into it gently, her hands on my shoulders. I put my head against Rose's belly and shook. Rose gathered me in her arms, humming still. Bina lit the gas stove to heat water. Rose smoothed my hair.

"Maybe tonight we should skip class? We could rest – it wouldn't be a sin," she said after awhile.

I looked up at Rose and then sat straight. Although she had poured herself around me like honey, her forehead was creased and I could see fear flickering behind her face. I noticed she'd torn one of her fingernails to the quick and it was bleeding a little.

"No, tonight of all nights we should go. There'll be news from Odessa and we can see if there are words in English for these things."

"English, Yiddish, Russian – how many languages do you need to

say anti-Semite?" Bina said through clenched teeth, pouring tea into glasses for us, with lumps of sugar to suck on the side.

Rose didn't want to sit across the room from Chava, but Chava motioned for her to take the empty seat by the radiator.

"Students, please!" Mrs. Kaufman hit the ruler on her desk. She'll need more than a ruler to keep order tonight, Rose thought as she pushed her way past the Italian girls who stood at the back of the room, uneasy, talking to each other. One of them, a girl who was taller than Chava, was chewing on a lock of her long hair. Rose wanted to tell them what had happened, but how? What did the Italians know about Russia, anyway? Probably more than she knew about Italy, she realized.

At first the teacher was reluctant to give up her lesson plan, but she gave in to the majority, as she called the Jews, to what they wanted translated from the Yiddish dailies. She wrote the words "majority rule" on the blackboard first. One of the shop owners from Houston Street was impatient.

"How do you say in English 'coward,' 'murderer'?"

"What about 'reactionary'?" Chava called out. Rose swiveled to look at Chava over her shoulder. Reactionary, she thought, that's too polite a word for what they did. But maybe Chava wanted to avoid words that would make others pry into her life. Rose blew a stream of air through her lips.

"Students, students, one at a time," the teacher begged. "Rose Petrovsky, what did you read that you want to translate?"

"Rape," Rose said, her face set hard.

Someone giggled. Chava stared at the girl so intently she started to cough and had to leave the room. Rose smiled at Chava, and they turned back to see that the teacher's ears were bright red. But she wrote the English word "violation" on the board for them.

Rose admired Chava's anger, the way she held herself, how she always had an answer or a question when someone was trying to push her around. She was glad she'd picked such a terrible word for the teacher to start with. Chava would know she could be serious too.

With her pencil Rose scratched Chava's name across the grain of wood on her desk, "Chava" standing out strong against the pattern of a hundred names scratched in before. She looked over the mass of heads to the coats on their hooks, the lace-collared jacket Chava had given

her as a present when she turned sixteen last week.

"Just because I'm sixteen?" Rose had asked.

Chava shrugged. "Yes, and for your new career setting in sleeves. Besides, you have been very kind to me," she said formally.

Chava's stiffness made Rose want to hold her the way she did at night after the bad dreams.

"I don't look for a reward from being nice to you – it's easy."

"You don't like the jacket?" Chava asked.

I love the jacket, Rose thought, looking at it in the classroom. But here I am, loving a jacket while people, Jews, are being killed in Russia. She felt bad for being so easily distracted, not as dedicated as Chava. Chava, she's seen real suffering.

Rose and I were allowed to close the door to our room because of Leon's presence – a boarder, a grown man, not just family – in the house. I sat fiddling with the laces of my boots.

"Tell me what you're thinking about, Chava," Rose asked.

Usually I said, "Nothing" or "Just how work was today." But Rose kept asking anyway. I guess she was lonely for a better conversationalist and every once in awhile I tried to do my part. That night it wasn't too hard.

"I was thinking about someone I met in Odessa."

"Someone I knew?" Rose stretched to unbutton her skirt at the side.

"I don't think you would know her. On the train ride from Kishinev, I was sitting next to my mother's midwife, Gutke. Do you remember when you met me at the station – they were there?"

"Who?"

"Gutke and – and Dovid." I realized I was lacing my shoes back up.

"No, I don't remember. Did you know them well?"

"Hardly at all, though probably she came to our shul. I only remembered Gutke a little from Sarah's being born, but my mother said if it wasn't for Gutke, I would have killed her for not wanting to come out. I was born feet first and stubborn, she said."

"She was right, absolutely right." Rose was folding her shirtwaist against her body. She came and sat beside me in her slip and corset.

I turned and knocked my knuckles against Rose's freckled shoulder. Rose hit me with the pillow.

"You don't understand what I'm saying," I whined.

"How can I understand what you're saying if you don't say anything?

Help me undo this corset, will you?"

I felt awkward, even though I'd done it a hundred times, and she noticed.

"What is it, Chava?"

"That man who was with Gutke – ."

"The one you met at the train station?"

"Yes. You don't remember?"

"Why should I?"

"Because he wasn't a man." I cleared my throat.

"What do you mean, he wasn't a man? What should he be, a dog?"

"Everything has to be a joke to you."

"Look who's talking. All right, I'm listening. So you met a man who wasn't a man – you have to admit it sounds like the beginning of a riddle."

"Hmm – I think it is a riddle." Her easiness made it easier for me. I pried my boots off.

"I give up already, so what was he?"

"A woman. He was a woman dressed to look like a man."

"Really? You know for sure?" She got up and put all her clothes in the bureau carefully, smoothing them out before she closed the drawer.

"I think so. I remember when we first got to the station, Gutke called him 'Dovida,' but 'Dovid' in front of you. And then Gutke winked at me. Yes, I'm sure. I'm sure it was a woman." I stared at a stain on the wall just to the right of Rose's shoulder. I figured I should have been undressing too but I couldn't seem to move off the edge of the bed.

"What a scandal! I never heard of such a thing."

"No, me either. That's why no one notices, I guess. They can't imagine it."

"Why would a woman do that?" Rose asked.

"I don't know. Maybe if she wanted to travel alone safely or if she wanted to be a bricklayer – ."

"A bricklayer? What girl wants to be a bricklayer? If she's going to dress like a man, she could want to be something better, a rabbi at least."

"Rabbis have to have full beards," I said. The words were a hot coal burning my mouth but I didn't want Rose to notice. "Maybe she wanted to be a student at the university."

"But wasn't he – she – old?"

"All right, maybe a university teacher or a grain trader. Men can go

anywhere they please to do business."

"Would you dress up like a man to do business?" Rose was studying me, her hands on her hips. For some reason I noticed that where her shoulder met her body, there was a little bulge of fat, just enough to curl a hand around.

"I don't know. I never thought of it, before then. I thought maybe in Odessa all kinds of strange things could be ordinary. But I never saw anyone else like that while we were there. At least that I could tell."

"I never heard about such a thing even here in New York." Rose put her foot on the bottom drawer and rolled her stocking down slowly, as if she were studying each hair on her leg.

"Maybe it's something they don't tell us about, because they think we're still children."

"Mama and Papa talk about everything with us, they think they're very modern. We shouldn't be ashamed of our minds or our bodies, they say. I don't think it's something they ever thought of either." She switched legs and rolled the other stocking off quickly.

"Well, maybe if no one can think of it, it would make it easy for them to stay invisible, keep out of the way."

"Oh, you're worried for them." Rose sat back beside me, putting her arm through mine.

"Aren't you worried for the girls you knew in Odessa?"

"Of course." Rose frowned, puzzled. "I know I should be more upset but Odessa seems so far away now, and the girls I knew – ." She moved her head from side to side. "I can only pray that God has been merciful to them. To them and to all the family we left behind." She paused, staring into the air, then she looked back at me. "Aren't you getting undressed tonight?"

"Yes, yes," I started to undo my shirtwaist. "Gutke's probably fine."

"Yes, probably." Rose started to say something else, stopped, started again. "Do you like being a girl, Chava?"

"Girl? I don't feel like a girl."

"I know, I know, you're all grown up and serious, studying so you can get out of tobacco. What I mean is, would you rather have been a boy?"

I looked at my hands, the way the yellow stain spread like an old map into the creases. "How can I know that? I could earn more money. The boys at my factory earn fifty cents a day more for doing the exact same thing I do."

"You think that's something? In garments, only the men can be

cutters, and some of them make $25 a week. You think that's hard to do? They should do what I do. But they get $10 more than the most experienced woman."

"They have families, though."

"And what? We have no obligations? We get to spend all our money on fancy waists with ribbons?"

"So maybe you're the one who'd like to be a boy?" Finally I got my shirtwaist off and stood to step out of my skirt.

Rose laughed. "No. Boys – I've had enough of them in my own house. You see how Mama spoils Harry, even when she knows he's taking advantage? And Aaron, so full of himself. Who wants to be like that?" She made a sour face for a second. "There's only one thing boys can do I wish I could."

"Oh," I smiled at her, turning the gas jets down after putting my clothes away. "What's that?"

"Kiss you." I froze, my back to her, for what seemed forever. "I'm sorry. I didn't mean to embarrass you," she said. "I was just teasing."

I turned around. Even in the shadows I could see her face was pink with blushing and her blue eyes glittering as if they were wet.

"Chava? I'm sorry, all right?"

"Don't be sorry. Just tell me the truth. Did you mean it?"

"Yes." Rose took a deep breath.

I took one too, sitting down beside her. "I also want to kiss you." I had the sensation of being on the sea again, pitch and roll, moving inside a different element, not attached to the earth anymore.

Rose leaned towards me, put her hand on my cheek to turn my face so we could see each other in the light that came from the street. I was worried, looking at her, at the olive of her face, but Rose appeared happy. "So if you want to and I want to, who starts?"

I pulled the tenement air down to the bottom of my lungs. This was harder than going out on strike. I moved my lips onto Rose's. Together. We had been lying in bed together for more than two years. Careful. Cousins. Left side, right side, I'm worn out, me too, goodnight.

No, I changed my mind as the kiss engulfed our faces and my hands found the soft flesh of her shoulders and pressed her close. This was easier than going on strike. This was easier than anything.

We didn't sleep. How could we? The borders of our bed were transformed, ran together. We had been separate countries with a

careful truce. Now I understood what internationalism really meant. I was still Chava and Rose was Rose but we traveled through each other, inside and out, without having to show identification. We opened – maybe Rose was always open and I hadn't known. Now this happened to us together. We opened and were recognized. In recognition there was a tenderness for which I was not prepared. Of course I'd heard the love songs of young girls, though mostly they were about waiting for a beloved who was unfaithful or some shlemil who went off to war. I ran my fingertip in the crease between Rose's lower lip and her chin. I wanted to ask and tell her so much, with my hands as well as with words, but we had to be silent, make all our noises sound like the ordinary sighs and moans of sleeping. Eventually, we must have slept for an hour or two before dawn.

I walked Rose to her new job at Schlessinger's Waist and Dress Company. Harry had wanted her to work for him after she quit Fine's, but even Aunt Bina agreed it would be better to keep his business separate. He laughed and said, "Well, at least if she doesn't work for me I can keep out the radical element!" I tried not to let Harry get to me. We used to have a rooster like him in Kishinev, all show of feathers, who'd run off at the first sign of trouble, leaving the hens to take care of themselves. At breakfast I got up to pour him coffee. He raised his eyebrows but I just smiled. Then he spilled the coffee down his shirt. Was it that easy to make all guilty men nervous?

On the street Rose and I didn't know how to act. It was as if the morning brought us into another world, almost exactly like the one we were in yesterday, full of stenches and exploitation. Yet this one also had soft-eyed chestnut horses pulling ice carts, the sweet taste of an apple in our mouths, clouds streaming by in the sky over the buildings, the sensation of her hand caressing my skin.

A hand! When Rose gave my hand a careful squeeze before she joined the crowd of girls going up to work, I stared at the long stains on my fingers. I didn't go to Polstein's. Instead I walked to First Street. The League door was locked and I turned to go, but then a key scraped from the inside and a woman leaned out. She looked me over.

"Nu?"

"Do you expect Lena Reznikoff today?"

"Are you a friend of hers?"

"We came together on the boat. She helped me after the strike at Samuels' box factory."

"Oh," the woman said, "you're the hero of the Children's Strike, I

remember. Come, come inside. I'm Rose Schneiderman and you're Chava, isn't that right?"

"Yes, Chava Meyer." I was surprised and pleased that she knew about me, calling me "hero." Another Rose. That I took for a sign, a good omen. At that moment everything was a good omen.

"Have you eaten? Can I get you some coffee, a roll?"

"Just some coffee, thank you." I felt very tall. Actually, I was taller than both Roses – Rose Schneiderman was very short – but it wasn't height, exactly. It was tall as if I had suddenly finished growing, was a person who had known both sorrow and a kiss, both of the big sides of life. And I was sleepy too, I realized, swallowing the strong coffee.

"Did you come down to join the League?"

"Really I came because Lena said she might be able to get me a job in a bindery. What does it mean, to join the League?"

This Rose gave one of those smiles that goes straight across the lips, without turning up. She had bright red hair, a long nose and a small, almost dainty mouth. She was much older than me, maybe older than my sister Esther, even, but she was welcoming.

"It's not always clear, even to me," she said. "Where do you work?"

"By Polstein's, stripping tobacco. A little more than a year now."

"There are good unions in tobacco, even for the girls. You have a union there?"

I showed her my local card. "But really, all we do is pay dues, nothing else."

"The union is there if you need it. You've got good conditions?"

"In tobacco I don't think there can be good conditions, because it stains you," I held up my hands to show, "and gets in your lungs. That's why I want to leave. But we usually only work ten hours, with forty-five minutes for lunch, not awful. Hard work, tedious – but where not?"

"And overtime?"

"We're supposed to get extra for overtime but usually the stewards pretend it doesn't happen." Rose made a little note. "Anyway, I would rather do something else."

"You think a bindery would be different?"

"It would be a change, and I want very much to work with books."

"Why not printing?"

I had a quick memory of the slogans on the ruined print shop wall in Kishinev. "Printing would be all right if you know of something."

"I don't. I was just asking. Myself, I used to line caps."

"You don't work in a factory any more?"

"One of the women from the League – a friend of Lillian Wald's, who started the Henry Street Settlement House – you know it?"

I nodded. Someone in my shop said they gave girls lessons in arranging flowers, which seemed very frivolous. But maybe Rose would enjoy that, to go to a settlement house and have ladies show us how to put flowers in a vase. They must have other lessons there too. Maybe she'd like an excursion to Henry Street.

"Working girls need unions first," Rose continued, "but sometimes settlement houses can help. This woman gave me a scholarship, she called it, so I could stop factory work, go to the Rand School and organize for the League."

A woman supported a working girl to go to school instead of a working boy? The whole world seemed turned inside out. I tried to imagine Aaron working so Rose and I could get an education. "What is this Rand School?"

"Socialist. I was supposed to take day courses, but it's easier to go at night. There's so much work to do among working girls during the day."

I felt a thrum in my body, a light-headed confusion. I looked at Rose Schneiderman and sighed, forgetting why I came. "If a working girl like me joined the League, what would she be expected to do?"

"Talk to the other girls where you work about the League and unions. If you're interested, we have lectures, English classes and committees."

"I'm not sure. It sounds like a good idea but I just really came to talk to Lena."

"Oh, Lena, of course. I'm sorry. Lena's in Chicago, at the national meeting of the League, with Pauline and Leonora. That's why I'm alone today. And you were looking for bindery work, isn't that right?"

"Yes." I sighed again, thinking of Lena taking a train to Chicago. How far was that? What did America look like outside of the tenement? It wasn't possible that everywhere was as crowded as New York. They had a map of the United States hanging in the high school. I imagined America was a palace, but they kept all of us immigrants standing outside, on the front steps, saying, "This is as far as you can go – isn't New York a wonder?"

Rose was writing something down again. "We have a girl on the executive committee from the bookbinders' Local 43. Already they have an eight-hour day, not a bad choice if there's work. Give me your address, and Lena or I will get in touch with you when we can find

something out, all right?"

I was still trying to grasp what it would be like to work only eight hours, six days a week. What would you do with all the time? I looked at Rose Schneiderman. Lectures, she said, committees, organizing. "Yes, thank you, and maybe I will join your League."

"Our League," she said, shaking my hand.

I was an hour and a half late to Polstein's. They said if it happened again I'd be fired; today they'd dock my wages through lunch. The forelady looked confused when I nodded pleasantly. I felt as if I was covered with fur and Rose's face kept floating beside me. Maybe I could get her something on the way home, a fancy orange wrapped in paper or a pastry from the Italian bakery. Would she like that or call me extravagant?

In between daydreams, I tried to listen to the reader. In tobacco, they had a person, usually the boss's wife or daughter or greenhorn relation, reading to the workers. Very nice. Sometimes it was just the newspaper or tales from Sholom Aleichem, sometimes even socialist essays. From one of Polstein's daughters we heard about the Haymarket Martyrs of Chicago. She was reading an essay by a Lucy Parsons, the wife of one of the men the police had killed in Chicago. What did he do? Gave a speech where a bomb was thrown. They said he caused the bomb to be thrown by his speech and they hanged him because a policeman died in the explosion. That sounded like the reasoning of the Tsar – who would believe a man threw a bomb at himself? The essay was in English but I was pretty sure I understood it all right. When there was a hard word one of the tobacco rollers would nod and repeat it quietly in Yiddish.

Polstein didn't know what his daughter was reading until she was almost finished. When he heard, he yanked her out by her collar and we worked in silence the rest of the afternoon.

All over the world at once

"A pig will study Torah before your high-society friends will knock on your door with a job," Aaron taunted. He had overheard me talking to Rose about getting a bindery job.

"They are not high society. They're working-class girls like me, organizers."

"Organizers, shmorganizers. You don't even know that most of your precious League is rich goyim."

"And how do you come to know so much, Mr. Failed-His-First-Exam?" Aaron had gotten into school last spring, finally, which made it easier to tease him.

"I heard about it in City College, from a friend of someone's sister who knows that woman, Mary Drier, who's mixed up in it. She's 'loaded,' he says."

Aunt Bina was listening while she worked. "New York sometimes is just another small town, isn't it? But," she frowned, "why would this 'loaded' – " she said the word carefully in English, mimicking Aaron, then switched back to Yiddish, "—lady get involved with union agitators?"

I took a little piece of white cheese out of the ice box. Aunt Bina had baskets she hung from the ceiling so the rats wouldn't get into our food. I reached up and pulled off a chunk of bread. "In their pamphlet they say the League is for sisterhood, for women helping women," I said as I chewed.

"That's nice," Bina said. "Don't snort like that, Aaron. Someday you'll be a married man. You should only be so good to your wife. But Chava, dear, I wouldn't hope too much on these ladies. You know what they say, 'Easy to promise, hard to fulfill.' " She peered at me across the

mountain of unsewn clothing pieces. "You didn't do anything foolish? Give up your place at Polstein's?"

"Don't worry, I know. 'If you stuff yourself with hope, you go crazy.'" Rose laughed to hear me trade proverbs with her mother like a yente.

I brought Rose a piece of bread and cheese too. I let my hand move slowly across her knuckles as she stitched, and she pretended not to notice. Usually she didn't sew at night – why should she? It was still busy in the garment industry, where she worked sometimes twelve or thirteen hours setting in sleeves. The factory wanted her there at 6:00 A.M., and sometimes kept her so late she missed night school. Then we had an excuse to go somewhere quiet, a rooftop corner behind a chimney, so I could catch her up on her lessons if she wasn't too tired and the night wasn't too cold. A little cold was good because no one looked twice at us sitting so close to each other, sharing a coat.

That night she was helping me sew a banner for the big event planned by the Jewish Defense Association, a memorial parade for the pogroms. Really, she was doing all the sewing. I designed the banner, picked out the colors from Aunt Bina's scrap basket and bought a purple background cloth from a pushcart on Hester Street. Rose embroidered where I drew the letters: "In memory of Rabbi Isaac and Miriam Meyer, murdered in Kishinev, 1903." I wanted to say something else but I was caught between quoting Torah and socialist tracts, so we left it simple. I knew Papa would have liked something from the Torah, but this way the message was clear and dignified. I didn't care anymore if people knew my parents had been killed in Kishinev. In fact, I looked forward to the opportunity of honoring their memory.

When we first heard about the parade, I showed Mama and Papa's photograph to Rose. Why I never showed it before I couldn't say. She touched the edge the way she sometimes touched my ears, gentle and curious. I was still hiding the photograph in Abramovich's verses. Rose read from the page: "And I? I suffer and keep silent./ Whom do I dare reproach?/ Whom may I embrace?" I could feel the blood rise up my neck in knotted ribbons when she read.

"That's like you are. You suffer too silently."

"I'm not always so silent."

"What you say in your sleep doesn't count. Let's put this picture on our chest of drawers. You don't have to keep it hidden."

I looked at our bedroom door. In the apartment everyone could hear everything, though if Rose and I talked fast in English, Bina, Isadore and the boarder, Leon, usually couldn't follow. But Harry knew even more

slang than us from always being out on the street, so we had to be more careful when he came in, which was usually very late.

I studied Mama's eyes. Would she mind watching how I felt for Rose now? Even if Papa could look, he wouldn't see. But Mama would have known. Maybe she would be glad I found comfort, someone to embrace.

"We should find a frame to protect it," I decided.

"On Orchard Street, we'll look tomorrow."

Just before the parade, I received a letter from Esther and Sarah.

Dear Chava,

Thank God everyone is well! I can't tell you how frightened we were this last year, with all the trouble from the agitators and intellectuals, and of course the rabble is so quick to fight on either side – anything to entertain themselves at our expense! There was a pogrom here again just four weeks ago, but all of us, thank God, came through all right. Nathan's family has a secret cellar near the river where they keep the provisions for their inn, so we were comfortable enough there, better than Shendl's chicken coop! Now that the Tsar has put down the revolution, we are doing a good business again. I am carrying my own first child. God willing, it will be born in early summer. I hope it can live without seeing the misery that we have. I was asking around for Mama's old midwife, who used to live by the spinster Golde who made my wedding dress, but no one has seen her for several years. Well, there are other midwives.

Nathan is talking about coming to America after the baby is born, but I'm not excited to go. I can't see to leave a good business behind and start all over in a new country with a newborn infant, or leave Mama's and Papa's graves. Bobe Malka is too frail now for the trip. She begins to live more and more in the past. I can't just leave her in a poorhouse or with some cousin she doesn't recognize. I know you wrote that Sarah would not have as much trouble as we were told, but I don't like to send her alone. If you tell me we should come, I will think about it again.

No one has heard from Daniel since Pesach. I'm afraid his politics may have hung him after all. We make inquiries discreetly and if we find out anything we will let you know. From Abraham we got a letter this summer. He married! He has two girls already, one and

two years old. He named the first one Miriam for Mama and the second is Rebecca. They are living in a place called Beersheba. So you and I are now aunts – mazel tov! I sent him your address in New York, so maybe he will write you also. All the violence here made me appreciate family more, so I wanted to let you know all that I could.

Your loving sister,
Esther

Dear Chava –
Esther said all the news. What is your news? I was scared in the pogrom but Bobe told me a story about how brave you were during the last one and I forgot to be scared most of the time. I want to see you again. I'm sending you a picture of me and Bobe I drew myself. Do you remember me?
Sarah

Did I remember Sarah? One footstep for Mama, one for Papa, one for Sarah, one for Daniel, one for Esther, one even for Abraham, two for my nieces I would never see, then I started again, counting in time to the beat of a drum way ahead of us on Bowery. Sarah was the third step of my marching, right after Mama and Papa. How could I forget?

It seemed as if there were a million people, as many watching as were in the street, even in this cold. I knew the East Side boiled with Jews, every day more coming from Russia, but it was something to see us all at once. Many of the marchers had political banners for the unions, the anarchists, the socialists, even for suffrage. I particularly liked the banners that had fringes on them, jiggling with the marchers' steps. And I was listening as well as looking. Even before we got to the platform for speeches in Union Square, people were arguing about how this was a memorial march, not a political one. Why didn't they ask me? It was my family. I took a deep breath and marched into the cloud of myself that formed in the winter air.

"Why couldn't they organize this for the spring?" Rose complained.

"Either it would rain or be too hot. Do you want to stop for awhile?"

"Just so I can get this pebble out of my shoe, do you mind?"

"Of course not." We stepped to the side and I took her pole, folding the banner in the middle. She put her weight on my shoulder, balancing to unlace her shoe. I stood still and serious, so no one should notice how much pleasure her closeness gave me.

"Chava!" I turned around as Rose bent over to lace up again. Lena was marching by with a group from the League. She handed her placard to someone and ran over to us. "I thought I would see you here. And who's this?"

Rose stood up and brushed a stray lock of hair from her face. "We've already met," she said.

"Of course, on the ship. You're Chava's cousin." Lena had forgotten her name. I could see Rose was annoyed. She was so social, discussing the weather and new corsets with every girl and pushcart lady on the street, that most people knew me as her cousin, not the other way around.

"Rose," she said, putting out her gloved hand very proper, "Rose Petrovsky."

"Of course, Rose, like our Rose Schneiderman, eh, Chava? I won't forget again." Lena noticed how Rose cut her eyes at me, how I smiled back. "So – ." She rubbed her hands together and jiggled up and down. Lena's jacket must have been even thinner than mine. "So I heard you had a nice talk with Rose Schneiderman?"

I nodded. "Under these gloves, my hands have turned to mud from tobacco so I went – "

"I know. I was going to come by after the parade and leave a note for you. Over at Harriman's Bindery they're hiring. They've got a couple of places now, from girls getting married. Go by on Monday morning, on Broadway by Spring Street. Tell them you're the one Nellie Quick sent."

"Nellie Quick?"

"She's the bindery union's representative at the League. If you last three weeks, you've got to join the union."

"I'm happy to. Thank you." I looked at her calm green eyes. "Thank you very much. I thought maybe you'd forgotten me."

"Forget you? No such luck. We're counting on you to lead the youth brigade of the revolution with Pauline." She clapped me on the shoulder as a comrade.

Rose hoisted her side of the banner pole. "We should get back in the march, Chava."

Lena looked at our handiwork. "Very nice," she said, looking at me as if to say, You see, I knew all along about your parents. "I have to go find the rest of the League myself. See you at headquarters. Goodbye, Rose Petrovsky, a pleasure seeing you again." She ran ahead, between the crowd on the sidewalk and the legions of marchers.

"What was that about seeing you at headquarters? And who's Pauline?"

"A girl our age who works over at Triangle Shirtwaist. They say she's already organizing strikes but I never met her. Lena didn't mean anything, she was just being friendly."

"Not just friendly. She got you a job, now she expects you to pay her back, you'll see."

"It's not like you to think the worst of someone. And what would be so bad if I did some work for the League? Do you know the bookbinders already have an eight-hour day? I'll have so much time now."

"You could do other things with your time."

"What? I would spend it with you but you're at work too. Don't be jealous, Rose. It's politics."

"I'm not jealous." A man carrying a banner from the landslayt organization of L'vov turned around and looked at us for a second. Rose straightened her pole and squared her shoulders, looking ahead. "I just don't want you to get swept away in some political fever, like Daniel and Saul."

"I'm not like Daniel or Saul."

She turned to show me her grin. "Thank God for that!"

The forelady at Harriman's, Miss Wolfe, was stocky and brusque, constantly taking in every detail. She was one of those German Jews who'd been here a generation already and fussed about the bad manners of us Russian newcomers. Right away I liked her, even if she wasn't so sure about me. A warmth hid beneath her suspicious nature, at least that was how I read her. Miss Wolfe showed me the different work stations. The only places for women were at the sewing table, gluing area and folding machine. What was I expecting, that they'd teach me how to make fancy decorations in the leather? It was just another factory, with noisy contraptions and sewing, no less. Also plenty of paper dust, but at least Harriman's was cleaner than anywhere I'd worked so far.

"Gluing or sewing?" Miss Wolfe asked.

The sewing machines looked like a cross between a weaver's loom and the machines Rose and Aunt Bina used. "Gluing," I said.

"Any experience?"

"I worked gluing in a paperbox factory – "

She cut me off with a sharp laugh. "Here we make books. You'll see

it's very different."

"Oh, I know. I always wanted to work with books. My brother is a printer."

"With whom?"

"In Russia."

She gave me a look as if Russia wasn't a word in English, not one that a lady would say. "Well. We'll see how you do. You have two weeks' probation. Gluers get $7 a week to start, $7.50 after probation, $8 after a continuous year. Reva will show you what to do."

Miss Wolfe abandoned me as quickly as she could. I stared down at my dress to see if maybe I still looked too much like a greenhorn.

"Don't worry," Reva said, "she's like that with almost everyone. She softens up if you're good at your job."

"I will be."

Reva laughed. "I'm sure you will. It's easy. Here, I'll show you."

By my seventeenth birthday I was making $7.50 a week. I had almost enough saved for a second-class ticket, though every time I went by the steamship company, they'd raised the price. Some American with his hair plastered down over his forehead and smelling of cheap whiskey would laugh and say, "Supply and demand, sweetheart."

"I'm not your sweetheart."

"You'll never be anyone's with that attitude."

I didn't pay any attention. In a year maybe I'd have enough saved. I knew Esther. If I sent the ticket, she wouldn't say no, because Sarah's leaving would relieve her and Nathan from making a dowry. Sarah was almost fourteen but I didn't want her to go right to work like I had. She should go to school and learn something besides factory work. Typewriting was good work for women, I'd heard, or maybe she'd like to be a teacher. If she went to school, what I brought in would have to be enough for both of us. The ticket would take up everything I had in the bank, so it was foolish to think of getting my own place now, when everyone said the economy was bad.

What made a bad economy? Something spoiled that capitalism had eaten, that gave it a sour stomach? New York was full of Russians who came after the failed revolution – they had to eat, sleep, work somehow. Wasn't that the way an economy worked? But maybe it was just the same as the Pale: not enough work to go around so everyone had to eat each other's fleas.

Good or bad, it was time to talk with Aunt Bina about having Sarah

live with us. We'd have to get a cot for her to sleep on in the room with Rose and me. But that wouldn't be so great, would it? What had I been thinking? Rose would be furious. How could it be all these months I had two people on separate sides of my mind – Sarah and Rose – and never put them together? Maybe I would wait until Rose and I got a place of our own, if the Petrovskys would ever let us. But would that be fair to Sarah? And Rose, would it be fair to Rose? And maybe Rose wouldn't want to leave her mama ... Oy!

"Hello, dear." Aunt Bina looked up for a second when I came in. "Did you get that fish for dinner?"

"Right here. But it looks like you were out already today." I motioned to the wall where a new portrait was hanging: Lincoln, in a thin wooden frame.

"I was just out for a few minutes. I can't sit all day like I used to, my legs fall asleep. And I have to get out now and then, find out what's new. Besides, Chava, you always pick out a good fish from Yankovich's. What they sell by Hester Street is only fit for cats."

"Mama, you're the best cook on Essex Street. Don't pretend you're not!" Rose came in from the bathroom, went to the sink to wash. Her shirtsleeves were rolled up and I watched a dribble of water flow down the outline of her arm, catch at her elbow, make a spot on the fabric. She looked at me over the drying towel and winked.

"You think you're paying me a compliment? All I should want in life is to be your cook?"

"Okay, so I'll cook tonight," Rose said. Rose was turning out to be a better cook than Bina.

"No you won't. You worked all day, you need a few minutes to relax. You don't go to class tonight?"

"It's Monday, Mama. I thought after dinner Chava and I would go to the baths. We could use a good shvits, but that doesn't mean I shouldn't cook. You're the one working all day."

"Didn't I just say I was out in the afternoon? Only slice some onions and garlic, all right, dear?"

Rose and I were chopping and flicking our onion tears at each other when Uncle Isadore arrived.

"So what's this?" Isadore asked. He didn't even bother to greet us. Rose shook her head. Bad news.

"It's a portrait of Abraham Lincoln, who freed the African slaves. I

213

got it in the Hester Street market for forty cents." Bina didn't look away from her needle.

"I know who it is. You think I haven't learned anything about this country? But you didn't ask me if you can buy a picture."

"Did I ask you about the curtains? Since when do you boss the walls around here?" She sighed and looked up. "You got laid off again?"

He shrugged, hung up his hat. I noticed a lot of stains around the brim. We would have to get him a new one if he had to look for a job.

"Slow season again, even by watches." Isadore picked up the *Forward* and rustled the pages, end of conversation.

"You know," I said slowly, not used to having so much room to form my thoughts, and hoping to change the mood, "just because Abraham Lincoln made the, the emancipation – ."

"Very nice, very nice English words," Uncle Isadore mumbled from behind the paper.

" – doesn't mean he would have been interested in freedom for the workers."

"What are you talking about?" Rose asked, making a little pile of our choppings as she heated up the frying pan.

"I mean, the President, any president, is still like the Tsar."

"You're calling Abraham Lincoln the Tsar? God in heaven!" Bina said, working a little faster now that she knew Isadore wasn't. When she shifted the pile of piecework, the dust made me sneeze.

"Remember we learned how the Tsar freed the serfs?" I asked.

"It's not the same," Rose stopped cooking and looked at me. "I learned in English class, like you. Abraham Lincoln was a great man who wanted to see freedom." I liked the way she stood with one hand on her hip. Still, I didn't want to be distracted.

"But I was listening to the anarchists talk in Washington Square – "

"Oy, the anarchists again, I might have known," Bina said.

Isadore snorted. "Anarchists, syndicalists, socialists – in the park you can listen to a hundred opinions, but opinions aren't onions. You try to take those Chaim Yankls seriously, you'll starve."

"But don't you think the state is just a big company, run to profit the rich?" I asked. "And the President is like the boss of that company?"

"I suppose a president is like a boss, but a president is elected by the people, the boss elects himself," Rose said.

"That's good, Rose, that's good thinking." Isadore glanced at her for a second, then raised the paper again.

"Still, the President is looking out for all the bosses," I persisted,

annoyed with Rose for taking her papa's side.

"And for all the workers too," Isadore said without looking up again.

"I think the President only cares about the workers enough so we don't revolt. So it looks like he cares. You know the government forces us – "

Now Isadore put down his paper. "Forces us to do what? Who's forcing you to do anything? You want to work for the unions, fine. I can see that working men, and ladies, have to band together sometimes, the bosses shouldn't take advantage of us." He stopped and grimaced, pulled out his pocket watch, made a show of opening and closing it. "You think we could do that in Russia without facing a band of Cossacks? You forgot already?"

"Isadore – ." Bina tried to shush him. I stared at his face.

"All right, that I shouldn't say to you. But we came here for freedom and freedom we got. We were always working people. Sometimes we had good times, sometimes not so good, like now. But I don't want any more of this anarchist talk in my house. Bina, I'm glad you bought that picture of Mr. Lincoln. It looks nice where you hung it – now I don't have to try to fix that hole. You, Chava, you," he shook his finger at me, at the same time turning his face away. "You're like Saul, always looking for trouble."

"I don't have to look," I said almost in a whisper.

"When I was a boy we talked respectful to our elders. Just because you get a paycheck doesn't mean you can treat me with disrespect."

"I don't mean to be disrespectful, Uncle. I just am trying to figure things out for myself." I noticed now that Isadore got laid off so often he wasn't quite the freethinker he had been in Odessa.

"For yourself!" Isadore's head bobbed up and down. "If you would take the trouble to learn from your teachers and your aunt and me, you would have a lot less problems in life, isn't that right, Bina?"

"Hmm," Bina replied. She had a mouthful of pins.

"You too are going to contradict me? I'm the only one who will stand up for America in this house?"

"I didn't say I wasn't for America, Isadore, really." Bina looked longingly for a second at her pins after she spit them into her hand. "The girls have to figure it out themselves. Chava can't know why the anarchists are wrong if she doesn't know what they're saying."

"She can take my word for it! I've had enough of this," he said. "I'm going out to talk to men, not to children. Just save some supper cold for me."

I looked over my shoulder at Rose, who gestured what-did-you-expect, and turned back to the frying pan.

"Goodnight, girls," he said, pushing the wobbly chair back, a little more cheerful now that we'd given him an excuse to go to his landslayt club. "Goodnight, Bina. Don't wear your eyes out doing that!" She gave him a look he couldn't see. As he went out the door Isadore looked at the wall. "And goodnight to you too, Mr. Lincoln."

While the fish was cooking I went down the hall to the toilet. I could see that Rose had cleaned it before I came home. It was almost never this bearable unless she did. The janitor was supposed to make sure it was sanitary, but that would have meant keeping a twenty-four-hour guard on every floor. The tiny room was the only private place in the building, providing someone wasn't banging to get in or you didn't find a rat keeping you company. It was the same size as a coffin and almost as dark. Sometimes I thought we'd be stuck on Essex Street forever.

"So, Mama, maybe we shouldn't go by the baths tonight, since Papa got laid off." Rose was setting the table when I returned. Neither of them seemed upset about the fight with Uncle Isadore. Leon had come home and Aaron was back from City College, reading his books. When all the men were home our kitchen was as crowded as a sweatshop, but just two of them wasn't too bad.

"Don't talk foolishness. We aren't so desperate that you can't keep clean."

I looked at Rose. She gave me a smile no one else noticed. Maybe she just said that to keep everyone from knowing how much we wanted to go to the baths. But then, it was coming on slow season and Rose might get laid off too. And Leon. And me, only binderies didn't have the same slow season, something to be grateful for.

Aaron looked up from his studying. "You know Mama, we heard this week a man from the police department give a talk – "

"They're going to teach college students how to beat up workers too?" I was trying to keep the mood light, only teasing him.

He scowled. "Everything by you is politics and you don't even know from politics." Aaron turned back to Bina. "As I was saying, he told us that after two years of college we could take the police exam and be hired right away."

Everybody looked at him in amazement. Leon, who liked to stay out of our family discussions, found his voice first. "The police? The police? My God, Aaron!" he could barely croak.

"Look, Leon, the whole Lower East Side's controlled by the Irish,"

Aaron said. "Why should they get paid to walk around our neighborhoods? I'd do a better a job."

"Think, Aaron, what kind of job they'll ask you to do," Leon implored.

"I know sometimes it will be hard."

"Hard?" Rose said, looking perplexed.

"Hard. But better me than some Irish man with a grudge against Jews in the first place."

"You're going to have to work with those Irish every day," I said.

He threw up his hands as if we were flies bothering him. "I knew I should have talked to Ma alone."

"What about finishing college? Your father was hoping you'd want to be a lawyer," Bina raised her eyebrows at him. It was the first time that night I'd seen her turn away from her sewing completely.

"College takes a long time," Aaron said, "and we all know Papa isn't doing so well here. You know what a beginning policeman makes?"

"Enemies," I said. He pretended he hadn't heard.

"Thirty dollars a week! On that a man could afford even to get married."

Bina stood up and stared at him. "You're planning to get married?

A guilty look crossed Aaron like a cold wind. "I'm just saying, Mama. Think of what a help $30 a week would be."

She shook her head. "Come and eat. I don't want to hear any more of this."

"But – "

"I said no more. I know you'll do what you want to do, the same as your brother did, but you don't have to spoil our evening. Speaking of brothers, where's Ephraim?"

"I saw him on Second Avenue, by the theater, missus," Leon said. "I'm sorry, I forgot. He said not to wait for him for dinner."

On Monday nights the Turkish baths were crowded. We sat together on the wooden bench, sweating, taking in deep breaths. I passed my chunk of ice to Rose and she licked it, knowing I was watching.

"Look," I said, holding up my hands, pressing my thigh close to hers, "almost all the yellow is gone already."

Rose retucked her towel and reached for my right hand. She turned it over, inspecting it in the steam. I closed my eyes. Every touch was loaded with double meanings. In the bathhouse women scrubbed each other's backs, slapped their friends' rears, pinched cheeks and

whatever fat they could get between their fingers, admiring, commenting. Women groaned and sighed taking off their corsets, running their fingers along the indentations left by the tight lacings, mumbling about what they went through for men.

"Men," someone said. "You just want to look stylish for the other girls in the workroom. You don't have a boyfriend."

"But I'm looking."

"Always looking," another voice registered, "is better than having babies and cooking."

"Look who's talking, Miss-Dances-With-Strangers."

"So I like to have a good time. With a hundred dance halls in my neighborhood, I should deprive myself? What Papa doesn't know doesn't start an argument."

The women laughed. A good time, the young women sighed. America was a balloon filling with the sighs of immigrant women. Here the world was open to us, we could go without chaperones, earn our own way, pay to stand in the Yiddish theater even if we sometimes nodded off on our feet. We could discuss politics with socialists, literature with published poets in cafés, and whether God was really dead with anyone who'd listen. If we didn't fall asleep. If we could find an hour, if there were more hours in a day.

I closed my eyes and listened. The steam seeped under my lids and gave me a dizzy image of women floating, laying their heads on each other's bellies, entwining their arms, rolling their breasts along each other's sides in a cascade of flesh. Could it really be only me and Rose who had this feeling for each other?

I blinked open in the heat. Everywhere, pairs and circles of friends. In the corner were the two women from our English class who ran the grocery on Houston, who said they were sisters. Grown women, maybe thirty or forty, one was rubbing the other's shoulders. No one paid them any attention. But usually when women rubbed each other, the rubbing one was distracted, concentrating on her job but looking somewhere else, at a spot on the wall. Between these two there was only a smiling that went back and forth. Were they really sisters? Did they hunger for each other? But of course they were old already, and they had their own shop. If they wanted each other, there they were.

"I see you're still biting your fingernails," Rose said.

"What?"

"Your hands look better, but you should file the nails, not bite them."

"Why?"

"So your touch is smoother," she whispered.

By the time they got home it was almost eleven. That was the trouble with going to the baths on Mondays, Rose thought. It made Tuesday a plague. Every week we vow we'll simply get clean and leave, but instead Chava gets asked to be in a poker game or I end up commiserating with a girl down the block about a terrible love affair or plead to stop for an eggcream on the corner until Chava gives in – actually, getting back before eleven was early. But it didn't keep her from complaining.

"I'm tired of these sweatshops, Chava, I'm plain tired. I still like sewing, but I can't keep working like this. We didn't work this way at home, not even the poorest people worked like this."

"How do you know how the poorest people worked?" Chava rubbed her face. Rose could see how the flicker of the gas jet bothered her. Chava wasn't the only one who wished the landlord would put the electricity in already – as if that miser would have wasted money on improvements.

"I never saw girls of sixteen work like we do," Rose said.

"I'm seventeen."

"All right, it's the same, isn't it? It wears us both out. Shlep, yes, we shleped – look, I had to make meals every day for all my brothers and mend their clothes. But we never worked on Shabbes, and no one would make us work in conditions like these."

"Conditions? Look at you, all clean and relaxed from the steam. So, we'll be sleepy at work. Tomorrow you be extra careful not to put the needle through your finger." Chava made a motion to kiss Rose's fingers but she pulled them away.

"I'm serious, Chava. Now that you're a bookbinder you get at least an extra hour a day than me, and you forget how important an hour is. We never grabbed at hours this way back home."

"Then we were lucky – and young. You forget all those beggars who lived underneath Odessa, in the catacombs. Some of them were girls like us. I know there were factories in Russia where whole families worked all day and then slept under their work tables in mud at night. My brother told me. What do you think the revolution is about? Why do you think we join unions? Everywhere around the world it's horrible what they do to us."

"That's all I was trying to say, Chava. It's horrible what they do to us.

You don't have to get up on your soap box and give me another lecture." Rose let her hair down, all crinkled from the steam in the baths. It took a long time to brush out on Monday nights.

"Maybe I do have to get on my soap box once in awhile. Is that so bad?" Chava took the hairbrush from Rose, standing behind her with one hand on Rose's shoulder, brushing slow, stopping to press the bristles gently into the middle of her back. Rose inhaled sharply, lifting her shoulders up.

"I used to think the revolutionaries were as much show-offs as anything," Chava continued. Rose wondered how she could concentrate on politics when her fingers felt so delicious pressing into her skin. "But now, if everybody feels this way, how can the bosses stop it? Wouldn't it be great if there was a revolution all over the world at once?"

Rose sighed. How come they could talk freely about revolution but not about how getting her hair brushed excited her, how she would rather have grabbed Chava's wrist and pulled her close? Rose answered in the language Chava was speaking, the language her family expected to hear coming from their room, if they happened to be listening.

"I don't know – it's not so long since the revolution in Russia was crushed, don't forget," Rose said. "And if it started up again, all over the world, it might be very frightening, more than you realize."

"It would be a great opportunity, an amazing time. Think how lucky we would be to be there when everything changed!"

"Ow! Be careful with that brush!"

"I'm sorry." Chava bent close to Rose's ear and whispered, "Sweetheart."

By then Rose was annoyed. "So what would happen in your great revolution? The old bosses get thrown out and then there would be new bosses."

"Just because your papa says that every time I talk about socialism doesn't mean it's true. Suppose the workers ran things? Suppose you and I got to run a committee?"

"At seventeen they're going to make you a big American committee lady? Who have you been talking to? Emma Goldman invites you over for dinner?"

"You don't understand. I heard at the league Pauline Newman's going to run for office with the Socialist Party."

"That's ridiculous. What man would vote for a woman? Give me that hairbrush."

"You don't understand." Chava sat hard on the corner of the bed.

"Don't keep telling me I don't understand. Just because you always have big ideas and talk strike with Lena Reznikoff and Rose Schneiderman doesn't mean you know everything." Rose could tell Chava was feeling sorry for herself from the way she stuck out her lip while looking at the floor, but whether it was because Rose didn't have the same passion for revolution or had taken away the hairbrush was hard to determine. Seeing Chava pout made Rose soften a little. Chava was so earnest, so dedicated.

"Well, I know more than you."

"That's not fair." Rose unsoftened, banged the hairbrush on the bureau and started to braid her hair up again.

"Rose, I'm just teasing you."

"Well, I'm tired of you teasing, and I'm tired of talking about revolutions that aren't going to happen and I'm tired. I'm going to bed."

"Come, don't be upset with me." Chava used her softest pleading voice. "Tell me what would cheer you up."

Rose stopped and considered Chava for a minute, finishing the second braid. All these difficult nights, where they had to sew their love for each other into hidden pockets in their flesh, as if they were still greenhorns in danger of being robbed on the way. On the way to where?

"Poetry," she was surprised to hear herself say. "Poetry would cheer me up."

"Poetry? Like Pushkin, you want poetry?"

"Well, you know everything, you have all kinds of words, you could have a little poetry for me." Rose sat beside Chava, taking her hand.

"Poetry!" Chava cleared her throat and thumped her free fist against her chest. "All right then, Russian poetry:

> *The eagles fly over foreign cities*
> *that were our homes.*
> *Little poppies on the steppes are in bloom.*
> *My heart is the mother country,*
> *and your eyes are the stories of my people.*
> *Come close and look upon me,*
> *that I may read my own history."*

Chava stopped, startled with herself. And then threw her head back. Seventeen and proud. "That wasn't so bad!"

"If you do say so yourself. But go ahead, write it down." Rose gave her a little push.

"See, you liked it." Chava looked over at the closed door. "But really, you know I feel that way about you," she whispered.

"Sha," Rose said, then raised her voice, focusing somewhere over Chava's head. "I have to get ready for bed."

"But Rose – ," Chava was beginning to whine. Rose could see that she was puzzling her. I puzzle myself sometimes, she thought. When I'm not too tired, when no one is in the house, it's easier to respond. But on nights like this it's hard to admit we kiss, stifle cries while our fingers go to each other's nipples under our sleeping gowns. I know I hurt Chava when I turned away. I didn't want to hurt her but sometimes I can't help myself.

Chava put her head in her hands as Rose went out the door to the toilet. When she got back, she found Chava at the kitchen tap, letting the rusty water overflow their washstand pitcher, watching the swirl go down the drain. Chava jumped when she felt Rose's hand on her back.

"Come read to me a little in bed, poet," Rose tried to speak calmly and quietly, as if this was the normal way cousins spoke to each other. Chava sensed the way Rose was relaxing towards her, and smiled. Leon coughed in his sleep or his awareness, while Aaron continued to snore.

Chava took the pitcher into their bedroom and Rose closed the door carefully. Then Chava found something very old fashioned to read and Rose lay on her stomach, smoothing the wrinkles in Chava's nightgown.

"Those girls," Isadore said, a few nights later.

"What is it, Isadore?" Bina was stitching, sitting by the air shaft, trying to extract breathable air from four stories of decomposing garbage. It was early still, 8:30 on a July night. The last bit of light made shadow patterns down the shaft. Sometimes she pretended it wasn't piecework, but just a little something she did when she felt like it, for treat money, to help out Ephraim. He insisted it was still hard going, getting his shop to operate at a profit. She knew he underpaid the greenhorns he found at the ferry docks. She sighed. What had Isadore asked her? "What about the girls?"

"They're getting too close."

"Too close!" She looked at the dust filtering through the air shaft and shook her head. "Maybe you'd like to buy us all an apartment building?"

"That's not what I mean. Don't you notice how they are together?

How Rose sighs when Chava reports about Emma Goldman's speeches? How Chava spoils Rose, gives her the best food from her plate? One night I think I heard them kissing."

"Kissing? Iz, really."

"Please, it's enough they call me Iz uptown. You don't have to use that silly nickname too."

"Excuse me, Isadore."

"All right," he cleared his throat, folding his newspaper carefully. "So, you were going to say?"

"Say? Oh, the girls. You know, in the bathhouses of Russia girls kissed each other all the time. Better they should try it out first on each other than some dance hall Casanova. It's their energetic time of life, and we should be grateful they have any energy left at the end of their day."

"All right, all right, you're the mama. What do I know about girls? Just what I read in this new Bintel Brief advice section Mr. Cahan started in the *Forward*." He put the paper on the table and tapped it for emphasis. "Sometimes I think I don't know anything about boys, the way Saul and Ephraim turned out."

"They're not so bad. We just have to keep praying for Saul, that he should be careful. But since he went to organize over in Austria, I think he'll be all right. And Ephraim – now he's an American boy, your Harry. Isn't that what you wanted?"

"A bum is a bum. I don't like the way he smart talks everyone. I want us to do well here, don't get me wrong, but I don't like his get-rich-quick schemes."

"You didn't have a few schemes once? Listen to you, Mr. Always-Upright. He'll be okay. By me, it's Aaron you should worry about."

"Just because he studies to take the policeman's exam? What a country, that a Jewish boy could join the police."

"You think the Irish of New York are better than the Russians in Odessa?" She stared at him. The easygoing, liberal watchmaker she married had disappeared – or been covered over, like a tenement wall with layer after layer of wallpaper. This new pattern was very plain, picked out by someone trying to piece together many different people's tastes, not following their own heart. She inhaled and took up her needle.

"That's the trouble with you, Bina, your nose is so much in that sewing. I wanted something else for him too, but I have to accept his decision. There are no pogroms in America. To be a policeman is honest, steady work. A living, even."

"But there are strikes. It could happen that he would have to shoot at his friends – or worse, God forbid, his own sister."

"Strikes! You're all the time shushing anyone who talks about the workers or revolution at your table, now you're going to let Rose go out on strike? You wouldn't let my baby walk a picket line?" He went over to her and lifted her chin from the sewing, trying to joke.

She exhaled, attempting to cover her amusement. "Rose isn't going out on any strike. Not now, but we won't always be able to forbid her. I'm just saying, what if?"

"What if? What if we got some sleep tonight, what if that, huh, missus?"

"It's early, Iz. I need to finish this."

"Again with the Iz?"

"All right, all right. But don't you let your drinking friends call you Iz?"

"It's not the same. In my house I want to be treated like a person, with respect."

"You know you have my respect, Mr. Petrovsky. Now let me finish."

"Finish, finish. It's my fault. If I could get a promotion – ."

"You're doing well, you work hard, no one blames you. You'll learn English a little better and they'll promote you, you'll see. We have enough to eat. In a few months, God willing, we can look for a bigger place, I think."

"A bigger place only means we'll have more boarders. I know you."

"We could get a flat on maybe the second floor, with our own bathroom. That would be nice, Isadore."

"Yes," he smiled and scratched his mustache. "You should have it a little more nice."

Bina put down the dress, the stitching done. "Go, lie down. I'll be there soon." She washed his dishes, packed up the piecework to exchange for new tomorrow, washed her own hands and face, straightened up a little. Rose and Chava were coming up the stairs with Aaron. They were almost an hour late. They must have stopped somewhere after night school, maybe in one of those cafés. Well, they worked the same as adults, but it was a shame to let girls go around a big city alone at this hour.

You can try a hundred things

First a dog got into the trash cans and rolled them against the cobblestones. Some men started fighting in the alley and then I heard the El tumbling through the night three blocks away.

"Rose?"

"I'm almost asleep, Chava. What is it?"

"You know I'm still saving for a ticket so Sarah can come."

"Sarah?"

"My sister."

"I know she's your sister. What about her?"

"I can't figure out where we'll put her."

"Oh," Rose yawned. "That could be a problem. Are you asking me this because it's Rosh Hashanah?"

"Probably. I've been meaning to for awhile," I confessed.

She shifted a little on her hip. "Did you ever ask her if she wants to come?"

Did she want to come? "Everyone wants to come to America."

"That's because they don't know what America is like. Gold in the streets."

"It's better than being in Russia."

"Hmm," she said. "Still, you could ask her."

"How come you're always right?"

"How come you always want to talk when I'm falling asleep?"

"I'm sorry, go to sleep. We'll talk about it tomorrow."

Rose was short and round and dark. When I curled around her at night I was curling around a lit coal. I remembered holding Sarah to me, those nights on broken boards in Kishinev. I was the big sister, the protector, her source of comfort. But when I curled around Rose I was

the one warming my hands, a homeless girl at a trash can fire, ashamed of my longing, unwilling to go without. *On Rosh Hashanah it is written, on Yom Kippur it is sealed, who shall stay at home and who shall go wandering.* When I was a child in the women's section of our shul, I imagined that the wanderers were all beggar men. I never thought it could be me. Rose seemed to be able to hear me think, even dream. Why not? Three years, every night. She half woke.

"Your eyes are still open, aren't they?"

"Yes."

She turned and pulled my head into her breast. "If you're restless on New Year's, you'll be restless all year. Go to sleep."

Sleep, she told me, as if she knew everything. We carried old superstitions with us like the seeds from our Russian gardens. Except in New York there was no room to plant cucumbers, only myths. The myths reminded us of Russian tsholnt and we forgot we only had words in our mouths.

"What are you chuckling about?" Rose asked, yawning.

"That was my stomach grumbling."

She reached behind her to rub my stomach. "You never eat enough, Chava."

"I eat all I can. Besides, I like feeding you better."

"You make me fat," she snuggled her behind into my curve.

"I love you fat," I whispered, scooping her belly under my palm. She sighed and relaxed. I listened to her breathing gradually return to a gentle snore. Her old nightgown was soft, worn-out cotton, the smell from beneath her arms sweet and sharp, copper and apples. I remembered dropping stones from the bridge into the Byk in summer, watching circles spread on the fast water. Then morning light surprised me.

It was the second day of Rosh Hashanah. Rose had to go to work, but the bindery was closed. Business probably wasn't so good and they were using the holidays to have an excuse not to pay us.

I walked by myself to the Williamsburg Bridge. Remembering the Byk made me want to look at a river. All right, it made me want to perform tashlikh. Religion was superstition, the opiate, etc., I knew. But all the water in the world was connected. Maybe what I threw into the East River would find its way back to the Black Sea, then turn to rain and fall on Mama's and Papa's graves. Can you throw your love into the water as well as your sins?

Most Jews were either working or in shul, though a handful of old

men and small groups of women were coming and going on the bridge's walkway, from the Brooklyn side as well, to do tashlikh, just like me. Maybe not exactly like me – I didn't even have a prayer book. But I probably had some of the same sins.

The Williamsburg Bridge was its own sin. Its construction, Lena told me, made hundreds of people homeless when their buildings were torn down. A little like a pogrom of progress, burning anything in its path, making Jews take to the roads with everything they owned on their backs, or move in with their relatives and landslayt, crowding more than we were ever crowded in Kishinev. At least it seemed that way. So many people in one building, so many buildings in one block. At home – was missing home a sin I had to empty out of my pocket or was it part of my connection to my family? My sins. I stood looking down at the river. Moving water carried our sins out to the sea, where they sank, I supposed, into the mud like stones. Centuries of sins at the bottom of the sea. Were they piled down there like pyramids while the fish pressed their bulging eyes up against them?

Fish didn't sin because they didn't have free will. I hardly believed in heaven at all, but I remembered asking Papa if animals had souls, and if they didn't, would we have to be in heaven without them? Wouldn't God want birds and cows and fish around? Weren't they all part of the creation? Papa said only a girl would ask a question like that.

"Then teach me," I said. He just shook his beard.

"I don't have time for all the students I have. You learn from your mother, like a good girl," he said. Mama answered most of my questions, but she also shook her head about the souls of animals.

"Certain things human beings were not given to know," she said.

"But the Talmud must have an answer, Mama."

"I'm sure it does, precious one, I'm sure it does." Then she'd change the subject or give me a chore.

If I didn't go to shul, was I committing the sin of not honoring my parents? I had gone the previous night with the Petrovskys. The blowing of the shofar was my favorite part. It sounded so ancient, setting my bones shivering against each other, the same as it did in Kishinev. The praying sounded different here, so many different accents. At home everyone always went to shul, at least all the men did, and the High Holidays were special, new clothes, new beginnings. For most of the people in shul here, like me, it would be the only time they'd go all year. Was that hypocrisy? The anarchists were going to have a dance on Yom Kippur. I thought it would be thrilling to go to a

ball instead of hearing Kol Nidre again, but Aunt Bina would be offended. It was one thing not to go to shul, it was another to make fun of those who did. And even if no one at the anarchists' ball would know I had survived a pogrom, it didn't seem right.

I didn't do anything else that dishonored my parents. No, I didn't think so. Papa wouldn't like my working or belonging to the union, but I took my place among all the other Jews here by doing these things, and what was wrong with that? Only about Rose, if they knew – but maybe lots of girls loved their friends, their cousins, maybe it was just something Mama had not talked to me about yet. Still, I could have done something more to honor their memory, saved more money for charity instead of buying treats for Rose or going to the theater.

I had such double feelings: I was sure that I sinned but not sure I believed in God. So if there was no God, what was the meaning of sin? If there was no Book of Life opened every year, did we have no destiny? Was it just an accident that Mama and Papa were in the wrong place in the wrong time? What about the real sins, the sins of the people who killed them? Could they get rid of a sin like murder just by emptying their pockets in the river? God took too long to punish murderers. It was no wonder human beings invented vengeance.

I felt a wave of nausea when I thought about vengeance, so I thought about Rose singing the prayers in shul. She had a good singing voice, not too high. She said the services were nice – she got to see other girls, some from her shop, in their best clothes, and the prayers were just prayers, maybe God heard them, maybe not, it couldn't hurt. She said I thought too much about God. What kind of disbeliever did that make me, anyway?

The cold, gritty winter reclined on the back of the wind circling the Williamsburg Bridge, gathering its force, grinning at the penitents, at me, as I turned my pockets inside out and threw one penny, a handful of breadcrumbs and some lint down to the dirty water.

19 Shevat 5667
Dear Chava,
It was so good to get your letter! We hadn't heard from you in such a long time I was afraid that you got lost in America. In school we learned it's almost as big as Russia. I like to look at the map of it.

But I'm not sure I would like to go there. Please don't think this is ungrateful, because I appreciate so much how you're thinking of me. I got into the girls' class at the Russian school here, imagine!

And I like it, the classes at least, not always the other girls.

Uncle Elihu and Aunt Shendl wrote from Warsaw that they're doing well – Uncle Elihu is a partner now in his brother's hat factory. They said if I wanted to go on to gymnasium, I would have a better chance if I came to Warsaw. Two of their boys are going to get in and their daughters are both engaged to be married. They want to share their good fortune with us, our family, they mean, because we were good to them when I was a little girl. I guess I'm the only one here they can share it with. Esther's happy having Nathan's babies. She's going to have her third at the end of summer and if I stay here I'll just keep being a nursemaid for them.

I read all your letters again, trying to decide. In America it sounds like life is as uncertain as here. I know a little Polish, and my German and Russian are good. I don't want to start learning English now. Does it sound like I have too many excuses?

I'll tell you my heart's secret. What I really want to do is to be an artist. Please don't laugh at me! Not many girls are artists, but a few. It's a new century – everyone says there will be so many opportunities, even for girls. And so much is happening in Warsaw now. At least, that's what our cousins write.

I know you dream of the revolution, like Daniel. I went to a lecture here by a Jewish artist who said he was one of "the wanderers" – they make art about what people's lives are really like, not just bowls of fruit. Art can also be part of a revolution, don't you think so? There's a school for artists now in Vitebesk. If I do well at the gymnasium, I could go there, maybe, or maybe even to Paris, which is my biggest dream. I never hear about artists in New York, only about work and money, but maybe I'm wrong. I count on you to help me make my decision. Of course I've never told Esther my dream. She's just proud because I do well in school.

I know your heart was always close to mine and I miss that now, but it also makes me think you will understand. Please write soon and tell me you understand.

Always your loving sister,
Sarah

February 15, 1907
Dear Sarah,
Today is my American birthday, the one they gave me at Ellis Island. Sometimes the immigration men get the date at least close,

but many times they give Jews Christmas as a joke. They did it to Aunt Bina. Some joke!

Now you are almost fourteen. I went to work in the box factory when I was fourteen. I was going to make sure you went to school as soon as you got here but people are talking about a bad economy. Rose is laid off again. Despite all the anti-Jewish laws in Russia, right now you might have a greater chance of getting your dream there than here.

If Warsaw is really where you want to continue your studies, I'll send you the money I've been saving for your ticket. You should have it for school and you won't have to rely only on Uncle Elihu. Don't protest. After all, I know what it feels like to depend on your relatives. I've been saving it in a real bank that a Jew owns here on the East Side. I was afraid if I kept it in the mattress that rats, or one of Rose's brothers, would get it. After three and a half years I have almost forty-five United States dollars! I expect you'll go to Warsaw after Esther's baby is born. Is that right?

A dream is always the best thing to have. I hope you will keep this dream instead of letting Aunt Shendl marry you off to the first yeshive boy she can find. But I think you are right about trying to get to Paris. Of course there is art and artists in New York, but the only art I see is on the painted sets for the Yiddish plays we go to when we can. They have a big museum for the rich uptown, and they just opened it on Sunday afternoons so working people might see what's there. But in my factory we work Sunday afternoons. It's not so bad, we get Shabbes off instead, and until your letter I wasn't even curious about what was in their museum.

When I think about your idea, I don't feel anymore like someone stuck in a factory. I remember that we are all young, and I feel youngness in me, that I can keep trying. You can try a hundred things in your life, and if nothing in those hundred makes you satisfied, you can still go on trying. Art doesn't have to be just for the rich, as you say. I look forward to seeing this new art you will make.

And somehow I hope we will see each other again. I keep you close to my heart always.

Your American sister,

Chava

On Essex Street and all throughout our neighborhood, everyone was

anxious about money. The rich bosses of the copper mines and railroads were doing things I couldn't begin to understand, though Uncle Isadore and Harry would argue about "economics" every time they found themselves at the dinner table together. More socialists and anarchists were out on street corners, lecturing us from their soap boxes. Their arguments were appealing to me but Rose had no patience for them.

"How is screaming from soap boxes going to change any boss's mind?" she asked. Part of me agreed, but still I believed working people could do big things if we stuck together, if we weren't always so tired and afraid.

Tension hit the neighborhood sidewalks like tiny icicles falling somewhere behind you, pop pop, making you shudder. Aunt Bina never seemed to sleep. The only time I didn't catch her sewing was if I got up in the middle of the night. Uncle Isadore was still working, but unless Harry was around to goad him, he barely spoke besides clearing his throat and mumbling from behind his newspaper. I missed the way he used to be so opinionated about everything. At Harriman's shop, we were just holding on. They let two gluers and sewers off already, which put me next in line.

Still, I was working, and not having to go in on Saturdays was fine with me. Since Rose was laid off, she was free too. Working on Saturdays wouldn't have bothered me – well, maybe a little, if I thought about Mama. No one in New York made their own challah, and even if they did, if anyone caught them feeding pieces to the oven for priests they'd be a laughingstock. I liked that word. Laughingstock. There were stockings, in English, and one could take stock of something, to consider it. How did consideration fit into a laughing stocking? English was hard to learn. The teacher said English was complicated because so many other languages contributed to it: Irish, German, French, Spanish, Portuguese, Greek. Even us Jews would probably change it, she said. "Better to change the life than the language," someone had called out from the back of the classroom, and we all laughed.

"Help me lace up this corset, Chava," Rose said one Saturday. She dressed slowly.

"You don't have to wear a corset today. You aren't even going to shul." I got up from bed to fumble with the laces. I liked to press my hand against the little ridge of fat that spilled over the top, along her back. I had one corset but I tried to get away without wearing it. What difference did cinching your waist make? It was hard enough to catch

a breath in this dark room without restricting my diaphragm. Besides, I liked the way Rose's flesh lapped and slid on itself. If she wore a slip instead, I could explore her body when we found ourselves alone. The corset was like a wall, the walls of Jericho that kept the Israelites out.

"Just because you think you're above being stylish doesn't give you the right to criticize me."

"I'm not criticizing. But doesn't it hurt you?"

"Only when you pull it too tight."

"If you say so." I brushed the back of my hand close to her underarm.

"Stop, that tickles," she said. When she turned, her smile was spreading a crescent across her face.

"We should help your mama," I said, making a flourish as I tied the last bow.

"You're going to sew?"

"I can do buttons, anyway. Things aren't so grim she has to work on Shabbes."

"Since when do you care about Shabbes?"

"I don't. She does."

Rose nodded. But when we told her we were ready to help out, Aunt Bina wouldn't listen.

"You, Chava, have already worked all week, and Rose has been out looking, or basting seams right next to me. That's enough. I had my boulevard days in Odessa. Now it's your turn. Go, find something to amuse you."

"Amuse us! We aren't children anymore, Aunt Bina." She smiled like I was a child to say so.

"All the more reason," she said. "You girls do plenty around here. I'm sure Monday Rose will find work again. Just go enjoy yourselves, but watch the traffic. You know that Breslau boy got his arm caught under a delivery truck only last Tuesday, crushed so badly they had to cut it off by the shoulder." She paused and tisked. "Is catching a ball worth an arm?"

"Mama, we're not diving into the street for balls," Rose said, patting Bina's shoulder.

"Well, it's easy to slip on the pavement in this weather. I only want you to be careful."

"We'll be careful, Aunt Bina," I promised, forgiving her for insisting on these bits of motherly advice. Bina tried to give us each a nickel but I wouldn't take it. She gave mine to Rose, who shrugged when she

caught my glare.

Out in the crowded street we peered over the heads of children building forts in the remnants of dirty snow. Where should we go?

"How about seeing what they do at the Henry Street Settlement House?" Rose asked.

"Why should we go there? We're already settled," I said.

She laughed and poked me. "I heard they have playgrounds, lectures, classes for girls, all kinds of things."

"And I heard it's all uptown women who come here to do us poor wretches good. You want to be another charity cause?"

"If they're snobby to us, we'll leave. They have uptown women at your League, don't they? They can't be all bad if so many girls go there. One of the girls in my last shop had a role in a play they put on. It can't hurt to look, Chava."

I tried to remember an argument about working-class solidarity from a socialist speech I heard at the park last week, but I got muddled somewhere in the middle. At the League I never saw any uptown women, though everyone said they were there. Certainly none of them would accuse us of being traitors for going to a settlement house; most of the people at these houses, the Jews at least, were socialists. Since Rose was willing to walk that far, I agreed. It was a pleasant day if you lifted your head above the stench of the street, warmth just beginning under the late winter cold, as if the world were blushing.

On Saturdays there weren't as many pushcarts as usual, but still plenty.

"Dancing fish!" a woman in an old, red shawl called out, "Beautiful live, dancing fish! Jewels on their fins, they've got! Your home will be blessed from these carp! Sparkling, dancing fish!"

We smiled at her. I slipped my arm around Rose, two girls out for a small adventure. Down Essex we bought two big garlic pickles for a penny from the pickle-barrel lady, Mrs. Guss, who instructed us not to drip on our shirtwaists. We leaned way over the curb, making loud crunches so she could see for herself how well behaved we were, but she was already selling to the next customer.

At Henry Street, we easily spotted the settlement house by the crowd of children on the steps, bundled up, resembling salamis with mittens. A girl a little shorter and older than me opened the door after we pounded the brass knocker for a good minute.

"Yes?"

"We came to see what you've got for girls here," Rose said in

English, perfectly at ease.

"Why don't you come in and look around. I'll find a club leader to talk with you." We followed her into a very clean, bright hallway. Pamphlets were arranged in neat rows on a polished wood table under a large mirror – not a crack in it. "Just poke around, girls. I'll find someone for you in a minute." She disappeared up the staircase.

Rose admired the furniture, picking up leaflets and putting them back without reading more than the English titles: *"Votes for Women"* and *"Maternal Hygiene"*. Down the hallway I saw someone turn a corner and I felt a familiar tug.

"I'll be back in a second," I said, clattering quickly down worn runner carpets. I saw a door close and I knocked. A tall, sturdy woman, at least fifty, looked out at me.

"Yes?"

"I thought – "

The old woman stared, chewing her lip, and then spoke in a familiar Yiddish.

"Oh, my! It's you, Chavele! You remember me, nu? Or has New York wiped you clean, so you don't remember your mama's old midwife from the Pale?"

I searched my memory for a minute. "Gutke?"

"The same."

"What are you doing here?"

"That's a long story. The short version is that I work with the nurses, examining the midwives' bags, attending a few births, helping out. In the tenements there's always something to do."

The Odessa station came back to me. I was trying to piece together a story without asking too many questions. Gutke cocked her head a little to the right.

"We left Odessa about a year after I saw you. Dovid had business contacts in New York, and he was worried about the way things were going in Russia. I told him if we had to move, I didn't want to go to Paris or Berlin, I wanted to go where all the children were going, to New York. So, here it is, New York. And here you are."

I felt dizzy with the confusion. Why was I meeting this old woman again?

"You want to come in, sit down?"

"Oh, no, I better not. I left Rose standing in the hall, she'll be wondering where I am."

"Your cousin?"

"Yes."

"Go get her and come in for a visit. No, I forgot, I have to go by Allen Street to check on one of my patients now. Next time. Just tell me quick, are you getting on all right?"

"Yes, I think so. It's not the golden city – we work too hard, but we do all right. I'm in the binders union and I'm going to night school for my English."

"Very good, that's very good. You remember to come back and visit me, promise?" She wrapped her cloak around her shoulders and picked up a black bag.

I felt bewildered, like the child I had been, on a train for the first time, not wanting to leave Gutke's side, anxious to get back to Rose. "I promise," I said after a long hesitation.

"Good. I'm going out the back – remember to come see me soon!"

When I found Rose, another girl was already there, talking about clubs and study groups. I heard her say something about Tolstoy and Shelley.

"Literature is nice," I said, impatient to tell Rose my news, "but we're workers. What we need is unions."

"This charming person," Rose said, raising her eyebrows at me, "is my cousin, Chava Meyer, who boards with us." She emphasized the word "boards," making the biggest possible distance between us. I grabbed at her blue eyes with my strongest look but she didn't blink.

"Very pleased to meet you, Chava Meyer," the girl said, politely ignoring our little scene, which I was sure she took in. "I'm Ellen Teller, and you'll be glad to know we have union discussions every other Monday and Sunday nights."

"You do?"

"Of course. We respond to the needs of all the people in the neighborhood, which includes us working girls."

I didn't like how this American-born girl said "us," but I didn't want to further antagonize Rose.

"It's important to work for our rights," Ellen went on, "but our rights have to include literature and art."

"Absolutely," Rose agreed with her, "it's not just the rich who should enjoy the good things in life."

I sighed. This was what I expected.

"Would you like to see one of our club rooms?"

Of course Rose would. And of course the club room was beautiful – a fire burning in the fireplace, a plaster bust on the mantel.

"We have a library in the next room, which you're free to use whether or not you join a club," Ellen said, looking at me, trying to be sympathetic. "The women's literature club meets tonight at 7:30, if you want to come back. You're welcome to stay here and look around as long as you like, but I have to see the children in the playground now."

"Thank you for your time. Maybe we will come by tonight," Rose said carefully, as if she were reading from her primer.

"That will be delightful," Ellen said, leaving us.

"Thank you," I called after her. Then, whispering, " 'Delightful!' and you – 'boards with us' – what is that supposed to mean?"

"Don't be so touchy," Rose said, inspecting her hat brim, picking at invisible lint. "You're the one who disappeared."

"And you'll never guess who I saw."

"Who?"

"Remember I told you about my mama's old midwife, from the train, Gutke?"

"No."

"Yes you do – the one who went with the woman dressed like a man?"

"Oh yes, I remember that. She's here?"

"Here, working with the settlement nurses!"

Rose gave me her I-told-you-so look, about what, I didn't know. "So where is she? Let's go see her."

"She had to go to one of her patients on Allen Street."

"She goes to the prostitutes?"

"I don't know, Rose. Not only prostitutes live on Allen Street, and besides, they deserve care the same as anybody."

"My sweet radical," Rose said, making as if to pinch my cheek. I shrugged her away. "Now maybe you too would like to come back for the discussion group?"

"You're willing to walk all the way home and back to talk about literature?"

She held up the nickels. "We can have dinner in a café and come back after. Mama won't worry. She knows I'm safe when I'm with you."

All over the East Side you could get a bowl of borscht any time of day for three cents, with bread and sour cream. I gave my sour cream to Rose, who put her hand over mine and sighed while I spooned it into her bowl. The best part about cafés was the eavesdropping. Groups of young people were always in the middle of spirited discussions. Girls the same age as us, at tables with men even, argued about the future of

Yiddish literature. I wondered if they read Yiddish authors at Henry Street or only goyim. Either way it was always men, men who were remembered for what they wrote. Maybe in the new world things could still be different, and women would be remembered too. No one remembered working girls – was that why women had children, so someone would remember us? I put down my spoon.

"Now what's wrong? Your soup is sour?"

"No, the soup is good," I said, taking a half spoonful to show her.

"You have to eat more, Chava, you're beginning to look a little flattened out."

"You're tired of how I look?"

"Did I say that?" Rose leaned her head left, letting her eyes run from my head to my breasts. "I just want you to stay healthy and happy."

"Happy?"

"You're not happy?"

"Oy, Rose, once I got in the binders union I thought I was going to be all set. Then I see the local for the gluers is like a ladies' auxiliary, almost only for social reasons and to get the scraps from the men or run their errands. And they keep telling me how lucky we are even to have a women's local."

"This is such news it should make you unhappy? You sound just like one of those street corner Isaiahs. Woe unto the unorganized!"

"It's important."

"I know it's important but you have to relax a little, at least enough to finish your soup."

A young woman in a brown shirtwaist and black tie walked by our table and smiled at Rose before she joined a group in the back. I watched Rose's gaze. "Would you like me to dress like that?"

"Like – ? Oh. No, it stands out too much. People call that look 'the new woman' but they aren't being complimentary. I like how you look now, don't worry." She squeezed my hand.

"Okay, I'll go back to worrying about the League."

"What's to worry about the League?"

At last maybe she was interested. Or maybe she was being polite. "The League wants to organize women so we can join the AFL, but the AFL doesn't do anything good by women that I can see. The anarchists say that's because even the workers are stuck in the idea of private property."

Rose shook her head, raising her eyebrows. "How'd the anarchists get into this?"

"I think what they mean is – ," I was trying to get it right while I traced a circle on the greasy table, "when men believe women belong to them they become a kind of capitalist. If the men are half capitalists and half workers, no wonder they never get anywhere." I noticed Rose's bowl was almost empty while mine was still full. I took a couple of spoonfuls. "That's why anarchists say they're for free love. Free love would be like a general strike against the property laws of marriage."

"A strike against marriage. I don't think that's going to go over well with the girls in my shop. Besides, it might sound good, Chava, but this free love they talk about, they don't mean it for us. I know what goes on in the shops. Every once in awhile some boss starts in on us about 'free love' – how if we want to sign union cards, we can't just go halfway."

"Bosses twist everything for their own selfish ends."

"And you think the anarchists are so pure?"

"Well, Emma Goldman – "

"All right, maybe Emma Goldman. But she's a woman. I agree with you, you know. We're not fighting." A waiter came by to take our plates and Rose waved him away. He shrugged off towards the kitchen. "If girls got the same wages as men then the men would have to take us seriously, that I get. But if a woman didn't get married, she'd have to take care of her children alone, or depend on whether a man liked her enough to help out, since he might not even be the father. That would be awful for women."

"You – "

"What, Chava?" Rose wiped at her upper lip, careful to remove the little borscht mustache.

"You surprise me, that's all. I didn't think you – "

"You don't think I listen? You think you're the only one here trying to figure out what's what? I just like going to the theater better than to your friends' speeches. So much of what they have to say is all the same. Marriage, free love – both don't sound so good to me."

"I'm glad to hear that." I rested my cheek on my fist, looking into her eyes. For all her talk about eating enough, I saw circles under her eyes too. They made the blue more delicate, echoing.

"For someone so serious you certainly have a talent for making every conversation into a joke."

"I'm not joking, Rose. How many do you think there are, like us? There can't be more than a handful. At the League, maybe a few, I think."

"I'm sure, at your League."

"So what other women besides – like us – are going to have the time and dedication to organize women? So many girls our age are married or giving all their attention to trying to be. Can you imagine if every girl decided not to get married or have relations with men? That would be a real general strike!"

"Shh," Rose warned, as a man stared at us from another table. She lowered her voice. "Who would ever call for such a thing? I heard they arrested Emma Goldman just for talking about preventing unwanted pregnancy. And you could never get enough women to agree."

"I don't know – "

Rose made a quick, angry gesture with her hand because I forgot to whisper. I lowered my voice and started over. "I don't know. If you want to change things, really change them, which end do you start with? Striking for better conditions? Making settlement houses? What makes a difference?"

It annoyed me to see Rose smiling at me, even though I knew she was loving, loving us, sitting in a café like everyone else, trying to solve the world's problems when we were only greenhorn workers. Everything was going so fast, and I could never tell whether it was spinning in a circle that trapped us, or was moving us towards the future.

Gutke found her journal at the bottom of her midwife's bag and opened it for the first time that year.

Even with my talent for visions, I never would have guessed half of what happened. I suppose that's part of why I started writing this diary in 1900, to see if an ordinary life had a pattern. Now I'm not sure that my life has been either ordinary or special, unfolding according to a particular plan. Still, when I thumb through the old pages, I recognize myself: Gutke Gurvich, born in the shtetl of Orgeyev, the fatherless bathhouse attendant, the midwife who married a woman masquerading as a banker and came to America. I am the pattern of my own experience. Yet that's really nothing more than saying I am the sum of my memories.

Memories. For every one I recorded, fifteen slipped away. On the steamship I spent days on deck peering into the waves, trying to make out the creatures that moved under the surface, visible for moments as I bent over the railing. I found why I disliked traveling, why I hung

back from so many of Dovida's invitations to join her in Vienna or Milan. In transit we enter one of God's antechambers, a fluidity in time where one's soul is either entirely in the present moment, unfastened from the past, or absorbed only in the goal, the destination. Travelers share no history, no place with each other – or all history, every place. Living out of steamer trunks made me dizzy, as if I had entered the realm of pure vision on which human hands had painted a flimsy veneer – here is your stateroom, madam, and here is your dining table – while the stench of steerage crept in through the portholes.

It made me wonder about heaven, traveling with Dovida. By her, everything had to be first class. She was a successful banker and I was her wife, uncomfortable in even the plainest Paris fashions she bought me for the trip. We even had a ketuba, the Jewish marriage certificate, inscribed by a friend of hers in Hamburg, that I carried in a small wicker box with my treasures: my mother's candlesticks, the field stone and talis vest Milcah gave me, Pesah's oil menorah and the multicolored shawl she sewed. Dovida gave me jewelry, pearls and bright gems. Blue ones I liked particularly but she was always chiding me for throwing them in the trunk with the rest of my clothes. I wore the gold ring. If the rest was stolen, my sympathy would have been with the thief. Money was good for buying safety for women like us. If Dovida had tried to go as a man in steerage, she never would have lived to see the shore. But first class was a harder masquerade than being Dovida's wife. After all, there was nothing untrue about our intimacy. Did every woman who got money through marriage feel this same unease?

To me, the steamship reflected the world's tiered conception of heaven and hell, whether Christian or Jewish. In the hold below, the mass of sinners, whose crime was poverty and desperation, prayed for relief from the crowding, the agony of their passage. In the middle decks, uncomfortable but hardly in pain, were those who lived in purgatory, counting every kopeck, balancing the small pleasures of adequate ventilation and relatively clean facilities against their fear of sliding into the abyss and their constant envy of those above them, whose parties they could actually hear. On top, the blessed reaped the rewards of industry and luck, of willingness to take advantage of others and circumstance, of turning opportunity into profit. Suppose in heaven everything was reversed? Those who sailed with such comfort would be thrown into the fiery pit, while those who had endured the hold were crowned as martyrs, heroes of the human condition. Did God really intend eternal reversal to stand as justice? I'd think God

would have as many reservations as I did about the ultimate foolishness of glorifying any one at the expense of any other.

I didn't like the journey but it did give me days to think, one luxury I was grateful for. Dovida had sailed from Frankfurt to New York once before, and many times in the Mediterranean and Black Sea. The ocean was simply another language she had to master, a dialect of winds and swells, and like in any other language, she was quickly comfortable.

Now I want to tell something else about Dovida. If being born a Polish Jew and a woman placed her in a narrow chamber, she found the door into the world by doing all the things that rulers traditionally allowed Jews to do: translate and handle money. She was the perfect product of our Diaspora, appearing to be at home everywhere, speaking any language, changing even her sex to suit the necessity of her ambition. But embracing the whole Diaspora in her own person, moving from place to place, always a guest, never rooted, had its costs. She, who professed not to believe in scripture, who admitted to being a Jew only because, as she said, it was written on her body – her olive skin and gorgeous nose – became as fastidious as the Orthodox. When I returned from a birth, she demanded I bathe before we touched, afraid of birth secretions and blood. I often thought her antipathy to dirt came from a fear that if she ever touched the ground she would weep for years over her lost tribe.

"Tribe?" she looked at me in disbelief. "Gutke, this is the twentieth century. We are not going to herd goats in the deserts of Judea. I, for one, take great pleasure in considering myself a citizen of the world. Commerce is a world without borders. Nationalism is an old superstition that we are now in the position to overcome."

"And so, Mr. Citizen of the New World, where is your home?"

She looked at me thoughtfully. "You are my home. Didn't you know?"

It was a big responsibility being someone else's home. Dovida was my comfort and delight, but Kishinev had been my home, the place where my life was shaped. And New York became home, the place I'd chosen to come. The streets, the people, the Henry Street Settlement House, our building on Suffolk Street, all these were parts of my home. But I also understood what Dovida meant when she talked about the twentieth century. In a blink, everything has changed. When I was a child in Kishinev, keeping a diary would have marked me as a witch if anyone had found out. Here, now, not an eyebrow would be raised. Every day, twenty diarists pass through Henry Street, along with all of

Miss Wald's reformer friends. Nurses, poets, organizers – all women. And so many like Dovida and me.

When, from time to time, I run into someone from Kishinev whose birth I attended, I feel as if my home has traveled with me, as if I am really part of a tribe. Today Chava Meyer, Miriam's second daughter, showed up at Henry Street, almost grown. I recognized her odor before I recalled her name, that smoky, slightly metallic scent. Not unpleasant but a little unsettling. She unsettles me, this young woman. Possibly because I know that we share the same feeling for women. I don't know how I know it, but I know. Just as I know that any minute now she'll be back to question me.

We returned to Henry Street a few minutes early. The girls' literary club leader told us they were discussing Tolstoy's story, "Kreutzer Sonata", that night. I never would have expected them to pick something about sex. Both Rose and I had read it in Russian a couple of years ago. The man at the bookcart didn't want to sell it to us and I had to give him a big spiel about the American Bill of Rights. First he said the Bill of Rights doesn't apply to Russian literature, but finally he gave in – since I was such a scholar and patriot, I could have it, but no bargaining and don't blame him. Another nudnik. Rose and I were then very excited to read the story and disappointed when it was just men talking on a train, Tolstoy expounding about abstinence and the sanctity of mothers, how sexual relations debase human beings and drive them insane. Which was why this splendid Russian killed his wife: sex made him crazy and jealousy drove him to murder. What an excuse!

I made my apologies to the club leader, saying I was going to take a look at their library, I didn't feel very talkative tonight.

"You're looking for Gutke, right?" Rose whispered.

I nodded. "You don't mind being left alone?"

"If you don't mind leaving me with all these new girls," she said, flirting with her eyes, scanning the room, which was filling up with girls about our age.

"Jealousy is a bourgeois male emotion."

"Go, go on. At least this time you have a good reason."

I picked through the books in the library. I wasn't looking at their titles but at their bindings, flipping open some of the more beautiful ones to see how they were put together. I was holding up the pages of a volume of Emma Lazarus's poems with an engraved frontispiece

when I heard someone clear their throat behind me.

What came over me? A sudden panic, the way I had felt when we were trapped by fire in the alley in Kishinev, cold and hot at the same time. Gutke looked so familiar standing there, as tall as me, but wider, stronger. I stumbled towards her, heaving, not crying, exactly, but gulping and discharging air as if I hadn't drawn a breath in ten years. She embraced me, one hand around my ribs, the other over my shoulder, patting my back.

"Please forgive me," I said, finally pulling away.

"What's to forgive?" Gutke motioned to the green wingback chairs separated by a little table. "Why this room isn't full of people studying now I don't know."

"They must have reserved it for us."

She laughed from her belly, the kind of easy laughter I hadn't heard in a long time. "Once in awhile," she said, "something that's meant to be, is. You didn't know I was going to be back here tonight, did you?"

"I just hoped – "

"Hope is good," she nodded. Her long, gray wool skirt, black laced boots and plain white shirtwaist gave her an air of dignity. Most women her age on the East Side still wore a wig or a kerchief but Gutke had her own hair in a stylish pompadour. She looked healthy, vigorous and sharp, and she smelled like black bread and hot samovars. I found my hands enclosed by her soft palms. Looking down I wondered if that was how she held a baby's head, guiding it through.

"So," she said, "tell me everything."

"Didn't I tell you everything already?"

"Only that you were learning English at night and are a factory worker in a – a bindery, right?"

"Yes."

"What do you hear from home?"

"Not too much. There was another pogrom in Kishinev, not as bad as the first."

"I heard." Her shoulders went to her ears and back. "A bad century."

"It's just begun."

"Indeed, we can always hope for better. That's why we all come to America, isn't it?"

"My sister Sarah doesn't want to come. She's decided to go to gymnasium in Warsaw and become an artist."

"You seem disappointed."

"I am. I wanted her to join me here."

"For her, or for you?"

"For both of us. For me. I suppose I was thinking it would be like having a little bit of Mama back again." I had to swallow to continue. "And it seemed important to get her out of Russia, to keep her safe." I stopped, trying to figure out which need belonged to whom.

Gutke was quiet, looking at me. "God willing, Sarah will be safe in Warsaw. And your sister Esther – she's a mother now, am I right?"

"Exactly right. Two girls and a boy so far. She married Nathan and they run a little tavern. She writes twice a year, at Pesach and Rosh Hashanah."

"What does she say about your brothers?"

"Abe married in Palestine. He has two girls and stopped living on a farm. I don't know what he does there but he seems to be settled. Daniel, we don't know if he's dead or alive."

"Not dead, I think."

"How do you know?"

"Just a feeling, a smell really. Death has a very distinct smell. "

I shuddered.

"I'm sorry. It's from being around all these nurses here." Gutke gestured to the walls, as if the settlement workers were hiding behind the roses in the wallpaper. "So let's talk about you. You're living still with the Petrovskys? Not engaged to be married yet?"

I squared my shoulders. That's what every yente always asked. "I'm not interested in getting married."

"What then?" At least she didn't press.

"I want to keep working at the bindery and do organizing."

"Organizing? Very good, very good. What kind of organizing?"

"How many kinds are there?"

She smiled. "All kinds. Here, for instance, they organize for children's health and education. Many women your age are organizing for women's suffrage. But you – "

"Yes?"

"You have other ideas, am I right? A dream you can't quite put a picture to, about union work, how women organized into unions will change the world?"

I felt breathless, though she was the one talking. "It's not just for better conditions, it's to own the means of production."

"I don't mean to be unkind," she said chuckling. "Here in America, and in Russia too, these words are on everyone's lips. But I've never heard of a factory yet where the workers unthroned the owners, took

it over and made a success."

"It's possible – ." I gripped the armrests of the green chair to keep myself calm.

"Yes, possible. Dovid and I argue about what's possible all the time. Usually I take the side you want to take so don't mistake me. It would be a miracle to live to see a real revolution, a welcome miracle."

"It won't be a miracle. It will be the result of educating the workers and changing the world ourselves." I felt a twinge of embarrassment for sounding so much like one of those street corner bombasts.

"Chava, I may look to you like an old woman who doesn't know what's happening in the world – "

"I never said – "

"Let me finish." She shook her head. "You must have read in the papers how in the western railroad strikes the government called in troops and shot the workers, and in the end the strike was lost. The world is too complex now for simple solutions." She stared off, rubbing two fingers against the side of her cheek.

"The unions are all we have."

"You mean the ideal union in your mind, not the AFL I read about in the dailies."

She was right about the union in my mind. "It's true that Sam Gompers doesn't want to antagonize manufacturers. He just wants a better life for working men and doesn't seem to care about women."

"So you are unionist and a feminist too."

"I'm not sure I know what a feminist is."

"You believe in suffrage?"

"Of course."

She raised her eyebrows, smiling. "You see how you say it, as if your certainties were the truth and anyone who made the slightest bit of effort to understand would agree with you."

"But it is true, I mean – "

"You're eighteen now?"

"Don't patronize me because I'm young."

"Not at all, Chava, not at all. But you will admit there's a difference between the young and the old?"

"Yes."

"This is our biggest difference: I don't believe anything I used to believe anymore, and not because I don't want to. I mourn the loss of the certainty you carry. And yet I have a sense, maybe now more of a wish than a belief, that all of us, pushing, needing things to be better,

will actually make the world better in spite of ourselves."

We both sighed, catching the wind of our thoughts. Something she just said – our biggest difference. I pushed my tongue against my teeth.

"What is it, Chava?"

"Dovid – "

She peered at me intently. "What about Dovid?"

Suddenly I was scared. What if I was wrong? What if I made up the whole thing? I was just a child then and so much was happening. Gutke interrupted my thoughts.

"Let me ask you something personal, if I may?" She fingered a button on her sleeve and kept looking at me.

"Anything." I was relieved.

"Your cousin Rose. In the tenement, you must have to share a bed?"

"We're lucky it's just two of us in the bed."

"And are you glad it's the two of you in the bed? I'm not being too frank, am I?"

"No. No, you're not being too frank." I wasn't wrong after all. It seemed so hard to put the words into the air. "I – am very glad to be with Rose. We share – everything." I looked down at a threadbare spot in the carpet underneath Gutke's chair.

Gutke cleared her throat. "Everything? Touch?"

I raised my eyes to the level of her lap, which made me even more uncomfortable, so I looked past her shoulder. "Touch," I whispered.

"But not the literature club."

"I was looking for you," I protested, finally looking Gutke in the eye.

"I'm only teasing. So, your question about Dovid was," she paused and looked past my right ear – could it have been as hard for her as for me? " – is Dovid really a man?"

"Yes. On the train I was sure you said Dovida."

"Did I? Dovida." She made a soft clicking noise in the back of her throat. "Moving back and forth, between lives, I make mistakes sometimes. Hardly ever, since we came to New York. People, women, sometimes guess. Lillian Wald, she knew from the minute she saw Dovid and me together."

"She did?" I had pictured Lillian Wald as someone too busy to notice the social details of people's lives.

"Nurses get a lot of experience you wouldn't begin to imagine."

"Oh." Then I had another thought. "Is Miss Wald—?"

"That's not for me to say. Besides, don't you think you've learned enough for one night?"

I blushed. But what did I learn, exactly? In the hallway there was a sudden rush of voices, girls talking in clusters, walking by.

"Here's your cousin now," Gutke said, standing, extending her hand. "Rose Petrovsky, yes?"

"I'm sorry, I don't know your last name, Miss – ?"

"Mrs. Greenbaum, I go by here." She turned and winked at me. "But you may call me Gutke."

"Pleased to meet you."

"The same. You and Chava must come to dinner with Dovid and me. We have so much in common. Next Saturday night?" Gutke found a scrap of paper on a side table and wrote out the address as Rose and I exchanged glances. "Unless you want to come to the literature class instead."

"We spent half the time arguing about whether Tolstoy was an anti-Semite," Rose said, both scornful and perplexed. "We can come back for the literature club another time. Next Saturday will be delightful."

"What's this?" Rose asked, fishing a crumpled wad of yellow paper she saw poking out from under our dresser. It was Sunday evening and we had a rare moment alone with all the men out and Aunt Bina called downstairs for an emergency consultation about a neighbor's sick daughter.

"Only something I wrote. Leave it," I said.

She was already smoothing it out on the bureau.

"Please just leave it."

"When did you become a writer?" she asked, sitting down on the bed.

"I'm not a writer. I'm a bookbinder, at least I was until yesterday. Sometimes words go through my head. Doesn't that happen to you?"

"Maybe," she said, not really listening. She started to read aloud. " 'I do not come from a beautiful people.' What's this about? You don't think I'm beautiful?"

"You know I think you're the most beautiful woman in the world. Just give it to me!" I felt like a bug some child had trapped in a jar.

"No. What made you write this?"

She wasn't going to let up, I could tell, so I gave in. "After I was laid off yesterday, one of the English workmen they kept on said he was glad they laid off most of the Jewish women, because the Jews are so ugly."

"He said that to you?"

"Not directly. To another man but so I could overhear him."

"I thought Harriman's was a Jewish place."

"They had plenty of goyim working there, the skilled men."

"So you decided to agree with him?" Rose put on her coldest face and rearranged her skirt.

"You're tormenting me, you know. I don't agree with him. I was thinking about your literature club, and I was trying to imagine what it is the Jew-haters see, that's all. It was just for myself."

"I want to hear what you wrote. Read it to me – no, I don't trust you – you'll tear it up. I'll read it myself." She smoothed the paper again and cleared her throat. I turned and stared at the wall. " 'I do not come from a beautiful people. The women of my race have long faces, or squat square ones with thick eyebrows, high foreheads, receding hairlines, chin and lip whiskers even among the young. Many have long, humped and hooked noses. We tend to be extremely fat or alarmingly thin, covered with freckles and moles, yellow-complexioned and wide-hipped.' " She stopped and gave me a look, "You really think this?"

"Rose, I told you, I was just trying something out."

"All right, let's see where you went with it. 'We are likely to sweat and hunch. Not known for grace, few of us are dancers or athletes. We vary from blond to very dark, we have in fact intermarried with every other race in the world and been violated for generations in the places of our exile and Diaspora. Still, we are thought to be marked, and visible to each other by the very character of our ugliness.' "

I started pacing with my hands clasped behind my back.

"Stop that," Rose said. I stood in front of her and let my arms hang down.

She gave me a sharp glance and continued.

" 'We are nervous. Often enough our generosity rouses suspicion: what guilt, what bribe lies coiled within our gifts? But when we withdraw, and are anxious to have enough for ourselves, we are called misers, usurers, petty. Typical. We are typically ourselves, laughing too loud where no one else hears a joke, abstaining in the midst of everyone else's pleasure, escaping whenever we can whatever fate you think is our justice. So we write theories, make music on street corners and study mathematics. We explain ourselves only to each other. If you overhear us, you never understand.' "

It was just a page, but her reading seemed to take a century. Rose looked at me as though she didn't recognize me. I stared at a hole in my left shoe and mashed a small insect into the floor.

She laid the paper on the table and drummed with her fingers. "It's strange to think of you thinking like this. You know what I mean? But it's also wonderful."

As I exhaled, I realized I'd been holding my breath.

She leaned over and kissed me on the cheek. "You should be writing books, not binding them."

"I'm not binding them, in case you forgot."

She pretended not to hear me. "Maybe you could send your writing to the *Forward*, or the *Call*. They publish literary pieces."

"It's not much of a piece, Rose. It was just an experiment." I reached for the paper. She had already folded it into neat quarters and ignored me.

"Maybe you're not ready. Or maybe you're afraid?"

"I'm not afraid. But that piece of paper doesn't make me any more of a writer than being a good dancer makes you a ballerina. Once in awhile I try to talk things out with myself on paper, like our night school teacher recommended. It's not meant for anyone else."

"You won't even share it with me?"

"I – you found it even when I thought there was nothing to share. You are always finding me, what can I do?" I lifted my arms and threw them back down to my sides, in a gesture of helplessness.

She laughed and reached to pull my hair back from my forehead. "I love finding you," Rose said, and brushed her cheek against my cheek, moving towards my lips. Appetite surged in me but just as we were about to kiss, we heard her mother's breath, heavy, rasping slightly from the stairs and the sound of her key.

The house on Suffolk Street was only five blocks from our tenement. I'd read in the *Forward* that the Lower East Side was the most crowded place on earth – visiting an individual home at the edge of our neighborhood made me more than uncomfortable, as though I was being called in front of a Russian provincial governor. I could make out the Jarmulowsky bank building, where I'd been saving for Sarah, poking up like a giant across Seward Park. I took the scrap of notepaper out of my pocket to make sure I had the right address. I looked at Rose, who was biting her lip. The jacket I had given her years ago looked out of style already. It strained across her breast and, unless the day was very cold, she left it unbuttoned. I considered getting her a new one out of my savings before I sent the money to Sarah, but now

I was laid off. Rose had a new job over on Hester Street for a small contractor, who knew how long it would last? In our apartment it was as though everyone was holding their breath, waiting for something terrible to happen – or for anything to happen at all. One of us could lose a job, one of us could get a new one. Like the new seesaws in Seward Park, we didn't go anywhere, only up and down.

Rose and I took a deep breath together. "This Dovida really dresses like a man?" she whispered.

"We're only going to have dinner with my mother's old midwife. It will be fine, you'll see."

"Uh-huh," she said.

Dovida answered the door. She was wearing pleated trousers with a long watch chain, a shirt with cufflinks, a tie. She still had a well-trimmed mustache.

"You must be Chava and Rose," Dovida said warmly. "I never would have recognized you. You've grown into beautiful women since our last encounter at the train station. Come in, come in!" She spoke in English, with a better accent than mine. Her voice was husky, probably from cigar smoking, and she had a spicy smell, something like cinnamon.

Rose's mouth hung open. She was usually so composed, always knowing the right words to say. I pushed her gently from behind and she seemed to wake up.

We came into a hallway painted a light blue, nicer even than the Henry Street house. Maybe because the air was full of delicious and familiar smells, tsimes and flanken, I thought.

"Gutke," Dovida turned her head, "our guests are here. Come out of the kitchen." This she shouted in Yiddish. Gutke appeared, wiping her hands on her apron, flushed with cooking, an ordinary baleboste.

"I'm so glad you came." She embraced me and then hugged Rose. "Dovid, take their coats, be a host. I'm just putting some finishing touches on dinner. I'll join you all in a minute. Go, sit, talk to each other." She shooed us into a parlor that reminded me of Rose's house in Odessa. Dovida put our coats in a hall closet while we settled into the soft, fancy furniture.

"So," Dovida said, again in English, wrapping the watch chain around her fingers, "how do you find America?"

"By sailing west," I said. Rose slapped me lightly on the knee.

"I'll have to remember that," Dovida chuckled, "very clever. It's a silly question, nu?"

"No, not silly. Just big to answer." I felt I was smiling too wide, and tried to recompose my face to be serious, adult.

"We've been here almost four years," Rose said, "and all we've seen is the East Side."

"We went on a picnic once to Central Park," I reminded her.

"Yes," Rose said, "we went on a picnic once to Central Park and twice I've been to Macy's department store. I know this is a big country, but by me, Odessa was better."

"You forget – ," I started.

"I don't forget. We came to escape pogroms and ended up going from sweatshop to sweatshop."

I'd never heard Rose describe our lives so angrily, certainly not to a stranger. Was it because Gutke and Dovida's house reminded her of home, too? Dovida's black eyes shuttled back and forth between us.

"America is certainly more than sweatshops," she paused, as if she was going to say something else, but instead moved her hand to her mustache, stroking it the way men do, as if they have important thoughts.

"Yes?" Rose prodded.

"I was just thinking about how I live." She paused again and fixed her gaze on Rose. "I gather you knew about my disguise already?"

Silence fell on us like tobacco dust in a sudden breeze. For a minute everyone's words were choked down. Finally Rose cleared her throat.

"It's a very good disguise – ." She hesitated, unsure how to address Dovida. "Mr. Greenbaum – ," she tried, but Dovida waved her hand in the air.

"Exactly the problem. How shall we discuss America and sweatshops if you don't know what to call me?" Her hand went back to her mustache. "Let's try 'Dovid,' all right? Mister is too formal for friends of Gutke's."

"All right," Rose said, but she didn't say "Dovid."

Personally, I preferred Dovida, yet I could see the problem about calling her the wrong name in front of others. I decided to steer the conversation away from sweatshops for the time being. "Are there many women who go about disguised as you do?" I asked.

"It depends on what you mean by many. In Europe I knew – ," she paused, squinting, while her fingers made a count, "maybe nineteen or twenty in the last thirty-five years. Here I've met, or know of, nine, yes, nine, I think. Of course there must be at least a dozen or two working-class women I wouldn't have the opportunity to meet. So, more than a minyan, not enough for a union."

That she said minyan surprised me. I had an image of my papa's shul on a quiet Saturday morning, with women dressed as men, davening. If women wore pants, could they also put on tfilin? Would God accept their prayers as though they were men, or consider them abominations? Did God look under your clothes to check your sex?

"Did you ever join a minyan?" I asked.

"I don't go to shul very often, but once when I was in Vienna I was moved to go one afternoon. It was very hot and the synagogue was quiet and cool. The rabbi enlisted me in a minyan for the evening service. I couldn't very well refuse." In her smile I saw a wistfulness for Vienna more than any idea of how shocking her story was.

"No one ever suspects you?" Rose asked.

"Women do, once in awhile, though mostly I fulfill their dream of a perfect gentleman, and they want so to believe that a perfect gentleman exists that they convince themselves I'm it."

"Perfect gentleman don't exist?" Rose asked, unconvinced.

"I've never met one. Some appear to be, of course, in front of women. We all know about the rules of etiquette between the sexes. But I can assure you that when men are together, especially in the upper classes, good ones are as rare as the philosopher's stone."

"The what?" Rose asked. I admired how she was never embarrassed to ask about a word she didn't understand.

"Ah – alchemists thought there was a magic stone that could turn lead into gold. Our species seems to have a fascination with metamorphosis – changing things entirely," she added quickly, "like a caterpillar into a butterfly."

"Or women into men?" I asked.

"Well, men aren't as exquisite as butterflies and certainly not as precious as gold, but that's the general idea. Appearances – ," Dovida wound her watch thoughtfully. "Take the case of our 'ideal gentleman.' Women can usually sniff the impostors out, but more often than not they hold their noses and dive in, believing the appearance to be more real than their own knowledge. I sometimes think gentlemen are more likely among the socialist types, who actually believe in equality."

The way she said 'socialist types' made me uneasy. I glanced around at the room and realized again how rich Dovida must be. On her own, Gutke would have been living in something like our tenement on Essex Street. Yet I wanted to know everything. How she did it, how she got that mustache, how she hid her breasts, how she talked, if she was afraid, ever.

"You look perplexed, Chava?"

"No, I just don't understand how you do it."

"How I do what? Oh – ." Dovida looked down at her lap and laughed. "The art of illusion is everything. Appearances, that's what we were talking about, wasn't it? Most people are concerned first with self-protection. Protecting their wealth or their religion or their self-image, whatever it may be. I look to see what they're protecting, and I make myself as agreeable as I can. It's actually remarkably easy to make people think you're a man. You just have to act like one, which is sometimes repugnant to me."

"Why repugnant?" Rose asked.

"Don't you often find men repugnant?"

Rose bit her nail. I could see she was thinking about all the sweatshop Romeos, or maybe her brothers. I had an impulse to put my arm around her. Finally she looked back at Dovida. "Yes, I often find men repugnant."

"Yes, I know," Dovida said softly. "When I was young all I wanted was my freedom. Being a man with money seemed like the surest way to be free. But I can see that both of you believe men with money are your enemies, am I right?"

"Well, yes," I admitted.

Dovida's head bobbled slightly. "It's not pleasant to appear as a villain to the very people you care most about. Of course, not everyone I care about thinks I'm a villain – ." She directed this to Gutke, who was standing in the doorway, folding her apron.

"Already with the politics. Now you all have to come eat dinner and not upset each other. It's bad for your digestion."

"We're not upsetting each other, dearest. Are we, girls?"

"No," Rose said, "though maybe confusing each other a little."

"Come," Dovida said, extending her arm towards Rose in a courtly way, "come eat and we'll try to banish confusion and care."

The dining room table was of heavy, dark wood with claw feet the same as the enormous sideboards. A blue oriental rug lay under the table and a small chandelier glittered above. All the place settings and dishes matched, and there were two crystal glasses by each plate. Gutke looked at my looking.

"The food will be familiar, I promise," she said.

And it was. Gutke had prepared a wonderful feast, plates of lettuce with sliced cucumber, which she called a salad, green beans, tsimes and flanken. Even at Pesach we rarely ate as well. The prunes in the

tsimes were as fresh as the ones from our own plum tree in Kishinev. I took a second helping while Rose beamed at me. Dovida offered us wine – wine like this I never had before, not syrupy or sour at all. It tasted like the wine of psalms. Both Rose and I let Dovida fill our glasses as often as she offered.

"So, Chava, Gutke tells me you're a bookbinder."

"I was," I sighed between mouthfuls. "I got laid off this week."

"There's a slow season for bookbinders?" Gutke asked.

"No, but the factory, Harriman's, never seems to be get enough business. Now people say there's going to be another depression. Almost all of us got laid off."

Dovida nodded. "They're right. A depression is already starting."

"How do you know for certain?" Rose asked as she took a piece of white bread to sop up the gravy on her plate.

"It's my business. Did you know that people can make a lot of money in a depression?"

"No." I reached down to pick up my napkin. For a second I thought I saw the carved wooden dragon spin the ball at the end of its claw.

"It's true. For one thing, a depression drives down the cost of labor, since people will work for any wage they can get. For another, it deflates prices – stocks and lands. So if you have money and you pick the right things to buy, when the economy gets better, the value of your possessions might have doubled or tripled."

"So you think capitalists make depressions?"

"I know they do."

"Is this dinner table talk?" Gutke interrupted.

"We're stuffed already from your wonderful cooking. We're just letting out a little hot air."

But I didn't think of it as air. "How can we stop them?"

"Stop them?" Rose looked at me as if I were fantastically naive. "Maybe we should write a letter explaining that it's too hard for us to go through another of their depressions, and they'll send a telegram right back, apologizing."

Dovida laughed. "You can't stop them. When there *is* too much suffering – so much that people start to revolt – that's a threat to social stability. Then someone, the government or the manufacturers, tinkers with the money supply until they can say 'Look, we've done you all a favor and gotten you through to a new prosperity.' Of course, it's not quite as simple as it sounds." She bounced her knuckle off her lip. "And sometimes it backfires. In the future I think depressions will be less

severe. They have too much potential for causing revolutionary fever."

"So they'll have little depressions, just long enough to crush the unions but not so long that everyone rebels?" I asked.

"Exactly. That's what I think. There are other interpretations."

"Like what?"

"Enough," Rose said. "This is as bad as going to a socialist lecture."

"Exactly," Gutke said.

"My apologies, ladies," Dovida bowed her head to the side, as if she were an uncle. "Let's have our coffee and Gutke's wonderful poppyseed strudel in the parlor. And don't you start cleaning up, Gutke. I'll do it later." Gutke narrowed her eyes but she left the dishes. Dovida brought out coffee and dessert on a lacquered tray. It was odd to see a man do a woman's domestic chore, even knowing who this "man" really was.

"Where do you work?" Rose asked Dovida when we were settled again.

"I have an office on Wall Street and I travel a lot."

"Too much," Gutke said.

"I am getting a little old to be wandering around the world – and a little bored."

"I'd like a chance to be bored like that," I said.

"In the end, most people find their lives are with the ones they care about," Gutke said, sipping her coffee.

Dovida's eyes wrinkled at the edges, smiling. "She's been trying to tell me this for years. But I've been stubborn. Actually," she glanced away from Gutke, "I'm glad I was stubborn. I have hundreds of stories now, to entertain us in our old age. And now I can give up my stubbornness."

"You always want everything," Gutke scolded, cutting strips of the poppyseed pastry.

"Everyone should want everything," Rose surprised me by saying. "Even if we know we'll only get a little bit, we wouldn't get that much if we didn't start out wanting."

"Just so," Dovida agreed. "I know I've been luckier than most and now I try to give back some of what I've gotten. You know, Chava, if you don't mind, I have a friend who owns a bindery that's been doing very well. I could ask him to consider you for their next opening."

"I – "

"Let Dovida ask for you, Chavele," Gutke said. "It couldn't hurt."

"You're going to just pester me until I agree, aren't you?"

"Of course," Rose took my hand, "of course we will, love." It was my turn to let my mouth fall open.

Gutke and Dovida got the pleased expressions of parents at a wedding, looking at us.

Stone soup

At the New World Bindery they already had enough gluers. Although the foreman was surprised when I said I didn't sew, he motioned across the room. "Ever worked on a folding machine?"

"It wasn't my regular job but I know how." Really, I had only stood beside the machine and watched in the early mornings, before the books piled up for glue. Sometimes, not always, they let girls work on the folders. I thought every shop had a list of machines girls might be allowed to operate: sewing, typewriting, pressing, folding – nothing with a blade, like the devices used by cutters and book trimmers. Maybe they were afraid to let us near anything sharp? The thought amused me but it confused the foreman to see me smiling, so I stopped.

He brought me over to the senior folder, Al. He looked Irish, and disappointed, when he saw me. Because I was a girl, a Jew or so plain? Al grunted "all right" to the foreman and started to explain what he wanted. By the loading dock were stacks of paper delivered from the printer, full sheets with sixteen separate pages arranged on one. If you put the sheet into the folder the wrong way, the book came out with its pages backwards, Al explained. I understood this already. I used to make folding models on my lunch hours, figuring out how the pages of a book ended up in the right place.

It was a very delicate operation, folding: a dance of straps and rollers, the turn of a cam shaft. It looked like a sculpture to me, the whole idea of industrial production neatly played out on an asymmetrical metal bar. I watched Al, who moved his arms as if he were another part of the machine, steady, pumping. He went by the rhythm of the machine, if not its grace.

"Grace," Rose laughed at me later that day, "an actress is graceful,

the drape of a skirt, graceful maybe, but a folding machine? You spent too many hours inhaling glue and tobacco fumes. Don't make a face. What else have you done in America? Your brain doesn't work so good anymore."

"That must be why I still bother to talk to you," I glanced behind as we walked down Pitt Street. No one was paying us any notice. I took her arm. Lots of girls walked arm in arm, holding hands, swinging them. Rose said that sometimes she'd see girls in her shop rub their cheeks against each other, sigh and give each other moony, tender looks – and then within a month one of them would be engaged to marry.

"You wouldn't – ," I said.

"I've already lived with enough men, thank you very much. Besides, you smell better than any man I've ever met."

"Even Dovid?"

She slapped me on the behind.

"C'mon," I said, "if you run with me to the corner I'll buy you an egg cream."

She held her skirt up, running after me, laughing.

But we still lived with men. When Uncle Isadore played with his watch chain at night, I thought of Dovida, sitting in her big plush chair, her feet up. Was being a man – or a woman – just acting, a series of gestures we learned?

"Daydreaming again, huh, Chava?" Aaron hit the back of my chair with his book. "Now that you make $8 a week you just like to sit back and take it easy."

"I haven't noticed that you do anything around here besides read your books."

"I'll have you know that today, this very day, I took the entrance exam to join the police force. Imagine getting $30 a week! And as soon as I pass the naturalization exams, even more."

"I remember that Judas betrayed Christ for thirty pieces of silver and then had to hang himself."

"You have to resort to Christian stories to insult me?"

"Children!" Isadore broke in. We turned to glare at him. "All right, all right, I know you're not children anymore – so stop behaving like children." He looked at Aaron, tapping his long nails on the table. "So how was this exam you took?"

Aaron shrugged. "An exam. All in English but I understood everything."

"Do they ask whether it's better to hit a striker in the ribs or in the head?"

"A lot you know. They don't have anything about strikers in the exam."

"Chava, leave Aaron alone. If he's made up his mind, his mind is made up. We have to respect his choices."

"Thanks, Pa."

"But I didn't say I approved." He sighed, looked at Aunt Bina, who was sewing by the air shaft. "We going to have dinner tonight, missus?"

"Where's Rose?" Bina replied. She relied on Rose, and me, more and more to take care of household things. I didn't mind, exactly, except that it was because she was always sewing for Harry, and Aaron and Uncle Isadore hardly did anything to help around the apartment.

"How should I know? I can barely keep track of myself, let alone these young people who board with us now," Isadore said.

"Chava?"

"She should be home from work any minute, Aunt Bina. When I stopped by Hester Street earlier they said they were only working an hour overtime tonight. Do you want me to go back and see?"

"No, I want you to put on water for potatoes and chop some cabbage."

"Potatoes and cabbage again, Ma?"

"You, Aaron, are not making $30 a week yet, I notice."

He made a show of standing, getting a new book, plopping himself down with his head in his palms, nodding over the page. He still looked like any young Talmud scholar, only clean shaven.

Isadore picked up the paper and went back to fiddling with his watch chain. I was halfway through the cabbage – it looked good on the outside, but had a little pocket of green worms, not too much to throw away – when I heard slow steps on the stairs. I put down the knife and went out to the hall, watching Rose's hatpins reflect the light from the gas jet on the third landing.

As she lifted her head I saw she'd been crying. I started down, met her on the middle step, clasped her shoulder.

"Nu?"

"Nothing. Fired again. Laid off."

"So soon?"

"They waited until the last minute to tell us, as we were putting on

our hats. They said to come back for our pay next Friday. But by next Friday the shop will be empty. I'll never see that money." She stamped her foot in frustration, then sniffled, wiping her nose on the back of her hand.

"Are you sure?"

"Oh, Chava, sometimes – ." She walked past me to the door.

I stood on the landing, looking at shadows for a minute, listening to Rose tell her parents the bad news. Aaron rushed past me.

"Where are you going?"

"Somewhere it isn't all potatoes and cabbages," he yelled, already halfway to the next floor.

The cabbage – I returned to the kitchen. Isadore was pacing; Rose had pulled up a chair next to Bina's. I started chopping again, glad that Leon was on overtime all week, even if he was willing to do it for free in order to keep his job.

"It's not good," Isadore was mumbling. He looked at us as if he hadn't seen us in months. "Mrs. Petrovsky, you're ruining your eyes and your back. You girls, you're ruining your youth. I left Odessa in the prime of my life and four years later I feel like an old man. It's my duty – it would be my pleasure – to see that you, missus, never picked up a needle again." He grabbed the overcoat that Aunt Bina was working on out of her lap and threw it on the floor.

"Isadore – ." Bina started to protest and then reconsidered, folding her hands in her lap, watching him.

"At home I had my own shop, my own house. To be reduced to this – ." He gestured at the stained walls, the pile of cabbage in front of me. Then he slumped into a chair, never taking his eyes off Bina's face, shaking his head back and forth, as if his thoughts could be dislodged like dirt from his ear.

"At home we had a few wonderful years, of great luck and privilege," Bina said slowly, picking up Rose's hand and stroking it. "But the whole street where your shop stood was burned out two years ago." She took a breath, making a dry smacking sound in her mouth. "Our fates catch up to us. You know, my Great-Aunt Rokhl told me that the Orthodox believe you can change your name when you're fatally ill and the Angel of Death won't recognize you."

"That's nonsense," Isadore said, reviving a little.

"Exactly my point. At least here we can hope for change, real change, not just a good spell between pogroms and the Tsar's edicts. You, thank God, still have your job." She held up her hand to quiet him. "And Chava

is now making $8 a week for the first time. Leon's still working and Harry pays me now, in addition to giving us board like Leon – "

"Oh Mama, Harry's a parasite!" Rose exclaimed.

"A parasite. What a way to talk about your brother. You're upset, I know. Go change, wash your face."

"Mama—"

"Go."

Rose looked at me and we traded identical shrugs. As she went into the other room, Isadore spoke. "She's right about Harry, I think."

"You too?" Bina said.

"I don't like the way that boy's turning out. He only shows up when he wants to take advantage of you."

"The money he pays me contributes."

"Contributes!" Isadore said, pacing again. "Maybe it's just as well Aaron is leaving City College for the police – we won't have to support him anymore."

"At least he should start paying you back, once he gets that awful job," I said, peeling barely edible potatoes.

Bina stood to retrieve the overcoat from the floor, as if it had merely slipped from her lap. "He has his own life to start now." She inspected her stitches, made a sour face and started up again. "As soon as Aaron gets that job, he'll move out." Her hand was flashing with a needle again. "I think he has a girlfriend."

"A girlfriend?" Isadore turned to stare at her.

"Sit, Isadore, all that pacing makes me nervous. He's twenty-three already. He would have two children by now at home."

"Why doesn't he bring her to meet us? What's wrong with him?"

"It's not him; it's us. I think he must have an American girl he met at school. He doesn't want to bring her here."

"A minute ago you were telling me everything was going to turn out fine, and now you're saying my own son is so ashamed of me he won't bring his girlfriend here?"

"Isadore, I don't know what to tell you. It pains me too. Talk to him. Tell him we can arrange a meeting in a café if he likes. We'll put on our best clothes and try not to look too green. I only hope she's Jewish."

"He's going with a shikse?"

"I didn't say that. I don't even know if he's going with anyone. Ask him yourself."

"All right, all right. I'll ask him tomorrow."

I threw the potatoes in the boiling water. "But Aunt Bina, even if

Aaron leaves to start his own home, is it right for him to leave without giving anything back?"

" 'When the father gives to the son, both enjoy good fortune. When the son gives to the father, both curse their luck,' " Isadore said.

"It's not like you to fall back on proverbs," I said, catching his eye for a minute.

"Sometimes the proverbs say it best," Bina said. "A man is a man, he makes his own way." She cut the thread, made a quick knot and turned to get another coat from the pile.

"What about the women who made his way possible?" I asked. "And what about daughters? They don't just drift off, even the married ones." When I started talking to Bina, Isadore took the opportunity to find his pipe.

"It's different with daughters, you can see that. Every day I thank God for Rose."

"You should tell her." I wondered if Rose was listening from the other room.

"If she doesn't know in her heart, what good would telling do?" Bina glanced to the door, sharing my thought with a half smile. "Chava, you know I try and keep up with you girls, with the world, but my people never talked about how they felt for each other. They would bring on the evil eye if they were happy, and if they were unhappy, well, unhappiness was familiar. At least they had their family, their place in the world. Now everything turns inside out one minute, sideways the next. I often think it's better for everyone if I stay steady and quiet."

"Too many women stay quiet, if you ask me."

"What do you mean by that?" Bina stared at me.

"No disrespect, Aunt Bina, I'm sorry. I just mean there are so many women working. If we all got together, think of what we could do."

"That's your League speaking, isn't it?" Bina rethreaded the needle.

Isadore made a show of packing and lighting his pipe, sucking loudly to get it started. He never liked it when I talked about the League.

"But it's common sense," I said.

"You're right, dear, and hard to accomplish, isn't it? When we were girls in Kishinev, your mother and I were told that if all the Jews kept Shabbes two weeks in a row, the messiah would come. You'd think when so many more people were religious, they could have agreed, just for once, to all keep Shabbes two weeks in a row – if only to see."

Rose came out of her room in a clean shirtwaist and a skirt with big

buttons down the side. "Jews could never agree about anything for a day, let alone for two weeks in a row," she said.

Isadore snorted, lighting another match. "You see how much you women understand?"

"What don't we understand?"

"The reason it didn't happen was because if they all had done it – just, as you say missus, to see – and the messiah *didn't* come, they'd have to give up their faith. So there was always someone who took it upon himself to keep that calamity from happening. It was faith in the messiah that was important, not the messiah himself." He puffed out a cloud of smoke and picked up his newspaper with an air of having completely won the argument. Aunt Bina nodded her head back and forth, as if commenting maybe yes, maybe no. I sighed.

"We're going to be late for class if we don't leave in ten minutes, Chava. What's going on with that dinner?" Rose pulled the spoon out of my hand, forked a potato, added some salt. In three minutes the cabbage and potatoes were on the table. I cut slices of black bread and the four of us ate quickly, without looking at each other.

We hurtled through the tunnel faster than a runaway team of horses, lights flashing at us from the walls. I pressed my eyes as close to the window of the front car as I dared. Rose squeezed my hand. Fear and excitement sparked between us. A group of workmen hurried to take refuge from our underground train, ducking into small, scooped-out grottos. This was progress, everyone declared. Thrilling, certainly, but I wasn't sure about progress. Maybe we were going backwards in time with all these new inventions, trying to hide inside the earth like moles. Going so fast, my brain was thrown around inside my skull, and surely that couldn't be good. Good or bad, Rose and I had wanted to ride on the train since it opened almost two years earlier, yet it always seemed an impossible extravagance.

Pauline Newman, who was sometimes at the League but usually worked with the Socialist Party, had organized a camp on the Palisades for independent girls out of work that summer, mostly seamstresses, so they wouldn't have to pay rent. I thought camping out with so many other girls would be a great adventure. But I was still working, and Rose played at being annoyed when I suggested she might like to go without me.

"I thought you liked me a little better than that," she said.

I liked Rose even better than the idea of a general strike, but I didn't

want her to miss the camp on my account. I considered abandoning my job, even though it was the best one I'd ever had. Then Rose threatened not to speak to me for a year if I quit. Finally we compromised on going for a weekend. We were lucky. The weekend we picked was in the middle of June's garbage strike. As the rats played tag among piles of fermenting debris on Essex Street, we were glad for any excuse to get away.

Saturday morning Rose waited a block from my bindery, standing guard over the provisions we were shleping, including a big bag of Shabbes evening specials we'd haggled for as the pushcarts closed on Orchard Street. I mussed my hair, pulled my shirtwaist half out of my skirt and ran up the two flights to the bindery floor. I'm not sure Al believed I had to take my cousin to the hospital for her consumption, but I must have looked so flushed myself that I scared him.

"Don't let it happen again," he growled. I was rarely late and never sick, so I figured I could get away with a lie once.

After the subway ground to its last stop at 157th Street, we trundled up the deep stairwell, glad, for a minute, to find ourselves blinking, bewildered by the bright day. After we got used to sunlight again, we transferred onto the Kingsbridge trolley to Dyckman Street and walked down to the ferry to Englewood. Luckily, the secretary at the League had given me detailed instructions. Except for our one trip to Central Park, I'd never been past the new Macy's on 34th Street, and this part of New York was as foreign as another country – a cleaner country, where a few trees straggled along the streets and the buildings weren't pressing their shoulders together, pecking like chickens at the clouds. Everyone looked like an American and I would have been shy to ask for help. Harry told us stories about uptown goyim who liked to trick immigrants by giving wrong directions, sometimes in order to rob and beat us. I knew he used these stories to support his personal religion of only looking out for himself, but that didn't mean the stories weren't true.

As we waited at the dock, I stood by our bags and bedrolls while Rose wandered around the landing slowly, playing with the curls of her hair, damp from the humidity. She was upset about how much the trip cost – thirteen cents each with the transfer, one way – I could tell from how she kicked at the rocks. After awhile she picked one up and put it in her skirt pocket. Then she felt me watching her and turned to meet my gaze, self-consciously tucking in her waist.

Once the ferry got underway, a breeze came across the Hudson and gave us relief from the heat. Children in britches, families with picnic

baskets going to Bloomers Beach, a few tramps heading for work on farms – all leaned over the railing to catch the wind and bits of spray. I remembered how tenderly Rose had fed me the orange when I was sick on the ship. I reached into the bag and found a ripe plum. I wanted to roll it across Rose's lips, hold it while she bit, to lap the juices dribbling down her cheek, but I settled for the glances we exchanged, the way her eyes held mine as she ate half, licking the exposed purple interior before she passed it back to me.

By the time we climbed the path above Englewood Basin, we were drenched with shvits even though we had rolled our shirtsleeves above our elbows. I didn't care how muggy it was. I was excited to be in our second American state, New Jersey, which appeared to be mostly river beach, cliffs and countryside. We stopped often on the pretext of admiring the view, though really because it was a long walk. We would have missed the last turnoff if I hadn't told Rose to watch for a red kerchief on a birch tree, which she spotted. Of course, the girls wouldn't want the whole city to know they were there.

As we neared the camp I could hear an accordion, someone playing "Tum Balalyke" – not expertly, but well enough that a chorus of girls' voices were joining in. Rose began to sing. Her face was flushed from the walk and from carrying so many parcels, yet her eyes reflected the blue brilliance of the summer sky.

"*What can grow without rain? What can burn and never be consumed? What can cry yet shed no tears?* Come, Chava, sing with me – '*tum-bala, tum-bala, tum-balalyke*'."

I'd never liked to sing. Papa used to laugh when I sang Purim songs. Mama said I had a sweet little singing voice but I never believed her. But with Rose – we made a turn in the path and saw a small shtetl of tents. In a meadow dozens of girls circled around the accordion player, while among the tents girls were hanging up laundry, sitting on crates and reading, gathered in groups of two and three, talking, chopping wood, hauling water, peeling potatoes over huge pots. So I started to sing too, and once singing I had a moment of wild, easy happiness. Anything was possible! We were so many, I thought, without knowing which "many" I was thinking of.

A girl with a bad complexion, shirtsleeves rolled above her elbows and one long eyebrow over her brown eyes, approached us. "New recruits!" she said in Yiddish.

I laughed. "Only for tonight . We have to go back to Essex Street tomorrow evening."

"What a shame. Well, one night's better than none," the girl said. "Here, let me carry some of those things."

"Thank you," Rose said but I didn't let her take any of my packages. I felt strong enough to carry mine and Rose's too.

"Are you Pauline?"

"Pauline Newman? Nobody's ever mistaken me for her before – you must not know her. I'm Sherna, Sherna Block."

We introduced ourselves. "I've always missed Pauline at the League offices, but Rose Schneiderman said to make sure to find her."

"You're League members?"

"I am – "

"I'm just a hanger on," Rose said.

"No one has to join the League, or even a union, to belong here," Sherna said. "The camp feels like a utopia."

"A utopia! This I have to see," I answered.

"Just look around. It's not the Ritz but everyone shares what they have and looks out for each other."

"And when it's not summer anymore?" I didn't want to seem sour, so I kept my voice light, hoping she would understand.

"Then we'll figure out what to do next – together," Sherna said, pointing to a space between tents and trees. "You can set up your things there. The kitchen is just through these tents and down that path, you can't miss it. Bring anything to eat?"

"Of course," Rose said. I could tell she was insulted that anyone would mistake us for spongers.

"It'll be welcome," Sherna said, oblivious to Rose's tone. "If you're still looking for Pauline, she's the one with short hair over there." She pointed to the edge of the singing circle, where a few girls stood to the side, talking.

For our tent we had two old sheets. We tied a line between trees and folded one sheet over, anchoring it with large stones. The other we used to cover the ground. It was an illusion of floor but at least insects would have to walk over it to get to us. We each had a bedroll with our featherbeds and another sheet . We rolled them out on our new floor and looked at each other. We'd left as much room between them as possible.

"Do you think we could move them closer?" I asked.

Rose shook her head, sighing. Was she thinking of all the ways we hid, until it seemed the real people we were hiding from were each other? Then she nodded her head, up and down, wise, warm and

welcoming. Stooped, we pulled the featherbeds until they overlapped. Our heads bumped and we fell, laughing, in a heap. We quickly untangled when we heard footsteps.

"Hello!" a voice called, "are you decent?"

"We're trying not to be," Rose called back.

I shot her an amazed look as I brushed off my skirt and crawled out towards the voice. Pauline was standing in front of our tent, her hands on her hips, wearing a cap like a workman's, a black skirt and a plain, pleated white shirtwaist, the shirtsleeves rolled as high as they'd go. As I straightened up, I saw she was my height.

"Are you Chava?" I nodded and she extended her hand. "I heard you were looking for me. You're a friend of Rose Schneiderman?"

"Not a friend exactly, but I know her from the Women's Trade Union League."

"I've been thinking about joining them," Pauline said, "but I go to all the meetings of the Socialist Party already. How many nights are there?" She shrugged and a strand of brown hair fell over her ear.

Pauline couldn't have been older than sixteen but she seemed to have the easy self-confidence of a grown union organizer. I looked directly into her eyes to show I wasn't intimidated, to show I was a comrade. "I'm drawn to the socialists but sometimes I'm confused about what, exactly, their program is, and if there's really a place for women to work in it," I said.

"Tell me about it!" She threw an arm around my shoulder, leading me towards the group Rose and I had noticed earlier. "Come, I'll introduce you to some socialists who organize women."

I turned around and saw Rose on her hands and knees in our tent door, peering up at me. I brought my shoulder up to my ear, as if to ask, you don't mind, do you?

"Go ahead," she yelled after me, standing, shaking the dust off her clothes. "I'll take a walk and look around."

Pauline observed our exchange and didn't miss a step as she led me forward.

Rose wandered through the camp on a path that led towards the cliffs. Usually she talked with everyone, anyone, but a rush of quiet filled her. She wanted to think. All the girls appeared to be Jews, since the only languages she heard were Yiddish and Yiddish-English, mostly Russian accents, but also Polish, Russian, Croatian, even some German and

French. She noticed at least a dozen blond girls talking Yiddish, which reminded her of old childhood whisperings that her grandfather must have been a Cossack, on account of her blue eyes.

How many hidden Cossacks were there in Jews? And what difference did it make, she wondered. Her blue eyes didn't change who she was. What Jews are – was it inside or outside? The path went around a rocky outcropping. Near the edge was a stone face that looked easy to climb: a toehold and you could swing a leg up, pull your whole weight after you and sit on a ledge on one of the dark columns of the Palisades. It took Rose two tries; she was glad no one was near, watching. The last group of tents was just visible through the trees and boulders, though the sound of girls' voices was close and stirred her.

Out of her pocket she pulled the rock she'd picked up at the Dyckman landing. The stone was flecked with soft, shiny bits that peeled off in small wafers. She compared it to the rock where she sat. They were so unlike, no bright bits on the reddish brown stone of the Palisades. She pried a wafer from the rock in her hand carefully, with her longest nail, and held up the miniature sheet to the light. The sun was beginning to set behind her, the horizon edged with pink, as if someone had woven ribbon through the hem of a tablecloth, laying it out over the sky, edges swaying over the city. The soft wafer pane could be a window in a miniature house. She pulled its layers apart slowly, letting it crumble by her side.

Songs drifted by as she sat, hugging her knees. Directly across, a river cut through a rounded hill. Far to her right, below the fields, New York City looked like a castle: a vast, low, rambling castle estate, its fingers pointing to the sky as if to challenge any idea that came from above instead of below, where so many toiled to make the castle rich.

Rose looked at the river, the rocks, the tents that from this distance appeared like flags from a fairy tale. Her heart had so many pieces that seemed uncomplicated at first, yet didn't quite fit together. She had a momentary sensation of longing for herself. The rock had been there longer than her life, and yet her childhood seemed like a wearisome dream she'd had, taking care of Papa's sons. They had been important – their ambitions, their ideas – important, in a way she never was, though Mama made her feel loved. There was a difference between being loved and being important, she realized. Her life had always been hard and soft at the same time. She favored smooth things: clean tablecloths with a little lace at the edge, carefully made-up featherbeds,

smooth gravies and strudel with cream, clean starched shirts, fine woolen shawls. Her own skin, she always liked her own skin, even before Chava. Touching it made her catch her breath – on the inside of her elbows, for instance, where the soft flesh was always warm, or her earlobe, a little sack at the side of her face made for fingering, like shells she remembered from the portside stores of Odessa.

She never complained about the work she had to do because Mama always tried to make it fun. "Imagine the mop is your dance partner," Mama said, "see how much of the floor you can cover, dancing." Mama taught her how to waltz, letting Rose stand on her feet. She knew girls with more brothers, whose mamas scolded them no matter how hard they worked. They'd get used to married life that way, their mamas said. Her mama said she didn't want that kind of marriage for Rose.

"Life is always working, of course, but it must have happiness," her Mama had said long before piecework banished happiness from the tenement. "You must find a way to fill your heart with the pleasure of everything around you. It's even a Commandment." Mama never told Rose which one. Something about not forgetting the way God moves through creation like the wind.

That was her childhood. When Chava came to Odessa, Rose was thirteen. She had just learned that the smoothness where her thigh met the opening between her legs was the best smoothness on her body. She remembered when Chava had been her slightly older, independent cousin who ran through Kishinev's streets, knowing all the shortcuts and alleys. Had she loved Chava since they were little girls? Chava had always been so serious – of course, because she was an orphan and saw her parents die.

What would she have done if *her* Mama had been killed? It would have been terrible to be alone with Aaron, Harry, Saul, Jacob. She tried to be as serious as Chava, to hold herself up because her cousin's parents were killed in a pogrom. Before Chava came to live with them she hadn't thought so much about being a Jew, even with everyone's Cossack stories. Now she thought about it all the time, trying to figure out if there was something different inside them, something they were born with, not just that their ancestors were Jews. And even if there was something different – if many had long noses, if they were ugly to others, like Chava wrote, or didn't believe in Jesus – was that a reason to make pogroms on them? Even in America, where Jews were supposed to be free, the American-born mocked them, and anyone who could took advantage. When Rose found herself on the wrong

street, she felt how mean their words were, even when she didn't understand their language.

Chava's heart must hurt her very much, Rose thought. When Chava came to them, she was hard as an elbow, always jabbing herself out into the air, as if to say, "Keep away." But Rose had seen how tender she was on the other side, so she let her be. With anything frightened, you had to be gentle. Even in the beginning, when she thought of being gentle to Chava, parts of her body fluttered inside. After a little while, being gentle with Chava was a secret delicacy.

Chava was brave but Rose was more sophisticated, she knew. She understood the world as a woman, even when they were girls. Chava knew about the revolution and suffering of course, but she was always putting suffering behind her as though it had nothing to do with all her grand political schemes. To Rose, the emotions of the world were more interesting, not intellectual life or abstract theories about economics and women's position. Anyone could know what women's position was just by opening their eyes. Who wanted to stare at that all the time?

All these girls, like Chava, had such a passion for ideas, their belief in a better life, a better way to organize living. What Rose loved, really – she looked up, noticing the pink clouds paling to gray – was their excitement. If Chava had, instead, a passion, a genuine fever, for buying property, Rose would have loved her for that. (Maybe – it was hard to picture either of them as landladies!) Ardent. That's what Chava was, ardent. Her need to change the world, that was what swept Rose into her.

Was she simply a log on the fire of someone else's passion? Rose rolled a pebble down the cliff. No, she was her own. She could make her own way. After all, she supported the family as much as Chava did, more until recently. Chava made her way through all those clawing shop foreman, the perils of the workplace, by simply not seeing them, not believing they were there, that they could be meant for her. Chava didn't really know herself as a girl, and she never had.

Rose shook her head, not sure exactly what this meant. She used to believe that fashion meant so little to Chava because she was in constant mourning, but now Rose understood her differently. And yet, Chava moved like a woman, felt like a woman: the softness of the inside of her upper arms, where Rose loved to reach in under the nightgown, and hold, while Chava's legs wrapped around her and rubbed over Rose's bone and belly, engulfed in a klezmer melody, the deep breaths they took sometimes melancholy and sometimes, in rare

moments when they were alone, as raucous as a wedding dance.

Weddings. Rose bit her knuckle. Her Mama and Papa expected her to get married eventually. They were starting to hint about consulting a shadkhn, "just for advice," in a year or two maybe, since they didn't want her to go with some dance-hall dandy or an impoverished tailor. How were they going to make a good match for their only daughter? In America their boys could, and were, taking care of themselves. If Rose happened to meet a college student or a young lawyer or even someone successful in his own business – but how would she meet this person?

They didn't seem to care about Chava the same way, and not just because she was only their niece. They appeared to have a little story they told themselves about how Chava was going to end up married to organizing, and in a way, they almost approved. Mama more than Papa. Mama had a respect for Chava. Maybe because she too saw how strong Chava was, and how sweet and good underneath that strength, how her idealism kept her connected – to the working women, to Jews. So many girls got buried alive in marriages. Mama wouldn't think of it that way but sometimes Rose saw her sewing, sewing, and saw that Mama was buried too.

If Rose had to get married, it wouldn't bury her. Chava would live with them, and – no, Chava wouldn't stand it, and Rose couldn't imagine seeing her, bewildered and wounded every night, even if they spent all their time together and everything else was the same. How *could* she get married? She'd only do it for Mama. And maybe it would be nice to have children, if there was enough money for them. She'd never make her girls into servants for boys.

Children. Rose looked over her shoulder and made out a few girls moving at the edges of the camp, some still singing, most doing evening chores, hauling armloads of branches, hanging out wash, sweeping up the pathways. She should have been helping with dinner. There was a familiar smell of onions and garlic in the breeze.

Maybe they should get an apartment together the way Chava wanted. They could get new lampshades, with fringes, and maybe she'd needlepoint some cushions for their chairs. Just the two of them would be such a luxury. Gutke and Dovida managed to live together very nicely. And many women lived together, at Henry Street, everywhere. They wouldn't need a lot of money. She hated to think of leaving Mama, but they wouldn't have to go far. And Mama could use their room for boarders, which would make up at least half of the wages they'd been giving her. Certainly they'd have to wait until this

depression ended. She'd rather live with Chava than with any man she'd ever met.

Rose's stomach gurgled. She gave it a little pat. "All right, then," she said to her stomach, sliding off the rock. "Let's go see what this bunch thinks of food. They can't all want to live off the air of ideas."

From our makeshift tent, Rose and I could see the occasional shape of a girl walking by. We lay in the night heat listening. Branches and dry leaves crackled as they were added to late cooking fires. Laughter, bits of song and discussion floated on the humid air. A layer of perspiration enclosed me like a sticky soap bubble, making me feel that no matter how much I wanted to touch Rose, she'd find me unappealing. A firefly flew inside our sheet-wall. I watched it try to find its way out again, blinking through the shadows. Rose took my hand.

"No one will bother us here," she said.

"I'm covered with sweat."

She licked my arm slowly. "Yes," she said, "salty."

"I don't smell bad?"

"You smell better than dinner to a laid-off seamstress."

A light breeze came up the cliffs from the river and dried my arm where her tongue had been, giving me a shiver. I leaned up on my side and looked at her. There was just enough light from the moon and the camp lanterns to see by. Her hair was pinned up off her neck and I could make out the small mole below her ear. She was wearing her lightest cotton slip, twisted tight across the mound of her belly. Sometimes her body seemed as far away as the moon when I watched her cleaning up on Essex Street or coming out of work with her friends. But tonight the moonlight was in the river and I could dip my hand in and drink it if I dared.

"Maybe I don't smell so good to you?" she asked. Her eyes, which had echoed the July sky all day, were gray in the dark. Even so I could see, now that I was looking at her body, her confidence leak away. I put my nose close to her armpit.

"You smell like the plum orchards of Bessarabia."

"You're a liar."

"You accuse me, your own cousin, of lying?" I poked her side lightly and she poked me back.

"At the very least, a flatterer," she said, pressing her hand against my arm.

"I know what I smell, and you smell delicious." I put my face under her breasts, resting on the upward curve of her stomach. In fact, we both smelled sweaty and smoky. How she really smelled was familiar and strange at the same time, the smell of a freshly bound leather folio, compelling. "Rose – "

"Yes?"

I turned my face up to look at her. "Would you take your slip off?"

She looked at me intently and we both sat up. All these years, we'd never lain naked together. We'd hardly seen each other's bodies unclothed except for the few seconds between pulling off our skirts and putting on our nightgowns, and when we let our towels loosen in the baths. I could feel a stone poking my thigh through the featherbed. I didn't care. From a few directions I could hear soft moans but no footsteps.

Rose heard the moans too and smiled. "Yes," she said as she pulled the slip over her arms. She folded it neatly. "Now you."

I peeled mine off and used it to wipe the sweat from my face before I threw it in the corner. Sitting, Rose's flesh made a generous fold above her belly. I slid my hand under the fold and squeezed her flesh upward lightly. Rose's eyelids trembled, her lips parted as an "aaah" crept up her throat, and then she opened her eyes wide, as if she were frightened.

"Rose," I said, leaning close to her ear, "you are my heart's desire."

"Flatterer," she mumbled into my check, relaxing as she kissed me.

Then we were prone again, naked on our bedrolls. And scared. Strangers surrounded us. Yet we were also beyond fear – the shop girls' camp was like a wall protecting us against our ordinary tenement life. I loved her softness, the resiliency of her flesh when I pressed my palm into it, the way a mossy riverbank springs back from your step. I rolled over on her body.

"I'm not too heavy like this?" I could feel the pressure of my chest flattening her breasts.

"No, you feel good."

We were sweating so profusely that I slid against her. I swayed into that sliding sensation, holding myself up on my wrists, back and forth, my small breasts tickling the pillowy surface of hers. We giggled when I guided my nipple exactly onto her nipple, and they both puckered, taking on the shape of ancient towers. I started to rock, my thighs slipping up and down hers. She pushed her belly up hard into mine and rocked with me.

"Put your whole weight on me again," she whispered.

I fell into her mouth, grabbing her thighs for balance. We kissed and swayed, slipping. My feet tilted off her calves and curled back around her toes. Between my thighs the sweat gave way to a different stickiness and behind my shut eyes a bright green flashed, seesawing my focus between mouths and lower limbs. Our legs tightened together, straining into each other, as if we wanted to get beneath the thin cover of our skins or melt the skin together, like candle wax. In a corner of my mind I could see the havdale candles I made as a child, felt my hands braiding the warm wax while it was pliant, two wicks intertwining, mingling with the sharp smell of the spicebox.

I opened my eyes to watch her face as she filled, moving beyond self-consciousness, moving with me. I arched to let one hand move between our bodies, supporting myself on my other arm. Rose seemed to hold her breath. I rubbed the curly hair below her belly, tugging it lightly until she gasped, and opened her eyes.

"Anything," she breathed, "anything you want."

"Anything you want," I echoed with the same urgency, "— everything." I turned my hand sideways, holding the fingers tightly together and entered the folds of her as I might slice through the uncut leaves of a book. I closed my eyes again, listening. Rose was taking short, hungry breaths and I could find the rhythm of her breathing in the pulse I felt coming up through her inside lips. I turned my hand again so that two fingers stroked her small mound. We called it the inner nipple, since it grew larger and harder when we excited each other and seemed connected to our other nipples by an invisible thread of flame. Rose grabbed my arm. Her grip was strong from years of sewing and carrying, and I felt almost faint from the pressure, from flooding. Rose was moaning and for the first time I didn't feel a need to shush her. I heard myself groan as I slipped the two fingers deep inside her and she tightened her muscles around me, clasping me as I shook and pumped.

For a moment Rose seemed to stop breathing altogether. Her muscles grabbed my fingers tight and her hips strained upward from the featherbed while her head rolled back. Then she gave a cry and jerked, gasping for air, relaxing and then squeezing my fingers and crying out a second, a third time. I felt my interior muscles contracting with hers, and cried out too. Then she collapsed in on herself.

Her laughter surprised me. At home she often pushed a pillow over her head when we got this far, to stifle any noise. I pulled my hand out.

A thin film made a web between my thumb and forefinger. I held it to my nose and sniffed, smiling at her strong smell, which carried a faint scent of the herring we'd eaten for dinner.

She took my hand and put it to her lips, kissing my fingers. "You are a blessing, Chava, my blessing."

Far away I heard another girl laughing, because of listening to us or her own pleasure? I rolled back onto my side, wiping my hand on the bottom sheet of our makeshift tent. Then I lay in her arm, nuzzling her breast slowly. What a pleasure to be naked. Rose stroked my hair, murmuring deep in her throat.

"And you?" she asked after awhile.

"I'm completely satisfied," I said.

"Completely?" She asked, moving her fingers down to the hair of my vee.

"Completely," I said, stopping her exploration. All I wanted was to lie there in the calm, feeling the liquid surface of my skin suffused with her body.

"All right, if you say so."

We played with each other's fingers for maybe a minute, maybe twenty. Every once in awhile I opened my eyes and saw the firefly blink.

"Would you like to hear a story?" Rose asked after a long silence.

"Yes." I felt some tender place tear open, an unused room, where the doorway was covered in cobwebs. Someone rediscovered it, clearing the debris, opening the shutters, bringing in the world. This was a welcome change, yet each cobweb was attached to a nerve in my breast bone and ached as it was wrenched away.

"Do you know the story about stone soup?" Rose asked.

"Stone soup?" I moved my hand down her side, stroking and pressing into her sweet fatness. Of course I knew the story. Who didn't? Mama used to tell us.

"You know, where the beggar comes to town and asks for something to eat – "

"A woman or man beggar?"

"I don't remember woman beggars at home, but for now we'll make it a woman, if you like."

"I like."

"Fine," Rose said. "So the beggar got thrown out of the first town she went to. The people threw rocks at her. She picked up one of the rocks and put it in a small velvet pouch she had found the week before."

"Where?"

"In the woods, near where the deer live."

"Did the deer make it for her?"

"I don't know, Chava. She found it, that's all." Rose poked me in the side. "Anyway, she comes to the next town and this time shows off her magic stone, which, the beggar bragged, you could put into a pot with some water and make the most delicious soup in the world."

"What town was it?" I asked, remembering Russia.

"Chava, it doesn't make any difference. Let's say it was – it was a shtetl, just a little bump of a town like you could see for a minute from the train."

"Okay, the shtetl of Bump," I said, tickling her knee.

"You're impossible," she said, swatting my hand. "Do you want to hear this story or not?"

"Very much."

"Then settle down," she said, ruffling my hair. "So in the shtetl of Bump the women all gathered around the beggar woman to see the stone. The beggar held up the velvet bag with a big lump in it. 'From this bag it must go directly into water,' the beggar said. 'Ah, if only I had a kettle of water.'

"Then one of the townswomen ran home for her kettle. 'But the water must be boiling,' the beggar said. And so the women built a fire and filled the pot with water from their pumps. When the water was boiling, the beggar woman circled the pot with her velvet pouch, mumbling words in a language the townspeople had never heard before. Then she made a quick gesture and the rock flew into the boiling water.

" 'Did you see that?' the women said to each other – "

"But they hadn't really seen anything, had they?" I asked. I looked beyond Rose's breast and could see that now there were two fireflies in the tent, winking at each other in the dark. Something crawled over my toe and I simply flicked it off. Rose nodded and continued.

" 'Ah,' the beggar said, bending over the pot, 'this is going to be delicious, if I do say so myself. But – .' The beggar took a big sniff. 'What?' asked a housewife. 'Well, if we could throw in some carrots, this soup would rival my grandmother's, of blessed memory.' "

"So the woman found some carrots, right?"

"Of course. And then onions, celery, salt and finally a chicken. One after another, the townspeople ran and got whatever the beggar woman suggested. Finally, the beggar said, 'One last thing, and the

276

soup will be done.' "

"What else could she need?" I nestled into Rose even more closely and she pressed back. Not a blade of grass would have found a passage between our bodies.

"Bowls and spoons, of course. And there was enough for everyone in the village as well as the beggar to eat their fill. When they were done, the beggar reached into the pot and pulled out her stone, which of course was gleaming from the soup and the chicken fat."

The fireflies appeared to be dancing for each other, signaling in some code I thought it might be possible to understand. "It was a miracle," I yawned.

"That's what the townspeople thought. A miracle that soup so good could be made from just a stone." Rose paused and ran the back of her hand along my cheek. I nibbled at her fingers with my lips but my eyes were too heavy to keep open.

"Sweet dreams, my darling," were the last words I heard Rose say.

"How was your adventure, girls?" Aunt Bina looked up from her sewing. In the gaslight I saw how her face was both drawn and a little puffy. Being in the fresh air for a day had changed my perceptions.

"Marvelous!" Rose said in English, and we all laughed.

"Where is everyone?" I asked.

"Leon's at his study circle, Aaron's with his girlfriend somewhere, Harry, who knows, and Isadore went to a union meeting. Is that everyone who lives here?"

"A union meeting?" I whistled. "Things must be really looking grim if Uncle Iz is ready to do more than pay his dues."

"If you're hungry, there's some leftover potato kugl," Bina said, pretending to ignore me.

Rose and I unpacked our bundles, going in and out of our bedroom. Rose pulled something out of her pocket and brought it over to Bina. "Look, Mama, what I found in this rock – little layers, like windows." She held up a stone about the size of a fifty-cent piece that shone in the small yellow circle of gaslight.

Bina stopped stitching for a second. "Nice, very interesting, a souvenir from the country." She sighed before starting to treadle again. "The stench around here is impossible, though the health department says they'll have the garbage cleared this week. I'm glad you girls got out for a little bit. You never have enough time to have any fun, just

working, politics, studying all the time."

"Us! Oh Mama, I wish you could have been there. You're the one who really needs a rest."

"You think this is work? It's nothing, nothing. I'm here in my own apartment, no bosses like you girls have. If I want a glass of tea, I have a glass of tea. I only hope we can keep the apartment."

I'd been cutting pieces of cold kugl. "What do you mean, keep the apartment?"

"What are you, an echo? The landlord is raising the rent again."

"Here?"

Rose gave me a look. "Where else would he raise the rent? On the moon?"

"You know the girls at the camp were talking about organizing a rent strike this fall. Maybe we should start right here."

"You want me to tell Mr. Abrams, I'm sorry, but we're on strike? He'll throw us out on the street in a minute," Bina said.

"Not if all the tenants do it together."

"Chava, it's one thing to talk theory, another to put us all in danger of being on the street. I don't even have a job." Rose looked frightened. Every day we passed people whose entire lives were open for public display to all their neighbors, sitting on their broken chairs, with a hat on an old milk crate for donations. Where did these people end up? With savings, we might find another place to rent but we'd have the same problems. And I planned to send most of what I'd saved to Sarah next week. Dovida had told me I should get my money out of the bank soon. Not a rush, she said, but soon.

I gave Rose her kugl, trying to tell her with my eyebrows that I would never allow her to be humiliated. We were too busy with our private interchange to notice that Bina's hands had stopped still in her lap. She was staring at something inside the wall.

"Rosele, it might not be such a bad idea, this rent strike of Chava's."

Rose turned to her mother in surprise. "First, it's not Chava's idea. It belongs to that socialist Pauline Newman – "

"Socialist, Republican, a good idea is a good idea," Bina said.

"Mama, you can't mean it."

"We wouldn't do anything foolish, I promise you, my heart. But we can talk. It can't hurt to talk to our neighbors. That new family who moved onto the third floor last week – "

"The Dropkins, I think that's their name," I said.

"Yes. I've never even introduced myself to her. What kind of world

is that, where we don't talk to our neighbors? Sometimes I think I can hear this old building breathe. Not knowing each other chokes us."

Rose plopped into a chair in disbelief. Love for Aunt Bina filled me. I could feel my muscles twitching, curving up around my mouth and eyes.

"What about Uncle Iz?" I asked.

She waved the thought aside as if it were a fly. "I'm the one who deals with the landlord and makes sure we have enough to pay the rent every month. If he doesn't agree, I know how to insist. You never know, he may think it's a good idea himself."

"But what will you say to the other tenants, Mama?" Rose was almost whining. She saw me watching her, and looked down, frustrated.

"I might be able to think of something. You think all your arguments have passed through me, that I'm some kind of sieve? No one likes to pay more rent and this increase is simply unfair. To think of raising rents when so many are out of work, it's inhuman. Who, in this building, wouldn't agree? We'll put together some kind of paper – "

"A petition," I said, "everyone has to sign it for the strike to work."

"You girls, you'll help. Chava, you'll write the petition up, and as long as you don't have work, Rose, you'll go with me to the neighbors. Maybe you'll bake some rugelakh." Aunt Bina went to her basket and removed two pieces of paper. She handed one to me and used the other to start a list.

"It's too hot to bake anything, Mama," Rose said, a sign she'd given in on everything else.

"All right, so maybe you won't bake. But you'll put a ribbon in your hair and you'll come, nu?"

Rose took a bite of her dinner. "I'll go with you, Mama. But don't blame me if you're the only one who thinks this is a good idea."

"She won't be the only one, Rose – that's just it. That's what Pauline and the girls were saying. We need to get our mothers and the housewives involved; we have to work for a better life on every level."

Bina finished with the list, put the pencil down and started running her sewing through the machine again. "And am I one of your levels?"

"No, I just meant – "

"I know what you meant, darling. You think of everything as a cause, you can't help it. And sometimes," she winked at me, "only sometimes, mind you, you're right."

No one believed, when we started, that the rent strike would be a success. Even Bina, whose enthusiasm was a bright, cool wind in the

hot days of September and early October, didn't think so many women would join. Pauline was thrilled. More than a year younger than me, she acted like a general in an army, sending her troops to every street, setting up housewives' committees for every block. Bina was chairman on our block of Essex Street. Many of the girls from the Palisades camp talked to their mothers, their friends, the people they boarded with – and the housewives enlisted more housewives.

We heard that Jewish housewives had held a successful meat strike shortly before we arrived in New York, when they forced the kosher butchers to lower prices. The women of the Lower East Side had tremendous energy – most of it leached out in doing piecework and haggling over every penny. Unorganized energy, that now seemed worth harnessing. They were angry. They worked hard and had no saloons or social clubs to go to in the evening like the men. The dance halls were for us, their daughters and sons. Was everything only for the children? Had their hopes for an American life been reduced to a few comic lines mumbled by a sentimental yente on the stage of the Yiddish theater, and even that glimpse only allowed them if everyone in the household was working for once and the boarder paying his rent on time?

Under the city streets there was a constant thrum of new electricity. Everywhere people studied for their naturalization exams – except the wives, who would become citizens automatically if their husbands did, and weren't going to be allowed to vote anyway. On almost every corner there was a man, sometimes a girl or lady, giving a speech. Most of the time Aunt Bina had to hurry by: the sewing, the cooking, the laundry, the shopping, the family waiting. But once in awhile she stopped for a few minutes to listen. Socialists, anarchists, suffragists, unionists – everyone had something to say.

And Aunt Bina, what did she have to say?

> *You asked me, I'll tell you.*
> *The day I started talking rent strike*
> *to the neighbors*
> *was the best day of my New York life.*
> *In Odessa we were progressive people,*
> *maskilim. My husband had the idea*
> *progressive Jews*
> *didn't bury themselves in Torah,*

made their own way,
while their wives stayed home.
It was the honor of a new age,
a mark of culture
not to live in the marketplace
where our grandmothers did,
prosperity measured
by how desperate you were
to sell an egg.
In Odessa I thought I was always busy but
when I unwind those years
it seems as if I owned a sky full of clouds
and each cloud was an hour,
time to discuss
with neighbors, cousins, aunts,
time to cook, mend, reflect,
look out the window,
time to teach my daughter to read and sew.
How could I have known the needle
was a prophecy?
In New York
every moment I look up from piecework
is bread stolen from my family.
An honor to stay at home!
I long for my grandmother's pushcart,
my daughter's factory –
to talk to someone casually
without counting pennies.
Finally there is a cause
that includes me
and gives me a reprieve from
these years of greenhorn isolation
on Essex Street.

Aunt Bina and the housewives of Essex Street got their rents reduced. Pauline told me about two thousand families succeeded. But later, in the cold of January, the landlords issued three-day eviction notices and six thousand families shuffled through the icy streets with bags and boxes, looking like they'd just gotten off the boat. Some of

the evictees told Bina the strike was still worth it, to at least raise their voices. Lillian Wald told Gutke it was time to pass a law that capped the rents so the landlords wouldn't get every cent we made. Gutke and I agreed it would be a long time before men would allow such a law to pass.

Underneath these words

<div align="right">January 12, 1908</div>

Dear Sarah,

Finally, finally I can send you money for your studies. This is what I saved for your ticket: forty-eight American dollars. Of course, you can change your mind and use it to come to New York. I would be so happy to see you.

I apologize for being slow to send the money. I almost lost it all! I was keeping it in a bank because I thought this was the modern thing to do. A person I know told me to get the money out last October. The day I went, the bank president himself was standing in the lobby in his top hat, begging everyone not to withdraw. Can you imagine? He was trying to act like a friendly uncle, joking about how saving is better than spending, but his face was pale and sweaty, like a garment worker with consumption. Two days later he locked the doors of his bank. I heard he died last month and the people who still had their money by him will never get it back. It's a big tragedy for hundreds and I feel lucky to be able to send this to you.

Because many of the Petrovskys were out of work last year I waited to send this – I was sure you'd understand. I was afraid I'd need it to keep a roof over our heads during the winter. But we scraped by and I only had to take $5 from the savings. Now I have a very good job in a bindery and I make almost $9 a week, so you shouldn't worry. I'll try to send you more in awhile but I'm not going to keep it in any bank!

I would be glad to get news of you. Esther writes but her letters are more and more formal. How are Aunt Shendl, Uncle Elihu and

all the cousins? Cousin Aaron is getting married in the spring. The rest of us continue more or less the same. You remember that picture of Mama and Papa you gave me? I have it in a little frame in the room I share with cousin Rose, and when I look at them I can see you and Esther (and Abraham and Daniel), the way you were when I left. But now it's almost five years, so quick! and each of us has grown. Since you're in a big city, you can get a picture taken and send it to me, so at least there will be one way I can keep you close. Underneath these words there are so many stories I wish I could tell you. Someday we'll be together again, I know.

Your loving sister,

Chava

Two months later I got an envelope with a torn scrap of paper. "I thank you with my whole heart," it simply said. In the envelope was a charcoal drawing of a young girl, her hair drawn back from her face, with one eye looking out the left side of the page and the other staring directly into mine. Written on the bottom were the words:

Sarah Meyer

Self-portrait

Warsaw, 1908

I tacked the drawing up in our bedroom, over a ragged hole in the plaster.

The metal had begun to dig into my rear, even through the layers of skirt and slip.

"You've been sitting out here for hours, Chava," Rose implored, "won't you come in to bed already?" She spoke in English, believing, as I did, that her parents couldn't follow what we said.

I brushed my knuckles against the railing of the fire escape, rapped my fingernails against the iron, plinking restlessly.

"Chava?"

I turned my head a quarter turn away, as if the sound of Rose's voice was heat, a shaft of air aimed at me, that I couldn't bear in early summer. Rose wiped the sweat off her forehead with her palm.

"Oh, Chava talk. If you can't talk, just come inside. I can't sit out there getting my skirt dirty like you, and my feet ache something awful."

"Sure, your feet ache so much you just have to go out dancing."

"Why is this such a big deal by you?" Rose pulled herself through the window and stood over me with her hands on her hips. She looked more exasperated than angry.

"Listen to yourself. You come out here asking me to talk, and as soon as I do, you tell me what I have to say is no big deal. If it's so unimportant, go back in. What do I care?" I folded my arms across my chest.

"We have to work in the morning, Chava, and people can hear us out here. Come in to bed."

"Into bed with the dancer? Suppose you kick me in your sleep? Better I should sleep on the couch Aaron left to get married. Or out here on the fire escape where the rats can dance on me."

"Oy, Chava, what a flair you got for dramatics. You should write for the stage."

" 'I have.' "

"You have?"

"No. You say, 'you have,' not, 'you got.' "

"All right, enough. I didn't come out for an English lesson, Miss American Lady."

"American lady? You're the American lady, going off to dances with factory boys."

"Chava – ." Rose stopped and listened. Uncle Isadore was snoring. Leon and Shmuel, the new boarder who took Harry's cot, were playing pinochle in the kitchen. Aunt Bina had the sewing machine going. She wouldn't be able to make us out over the snoring and the noise, and anyway, her English would have failed her. Still Rose whispered, and her whisper was angry.

"Chava, Reuben is nothing to me, you know it. Why do you make me say it here, over the street? Maybe you want I should yell it, yell what's in my heart to everybody on Essex. Maybe I should paint it like an advertisement on the side of a building. Come inside, I don't like this. Please, Chava, come inside." Her frustration became a small wind, begging at my back.

I turned to her. My mouth twitched as I tried to keep a serious face, looking up into Rose's eyes. "Really?"

"You know, really. Come on, don't be such a baby."

"I had a surprise for you." I had meant to sound romantic, but it came out more like part of my complaint.

"And now I suppose it's my fault for spoiling it?"

At least Rose sounded amused. "No, I didn't mean to imply that," I said.

"Nu?"

"I was going through my old clothes to give to the ragman, and I found something Gutke gave me when I first met her."

"When you were born?"

"No," I said, impatiently. "When I met her on the train."

"Will you never learn to take a joke?" Rose asked. "So what is it already?"

"That was the surprise."

"Come inside and show me, then," she said, holding out an arm.

I grabbed onto her, pulling myself up. "Oy, my foot's gone to sleep."

"Just stand here for a minute, shake it a little."

"Won't you rub it?"

"When we get inside, you tease," Rose whispered.

I shifted back and forth, wincing, then followed Rose through the window.

"Don't close it," Rose said, "there's still a breeze. Are you going to drag this surprise out all night?" She spoke so softly now that we were inside I could barely hear her. I limped over to the bed and pulled the old bundle out of my pocket, making a show of unwrapping it.

"This is lovely," Rose exclaimed, picking the ring out of my palm. When she held it up to the light I was glad I'd polished it up for her. "Gutke gave you this?"

"I don't know why," I said, shrugging. "She told me I had to indulge her, so I did. I didn't think I'd ever see her again then."

"Why didn't you ever wear it?"

"Too big," I said, lying, although it was. I had no idea why I didn't wear it – except maybe that my hands had been stained or rough from work the whole time we'd been in New York. "But I think it will fit you."

Rose slipped the thin silver band on her finger, admiring the garnet. A perfect fit. "You really mean to give this to me?" She frowned, looking perplexed.

"All you have for me is questions?"

She pressed my hand. "I have a few answers for you too," she whispered.

As I leaned against her I felt a twinge. "My leg is still a little numb," I said.

"I'll take care of that in a minute." I noticed how Rose's grin mirrored mine. She stood and took off her skirt and shirtwaist, letting down her

hair, putting on her nightshirt. She was always so fast, her movements hardly gave me a chance to appreciate her. I drifted back to how her body looked that night on the Palisades.

"Come back from your trance, Chava. Get in your nightgown and I'll rub your leg. And other places," Rose whispered, holding the hand with the ring out in front of her for another look before she gave me her full attention, "if you promise not to be jealous anymore."

"Promise not to give me a reason," I said, reaching for her waist.

"There is no reason, love," Rose breathed into the tunnel of my ear.

It was Saturday morning at the New World Bindery. We had a big rush job for Emma Goldman, herself, no less, a pamphlet to fold and staple. The radicals didn't always pay on time but most of us put extra effort into their jobs. Mrs. Shapiro, the boss's wife, had picked up a big contract to bind schoolbooks, which was half our work now. We were lucky to have the schoolbooks, the other girls said, since none of us were laid off during the hard times of the previous year.

In the middle of Goldman's pamphlet, all the folder tapes tangled and the whole machine broke down. I'd watched Frank, the mechanic, fix the problem, ten, fifteen times already – but Frank wasn't around.

"Where the hell is he?" Shapiro wanted to know. "Mechanics – they think they can go on a drunk and still have their jobs waiting for them."

"Maybe he went to shul," one of the new gluers suggested, which made all the girls laugh.

"Frank's Catholic," I told the new girl and she blushed. Shapiro was standing with his hands on his hips, surveying the mess.

"Mr. Shapiro, I think maybe I could fix it, if you let me try." My voice went up too high when I spoke, even though I wanted him to have confidence in me.

He swiveled and looked at me, looked at Al, the folder supervisor. Al didn't like to get under the machine with the oiling can, even. He knew how to adjust everything, the tension and the speeds, but for anything serious he always called over the mechanic. Nora and I were the only girls who ever worked by the folder, and today Nora was sewing. Al appraised me, turned back to the boss.

"Can't hurt to let her try," he said. "I don't see a way she could make it worse."

"All right, see what you can do," the boss grumbled. "Frank's tools are in the closet beside the men's washroom. I'll give you an apron you

can put over your dress."

I tied the apron tight and low, to gather in the folds of my skirt as much as possible, and crawled under the legs and bracings of the machine. It would have been easier in Dovida's trousers. She'd have been proud to see me under here, I thought. I repositioned the tapes and rocked the cam shaft back and forth. Some parts were loose and I could see a chip on one of the humps, probably why we'd been having so much trouble lately. I pointed out the chipping to Al, and tightened everything up. The boss was watching, sticking out his lower lip. Finally I crawled out and turned the switch. There was a little clunk. I flicked it off. I knew exactly where that sound came from, so I crawled back underneath and secured the part in place. Then I oiled everything good. When I turned it on the second time, the tapes ran smoothly.

"I think it's okay now, but soon we're going to need a new cam, the one I showed Al," I told Shapiro. He waited. Al fed a sheet of paper and another. Perfect.

Al shook his head. "Never seen anything like it."

Suddenly all the sewing and the gluing girls were clapping. I faced them. What could I do? I made a curtsey. I had oil on my shirtwaist sleeves and a lock of hair fell over my face.

"That's enough," the boss shouted. "Everyone, back to work. Chava, you come with me."

Except for payday, I had never been in the office before. Shapiro sat behind his desk and stared at me. "Where'd you learn to do that?"

"Just by watching."

"I don't pay you to watch. I pay you to work."

I thought he was pleased. I did him a favor. All right, let him fix it himself next time. "Then I should get back to work – ." I moved as if to leave.

"Hold on." He made a fist with one hand and slapped the top of it with the other. "Can you read English?"

No, I just folded pieces of paper like a trained bear. I stared at him. "I've been going to night school. Next year I'll be eligible to take the naturalization exam. I read."

He went to his bookshelf, picked out a book and threw it at me. "Sit down. See if you can follow this."

It was the instruction manual for the folding machine – diagrams and illustrations followed by pages of text that said things like, "Refer to Figure C, Part 13." What a wonderful book! I found the page that explained about the parts I just worked on, and went back and forth

between the text and the illustration. "Oh," I said, "uh-huh."

"That's enough," Shapiro grumbled. "Well?"

"I understand it." Then I said it again for myself. "I understand it." I wondered if my brother Abe, studying Talmud, had experienced a moment like this, when everything came together, when you found there were names for every part, every part was designed to work with the next and the way it worked could be understood. "Can I maybe borrow this book from you? Or read it at lunch?"

Shapiro shook his head and laughed. "Listen, Meyer," – this was the first time he called me by my last name – "as long as you work here, that book's going to be yours. And I got some others you might like too. That is, if you want the job of mechanic."

"Me?"

"You see anyone else in this room? Am I talking for my health?"

"I would very much like the job of mechanic – ." I frowned, trying to take what he was saying in.

"Oh, you want to know about the money? Okay, okay. How much do you make now?"

"Eight-fifty a week."

He looked something up in a ledger on his desk. "I can't pay you as much as Frank was getting, you understand? Besides, you have a lot of studying to do. I want you to take that book home and read it from cover to cover. Got me? Okay, let's see. I guess no one will kick too much if I start you at $12 a week."

"Twelve dollars?" I never imagined I would make so much. But he misunderstood me.

"All right, thirteen – if you don't mind being paid an unlucky number. I'm not going higher."

"Thirteen, thirteen is fine."

He cracked his knuckles, looked out the window, looked back. "You know this is an experiment." He cleared his throat. "If the men start to give me trouble about it, I'm going to have to put you back to folding. I'm a forward-looking man, in this business you have to be. I can see you have a natural talent, don't think I can't. And I remember we took you on Mr. Greenbaum's say so. But it's a hard time. Hard times out there, still plenty of men looking for work. I could get in a lot of hot water for giving this position to a girl, and I don't want any strikes in my bindery. How would it look?"

Suddenly I realized that Frank must have been getting a lot more than $13 a week. By giving me this job Mr. Shapiro was giving himself

a big savings. At the AFL, they could say it was like scabbing, because I would be undercutting men's union wages. At the League we were always arguing that if the men cared so little about women, why were we trying to join their organizations? Would the men even let me join their mechanics' union?

"I understand," I said. "This is an experiment."

Gutke turned on the new electric lamp in her third-floor study, and continued writing:

How comfortable the girls have become visiting Dovida and me on Suffolk Street. They come over often on Saturday nights now, giving the Petrovskys the impression they've gone to a settlement house lecture or a club. Our home is a club, in a way, isn't it? And tonight we actually went to a hall and sat through two speakers, Emmeline Pankhurst and Harriet Stanton Blatch.

"Why do we keep going to these suffrage talks? We agree, and we still can't vote," I said, heading for the kitchen to put water on for tea as soon as I took my shawl off.

"You can't vote, my dears, but as a brand-new American, I can." Dovida steered Chava and Rose into the parlor. Dovida was naturalized in early spring as Mr. Greenbaum. Even knowing her as I do, that she would take an oath as a man astonished me. But she said if it was a choice between making a lie that only we would ever know about and appearing to be ungrateful to America, the lie would hurt us less. Everything with Dovida was relative.

From the kitchen, I could hear the girls talking. Rose sounded annoyed.

"You think the solution is for us all to wear trousers and go about as men?"

"Ah, Rose, you always cut me down to size," Dovida said.

"And it's a good thing she does, too," I said, coming back to check that everyone was settled while the water heated. "Sometimes I wonder if acting like a man all these years hasn't gone to your head."

"Or my pants?" Dovida's audacity made Chava laugh.

"We have to go to the lectures so we can remember the arguments," Chava said. "Each of us comes into contact with so many people that it's easy, for me at least, to get confused in an argument. The more of us who can offer a good quote, the more who turn around and pass it on."

Chava's sensibleness pleased me.

"Exactly so," Dovida said, clipping the end off a cigar, offering the box to Chava and Rose. Years of Chava's life as a worker were in that box, gluing, stripping tobacco. I could see the shadow of early weariness pass over her face. Would she be able to taste herself in the smoke?

She started to pick one up, examining the union label. "Don't you dare!" Rose said and she dropped it back in the box, looking sheepish.

"It's a bad habit – and expensive, better not to start," Dovida said, winking at Rose. "But you're right about the panel. When I tell my associates I'm going to vote for suffrage, first they give me a strange look, then they want to know 'whatever for?' When I'm fresh from one of these discussions, I know what to say. Sometimes they even listen."

"But how do they vote?" Chava asked.

Dovida shrugged.

Rose picked up a knickknack we had on the end table, a pink bird, made of quartz. Dovida was always bringing home these tshatshkes. I could have lived without them. I noticed then that the garnet ring Rose was wearing was the same one I'd given Chava on the train. I was gratified to see her wearing it, yet had a sudden unpleasant buzzing in my ears.

"Didn't Miss Wald look lovely tonight?" Rose's voice made the buzzing stop.

"Oy!" Dovida slapped her forehead, "Gutke, I forgot to tell you. I invited Miss Wald and that nice young woman Rita Morgenthau over for tea – "

"You didn't! I haven't had time to clean up in days."

"Everything looks fine to me," Rose said, setting the bird back down carefully.

"Is there anything I can do to help?" Chava asked. The girls didn't seem surprised anymore by who dropped by, whether famous reformers or financiers. Their main concern was deciding if our guests knew Dovida's secret. Only one or two did, of course, but I could see it was a form of entertainment for them, looking for clues. Dovida or I would try to give them a sign, yes or no. Their preoccupation with the ruse helped them get over Dovida's guests' rudeness. Most of them, even the women, paid very little attention to me, let alone Chava and Rose, once they realized they were just East Side factory girls. Sometimes Dovida described them as "Gutke's Henry Street protégés." Whatever that was supposed to mean, it seemed to satisfy the important and the rich.

I turned to Chava in resignation. "Come help me bring in your tea.

We have no idea if these women are going to even show up."

"I always come when I'm invited," Rose said.

"Because you, dear, are our friend," I answered.

"And Miss Wald isn't?"

"Technically, she's my employer, and I'm not sure whether friendship is her motivation when she comes."

"What then?"

"Fundraising schemes, a haven from everyone grabbing for her attention at the Settlement, curiosity about Dovida. Ah, this Rita, she doesn't know." I paused to make sure they understood my meaning. "Come, Chava, help me see if there's something fit to serve if they do show up."

Rose was fluffing pillows and straightening the parlor when we heard the knocker, and then Dovida – Dovid, her voice low and formal – welcomed the new arrivals. I'd just put a plate of store-bought kikhl on the coffee table.

"I thought we'd never get away. I hope our invitation is still good, Mr. Greenbaum?" Lillian Wald asked as she came from the hallway, pulling up her veil and setting her flowered hat gently behind the sofa. She looked elegant, as always. Even in the middle of summer, every hair was in place. Lillian Wald emanated a purposeful calm. I knew she went as a nurse into the same tenements that I did, but I felt like an old world bobe when I looked at her, corseted and in style. I *was* an old world midwife after all, nothing to be ashamed of in that.

"My, you look thoughtful tonight," Miss Wald said delicately. It took me a moment to realize she was addressing Chava, not me. "Thinking over the speeches, I hope?" She gathered her skirt from behind as she sat down.

"I, I was thinking about women," Chava managed to sputter. That was enough to satisfy Miss Wald.

"We should have had the vote a hundred years ago," Rita said.

Rita was only a few years older than Chava and Rose. I'd seen her at the Settlement, always rushing by or showing benefactors around. They said she was one of Miss Wald's pets. Chava was staring at her intently. In the calm of the parlor, she looked particularly pleasing, not the haughty rich girl I took her to be.

"I don't see how we'll ever get the vote if we can't vote for it," Rose said, giving Chava a where-are-you look.

"But surely Mr. Greenbaum will vote for it, won't you?" Miss Wald turned to Dovida.

"Surely, Miss Wald. It makes perfect sense to me. Either we have a system of nobility or we have a true democracy. If women don't vote, men have the position of nobility in relation to women. I have no desire for Mrs. Greenbaum to be a serf in relation to me."

"But you don't mind if I serve our guests, do you?" I went into the kitchen to get our best silver tea service.

"Let me get that for you, my dear," Dovida was on her feet, relieving me as soon as I returned.

I had to chuckle. "Always a gentleman for company."

"Where else?"

"Mr. Greenbaum is a perfect gentleman," Miss Wald emphasized "perfect" in a way that made us all nod in agreement. "Don't you think so, Rita?"

Rita looked a little puzzled. Our parlor had become like a play I saw once – Molière in Yiddish, though Miss Wald's Yiddish was nowhere as good as her manners. Rita mumbled agreement.

"I'm so impressed with Harriet Stanton Blatch, aren't you, Mr. Greenbaum?" It was beginning to grate on me, that Miss Wald gave so much attention to Dovida. Didn't she care what I thought? I was the one she turned to whenever the nurses and midwives had a disagreement. I didn't give Dovida a chance to open her mouth.

"What's impressive to me," I said, "is how she broke with her mother, after Mrs. Stanton said all those regrettable things." I wanted to let the girls know I had followed contemporary politics.

"What things?" Rose asked.

I sighed. "You know the National Women's Suffrage Association has taken the position that by giving women the vote, women will be able to counterbalance the influence of Negroes and immigrants – "

"I never have understood that argument," Rita said softly. She had very thick, long eyelashes. I watched her lower them. Chava responded by looking at her own knees.

"It's true that when you take it apart it doesn't make all that much sense," Miss Wald said. "They believe, I'm sure, that it's a tactic to win the Southern vote."

"There are plenty of people in New York against immigrants," I said.

"You wouldn't believe how many anti-Semites and anti-Negroes I meet in my business," Dovida agreed. "Of course they would never describe themselves that way because it's too much of the foundation of their thought."

"We're always the last to see our own prejudices, I'm afraid," Miss

Wald said. Everyone looked at her, wondering what she meant, exactly. She took no notice. "And yet you can see how Miss Pankhurst's radicalism has influenced Mrs. Blatch."

"Well, I like how she said that working women can offer more realistic solutions to our problems than the rich," Chava offered.

"Exactly, dear," Miss Wald said. She could agree with Chava and be patronizing in two words. "That's why she founded the Equality League. Did you know that Rose Schneiderman is already one of their most popular speakers?"

"How come she didn't speak tonight?" Rose asked.

"She's out of town, organizing, I think."

"Are you going to join the Equality League, Miss Wald?" Dovida asked, stretching her legs out. Chava snuck a sideways glance at Rita, who had her hands folded neatly in her lap.

"Oh, Mr. Greenbaum, I'm asked to join every suffrage group, to lend the weight of the Settlement's good name to it, and so I'm afraid I must join none."

"But don't you think by joining none your intentions might also be misinterpreted?" I asked, pouring myself another cup of tea. The rest of them could help themselves.

"I doubt anyone would suspect us of betraying the immigrant's cause, if I understand your implication."

"No," Dovida said, "everyone knows the good work of the Settlement. I can understand why Miss Wald chooses not to make an official alliance in this, dear."

"And," Rita added, "so many organizations come and go. We want to provide a forum for them, while avoiding any internal strife that might come up."

Miss Wald nodded at Rita, approvingly. "Of course everyone knows we believe in, and work for, the advancement of women. I do serve on some other boards when duty calls, but I must reserve most of my attention for Henry Street."

"Duty," Rose said, standing, "that reminds me that it's my duty to get up at five tomorrow for work. You'll excuse us?"

"Of course," everyone murmured. Dovida started to rise, but I motioned her down. "I'll see the girls out tonight, Dovid."

"That wasn't too bad, was it?" I said softly as the girls hugged me goodnight.

"No," Chava grinned at me. Rose just raised an eyebrow as she pulled on her gloves.

"Now be good to your cousin," I whispered in Chava's ear, amused at the confused look she shot me.

When I returned, Lillian Wald was appealing to Dovida for funds. Sometimes I felt Dovida was paying my wages at the Settlement. That was the odd circle that money imposed on our interactions. Dovida's generosity made it easier to waive the $5 I was supposed to charge tenement women for delivering their babies. Within a half hour, Lillian Wald and Rita said their goodbyes.

I ruffled Dovida's hair as I started to clear the dishes. She pulled me into her lap.

"Did you see that flirting?" she asked.

"It's nothing, Dovida. Chava's dedicated to Rose."

"I didn't mean them," she said, tickling me with her mustache.

I kicked through the piles of autumn leaves on the sidewalk, feeling light and easygoing for no reason at all. On our street there were no trees, so I liked walking home by Seward Park.

"So," said Rose, "what was that about?"

"What?"

"What? What! You couldn't stop looking at her all night."

"Miss Wald?"

"Chava – ." Rose scraped her foot along the pavement in frustration.

"Rita? You mean Rita?"

"No, Gutke. Of course I mean Rita."

"I was just looking at her."

"So I noticed."

"You think I – ." I stopped, realizing I did, I was – that whatever Rose was accusing me of, I was genuinely guilty of it.

"It's only because we happen to share a bed that you want me, isn't it?"

"Rose, I wouldn't. How can you think such a thing?" The shop signs threw shadows over our faces.

"You know I could never feel for some dance hall boy the way I feel for you. But when I saw how you looked at Rita, it really scared me. Not everyone stays with their first, I understand that."

Her face was tight, composed in the faint streetlight. She picked up a brown leaf and crumpled it slowly. I took her hand.

"Rose, I'm not saying you were wrong in what you saw. But what you saw was only looking."

"But how long before one day you look at someone like that and decide you want to leave me?"

"I can't imagine leaving you."

"Then you have very little imagination."

"You're confusing me."

"It's not hard to do." She made a fist with her free hand and pushed a little at my shoulder.

"I want to be with you. I want you to want to be with me. If I tell you every morning when we wake and every evening before we fall asleep, will you forgive me if I sometimes think of other things during the day?"

"You want me to give you permission to spend your days swooning after other girls?" She squeezed my hand tightly.

"That's not what I meant."

"I know, sweetheart." Her face softened. I took her arm and pulled her close to me. As we walked, I was careful to match my long stride to her shorter step. We were silent, the street curiously quiet, a few animals rummaging in garbage, distant shouts. By the time we got home I felt like we shared the same body, separated only by skin.

On the second landing, I turned to her. "I love you," I whispered.

She gulped, gesturing at the stained, pressed tin walls. "You always tell me in such romantic places."

Pleasure is my answer

November 22, 1909, the day before Rose's birthday – at last we would both be done with our teen years – we arrived at Cooper Union two hours early. Already every seat was filled so we found a position, not far from the stage, where we could lean against the stone wall. Rose had been working in the garment industry for more than five years and she knew hundreds of the girls – it seemed like hundreds to me.

Rose had been feeling both guilty and glad that she didn't get hired at Leiserson's. She'd wanted to work there at first: they had electricity, not gas, for light. Now Leiserson's had been out on strike for at least two months and probably nothing was left in Local 25's strike fund. Rose had been working at Moss's, which had the same conditions as a basement sweatshop, with two hundred girls. But it was better than working for Harry – and for Leiserson's too, as it turned out.

As the hall filled up, we could tell that many would be left outside. I felt bad taking up a garment worker's space, but then I saw Mary Drier, the head of the League, step onto the platform with Gompers and the other men, and I remembered that we were all workers together. I was there to be with Rose. Packed in with the others was the first time I'd felt really warm in a month. The newspapers said it was going to be an especially cold winter.

I enjoyed hearing Miss Drier speak, even if she addressed us in English, throwing in the few Yiddish words she knew, for solidarity. It made me proud that the AFL and the socialists took us seriously enough to have her at a mass meeting. But the speeches seemed to go on forever. Words rippled through the arches of the big hall and I got that slightly seasick sensation again. Rose slid down to the floor, hugging her knees, and I followed her. When she bent over, I rubbed

her neck. A young woman standing next to me smiled, then pointed to her mouth, opening it wide in a yawn. I nodded. Was something really going to come of this?

Suddenly there was a commotion in the middle of the seats, almost directly beside of us. We stood to see what was going on. A small girl yelled that she'd been picketing Leiserson's all this time and demanded to be heard. "Let her through," people were saying, and as she dashed by us Rose whispered, "That's Clara!" The girl leaped onto the platform.

"I am a working girl, one of those who are on strike against intolerable conditions," Clara said. "I am tired of listening to speakers talk in general terms. What we are here for is to decide whether or not to strike. I offer a resolution that a general strike be declared – now!"

Everyone was out of their seats, shouting and yelling. A small group of Italian girls in the aisle behind us looked puzzled and I heard someone quickly translating for them. They had lasted through all these hours of Yiddish and English rhetoric. I knew that lots of Italian girls had worked with Rose but I didn't see many in the hall. Of course, in American clothes, Jews and Italians often looked like cousins. The shouting drowned out their translator. Rose was waving her arm in the air, yes, yes. The Italians got the idea and they started waving and shouting too.

A strike! All the garment workers, the whole industry, thousands of – thousands of girls! Suddenly I realized what was happening and my whole body tingled, as if someone was making sparks against my skin from the inside.

Gompers looked like he was going to explode. Hadn't he just advised everyone to be cautious? In his black boxy hat and long black coat he looked like a beardless cantor who'd been upstaged by a choir. The chairman, Feigenbaum, kept calling for order but no one paid attention. When he asked for a second to the motion, the whole room started to yell again. When there was a pause in the noise, Feigenbaum called out, "Do you mean faith? Will you take the old Jewish oath?"

As if we were transported to a synagogue, with the Italian girls gaping at us, all the Jews intoned, "If I turn traitor to the cause I now pledge, may this hand wither from the arm I now raise."

"Chava, you're crying," Rose said as she turned to me. She was beaming, excited. She put her hand up to my cheek to show me.

"I guess I am," I sniffled.

"Don't, sweetheart. It's my birthday now, the best birthday I've ever had." No one paid any attention to us in the din, though I was vaguely

aware that the people on the platform were giving out instructions, where to go to join Local 25, how to find the Women's Trade Union League. Rose and I already knew.

I told Rose I'd do her early picket duty for Thursday morning before I went to work. She could come relieve me at seven. I was a member of the League, if not the International Ladies Garment Workers Union, and we were all in this together. Why shouldn't I help?

It was 4:00 A.M. when I woke. Rose was a soft series of mounds. I squinted at her and pretended she was the shape of Russia from the boat. Only her I got to keep by me, more steady than any country.

When I crawled out of the bed it was bitter cold. Maybe the gas lines had frozen again. Picketing before dawn was so unpleasant, but I was glad to do it for Rose, she needed to sleep. Everyone was stretched beyond what they could take. Besides the scraps Harry threw us, it was just my wages keeping the household from the street. Bina kept taking in work from Harry, even after Rose told her it was like being a scab. Bina said she wasn't crossing a picket line, she wouldn't do that. But Harry had to get through this strike too; the preparation she did would help the union girls when Harry settled. She would make sure he was among the first to sign a contract, so what was the harm? Rose had walked out on Bina and I followed her. I began to understand how people in families stopped talking to each other. Of course, we were talking to Bina again within the hour, but we gave Harry the cold shoulder. Thirty thousand girls were out. What would it have been like if we could have organized the homebound pieceworkers too?

I got by Moss's at 5:15. I was the first one there. At 5:30, several carts came up and maybe thirty Negro women jumped off, forming a queue. It was me and my one picket sign, them and two guards. One guard was by the front door, unlocking it. The other waved at me with his club from the front of the line.

I caught up to the last woman. I had never been that close to a Negro before. Her nose was broad like my Aunt Shendl's. In the Yiddish press I'd read how white people in the South hung Negroes – lynching, they called it. "Sister," I whispered to her, "don't scab on the union."

She turned and glared at me, sharp. "Sister!" The cold air made a cloud that hung between us. "You going to feed my children, sis-ter?"

"Join the union. The strike fund will give you food." I wanted to talk to her about how alike our plights were, how the world made pogroms

on us both, but I lost my footing on the ice and had to hurry to catch up with her.

She kept looking at me. "You going to give me a union card?"

"Why not?"

She shook her head. The guard was getting closer as we got near the door. "Either you just got off the boat, honey, or you're blind. Your union folks won't sign up a colored woman."

"I would."

She squinted at me. The new electric lights weren't much brighter than the old gas ones. "I believe you might," she laughed.

"Get along, you – you know what we do to your kind!" The guard yelled and swung his stick an inch from my cheek. I jumped back. He grunted, satisfied.

When I got off work from the bindery later that day, I walked all the way up to East 22nd Street, to the League strike center. I recognized some of the rich women from the speeches. Leonora O'Reilly and Rose Schneiderman I knew already from the League office. Lena was there too, on the telephone, as usual, but she looked up and waved at me. Everyone was talking, drinking coffee, gesturing, campaigning. At least it was warm, mostly from the heat of our bodies. Some of the girls probably joined the union just to feel all right about attending their meetings, thawing out. Finally I made my way over to Leonora.

"I've got to ask you about something, about the scabs?"

She turned. I could see she recognized me but didn't remember my name. Thousands of girls were walking in and out of the center every hour, but still, I'd been to three executive meetings, since the girls in the bindery nominated me as representative. "Go ahead," she said. It would have been easier to talk to Lena Reznikoff instead of to this American, even though Leonora used to be a working girl. Maybe I wouldn't know how to say it right. Somebody was already asking her a question about bail money for the girls in jail.

"In a minute," she said to them and turned back to me, raising her eyebrows as a question, waiting.

"Is it true the union won't sign up, up – ," I fumbled in English.

"Who?"

"Women who used to be slaves?" I thought she would understand but she didn't.

"All of us are wage slaves here. Who told you somebody wouldn't sign them up?"

"That's not what I mean. I mean the Negro women."

"Oh." She frowned, looking over my shoulder at the crowd. I looked too. Almost all the girls were Jewish, some Italian – that was who worked in the needle trades. Where did the Negro women work?

"You know I belong to the National Association for the Advancement of Colored People myself," Leonora said.

"No. I didn't even know there was such an organization."

She nodded, patiently, the way she always did. "I've taught Negro girls sewing at the Manhattan Trade School. I agree it's of the utmost importance that the League support the Negro cause. Many misunderstandings and injustices keep us apart. If they came up here to join the union, surely we'd sign them up. I'd sign them up myself. But they don't, do they?"

"A woman I talked to this morning said we wouldn't give her a union card, so maybe they don't know. We should send an organizer to where they live."

"I can't find but a handful of organizers for the Italian girls. Now how I am I going to organize Negroes? Are you going to do it?"

"I'm the only one at home bringing in a paycheck now. I work for a bindery," I added quickly, in case she really didn't remember. "How could I?"

"There you have it. Now I have to see about this bail fund."

"But – "

"Come talk to me after the strike's over. I know most of your people are like-minded on this, and after the strike we should make every effort to extend our services to Negro women. But I have five thousand girls to feed tonight and another thirty I have to arrange bail for."

The month jumped out of our hands like a starving alley cat. One night Rose and I went to hear Mother Jones speak at the Thalia Theatre. Guss's pickle stand was closing up as we hurried past, and Mrs. Guss offered us a pickle. "If you're strikers, it's on me," she said.

"Only her," I said, motioning to Rose.

"She's done picket duty too," Rose said, reaching out her hand. Mrs. Guss grinned as she handed me a pickle.

"Glad to help you girls," she said in Yiddish. "I was a seamstress before I married. Pickles are easier, even with the smell. Come by any time for a nice pickle, all right?" We nodded with our mouths full, the pickles so cold they tasted like garlic icicles.

There were a few seats left at the Thalia. Rose and I had read about

Mother Jones. She'd been a hero to coal miners for years, and that night she told us that every strike she'd been in was won by the women. The men in the audience looked a little doubtful, but they clapped for her just the same. I suppose you could think of the sweatshops like mines, of women going into their bleak, dangerous caverns, forced to hard labor that no one recognized, every day.

I was confounded by how many women were in the streets, how many were willing to march right up to the mayor's office, how many linked their arms when the company gorillas charged the picket lines. Pauline called it a fantastic awakening. She picketed by Triangle Shirtwaist every day, except when they sent her to raise strike funds from the wealthy. The rich were among us so often I began to remember lines from the Dickens novels I'd read in Kishinev. We were the smudge-faced poor, holding out our hats, begging "please, ma'm, for the suffering widows and orphans." Emma Goldman wrote that wealthy women were just trying to get our sympathy for the vote and that when we got the vote, they'd turn their backs on us. But we needed their help, didn't we? Some even got arrested on the picket lines – the judges hated that.

I weighed fifty different opinions in my mind. Some days I felt despair about the babel the strike had created, but on other days the idea that girls could have such power exhilarated me. Probably that was what gave so many the strength to go on – the other women. I hated having to spend so much of my days tinkering with machines, while Rose was pounding the pavement in the cold.

Usually she was home from picketing by the time I returned to Essex Street. They didn't bring scabs in for the night shift, thank God for small favors. But one night, instead of Rose the first thing I saw was Aaron's uniform, Aaron holding his hat in his hand, his head bowed, looking at the floor. I wanted to beat on him, the way I'd seen police beat on the girls, but I managed to hold my temper.

"Excuse me," I said, "I must have the wrong address. This is a striker's home."

His face was ashen. Aunt Bina was sitting at the table with her hands folded, staring at the side of his head. "Tell Chava, go on, tell her what you told me. If I hear it again, maybe I'll believe it."

"Rose is in jail."

"You arrested your own sister?"

"Not me! My partner. I didn't even know she was there."

"How could you not know?"

"I didn't know where she was working." He pulled at the bottom button on his jacket.

"You knew she was working somewhere, that she was out on strike with all the other girls. You and Irene were here for Shabbes two weeks ago. How could you not know?"

"I'm supposed to say, 'Sorry, Sergeant, but I need a desk job until the strike is over'? They need every man out there – "

"I bet they do."

"Listen Chava, I don't like it." He stared up at me for a minute and I could see he had groomed his mustache into handlebars, like the Irish. Then he looked at Bina, pleadingly. "I thought being on the force, I could help keep the other men from using their batons on the girls, talk reason to the strikers."

Bina shook her head. He turned back to me and I could see why he wouldn't look at her. His stepmother was crying.

"Reason? You thought you would be the good police, who help us all through times of civic strife?"

"You can't understand – "

"I understand exactly," I said, pulling a chair up facing him. And I really did, experiencing a rush of understanding for Aaron I had never felt before. "You think that the law in a democracy is basically good, with a few leftover injustices that can be fought using the law, and being a policeman is honoring democracy, am I right?"

"Basically." Aaron looked confused and held his hand up as if to say something.

I didn't want to hear his version. "And that having a good guard helps the prisoner, and you could be that good guard?"

"Yes, I think that – "

There, I had him. "The idea of a good guard destroys real progress, Aaron. The prisoner comes to depend on the guard and forgets to make alliance with the other prisoners – "

"What?" He turned back to Bina. "Ma, what's she talking about?"

Bina sighed and wiped her cheeks with her apron. "Darling, I know you want to change the world but you're not going to change Aaron. Maybe instead we should try and get Rose out of jail?"

I jumped up. How could I have been so wrapped up in fighting Aaron that I would forget Rose? "I'll go right to the strike office. I'm sure I can get the bail money – "

"I brought money for bail, Chava," Aaron said softly.

"You?"

He looked like a combination of thug and whipped puppy. "Irene's – we've been saving everything because – "

"Irene's expecting," Bina said.

"Since when?"

"Two months," Aaron cleared his throat again. "I don't want to go down to the jail – "

"You're ashamed to see your sister?"

"I have to get home to Irene. I've been working double shifts." He stood and threw an envelope on the table. "This should be enough."

"Chava shouldn't go down there alone, Aaron," Bina said.

"Then wait for Pop to come home, or Harry."

"We don't see Harry much these days, except when he scuttles in like a cockroach with piecework for your mother," I said, looking at the envelope lying on the table, grubby from Aaron's grip.

"Don't start about Harry now, Chava," Bina said.

"I'm sorry. It's a hard time."

"It's hard for all of us, Chava," Aaron said, extending his hand, as if to shake hands was to make peace.

He may have been my cousin but there he was in uniform. A man in a uniform who arrested his sister. "I can't. Not while you're dressed up as police." My voice was almost apologetic, which I regretted.

"All right then. Mama, I – "

"Don't whine. Go to your wife." Aunt Bina stood up, looking around the room for some work she could do next.

"I'll bring by some food later this week."

"We've accepted the bail money as retribution but we don't need your charity," I said.

"This is *my* family, dammit."

"Don't swear, Aaron. And I agree with Chava on this. We don't need charity from you. If you want to be family, be family. Invite us for Shabbes – "

"Don't arrest your sister – "

"I gotta go." He shoved his hat on his head, stuck his hands in his pockets and left. We could hear him moving like thunder down the stairs.

"I'm sorry, Aunt Bina, I can't help it. I can never believe he joined the police."

"I understand, sweetheart. This strike – "

I picked up the envelope. "I'll be fine at the precinct, don't worry. If Uncle Iz comes home, tell him to meet me there."

"Be careful."

"Thank you, thank you, thank you, thank you." Rose kissed me on the cheek, a proper, cousinly kiss.

"Actually, you have to thank Aaron. It was his money."

"You took his money?"

"I consider it part of the union's bail fund. He'd never give $40 any other way." Rose laughed, linking her arm with mine as we left the precinct station. "I'd have been here a little sooner but I was arguing with him."

"That's okay," she said. "We were singing and sharing stories. It wasn't so bad."

"You want to go back?"

"Not a chance. I want to go to the deli for a pastrami sandwich."

"First, we have no money, and second, your Mama was going to send your Papa down to chaperone us. We have to get back before he leaves."

"You're no fun."

"Fun! How can you talk about fun?"

"If I didn't talk about fun, I think I'd go out of my mind. You know what I heard?" Rose's breath came out in frosty gasps as she struggled to keep pace with my stride, talk and look in the store windows all at the same time.

"How would I know?"

"One of the judges, Olmstead, told a girl she was 'on strike against God and Nature' and sent her to the workhouse on Blackwell's Island for thirty days."

I stood still. "Oh God – "

"They've sent fifteen or twenty girls to the workhouse already." Rose caught her breath and looked me in the face. "Thank you for coming to get me."

"You knew I would, didn't you? Even if Aaron hadn't given us the money, I would have found it. I would never let you spend a night in jail if there was anything I could do."

"That's why I'm thanking you."

"Oh." I blushed and pulled her along the street with me. It was too cold to stand still.

What Rose Didn't Say

I am always instinct
when they write this drama—
appetite, kindness, sociability.
I grumble to get out of bed early,
walk in a circle
yet I do the picket duty.
I fix my hair, wear
my best clothes on the line.
If a girl is taunted
I link arms with her, try
to keep us clear
of bullies and police.
But if the police raise their batons
I stand firm.

It's not what you'd call courage.
I'm too soft for courage.
Like so many of the girls
I rise to embrace
what's mine—
an ordinary, loving life.
We learned in night school
the Constitution of the United States
says: pursuit of happiness.
Happiness is my courage.
It fills me unexpectedly
in tenements where
life is lice and broken promises.
Pleasure is my answer.
What difference, then,
a night in jail?

I talk to prostitutes, other strikers
about what clothes they like, which colors,
what they hope
in private.
I could want to save the world
but the world is going to listen to me?

Maybe it's selfish, this thing radicals deride
as a yente's tendency
to only work "for me and mine" –
but I do my part.
It's a bit part,
a member of the crowd scene,
a walk on, and that's fine.
Where would all the heroes be
without me?

The temperature was front-page news along with the strike, the coldest winter anyone could remember. I would stand on the corner of Delancey with a group of women, selling the *Call*, shifting from foot to foot, afraid if I stopped moving my shoes would freeze to the sidewalk. The newspaper donated two editions for the strikers' relief fund. All over the East Side women were out with white banners across their chests, supporting the strikers.

This was the least I could do while Rose was picketing. I sold papers before going to the bindery, and as soon as my shift was over I started again with a fresh bundle. Gutke saw me early the morning of the last day of December and bought three copies. She rubbed my cheeks until a little warmth came up in them, pulled my coat collar tight around my throat. At moments like this, I thought Gutke was my personal guardian. She always stayed exactly long enough to cheer me without interfering. Maybe Mama sent her. Who knows? I liked to think Mama still remembered me in the corridors of the dead.

I had only seven papers left to sell, though I had already turned to ice. I'd promised Rose I would take her to the Anarchists' New Year's Eve Ball – I was a stiff enough partner even without frostbite. How long could the strike last? What the judge said, "On strike against God and Nature," came back to me. Nature fought as bitterly as any capitalist. We were lucky to have heat and food; so many were freezing to death now. They said the poor only had two bad times a year: summer and winter.

"You're going to stand out in the cold all night?" A man yelled at me from an automobile.

"Paper? Support the striking girls, buy the *Call*."

"I'll take everything you have left."

"Dovid?" Gutke probably told her to look for me here. I wasn't sure

whether I was grateful or annoyed.

"Come, get in. I'll drop you off at home. Don't just stand there gaping, young woman. The auto won't bite," she yelled.

As soon as I was on the leather seat I felt guilty. Riding in an automobile. Sometimes the uptown ladies brought them for suffrage parades, but to actually ride in one! It jolted up and down, even a little sideways, as we made our way.

"Well, what do you think?" Dovida asked, stroking the instrument panel proudly. "Oh, I can tell. You have that look in your eye."

"What look?"

"Whenever you're about to go moral on us, you retreat ten feet behind your eyes – ." She swerved to avoid an old man pulling a pushcart across the street. "So you don't approve?"

"It's not for me to approve. But – "

"Uh-huh, now we'll have it."

"With so many girls on strike, how could you think to buy an automobile?"

"Ah, I should donate every extra penny to the strike fund?"

"Well, yes."

She patted my hand with her black leather glove. "Maybe so, maybe so. But the fact is, I'm not going to. It's not human nature. It's not my nature, at any rate, to leave nothing in reserve or to go without. This I got mainly for business. I have to keep up many kinds of appearances, you know. I'm garaging it uptown but I wanted to have it out for New Year's Day. I'm taking Gutke for a country ride."

How could she understand? That she should have so much while the strikers lived on scraps of bread and charity. Dovida gave me a quick look.

"I see you're suffering over this. If it's any comfort to you, I have given quite a bit to the League and the union, and I'm putting whatever pressure I can on this new Manufacturerers' Association the bosses have cooked up. You have the numbers and it's remarkable to see how you're using them, remarkable. Numbers, though, don't always translate into power."

We were driving past Yonah Schimmel's Knishes on Houston, and I had an impulse to duck. What if anyone saw me, riding around like a big shot? "In a democracy –," I started.

"You don't live in a democracy," Dovida cut me off. "Not the kind they teach you about in night school. The revolutionaries, they know. Power is a ladder, and you can't climb it with hundreds. You fight through the hundreds to get on the first rung. It's not easy to knock the

ladder down. People have been trying for centuries. Only once they get to the bottom, they get curious about the view, and the next thing you know, they're climbing too."

I hated to admit it but riding in her auto was exciting. I was curious about the engine underneath, the mechanics of what made it move. "So," I sighed, "how *is* the view?"

She laughed. "It depends on what direction you look. When I look down, I don't like what I see at all."

"Uh-huh."

We turned onto Essex. "Chava," she said, pulling over, "you lash out at the world because the world is cruel. It killed your parents."

I was surprised that she came right out with it. Everyone else danced around the subject when they wanted to remind me I was an orphan.

"But most of us, even those of us you perceive to be morally compromised, don't set out to hurt or oppress anyone. I'm getting to be an old man – " she cleared her throat at the look I gave her, " – so, even I forget sometimes, out on the street. Maybe I make too many excuses because I've spent my life playing both sides of every role. I may not deserve it, but I want a comfortable old age among the women I care about."

"But that's it. It's not that you don't deserve it, everyone deserves it. My Aunt and Uncle. Me and Rose." I looked down at the pile of newspapers between us on the seat.

"Even your cousins Aaron and Harry?"

"Them, I'm not so sure about."

"I'm glad to see you can still make a joke. But I take your judgments to heart, and I'll think about what more I can do to help with this strike."

"I appreciate your goodwill, Dovida, but it's not what you can do for us, except to step out of the way when working people unite."

"Yes," she said, smiling at me. "I've heard this slogan. Don't worry. I've made a career from knowing when to step out of the way."

Arguing with Dovida was like punching at a pillow or a shadow. She always yielded and changed shape. Yet she felt almost as familiar to me as my brother Daniel or Rose. I slipped a little on the icy pavement as Dovida handed me a five dollar bill for the newspapers. I held onto the automobile door, looking at the money.

"Be careful there. We wouldn't want to lose a talent like yours!"

Thanking her didn't seem right. "Enjoy your automobile," I said instead.

"Thank you. And you enjoy the Anarchists' Ball. Come by me and Gutke soon. If you or your family needs anything during this strike, let us know. I consider it an honor to be allowed to help any way I can."

I had to laugh at how carefully she put that. This time I did thank her. Only as I was climbing the stairs did I wonder how she knew we were going to the ball.

It must have been the AFL that declared the shirtwaist strike officially over in February, because it certainly wasn't the strikers. Rose's shop, Moss's, held out the whole time, sending their work on the sly to small jobbers like Harry, who had settled relatively early. I knew he got pleasure out of looking like a mentsh while really scabbing for the big manufacturers. Rose was on a list of union hotheads since she'd been arrested. Moss's wouldn't take her back and she couldn't find work anywhere else.

At the end of February there was a victory dance at Clinton Hall. I wanted to take Rose out, get her mind off job hunting. Usually she'd leap at any excuse to be on the dance floor but this time I had to play on her sympathy.

"My birthday got lost this year in all the commotion," I complained, trying to look downcast. "Please come out with me."

Rose stared at her hat, which lay like a cat that had fallen under the wheels of an ice cart. "I'll fix it up," she said, "one more time."

Aunt Bina supplied a bright scrap from a house dress she'd made the year before, and Rose turned it into a sash that made the hat look almost fashionable again. She mended the torn lace collar on her threadbare overcoat. Our great grandmother's cameo, one of the only things from the old country Aunt Bina was planning to pass on to her daughter, was fastened at the throat of Rose's best shirtwaist, and she was wearing the garnet ring on her left hand. I thought she looked grand, certainly as good as J. P. Morgan's daughter, who had been in all the newspapers with her strike support until the girls voted down the manufacturer's proposal. The union had been infiltrated by foreign radicals, she then proclaimed. Now Anne Morgan was probably dancing uptown in silk and pearls.

It was a whole dime each to get into the dance. I supposed they thought all the strikers were back at work. We probably could have told the ticket taker that Rose was still looking and likely he would have let her in for free. We stood on the sidewalk watching people go

in and out, some with bottles of beer and sandwiches, trying to decide what to do. "Maybe we shouldn't have come," Rose said, fingering her earlobe.

"You like to dance and I'm happy to treat you," I said.

"You're sweet," Rose sighed, her breath coming out in a cloud. "I don't know why I'm in such a mood."

As I leaned to whisper into her ear about moodiness, a woman called my name. It took me a minute to recognize Lena Reznikoff. As she approached, she peered at both of us from above her spectacles. "It's Rose, isn't it?"

"I'm glad you recognized me this time," Rose said, extending her arm, which Lena pumped in a vigorous handshake.

"I noticed you picketing several times but I couldn't get close enough to talk. Are you going to the dance?" Lena asked.

"We're trying to decide," I said.

Lena appraised us carefully. "I think it's overly optimistic to declare the strike a victory, but I can understand why people need to feel good about all the work we did."

"You don't feel good about it?" Rose asked, a faint bitterness trickling into her voice.

"Don't misunderstand me. We all did great things during the uprising, didn't we? It's important to hold on to some of those feelings of solidarity, the way we stuck by each other – "

"Hmm," Rose said.

Lena peered at her. "You're out of work still?"

"Still," Rose said.

"Listen, I'm on my way over to the Grand Theatre myself. Why don't you both come with me?"

I looked in at the bright dance floor, boys and girls dancing together, and thought maybe standing beside Rose in the dark theater instead wouldn't be such a bad idea.

"If I can't afford the dance – "

"Please!" Lena interrupted Rose. "I don't invite you so you should have to pay. I got an organizer's wage through most of the strike, and I share an apartment with one other girl, no family to give my pay packet to." Lena said, anticipating my objection. "It would be my honor if you'd both be my guests."

"What do you think?" I asked Rose.

"The dance was your idea," she said. "Now that I'm all dressed up, we should go somewhere."

"Exactly," Lena said, getting in between us and marching us down the street.

"What play are we going to see?" Rose asked.

"It's Sholom Asch's newest, *The God of Vengeance*. It's supposed to be scandalous. Just the diversion we all need, eh?"

It was a busy night at the Grand but there were still rail tickets left, standing places at the back. Rose and I had yet to sit in a theater seat in New York, except for sneaking a rest during intermission. The Grand Theatre lived up to its name. Passing through its columns, I felt as if I were entering a kind of temple, where all the prayers were in Yiddish.

And this play! A girl actually kissed another girl on the stage. They made it out she was a prostitute seducing a good girl into a life of sin, but the good girl went willingly. The father and mother kept the brothel, and so they were being paid back for their evil ways because their daughter kissed another girl. Rose and I exchanged astonished glances, hoping that Lena wouldn't notice.

During intermission we were unusually quiet. Lena, who I always thought could talk about anything, only seemed to be able to discuss the weather. We overheard a few arguments on the difference between mother-love and sensuous-love. We were back at our places well before the signal. For me, it was thrilling and terrifying. I had always thought that as long as no one knew about Rose and me, no one would pay us any attention. We were merely cousins, in the world's view, cousins who were very fond of each other.

Now that anyone could see, for the price of a ticket, how love between girls could make them disobey their families, even drive them into the arms of prostitutes – would they look at us differently? I couldn't decide whether or not to be angry at Asch for taking it upon himself to write this play. Why did the world need to know?

Lena invited us out for eggcreams after the play, but Rose insisted she'd been generous enough. So we set out for home, walking in the same direction in silence. Finally Lena spoke.

"I don't like how Asch implied that it's God's vengeance for two girls to love each other," she said slowly.

"You don't think it's a sin?" I asked her.

"Maybe somewhere in the Bible. But worse things could happen to a girl than that," Lena said.

"Much worse," Rose said. The lightness in her voice surprised me. Lena too, I noticed.

Lena cleared her throat. "I – ," she started and stopped.

"It's all right," I said, and pressed her hand.

"I myself – ," she tried again.

"You?" Rose said, but she didn't sound very surprised.

"Well, I never actually. But during this uprising, I was so impressed with all the women and girls. And sometimes when I look at them – ." Lena was several years older than us, but suddenly she seemed younger, tentatively groping for words. "Sometimes I'd look up from the phone and see Leonora O'Reilly taking charge of one impossible situation after another – "

"Leonora?" Her choice surprised me.

"Don't you know her?"

"Of course," I said, and turned to Rose to explain. "She one's of the Irish leaders of the League."

"An Irish woman?" Rose caught my surprise.

Lena looked indignant. "I thought you'd understand."

"We understand," Rose laughed, "really, we understand." She linked her arm with Lena's. "I didn't expect to be taken off guard by an interfaith alliance between women, that's all." I could feel my face flush from Rose's bluntness.

"I wouldn't exactly call it an alliance," Lena said.

"Leonora doesn't know how you feel?" I asked.

"You're the first people I ever told."

"Oh," Rose said, pleased. "You know I'm mostly an observer of your League, but I don't believe you are the only one there to have these feelings."

"For Leonora?" Lena sounded distraught.

"For Leonora, I wouldn't know. All I'm trying to say is that I don't think she would be shocked if you told her how you felt."

"Really?"

"Rose has always wanted to be a matchmaker," I said. "But I think she has a point, Lena. If you never ask, you'll never get an answer. And what's the worst it could be? Like Rose says, I don't think you'll shock Leonora."

Lena took a deep breath and expanded from the inside. "Thank you. I'm going down Orchard here. You've given me a whole new way to think about this."

"Our pleasure," Rose said. "And thank you for treating us to the play."

"Best thing I've done all week," Lena answered, waving goodnight.

Rose stopped to adjust her hat in the reflection of a store window. "What a good idea of yours this was, Chava, to go out dancing."

"Dancing?"

Rose laughed and pulled my arm around her waist. We waltzed under the streetlight at the corner of Grand and Orchard, not caring for a minute who saw us or what they thought.

By the following December, our dingy rooms on Essex Street were looking and feeling particularly bleak. No matter how exhausted Rose and I were from work – she had found a sewing job at Triangle Shirtwaist in the summer – we made every excuse not to get home until we dropped directly onto our bed, too tired to do more than hold each other's hands. When Rose complained about our cheerless surroundings after Shabbes dinner one night, Aunt Bina grimaced.

"I don't mean it as an insult to you, Mama. But weren't we only going to live here a year or two until we could afford better? I'm working again – "

"As long as those mamzers at Triangle don't find out you're in the local," I said.

"They're mamzers, as you say, everywhere. You ever been in a shop run by saints? Socialists, even?" Rose said, only to be interrupted by Harry.

"Still in the local, huh?" he asked, picking his teeth with a fish bone. He had a room next to his own factory and only came by on Friday nights.

"Don't bait you sister, please," Uncle Isadore shushed him. "Very nice meal, Mrs. Petrovsky, very nice. And as for you, Rose, you know how hard your mother works to fix this place up."

"Rose does too, Uncle Isadore," I said quietly, hoping to sound respectful.

"Yes, well, a girl should help her mother, not criticize."

"I wasn't criticizing, Papa."

"Maybe you were really criticizing me, eh? But don't worry," he leaned over and patted her hand, "now that I'm a foreman at Stern's, I think finally our luck is changing. I'm not going to make any premature announcements, but this year, God willing, will be the year we move. Unless of course you get married first."

Rose gave a loud sigh. An unusual moment of silence enveloped the table. Only Harry made little smacking noises while he continued to

pick his teeth.

"Rose, dear," Bina finally said, "I was thinking how it would be nice to have a special Chanukah dinner, have everyone together."

"Everyone?" I asked, grateful for even this change of subject.

"Yes, everyone. So we have our disagreements. We're all still family. I don't get the opportunity to see my new granddaughter often enough."

"Chanukah," Isadore said, stroking his chin in approval, "a good idea. We haven't celebrated Chanukah in years."

"What's the big deal?" Harry asked, lighting a cigar.

"You're content to come every Shabbes for a free meal, I notice," Bina said. "Would it hurt you to come one extra night and sit with your brother, your new niece?" When she made a motion to start clearing the table I jumped up and took over the job.

"Aaron's the family type, not me," Harry said. "Anyway, you probably don't even know when Chanukah is. God knows, I don't. And you know what, Ma? I don't care."

"What kind of way is that to talk to your mother?"

"That's another thing, Pop. She's not really my mother."

Isadore leapt up like a watch spring and hit Harry on the cheek with the back of his hand. Bina's mouth fell open in disbelief, but whether from what Harry said or what Isadore did was hard to tell.

"Ephraim!" she managed to exclaim.

"Okay, okay. I apologize." He put his drinking glass up to his cheek to cool it off. "That's some wallop you got there, Pop. You should have been a fighter."

Isadore glared at him and turned to run his fist under the brown water from the sink.

"Your father is a fighter, Harry," Bina said softly.

"Ma, I'm apologizing, all right? All this old country holiday stuff just rubs me the wrong way."

"You want instead to celebrate Christmas?" Rose asked, trying to joke.

"It wouldn't be such a big crime. One of the guys I play poker with is going to get himself a regular Christmas tree."

"A Jewish boy?"

"We're all Americans now," Harry said.

Isadore rubbed his knuckles and slumped back into his chair. "I never thought it would lead to this."

"What would lead?" I asked.

"My father was shocked by me when I trimmed my beard," he said. "I shocked myself when I stopped going to shul here. I suppose my son has to follow in my footsteps, but I didn't think I was walking into apostasy."

"No one's talking about apostasy, Pop. C'mon, you gotta admit that all the lights they put up for Christmas in this town are impressive."

"You can be bought for a string of lights?" Isadore asked.

"Listen, I'll come for Chanukah, all right?" Harry grabbed his hat. "I gotta go put some snow on this cheek before it swells up." He walked over to the pile of jackets Aunt Bina had been working on before dinner, trying to judge how close they were to being finished. "Ma, it's all right between us? I'm sorry for what I said."

Bina looked over at the jackets like a prisoner looking at bars. "Chanukah dinner, the Monday night after your Christmas, at seven o'clock."

"Seven?"

"It wouldn't hurt you to let your workers out a half hour early. For a Jewish holiday," she said.

"Okay, Ma. Whatever you say. And thanks for putting the rush on these."

Rose's eyes almost popped out of her head at his arrogance, but Harry grabbed his hat and was down the stairs before anyone could give him more grief.

On Sunday Rose and I went to Sinsheimer's Café at the far end of Essex Street for soda water after seeing a picture: *The Great Train Robbery*. Usually I was the one who argued for new inventions, but the moving pictures made me uncomfortable.

"A photograph makes a portrait of the soul, one moment of the soul," Rose said, excited, "But a moving picture is a record of a soul in motion."

"Yes," I agreed, trying to find a way into what bothered me, "and still it stops somewhere, so it has the same effect as a photograph. It has a beginning and end in time."

"But if I hold a photograph in my hand, what's moving in the photograph is my own feeling. The photograph is full of secrets. It's a ghost, a bad night or a good afternoon," Rose said, flushed with thought. "The moving picture is public – these people we never knew are now part of our lives. They move forward and drag us with them

into the future."

"You think the moving pictures are the future?" I asked.

"Of course. The life we live is like an old photograph, it's dirty and crumpled." She took a long sip of her seltzer. "You think our condition can be changed by many people acting together – "

"It can be, Rose. It will be," I said.

"Well, I hope you're right. But think if people saw it in the nickelodeons, all over America, in little towns – "

"A moving picture about women striking?" That was a new idea. "You're saying if we made a moving picture about women striking we would gain the sympathy of the masses?"

"More quickly than any pamphlet your socialists produce." Rose turned and looked at the counter. "Do we have enough money for a piece of cake?"

I checked my pocket and held up a nickel. "Get me a piece of apple strudel."

She came back with the strudel and chocolate cake. "You never get a stomach ache, do you?" I asked.

"Only when we argue," she said, though I knew she didn't mean it.

I was trying to imagine a political picture. "I don't know if we could get people to come to a moving picture about sweatshops. People go to these for entertainment – "

"To you everything is in a box," Rose said, her mouth full of cake. "Entertainment is one box, politics another and our friendship something else." She waved her fork in the air to illustrate the separate places.

I made a face about the last category but tried to let it go. I picked a little at my strudel.

"Why do people come to a speech?" Rose continued. "A speaker has to know tricks, tell jokes, or stories at least. Emma Goldman's magazine *Mother Earth*, for instance – each month it starts with a poem. I read those poems even if I don't read the tracts. Moving pictures draw people in. If you can tell a story the right way, it should be able to keep moving inside people after the show is over. Don't you think that would be true?"

"You might be right, actually." I wanted to embrace her right there. "But Mr. Carnegie isn't going to give us the money for it. How would we ever make something like that?"

"We won't. And that means we won't really be part of the future," she looked over my shoulder into the street and put her fork down.

"Oh, listen to this! When did you become a pessimist? Even if I agree with you that motion pictures are the future, and I'm not saying the future of what, even *if* – they still have no bearing on the world outside themselves. Everything has a future, its own future, lying inside it, waiting to tumble out with the days. A few inventions don't gobble up the personal meaning of that. The automobile—"

"Yes," Rose said, smiling again and finishing her cake, "it's exactly like the automobile."

I thought she was agreeing with me and I relaxed, making little balls out of the strudel crumbs, like I used to with candle wax. "Right. The automobile does not eat up the future of that horse across the street. That horse lives and has its own work and its own future."

"That's where you're wrong, Chava," Rose said. "The automobile does eat up the horse, and the moving pictures are eating us – if there's anything left after the sewing machines get us. You're the mechanic, you ought to understand. I'll make you a wager that in five years you'll agree with me."

"And what are you going to wager me?"

"Let's see." She looked back over at the case of kugls and salads. "A whole fancy dinner out, anywhere the winner wants to go."

"You think you'll be able to afford that?"

"Who knows? But I'm sure you'll be paying." Rose ran her tongue over her lips and laughed. "Are you going to finish that strudel or just play with it?"

"Here," I said, pushing it across the table. I felt excited and let down all at once, and I turned to look at the horse across the street again, stamping its foot, its breath condensing into cold white clouds under the curve of the street lamp.

Melt the world

"It can't be 5:30 already," I groaned.

"You say this every morning, yet you're usually the first one out of bed."

"But Shabbes, Rose, they could at least let you sleep until six."

"Shhh, you'll wake Papa." Rose laid her finger on my lips and I kissed it. Then Rose moved her finger along the line of my cheekbone and over my eyes. "You can sleep today. You enjoy it, lazy girl."

"I'm not lazy – "

"Always an argument. Next you'll get mad, you'll say you won't come to meet me after work." Rose stretched, sat up in bed.

The room was so dark. It would be nicer to have our own place. But the money, the Petrovskys. Everything was always waiting. Working and waiting.

"So who wants to go all the way over to Washington Square just to see you?" I said, giving her a little poke in the thigh.

Rose turned towards me, trying to make out my face in the bit of streetlight that filtered past the fire escape. "You're teasing me, aren't you?"

I tried to pull her back down and she clicked disapproval. "Oh babychins," I whispered, "just a little – ," and Rose was back against me, the top of my head pressing into Rose's neck, my hand kneading flesh through the nightgown. So quiet.

I remembered last month, on the Greene Street sidewalk where she worked, Rose had said, "When you touch me, I try to imagine we have a secret cave in the snow, and there's no sound at all in there, only this fabulous warmth of you all over me. We melt the cave, we melt the world, until finally the sound comes out and there's a place where I can say 'I love you.' "

I laughed then because she'd said she loved me, right there on the street. We had been walking towards Washington Square Park as we usually did on Shabbes after Rose got off work. None of the other girls were near us.

"You know what I mean?" Rose had asked.

"Yes," I said, "you mean you want to go somewhere right now where you can express your animal nature with me." Rose banged her pocketbook against my rear.

Now in the dark Rose's face came close and her lips were suddenly against me. I shied away. "I don't taste good."

"I don't care," Rose said and pushed my mouth back to hers, just a moment. Just a quick, thick morning kiss.

"If we lived alone," I whispered in her ear, "I would have time to eat a peppermint first. I'd have time to buy flowers – I'd buy all the flowers in Mrs. Berger's flower stand and fill the bed with flower petals. Then – ," I yawned, half dreaming, "I'd roll you down on them. Hmm. You'd get flower petals stuck everywhere."

Rose stiffened, moved away, then turned back. "What makes you think we'd have more time if we lived alone?" she whispered in my ear.

"At night, anyway, at night we would."

"Stop. We're going to argue and that would wake everyone up. Just go back to sleep now."

I shook my head, teasing with mouth and eyes, "No, I'm going to watch you dress, and you know it."

"You can't see anything in the dark, just sleep, all right?" and Rose slipped out of bed. I could make her out, changing into a white striped shirtwaist, bright, outlining her full breast, her thick arms and wide shoulders. She wound her hair in a loose braid and pinned it up.

She seemed so strong, so tender. Sometimes when I looked at Rose, the pain I felt, in my stomach, in my shoulders, disappeared. Drained out of me somehow. Look, I wanted to say, you've cured me, I can eat pancakes for hours just because you make me happy. That would be nice, maybe I should make pancakes for supper, for everyone, all the Petrovskys. They'd like that. Everyone would relax, Uncle Isadore would wind his watch, Aunt Bina would complain I was giving Rose too much, I was eating too little, the boarders would drip syrup on their shirts, it would be a lot of fun. They would like it. Rose would like it. She'd say she could still taste the syrup when she got into bed ...

I curled up on my side. Rose, dressed, leaned over me and kissed me goodbye.

Someone was singing "Let me call you sweetheart" in an apartment on Mercer Street as I walked by later that afternoon. It was a beautiful spring day, the second Saturday after Purim. I swung my arms, humming along in English, *I'm in love with you*. Then I heard a muffled boom close by and my stomach flopped against my ribs like a fish gasping for air. When I turned the corner onto Washington Place, an old man, running wildly with his hands flailing above his head, almost knocked me over.

Suddenly noise was everywhere, the noise of panic, confusion. Horses pulling a fire truck clattered past. I don't know why but my hand went to the brooch Rose gave me last month for my birthday: a woman's head in relief like you can buy in half the stores on Hester Street. We called her our little Gitl, and Rose had said to brush her tiny lips with my fingertips when I needed to remember.

I stood flat against a brick wall with my hand over the brooch, over my throat, trying to make sense of the people running and the noise. "The factory! It's the Triangle factory!" someone yelled just as I saw a snake of smoke rise out of the upper windows of the Asch building on the corner of Greene Street.

No. I picked up my skirt and started to run towards the commotion and smell. In front of the building firemen and police were holding people back, holding people screaming. The street was full of screaming, smoke was pushing against the windows up there, on the top floors, breaking the glass as if the smoke had grown fists.

Mrs. Goldman stood in front of her café, gripping her broom.

"What do they think they're doing?" she shouted. "Throwing those burning bolts of cloth – Oh my God!" At the same moment she and I saw the legs scissor open as the smoldering girl smashed onto the pavement. I looked up. Girls were standing on the ledges. I counted the stories. Two groups were pushing through the jagged panes on the eighth floor.

Rose worked on eight.

More girls balanced on the ledge above. Some were screaming too, but most seemed quiet. The real yelling was down on the street, which was jammed with people who had been in the park and then with the Triangle workers who had managed to escape. One girl's hair was burnt around her neck, another was stumbling, trying to see out of a pair of smashed eyeglasses. I scanned their faces, then looked back at the ledge.

Where was Rose?

I grabbed one of the girls by the shoulders. "Rose Petrovsky, have you seen Rose Petrovsky?" She stared at me as if she'd seen the fearful face of God and started sobbing, bleating out something in Italian before she pushed past me. The firemen were stamping furiously beside their trucks. They had extended the ladders as far as they could go – the ladders stopped two floors short. The water from the hoses couldn't even reach the women on the eighth-floor. A terrible shrieking was coming from the side of the building.

Then sound stopped in my ears. Looking up, I could make out two women taking each other's hands as a spear of flame prodded at their sides through the broken glass. They plunged into the air, kicking their legs, as if to keep themselves aloft. The firemen held out a net, slipping back and forth through the wet red street, trying to stay under the jumpers. They managed to get the net right below the two girls, but they broke through as if it were tissue paper and smashed on the ground. Where were their sounds? Where was – ?

I looked up again and realized a woman was holding me. Her mouth was moving but if she was saying something, I couldn't hear. I should have been screaming, yet nothing escaped my throat, everything was caught inside, shaking, cold. The woman I'd never seen before was trying to hold onto me but I felt I was exploding and wrenched myself free. The green metal sheets that opened up the sidewalks for basement deliveries were stained black. Firemen piled bodies on top of each other like logs. The gutter was running blood.

Running blood. Somebody should have been helping them – . The woman who had been holding me disappeared, came back – no, it was Mrs. Goldman this time, with a cold rag. With many cold rags. She pressed one to the back of my neck and I took a deep breath. A terrible stench filled the air, burning machine oil, clothes, hair, flesh. Gutke said something to me about the smell of death, what was it? I shook my head to clear it and squeezed Mrs. Goldman's hand. Then I walked up to every woman in the street, everyone coming out of the building. Women and men were crying, holding onto each other, their skirts and blouses torn.

"Rose Petrovsky, do you know her? Have you seen her?" A woman looked up at the ledge, covered her eyes with her hands and didn't remove them. I saw Clara, who gave the speech in Cooper Union that started the Uprising. Clara was frantically moving from one group of bodies to another, wailing and laughing with the same breath.

A man was watching Clara from the other side of the street, taking

notes. Another tall, skinny man chewed a cigar. "Let them burn," I heard the skinny man say to the notetaker. "They're a lot of cattle anyway." The notetaker's mouth opened and shut in surprise.

The taste of blood filled my mouth. I couldn't look at the other lookers anymore. I tried to get close to the doorway but a policeman stopped me. "Can't let you past here, miss," he said. "We're doing the best we can. If you want to be useful, go look over there by the fire carts and see if you recognize any bodies."

The street was full of bodies, so many bodies in just one little street. They were being piled into ice carts and delivery trucks, into fire and police trucks, ambulances. At home it hadn't been like this, all together – just one, then two – just one and – . I closed my eyes. No. Not Rose. Not Rose. Not Mama. Not Rose.

Sound stopped again. There was a different smell. Rose's perfume and the smell of something I couldn't place.

Flame spikes up through the floorboards.
Everyone is running
 yelling
 you can hear it
 even though the flames are moving faster than sound
 open mouths

let me out of here I have to get downstairs don't you understand?
let me through let me through

how can this happen to me?
 how can this
 how can it to me? *to me?*

I was good I lit the Shabbes candles
I was about to meet my lover I was engaged to get married
I was pregnant I was bringing my pay check to Mama

I'm trapped by the wall window coat hooks door elevator
beating on the locked door

I'm too young
 can't you hear we're too young we're just girls

 we are just girls
 this can't happen
 an hour from now the floor would be empty
 this –
look at us
 we came on ships
 from small towns in Italy Russia Poland
 from big cities where there were no jobs
 we were grateful for these jobs last year
 I kept my machine oiled and never talked back
 I had such a good stitch

 unlock the door! enough already
 let us out

 someone drags a girl to the window a rag doll
 breaks the glass pushes

my lover is downstairs waiting for me
 I don't want her to see me like this

Chava I worked sewing since I was fourteen
 seven years in sweatshops
 and still I had pride in my needle

Chava I went to the window but I saw what happened to the girls
 who jumped
 I tried to get back to the door
 the black stripes on my shirt
 burn first

Chava wait wait for me this heat
 my face cracking crackling

there's another story where I get back to you
 where I'm on the last elevator that makes it down
 where I crawl across the roof
 where I fall onto a fire escape and rave in the hospital for a week
 but survive
 Chava I tried the door of all these stories

　　　　　　but each was locked from the inside

I'm scared　　　　　　angry
it's too hot here　and I can't breathe　　the fire is on my hair
oh god　　I'm batting at it with my hands but
my skin is peeling back in strips
　　it hurts　　it burns inside my lungs　　my lungs are going to burst
if I close my eyes　　Chava　　　Mama　　　Mama
　　this can't be happening to me

Chava　　　don't let this happen to me I can't
　　　　　　I can't open my eyes　　　I can't

Rose touched my cheek.

"So fast, Chava, you wouldn't believe how fast it is. I tried so hard to get to you. I knew you would be out in the street. I didn't want you to see me fall. The doors – I pushed and pushed, but they were locked, we couldn't break through. I got trapped against the back wall. They'll find me there. You'll be able to identify me by the ring you gave me. I clutched it tight in my hand, I never let go. Oh Chava, I wanted my life. I wanted my life. I'm so sorry."

Ash was blowing through the streets. There were no more falling bodies. The eighteen minutes were over. One hundred and forty-six had died and their spirits were filling the small street, the streets beyond Washington Square, teaming, pushing, trying to get home, trying to speak with their last energy, almost all young Jewish and Italian women trying to get to their mamas, to their families, to say: Don't worry, it was fast, I died quickly, keep me with you, keep me alive within you, I didn't know this morning to say goodbye, to say I love you, remember me, Mama – *how could this happen to me?*

The spirits were called quickly. The mothers in their kitchens sat down. Everything was suddenly wrong. They didn't know why and then there was shouting in the street below the window.

I bent over and put my hands in the gutter. They came up red and black. I smeared my face, my shirtwaist, with the dirt. The man with the notepad came up to me probably thinking I was one of the ones who fled the building. "No, no. I have to go home now."

I made my way to Houston Street. How was I going to tell Aunt Bina? How could I go back to our room, our bed, our – . I slumped

against a wall.

I'm not sure how much time went by before I felt someone put their hand under my chin, lift my face up. Blue legs, blue coat, blue cap. I swatted the hand away.

"Chava." A familiar voice. Aaron. "Chava," he said again. "You weren't in the building, were you?" His voice shook. His face was out of focus. I looked at my arm and saw that my shirt was torn and covered with blood.

"No, they wouldn't let me in."

"I just came from there. The firemen couldn't get in themselves until a couple of minutes ago. Did you see Rose?"

"Rose is dead," I heard myself say, letting my head drop back down.

"We don't know that," Aaron's voice broke. "She could be in the hospital or someone could have – "

"Rose is dead, Aaron, Rose is dead. Gutke said there's a smell – here, smell, smell it." I shoved my palm under his nose.

He forced his arm under mine and pulled me up. "C'mon, Chava, can you walk? Good. Come with me. Here, take my arm."

"No, I can walk myself. I'll come." I walked very slowly, shuffling, kicking at the dirt on the sidewalk. I felt faint but I didn't want to admit I needed Aaron's help.

"Look, Chava, are you going to be okay to get home?"

I nodded.

"Are you sure? I have to go down to the pier and help – "

"I gave Rose a ring," I mumbled.

"What?"

"A little silver ring with a garnet. It's in her hand."

I felt Aaron shiver. "All right, I'll look for it. You sure you can make it back to Essex Street? It's a long walk."

"Go ahead, Aaron, do what you have to do. I'll be fine." I started to cry and Aaron put his arms around me.

"Take it slow," he said after I calmed down. "Tell Mama I'll come by as soon as I can. Tonight." As he ran back towards Greene Street, he kept turning his head and waving.

I picked my way along the cobbles in the street. Everything was greasy with ash. The street – I had to fight a desire to lie down and rub my hands over the paving stones.

I found myself standing in front of our building. Looking at the fire escape. Rose. Everything was so close at this minute. Rose was so close to me. Maybe she went home early, sick, maybe she quit like she

always said she was going to, maybe they fired her, oh please, let them have fired her at noon, let her be there, waiting for me, crying for all the girls.

Rose floated above the fire escape, her head circled in flames. Rose beat against my chest in the street until we were both sobbing, heaving.

"Chava," Rose cried, "you have to be brave now for my Mama. Chava, please, please, don't let me go."

A Law of Physics
Saturday, March 25,1911

One body falling alone is its own weight
times distance.
Two bodies falling alone are their own but
if they hold hands
their weight is multiplied.

Here's a for instance:
Two girls are on a ledge.
The building is burning.
There are nets below.
The girls are young and for the purpose
of this example
thin and frightened.
It is eight stories to the ground.
The net can hold 90, 120, 150 pounds
times the distance but
holding hands
they become 11,000 pounds on impact.
The net breaks.
No one knows the price
of comfort,
how much they loved each other
and expected, by jumping,
neither to live nor die
but fly
released
from the Triangle Shirtwaist Factory.

Days went by while they identified bodies at the 26th Street Pier, where the city set up the morgue. Harry came into the bedroom and sat on the bed for awhile, running his hands around the brim of his derby. He told me there was a hailstorm the first night that smashed the glass roof at the pier. Who was angrier, the living or the dead? I noticed he was observing shive by not shaving. Aaron was in and out of the apartment for a couple days. I mostly stayed in the room. In our room. Yesterday Aunt Bina came in with the little ring clutched in her fist.

"Is this the ring you told Aaron you gave Rose?" Her eyes were red, her hair a tangle around her shoulders. She held out her arm and opened her palm. The fire had turned the silver a golden black.

I had only memorial candles for light, still I could see that someone had rubbed off the burnt skin. "Yes," I said, "this is the one. They found it in her hand?"

"In her hand," Bina said, choking. "Aaron and Harry both looked but they couldn't make out her face."

"Should I go down there?"

"You don't have to. If this is the ring, they're sure now it must be her."

"Do they need the ring back?"

"No. Aaron says you can keep it."

"If you want it, Aunt Bina." I extended the ring to her. Tears streamed down both our faces.

"No. I can't," she said, backing out of the room. I heard Aaron talking in the hallway, his feet thudding down the stairs.

All my life I wanted not to cry in front of anyone. Now there was no one left to watch me not cry. I sat on the edge of the bed and couldn't stop. Rose. Mama. Papa. All those girls. The woman in Kishinev with the nails through her eyes. Rose. I clutched the ring in my hand, with the other I wiped tears off my face. I put the ring under my pillow. Imprinted under my eyelids was the after-image of the bodies on Greene Street. I coughed the paper dust of the bindery. My face was still wet, my hands, my shirtwaist – I ripped it apart. I sucked air in and when it came out I moaned *Rose*, shaking my head back and forth, closing my eyelids, dropping my chin, shaking, sighing. Lamentation was my only relief.

My aunt sat at the kitchen table, sewing again. She watched the needle piercing the cloth, in and out: How many stitches in a life? She had only had one daughter and America swallowed her whole. She had been afraid of losing Rose bit by bit to dance halls, strangers,

English. America took whatever it wanted. It didn't ask, it didn't even make a law, it just reached out, like an eagle in the pictures of America, on its money, reached out with its big muscles, its claws, and grabbed. Grabbed her daughter, shook her one way and then the other until she was dead.

Bina must have realized the apartment was full of my crying, a wind inside, banging on the doors to get out. She stopped the sewing machine. The boarders were at work, Uncle Isadore with the funeral committee, Harry was back at his shop. Just her and me, sifting through the ashes of our grief. Did Bina think, "Like a lover, she mourns Rose"? I felt her pausing, wondering.

Everything had become so slow. Could Bina finally hear what she was saying to herself? Of course. Like a lover.

It took Bina a long time to stand up. Everything ached. It was only a few steps down the hall. So pleased they had been, to have a hallway with a closet. I sensed Bina looking in at me, curled on my side on top of the featherbed, my hands covering my face. She came around the other side of the bed and lay down next to me, embracing, holding. I turned towards her, weeping. The force of my tears made Bina cry again herself. She unbuttoned her shirt and pulled me to her, cradling me and stroking my hair.

We lay in the dark bedroom, crying and rocking, until she heard the outside door slam.

"Bina," Uncle Isadore called. Aunt Bina didn't hurry. She sat up, buttoned her shirt. She looked at me in the dusk and I returned her gaze, opening my swollen eyes as far as I could. She rubbed and patted my hand, balled up as it was into a fist.

"I'm sorry I didn't understand," she said, before she left the room.

Gutke writes ...

Dovida wanted to drive her auto in the memorial procession, an idea she had about showing the workers they had allies.

"The workers – and Chava – don't care about allies right now," I told her the evening before. "You always want to show you're different from the rest of the world. But I'm not. The entire East Side is in mourning and I want to be another old woman, walking with the nurses of Henry Street and the poor people I came from." Dovida ran her hands through her slicked hair and dropped her chin to her chest. Grief doesn't always bring people together.

Still, we had been sharing life for almost twenty-seven years. And no matter how separate we were at any particular moment, her touch comforted me, brought back Golde and my mother, the old horse that pumped water for Pesah's bathhouse. Golde, at least, was still alive. She sent me a letter with a little bit of handmade lace every Pesach.

Pesach, the feast of renewal. What a terrible thing to have to bury all those children in the spring. My hand trembles as I write. Besides Rose, I knew one other girl, Sophie, who died in the fire. She had been taking nursing courses at night and often assisted us at Henry Street on her day off. The morning of the funeral, rain woke us, hitting hard against the windows. I was glad for the rain and glad that Dovida didn't use it as an excuse to bring up the automobile again. She handed me my black umbrella. As we left the house, she ripped her sleeve. This drew me back to her and we linked arms, joining the thousands who were walking towards Fifth Avenue through the wet streets.

Some days are long enough. Somewhere ahead of us horses pulled coffins to the Workmen's Circle Cemetery. We walked and walked, silently, listening to a slow drum beat. Others watched from the sidewalks, mostly somber and dignified. A few miscreants worked the crowd, selling hat flowers and necklaces they said had belonged to the dead. Whether they had stolen them on the pier or made up their stories didn't matter. People actually bought. Why? The same reason people came to Milcah and me for potions that would cure their troubles. A keepsake from the dead, a souvenir of disaster that might keep disaster away.

It was during the memorial service at the Metropolitan Opera House that I saw Chava, but I don't think she noticed me. She was sitting with a short, freckled woman and two men, clearly a father and son, the father with a clipped, modern beard, the son beardless. They must have been Rose's family. The mother was round-shouldered, no doubt from piecework. Or sorrow. Most of the backs in the great hall were bent with sorrow.

The talis vest that Milcah made hadn't fit me in years, but I'd opened the seams and wore it around my shoulders, under my dress. I didn't want to take any chances on bringing the specters of those burned girls into the memorial. Their charred and smashed bodies were vivid enough without being dragged back from the realm of the dead.

Even so, when Rose Schneiderman said, "Too much blood has been spilled," I glanced over at Chava and was horrified to see blood covering her face, running down her chest. I must have gasped.

"What is it, dear?" Dovida whispered.

"Chava," I said, nodding to where she sat.

When Dovida looked at Chava and back at me, puzzled, I realized I was the only one who was seeing the blood. I kept glancing at Chava during the speeches. Gradually the blood drew back from her face and the stains on her clothes dissolved. By the end of the memorial I stopped holding my breath.

It is customary not to return to a cemetery for thirty days after a burial. I had never been one for visiting graves. I did think to lay stones on my mother's and Pesah's graves before I left Kishinev, only once. I had to go to too many funerals as it was, since mothers expected me to attend when a baby died in childbirth. I wanted to show respect at those times, of course, but also that I wasn't in league with Lilith and that no demons were involved in the tragedy – at least none that entered with me.

So it seemed odd to find myself taking the trolley back to Workmen's Circle Cemetery in May. At first I attributed my desire to visit the graves to growing sentimental with age. Or perhaps I had unfinished business with the dead that only being by their side would reveal. When I saw the cloaked figure kneeling by a fresh mound, I realized it had been the living who called me.

At first I thought it was Chava but the woman was too short. I stood back some distance. Finally the woman straightened, brushing dirt off her skirt. When she turned around, I recognized her as the freckled woman sitting beside Chava the night of the memorial.

"Mrs. Petrovsky?" I asked, quietly.

She looked startled and drew her cloak around her throat.

"Do I know you?"

"No. I knew your daughter, Rose."

"Rose?" She looked perplexed.

"From the Henry Street Settlement. I met her there with Chava Meyer."

"Oh," she said, relaxing. Many strangers were showing up at the doors of the families of the dead, soliciting funds for unneeded grave markers or fake charities.

"I was also your sister Miriam's midwife in Kishinev," I added.

Her hand went up to her throat. I glanced around and motioned to a stone bench not far from where we stood.

"Excuse me," she said. "I'm not usually easy to startle. I spend so much of my time with only the family at Essex Street. Mr. Petrovsky belongs to a landslayt association, of course, but I hardly ever meet someone from home." She paused and looked at the mound where the unidentified Jewish Triangle workers lay buried together. "My daughter, my sister – ." She raised her eyebrows and stared back into my face. With her dark brown eyes and fair complexion, she looked more like her sister than her daughter. Even in the extremity of her emotion, she had a clear, strong gaze. "I'm sorry, I didn't get your name."

"Gutke – ," I was about to say Gurvich and quickly switched to "Greenbaum. Your daughter and Chava came to my home several times."

"She did? Why?" She regarded me carefully.

"I invited them after lectures, things like that. Mr. Greenbaum and I have no children of our own, so we appreciate when young people honor us with their presence."

Mrs. Petrovsky smiled faintly. "It seems I took my daughter's presence for granted."

"I didn't mean to imply that," I said.

"No, you didn't. I just see that we never know what blessings we have until – ." She started to cry and I reached for her hand. "I don't want to talk in proverbs," she said after awhile, wiping her face. "Tell me about my daughter, how she was in your home, at the settlement."

I didn't realize how many stories I had to tell Mrs. Petrovsky. Not only about how generous and lively her daughter was, but about Miriam and our old life in Russia. We stayed on that hard bench for hours. Only at sunset did we catch the trolley back to the Lower East Side, holding hands like old friends.

"Not guilty! *Nisht shuldik!*" the newspaper boy in front of the bindery called out. Across the street, another boy yelled, "*Non Colpezole!*" holding up what I took to be an Italian daily. "*Nisht shuldik!* Read all about it. Not guilty! Paper, lady?"

"Give me both the *Forward* and the *Call*," I said, handing him a dime. Little snowflakes fell on the headlines as he pulled out the papers I wanted. I skimmed the words but they were too hard to believe and I rolled the papers back up, tucking them under my arm. The wind was stronger. I pulled the scarf tight around my throat. If I

had been on that jury I would have hung Harris and Blanck. Personally. Didn't they used to burn people at the stake? I would have lit the fires underneath their feet. I would have stood close to the fires and watched their ugly faces: *Now do you know what you did to those girls?* Only when their hair caught on fire would I have looked away.

My feet packed the light snow down on the pavement. I felt each footstep, furious, deliberate. At the top of the steps to our tenement door I looked back, expecting sulfurous smoke to rise from where I walked, but the print of my overshoes was melting unremarkably into brown December slush.

Bina, Isadore, Leon and Harry were eating dinner. Shmuel had left for a chicken farm in California almost six months ago. Harry started coming regularly on Shabbes after the fire, and some other times during the week when I was at the bindery, to pick up and drop off Bina's piecework. On the sideboard the Shabbes candles flickered.

"You're later than usual. Did they keep you overtime?" Isadore asked.

"Overtime?" I left the bindery exactly at 5:30, as always. Where did I go? "No, just walking. Did you hear the news?"

Bina looked at Isadore and then up at me. "Yes. Come, sit, eat. I made kneydlekh." She got up and spooned out a bowl of soup.

I shook out my coat, hung it up. For her, I sat down. Leon passed me the challah. There was only the clink of spoons in bowls, slow, tense. I couldn't join in this old music of sigh and slurp. Instead I made marbles out of the soft white challah, the way children do, rolling it under my fingertips.

"I don't understand," Isadore finally said.

I guess the strain got to Harry. His father had asked a thousand questions that he never deigned to answer – but this, that wasn't even a question, he had to jump on.

"Maybe you didn't follow the trial closely," he said in English.

"What's to follow?" Leon asked, then blinked as if he hadn't meant to get into this.

"Harris and Blanck said they were being singled out for all this publicity because they're Jews. That's anti-Semitism," Harry said.

"Singled out because they're Jews! Imagine trying to claim that as a defense, as if they were Dreyfus. Who singled out all those Jewish girls to die – were they planted in the factory by anti-Semites?" Isadore let his spoon clang into his dish.

"All right, Pop, but you have to admit it looked like the girls'

testimony was coached – "

"Most of the girls don't speak any better English than Aunt Bina, no offense," I said and Bina waved her hand in the air to dismiss any idea of disrespect, "and they were scared, still shocked. What difference does it make if they're coached to tell the truth?"

Harry put his palms out, bunched his shoulders up. "Chava, I'm only saying it didn't look so good. Everyone knows there are always girls in factories not as smart or clean as they should be."

"What's that supposed to mean?" Isadore stared at his son. "The boss is responsible, that's that."

"Pop, I feel as bad about what happened as anyone. But in a factory there are always accidents. The girls get sloppy. We had a fire even in my place last month – "

"In your factory you had a fire?" Bina stared at him, her eyes wide.

"It got put out, Mama. I only lost one rack of pants."

"You lost a sister, or maybe that doesn't count as much as pants to you?" Isadore pushed his soup bowl to the center of the table.

"You're deliberately twisting what I'm saying. All I meant was an owner can't be everywhere at once, making sure there's not a single oily rag left in a corner – "

"In your factory you allowed a fire?" Bina said again. She moved slowly to the sewing machine, tore the pair of trousers she was working on out, threw it on the stack, picked up the fifty-pound bundle, finished and unfinished, and dumped it by the door. "You take these out of here. You don't bring me sewing ever again, do you hear me?"

Harry got up. His face was splotched, red where his anger rose and yellow where his little-boy fear overcame him. "If that's the way you want it. But you're making a mistake – "

"You're the one making a mistake. I hold you responsible for every hair on the head of every girl who ever works for you, you understand, Ephraim? Every hair!"

"Pop – " Harry turned to Isadore.

"Don't look at me. I back your mother 150 per cent! You want to be an owner, fine, but if you can't be an owner and a mentsh at the same time, better you should be a pushcart peddler. The boss is responsible for the safety of the workers, and that's that." He folded his arms across his chest.

Harry shrugged, got his derby, picked up the bundle and kicked the door open. "I miss Rose as much as you do!" he shouted from the

landing. "You don't have to take this out on me!"

Leon looked at me. I looked away, got up, cleared the plates. Aunt Bina went into her bedroom and slammed the door. We could hear her pacing back and forth. It didn't take Isadore more than a minute to follow her.

"Guess I'll go out. They say there's a new picture show, almost forty-five minutes long, at the theater on Broadway. Want to come?" Leon asked.

I knew he was trying to be polite, but I was shocked by his insensitivity. I said no. Leon hurried out into the night, a lost beetle of a man, still looking for a way to be at home in a country he only pretended to understand.

What was I doing in this place? I listened to Bina's and Isadore's voices in the next room, the anguish, anger and grief beating against the walls of the apartment. By now the griefs we suffered should have knocked all the timbers loose, the tenements should have been crumbling under the blows of our losses. I couldn't stay much longer. I'd been holding Rose's shadow for nine months, trying to calm her, to be a salve on the wounds of her sudden death. I walked into our room and looked across the bed to the window, out beyond the fire escape. Rose was gone. I lay down listening for her heartbeat, the way I'd heard it filling the world every hour since the fire. Tonight there was only my own heartbeat and the sound of wind blowing snow across the metal grates.

"I don't know what to say to her, Gutke, you talk to her," Dovida said.

"It's too much for a young person."

"It's too much for anyone but she can't fold up forever."

I could hear their voices from the kitchen. Lately it seemed I heard much better. I could distinguish the sounds of every gear and strap in the folding machine from the sounds of the binder's engine. I knew which horse was coming down Essex by its hoofbeats and its cough. The chestnut mare of the iceman, for instance, paused for a second before putting its leg down, as if it couldn't believe the road would still be there. Before it had only been noise to me. Now I heard how silence coiled behind the city, below the noises. I found it first at the fire. Gutke could hear it too, I knew. She told me she'd never had such a bad headache as the day before the fire.

If I could make a way to the silence, I could sometimes hear the

dead. The dead were all around us. Cities had to make so much noise to cover them up, so we wouldn't be distracted from maintaining the engines that drove the machinery of profit. In Kishinev, I realized, we had more room in our ears, in our habits, to live with our ancestors –

Gutke was in front of me, offering me a handkerchief. I'd been crying again, unaware. She sat down on the other side of the sofa. I imagined the beams of an X-ray were like her eyes, the black one, the gold one, only they took pictures of our spirits, not of our bones. What does a spirit look like without its body? I let myself be drawn into her eyes, let her see whatever she wanted. What difference did it make?

"Chava, it's almost a year – "

"Eleven months and nine days by the Christian calendar."

She nodded. "There is a proscription for the length of mourning."

I was the rabbi's daughter – she thought I didn't know? You said kadish for eleven months to help the departed enter heaven, then no more, except on the anniversary of the death, because you didn't want people to think the dead person was so unrighteous they'd need a full year of kadish said for them. Rose, Mama, Papa – how long before our prayers helped clear their way to heaven? None of them could have needed more than a week. Heaven –

"Something is perplexing you?" Gutke asked.

"If there is no God, where do the dead go?"

"No God! Child," she opened her mouth, closed it again. "All right, we don't have to argue about this now. But don't you see how much comfort you could have, if you believed?"

"Comfort? Comfort!" Suddenly I was on my feet, pacing. "Comfort in God? God gives and God takes away, blessed are the mysteries of God? That God? Or the God who strikes down the enemies of Israel – where is He? God, if God has any feeling, how could He, how could –" I stopped. I saw my Mama lying over my Papa's body in the marketplace. I heard the sound of the wagons where they piled the bodies, those old creaky wheels. I stood there, listening. Then I heard Gutke take a deep breath.

"These things are not what God did, but what men do, out of neglect, fear and something horrible inside them we can't understand."

"But once they've shown how terrible they are, why are they allowed to go on? No one punished the men who killed my parents, and Harris and Blanck are back in business. No one cares about the girls who work for them."

"But you do," Gutke said.

"What?"

"You care about the girls and you care about justice. Justice, not vengeance. When we dedicate ourselves to justice, we honor not only the past but the future. When we become obsessed with vengeance, we get caught in the traps of those who do evil. Do you understand what I mean?"

"Not exactly." I sat back down beside her, feeling very weary.

Gutke folded her hands in front of her face for a minute, looking beyond me. "These men – Harris, Blanck, the Kishinev murderers and all the others – you don't want to spend the rest of your life living with them, do you?"

I motioned her to go on.

"You shouldn't forget them or forgive them – "

"Forgive them?" My hands curled involuntarily, my nails pressing hard into my palms.

"I just said, didn't I, you *shouldn't* forgive them. They are responsible for what they do and there is no forgiveness possible for such brutality. But if you are to go on living, you want to live with the people you loved, not their destroyers, am I right?" Gutke said, taking one of my hands and softly prying it open.

"The people I loved are dead."

"Yes, but you feel them, don't you?"

"All the time. More and more." Her palm was creased and soft.

"I thought that. All right, that's good. If they are with you, what is it they want from you now?"

"I – ." I looked away from Gutke. Rose wavered in the air in front of me, and behind her Mama, Papa stroking his beard, Bobe Malka who, I realized, when I saw her there, must be dead too, though Esther didn't mention it in her last letter. The faces of the dead became clearer. Rose put her hand out towards me. She didn't open her mouth but I heard her whisper, "I need you, Chava. I need you still." And then they all disappeared. I turned to Gutke.

"Did you see that?" I asked.

"Only some shadows by you."

"She said she still needs me."

"Do you understand what she means?" Gutke asked.

"No."

"May I tell you what I think?"

I nodded.

"You've been living in yourself as if you were dead, too. As if

337

everything you needed died with Rose in that fire."

"That's the way I feel most of the time." I pulled my hand away and started picking at a loose string on the sofa's arm cover.

"You understand that when Rose says she needs you, she doesn't mean for you to come to her by taking the gas?"

"No, she doesn't mean that." Rose would never have wanted me to kill myself, I realized.

"Good. That's good. So you have half of it." Gutke pressed her hands together with a clap.

"Half of what?"

"They need you to live, not to live 'for' them, exactly, but to live with them, to hold them in your living, to do what you would have done with them if they had been able to stay with you."

"But – "

"Sha." Gutke appeared to be listening to something herself. I couldn't hear anything except Dovida pacing in her study, the noise of traffic in the street. She cleared her throat, snapped her head around. "Your aunt. What is she going to do now?"

"Aunt Bina?" This change of subject confused me. It took me a minute to remember our apartment. "She's been saving money all these years, penny by penny. With that and the death benefit – ." I clenched. How much were those girls worth? Less than a sewing machine.

"Go on."

"Uncle Iz has the opportunity to buy a small jewelry store in Yonkers now. The man who had it, a landsman, is retiring. His sons didn't want to be in the business. Aunt Bina says it's a relief to be able to leave Essex Street, too much there reminds her. So they, we – "

"You were planning to move to Yonkers with them?"

"I guess I wasn't planning anything." I pulled out the thread I'd been worrying and wound it around my finger.

"So maybe you'll come by us until you know what you want to do next?"

"Live here?"

"Why not? There's an extra room where we put our guests. You wouldn't be a guest, exactly, but you could stay there."

"Dovida – ." I heard Dovida clear her throat in the doorway.

"I wouldn't mind if you stayed with us for awhile, if that's what you were about to ask," she said, stepping into the room. "It's better you should be in New York than in Yonkers. More opportunities."

"Opportunities?" What did I care about opportunities?

"She doesn't mean in business, dear," Gutke said. "Through Henry Street or the League – "

"The League?" I hadn't gone to the League since the fire. I meant to, but every day when I got home from work I was too tired.

"You have to repeat everything we say? You remember the League, surely," Gutke said.

"I was talking to Paul, Pauline Newman just a few weeks ago when I was in Chicago," Dovida said, sitting down in the easy chair across from us. "She said after the fire she couldn't do anything for weeks. Couldn't read, write, give speeches. Schneiderman and Reznikoff persuaded her to keep going and she went on to Cleveland, organized the cloakmakers there. She keeps resigning, but the garment workers keep asking her to come back. She's their only woman organizer, you know." She tapped the case of her pocket watch. "But she keeps on, and her life's not an easy one."

"She didn't lose – , " I started.

"You can't say that, dear. Pauline worked at Triangle for years. You don't know who she might have lost." Gutke raised an eyebrow at me.

"You're right, I don't know." I remembered Pauline on the Palisades, the knowing look she gave Rose and me. "Still, what's that got to do with me?"

"Everything," Dovida said, "don't you see? These women need you – Pauline, Lena, Rose Schneiderman, Lillian Wald – "

"Stop, Dovida," Gutke said, "you're overwhelming her."

"No, it's all right. It's – ." I got up and went over to the window. Across the street children were playing, people were strolling, arguing, gesturing, even though it must have been nearly freezing. "What can I do? All *I* know is gluing and machines."

Dovida snorted. "All these years of lectures, debates, marches, strikes, and all you know is gluing and machines?"

I turned around to face her, angry. She was smiling at me.

"Come," she said, "let's go look at your room. You'll tell me if there's anything you need. Then we'll go with you over to your aunt's, so she'll see you're moving in with a respectable bourgeois couple."

"She'll have trouble believing I know any bourgeoisie."

"Don't worry," Gutke said. "I already met your aunt, a very good woman. She'll be glad to know you're staying by us. I was your mother's midwife, after all, so to her it will be the same as family."

Dovida and I looked at Gutke in surprise, but she wouldn't say anything more.

● ● ● ● ●

Living with Dovida and Gutke was harder than I imagined. Everything in their home was either clean and new or old and valuable. It was easier to be a guest for tea. Going to the bindery then coming back to an impeccably kept house every night was unnerving. I started going over to the League offices in the evenings again. Not many of the allies were around at night, just working girls.

But things weren't going so well at the League, either. The allies, and even some of the American-born working women, thought Rose Schneiderman was spending too much time organizing the Jewish working girls.

"Too much time!" she said to me. "Maybe if I'd spent more time – "

"They don't remember your speech after the fire? That was the most moving speech I ever heard." Rose Schneiderman could always find something for a volunteer to do. I was filing papers for her.

"Thank you," she said, without smiling. "But speeches don't seem to change much. You don't know what I have to swallow to work with these American-born. Now they've hired an organizer who supports immigration restrictions, as if immigrants cause all of America's labor problems."

"That doesn't make sense."

"Everyone wants someone to blame. Organizers know that the easiest way to get group solidarity is to find a common enemy." She handed me a fresh stack of paper. "Only I thought we had agreed our enemies were capitalists, not poor people escaping pogroms."

"I agree." I had to keep repeating the English alphabet to myself under my breath while she talked.

"Yes, but you're not even on the executive committee anymore, are you?"

"What? Oh, no. When I stopped going last year, they replaced me."

"With an American girl?"

"Yes, now that you mention it."

She sighed, starting to sort a new stack. "Our secretary said, at the last meeting, 'The Russian Jew has little sense of administration. We have been used to ascribing their failures to their depending solely on their emotions and not on constructive work.' "

I turned around and looked at her in disbelief. "She said that? After everything you've done, all the work Pauline and Lena have put in, all the Jewish girls?"

"It's plain anti-Semitism," she said, getting up and pacing. The room must have been as familiar to her as Essex Street was to me. Desks,

telephone, American flag, photographs of the League presidents in other cities. "I have to resign. I can't let them think this kind of slander is acceptable, can I?"

"No," I said fiercely.

"The suffragists have been asking me to go to Ohio to stump for the referendum there." She sat behind her desk, picked up an eraser and started bouncing it nervously.

What must it be like to work for women's unions, and if that didn't work out, to work for the vote? Everyone wanted Rose Schneiderman because she was such a wonderful speaker. Even when she couldn't give you the answer, she could lay the problem out as quick and clean as you'd gut a fish.

"So what do you think?" she asked.

"About going to Ohio?"

She caught the eraser in her fist. "Probably it will do me good to get out of New York for awhile. And there's no doubt we need the vote. I think I was born a suffragist but if I wasn't, the conditions of working girls in New York would have made me one."

"You're already working on your speech," I said, turning back to the filing cabinet.

She laughed. "I'm sorry, I'm used to soap boxes. But the more I try to organize women, the more I believe we need the power of the vote."

"Last week I heard a speaker over by Delancey Street say that suffrage is a sidetrack, we can't depend on the state for solutions." I had listened to his whole speech. Nobody was waiting for me at home.

"That sounds like the Wobblies. They've done some wonderful things, but you saw what happened after 1909, how the momentum dissipated," Rose said with authority. "We have to be able to influence legislation, to make laws to protect women and children, or we'll never be safe at work. I know there are contradictions but we have to take the world where it is. If we start, maybe the next generation will be strong enough to fix our mistakes."

She fell silent, bouncing the eraser. Was it better to make practical compromises or hold out for the ideal? If you could agree on what the ideal was – my finger slipped among the papers and I had to start over again: A, B, C ...

"Rose Schneiderman is going to Ohio for the vote, is she?" Dovida folded her napkin carefully, tucked it into her shirt for a bib. Gutke had

made chicken fricassee for dinner, with baby carrots. "She's some firebrand."

I looked at Dovida to see if she'd heard herself, but she was busy sucking a neck bone. Gutke was watching, though. Rose Schneiderman's red hair, her anger, did make her seem like a torch, sometimes. Roses going up in flames. Except Rose Schneiderman didn't get consumed.

"Eat, darling, you've hardly touched your dinner. It doesn't taste good to you?"

"It's delicious, Gutke. Everything you make is better than the last."

"She's something, isn't she?" Dovida beamed at Gutke.

Suddenly I felt that I had witnessed too many of their private moments, that I couldn't stay with them anymore than I could still live with Aunt Bina and Uncle Isadore. "Maybe I should go with her," I said on impulse.

"To the kitchen?"

"She means with Rose, to Ohio, Dovida," Gutke said.

"I knew that." Dovida took another bite of chicken. "That's not a bad idea."

"You're ready to get rid of me?"

"Not at all, not at all. But it's good to have a change of scene. And working for an idea you believe in, that's the best kind of work there is." Dovida said.

"Nobody's offered me a job to do this."

"No?" Dovida sucked her teeth for a second. "Maybe I should hire you."

"You? I couldn't accept that. You've been too generous already."

"You know many of the working girls at the League, in the Socialist Party, get their wages paid by patrons who believe in what they're doing."

"Some people would say you buy the leadership now, so you won't have to worry later," I said, looking at the gravy on my plate.

Dovida screwed up her mouth, bobbed her head. "Good argument. I'll remember that. But we're not so worried about later, are we, Gutke?"

"Later takes care of itself, I've found out," Gutke said. "I don't think Dovida's offer comes from bad motivation, Chava."

"I'm sorry."

"No, don't be sorry. You should always ask what someone expects in return when they give you something." Dovida paused, chewing. "And I do want something in return."

"Which is?"

"I want you to keep working until the cause is won."

Both Gutke and I laughed. "Which cause do you mean?" I asked.

"The vote, to start. And then everything else you believe in – "

"But that would take my whole life," I protested.

"Exactly," Dovida said. She turned to Gutke. "Did you have time to bake today?"

Gutke raised her eyebrows. "Really, Dovida. I was working with the nurses from six o'clock this morning. You're lucky you got this."

"You didn't happen to bake, did you, Chava?"

I stared at her. For a second I remembered making challah with Mama. It had never occurred to me to bake anything in America.

"Just making sure." She whipped her napkin off, went into the front hallway and came back with a pink baker's box tied up with string. "I picked this up for my working girls," she said, pulling out the most beautiful pie I'd ever seen. "If I can remember how to turn the oven on, I'll heat this up and we can have it with tea while we discuss your trip to Ohio."

The pie, cherry, was so good we each ate two pieces.

"I hope you won't be disappointed if the food isn't so good out West," Dovida said. I realized we were taking it for granted that I was going. I cracked my knuckles.

"That's not the most ladylike habit, dear. I don't mean to criticize, but traveling with suffragists won't be the same as being a mechanic at the New World Bindery," Gutke said.

"You know – ." Dovida poked her finger into the air, stopped, looked at me. "You don't have to travel as a woman, you know."

"Dovida," Gutke warned.

I knew exactly what Dovida meant. "I always wanted to know how you pull it off."

Gutke cleared her throat and started to remove the plates. "This is not the world's best idea."

"I just want to know how it can be done, that's all," I said.

"She should have every option, don't you think, Gutke? Or am I still such a freak to you?"

Gutke dropped a dish. "Never – Dovida!"

"Let me clean that up," I said, while they were untangling each other's meanings with looks and gestures. I found the broom and started sweeping.

"Dovida." Gutke pulled a chair next to her, took her hand. "You

can't believe I ever thought of you like that."

"Then why are you so against it?"

"Because it's dangerous. I was thinking of Chava, not you. You've been doing this for years and you're a banker. Remember what happened to Oscar Wilde."

"That was different. Oscar Wilde went out of his way to provoke censure and thought no one would ever take him up on it. We know how the mob thinks and we know how to avoid giving them reason to think it. I'm not suggesting Chava do anything that she feels uncomfortable with."

"Think what would happen to her if anyone found out."

"She should have a good teacher, then, to make sure she doesn't get found out – *if* she decides to do it. What do you think, Chava?"

I leaned the broom against the wall. "I'm not sure. How do you think Rose Schneiderman would feel if I suddenly turned up as a man?"

"A very good question. What do you think, Gutke?"

"I think she would blink and then go on with whatever speech she was making. Rose Schneiderman is the last person I'm worried about. But something about this bothers me. For Chava," Gutke emphasized.

"Chava?" Dovida cocked her head to the side, looking me up and down.

I took a deep breath. "It would be easier to get a job as a mechanic."

"It will always be easier for men to get jobs as mechanics," Gutke says. "But you got one already as a woman."

"Yes, I did," I said, thinking about leaving the bindery, leaving New York, saying goodbye to Aunt Bina a second time. "Well, you could show me how and I can still decide later, can't I?"

"Absolutely," Dovida said. "Come upstairs with me."

There must be a road away from death. I came across seas to find it, leaving my mother's wig in the dust of Kishinev. The boat stank, the shops were filthy. We thought in America it would be different but only America's manners are different, and its clothes. Underneath all countries lies the same greed. Let me call it what it is – I'm not ashamed. How can I be ashamed anymore after I saw Rose in the fire?

She was soft and good to me. I tell myself stories about how good she was. I'm not always sure now that she really did rub her palm along my cheek. Her blue eyes – nothing else in life was that color, because the color in eyes changes on you: in a person's eyes, all of a sudden,

some feeling shuts out light. How can that happen? When we were children we'd pretend we could control a candle flame by thinking: – *now I will it to be small –*

How can I stop thinking about fires?

I tell myself stories about her goodness. The heat in our room was unbearable, but at least it drove everyone else to the fire escape. And if we lay with only our slips on, our breathing noisy, labored, who would think anything was wrong?

The engine strains against the train cars, eager to be off. I never would have believed the world stretched so far beyond the Pale. I still can't bring myself to speak about the sea, crossing the sea. I pretend I dreamed the crossing and if I try hard enough, I believe it, although my stomach is bad after that dream.

My stomach is bad. She would stick her finger in the cream at the top of the milk bottles and hold her hand out to me. She pulled my lip down and ran the cream against my teeth until I couldn't stand it anymore and I bit and licked her fingers. We were so lucky.

Listen to me! They murdered her when they locked those doors. All I can do is start moving again, preparing to learn America, traveling West.

This morning I looked up leaving the tenements of the East Side, catching bright blue between buildings at sunrise. A nice color but there was no color, really, like her eyes.

As the conductor yelled "All aboard!" I closed the notebook Gutke had given me as a goodbye present. She told me she'd been keeping a diary since she was forty. Forty! I thought, but said, "How will I live that long alone?"

Gutke smiled. "You won't be alone. Everywhere you go now there will be women to meet you."

"That's not what I meant," I said.

"I know what you meant," Gutke said, pushing a lock of my hair behind my ear. "You'll see. I know what I'm promising you."

I ran my hand over the notebook's rough brown cover and looked at my shirtsleeves. Rose might have made this very waist. I had decided to wear my own clothes, even after Dovida's warnings about traveling as a woman. If I'd made it across three seas, I could survive a train to Cleveland. Dovida was wonderful, and I was grateful for all she was doing for me, "for us," as she kept correcting. But after seeing my

costumed male reflection in her mirror, I realized I had no desire to enter into men's worlds. Women who didn't know Dovida's secret treated her deferentially, coquettishly, and I didn't want women treating me that way. I wanted to do my part in whatever lay ahead as a woman among women. So what if it was going to be hard? What hadn't been?

The train left the dark tunnels under Grand Central Station. I closed my eyes and felt surrounded by gentleness. Mama, Sarah, Aunt Bina, Lena, all the women of the League, Dovida, Gutke.

Rose.

Glossary

The following words are from the Yiddish, Hebrew, Aramaic, Russian and English. Yiddish words generally follow the YIVO Institute for Jewish Research modern transliteration guidelines, with a few exceptions (for instance, challah and mazel, which should have been khale and mazl) where the author found herself too attached to the old misspellings.

Transliteration Guide:

a = f*ar*, c*ar* ey = b*ay*, gr*ey*
u = b*oo*t, r*u*de oy = t*oy*
i = m*ee*k, l*ea*d kh = a*ch* (as in German)
e = b*e*t, r*e*d zh = bour*g*eois, mea*s*ure
o = m*o*ther tsh = *ch*ildren, bea*ch*, whi*ch*
ay = *eye*, wh*y* ts = le*ts*, *ts*ar

BABUSHKA. A kerchief or scarf worn on a woman's head and tied under the chin (from the Russian for grandmother).

BALEBOSTE. Homemaker (complimentary).

BAR MITSVE. The traditional ritual which marks the adulthood of thirteen-year-old boys and their taking on the full responsibilities of "men" in the Jewish community, e.g. communal prayer, Torah reading, etc. Most contemporary Jews allow a bat mitsve for girls at the age of twelve; this was not the practice at the turn of the century.

BAT KOL. "Daughter of a voice" (Hebrew), a voice believed by some religious Jews to emanate from God, angels or heaven, directing people towards some truth.

BENTSHN LIKHT. To recite the blessing over Shabbes or holiday candles; traditionally a woman's duty.

BESSARABIA. A province of southwestern Russia during the time this novel begins, bordered by Rumania on the west and the Black Sea on the south. The region often changed rulers and was detached from Moldavia in 1812.

BEYS MEDRISH. House of study, often a part of the synagogue.

BIRZHE. A gathering of workers, often secret, where leaders distributed jobs in factories and strategized about various workers' actions.

BUND. Founded in Vilna in 1897, a Jewish socialist workers' organization, which rejected Jewish observance and advocated instead for Jewish national cultural autonomy and the Yiddish language.

CALENDAR. The Jewish calendar consists of twelve lunar months within the solar year, with a "leap" month inserted seven times every nineteen years so the holidays remain seasonal. The Hebrew months are: Nisan, Iyyar, Sivan,

Tammuz, Av, Elul, Tishri, Kheshvan, Kislev, Tevet, Shevat, Adar and, on "leap" year, Adar II.

CHAIM YANKL. A Joe Shmoe, a nobody.

CHALLAH. Braided white bread made especially for Shabbes and holidays.

CHANUKAH. The eight-day "festival of lights" commemorating the victory of the Macabees over Greek invaders in Palestine in 165 BCE. Chanukah usually occurs sometime in December (see calendar).

CHAZAN. The cantor, a trained liturgical singer who assists the rabbi in leading the singing for religious services.

CHUTZPE. Arrogance, presumption, nerve, exceeding gall; while usually negative, sometimes pronounced with grudging admiration.

DAVEN. To pray. Davening is often accompanied by a bobbing motion.

DI ALTE HEYM. The old homeland.

DYBUK. An evil spirit, usually the soul of a dead person, that possesses the living and drives them mad.

FLANKEN. Potted beef brisket.

GEHENE. Hell.

GOLDENE MEDINE. The golden land – that is, the United States, where the streets are paved with gold.

GOTENYU. Familiar, affectionate, intimate form of addressing God.

GOY (s.), GOYIM (pl.). Non-Jews (pejorative).

HASKOLE. The Jewish reform/enlightenment movement started in Germany by Moses Mendelssohn in the eighteenth century, promoting modernization of religious Jewish practice, secular and scientific education, and the full participation of Jews as citizens in the countries in which they lived.

HAVDALE. The ceremony that marks the end of Shabbes on Saturday night, using wine, a spice box and a special twisted double-wicked candle.

KADISH. The prayer for the dead, traditionally recited by sons (or other male family or congregation members) during the eleven months after a parent has died and on the anniversary of her/his death.

KAYN AYEN-HORE. "Without the evil eye" – verbal antidote to jinxing something that has been praised as successful, good or beautiful.

KETUBA. The marriage contract, often an elaborate, decorative scroll.

KHEDER. Literally "room"; refers to the first school that Jewish boys attended between the ages of three and six; some towns also provided girls' kheders.

KIKHL. Little cookies, usually very plain.

KISHKES. Intestines (to refer to your stomach or intestines as kishkes is considered coarse); also, a sausage-like food made from beef intestine stuffed with grain, chicken fat and spices.

KNEYDLEKH. Matzoh meal dumplings, usually served in chicken soup.

KOL NIDRE. Literally, "all vows" (Aramaic); the solemn prayer recited at the beginning of Yom Kippur, chanted three times by the chazan.

KOSHER. The Biblical dietary proscriptions, the most common being not to eat meat and milk at the same time (keeping separate dishes for each), to eat only certain kinds of meat and fish, and to slaughter animals in a special way.

KREPLEKH. A triangular dumpling similar to ravioli.

LAMED VOVNIK. "One of the thirty-six" (Yiddish), from the belief that in every generation there are thirty-six hidden righteous people on whose merits the world depends. Based on the letters lamed (twelfth in the Hebrew alphabet) and vov (sixth), which have the numerical value of thirty- six when written together.

LANDSMAN (s.), LANDSLAYT (pl.). Someone who comes from the same town or region. There were dozens of landsmanshaftn organizations in New York alone.

LATKE. A potato pancake fried in oil, usually cooked on Chanukah to celebrate the miracle of the oil that lasted for eight days though there was only enough to keep the eternal flame lit for one.

LILITH. The legendary first partner of Adam. When Lilith found she couldn't achieve the equality with Adam that she demanded, she pronounced the secret name of God and chose to become a demon. Lilith often appears in the form of an owl and is considered a thief of souls, particularly children's. Feminists and lesbians have reclaimed her as a symbol of rebellion against male authority.

LUFTSMENTSHN. Those who live on air – poor people with no jobs or visible means of support. Shtetl dwellers were usually considered luftsmentshn because of the terrible economic conditions of their towns.

MAGIDIM. Itinerant preachers, often with reputations as good sermonizers.

MAMZER. A bastard.

MASKIL (s.), MASKILIM (pl.). The followers of the Haskole (see above) – enlightened, liberal intellectuals.

MATZOH. Unleavened bread, eaten during the eight days of Passover (Pesach) to symbolize the bread the Israelites baked when fleeing slavery in ancient Egypt.

MAZEL TOV. Congratulations.

MEGILE. Scroll, lengthy document; one of the five books of the Old Testament:

Esther, Ruth, the Song of Songs, Ecclesiastes and Lamentations, which are read on certain holidays; especially the Book of Esther, which is read on Purim. It has also come to mean any long or complicated story or proceeding.

MENORAH. Candelabra; usually refers to the eight-branched candelabra lit on Chanukah.

MENTSH. An upstanding, honorable person – someone to admire or a state of being to aspire to.

MESHUGINER. A person considered "crazy," wild or absurd.

MEZUZE. An oblong container attached to the right side of a door post, containing the first two paragraphs of the Shema (see below) and indicating a Jewish home.

MIDRASH. The exposition of Biblical scripture in which the text is explained differently from its literal meaning.

MIKVE. Women's ritual purification bath, taken before marriage and after menstruation or childbirth, and composed of natural (rain or spring) water .

MINYAN. Quorum; for religious rituals, ten males past the age of bar mitsve are traditionally required.

MITSVE. A good deed one feels commanded to do, a virtuous act that expresses God's will.

MOLDAVIA. A province in eastern Rumania bordering, and sometimes including, Bessarabia. The majority of the native population was rural and poor.

MOUJIK. A Russian peasant.

NARODNIK. A member of the Russian populist agrarian socialist movement that proposed a loose confederation of local cooperatives to replace the state. Active between the 1860s and 1900, Narodniki were replaced by the Socialist Revolutionary Party. The terrorist wing assassinated Tsar Alexander II in 1881.

NU. The verbal equivalent of a shrug, a frown, a grin, a grunt, a sneer or a sigh; an all-purpose interjection or interrogative.

NUDNIK. A real pest, an annoying and exasperating person.

THE PALE. The Pale of Settlement, the large area in western Russia to which Jews were restricted from 1791 to 1917. Jews were also forbidden to enter the "holy cities" of Kiev and Moscow within the Pale. Its boundaries changed according to the liberalism or anti-Semitism of the tsars.

PAYES. Unshorn ear-ringlets and sideburns worn by Orthodox Jewish males.

PESACH. Passover, the spring commemoration of deliverance from enslavement as recounted in Exodus; a major Jewish holiday.

PURIM. A holiday occurring about a month before Pesach, commemorating Queen Esther's triumph over Haman, who intended to destroy the Jews of Persia.

REBITSIN. A rabbi's wife.

ROSH HASHONAH. The Jewish New Year that begins the High Holy Days period, ending with Yom Kippur ten days later (see below). Rosh Hashonah usually falls in late September or early October. During the High Holy Days, the Book of Life is said to be open, and humans can affect what is written there by sincerely repenting their sins and directly righting the wrongs they've done to others.

RUGELAKH. A crescent-shaped pastry stuffed with nuts, fruits or jams.

SHABBES. The weekly Sabbath, beginning with the appearance of the first star on Friday and ending at sundown on Saturday; a time of rest and spiritual reflection.

SHABBES GOY. A Gentile who is asked or hired to perform domestic tasks, such as lighting fires or putting out candles, which are forbidden to Jews on Shabbes.

SHADKHN. A Jewish professional marriage broker.

SHAYNE MAIDELE. Pretty girl.

SHEMA. The first word of the Jewish prayer recited every morning and evening; literally, "hear."

SHIKSE. A young non-Jewish woman (usually pejorative).

SHIVE. The prescribed seven solemn days of mourning immediately after the funeral, where Jews "sit shive" in the home of the deceased, during which mirrors are covered, garments are rent, hair isn't cut and low stools or boxes replace chairs, among other customs.

SHLEMIL. A fool or a born loser; someone who's clumsy.

SHLEP. To drag or carry a burden.

SHMALTS. Literally, "rendered fat" (usually chicken); metaphorically, excessive sentimentality; commonly used in both senses.

SHOFAR. A ram's horn blown during the High Holy Days of Rosh Hashonah and Yom Kippur.

SHTETL. Small village or town in Russia and Eastern Europe where Jews were either a majority or inhabited significant Jewish quarters.

SHUL. A synagogue.

SHVITS. Sweat.

SIMKHE. A celebration or party.

TALIS (s), TALESIM (pl.). A striped, tasseled shawl, traditionally worn by men during certain prayers (some contemporary women have begun wearing them as well).

TASHLIKH. The symbolic casting away of sins into flowing bodies of water during the first two days of Rosh Hashonah.

TECHINOT. Women's prayer collections in Yiddish, often written by women.

TFILIN. Phylacteries – small boxes, containing passages from Exodus and Deuteronomy, strapped to the left arm and the forehead during weekday morning prayers by observant males.

TREYF. Any non-kosher food; hence anything unclean or anyone untrustworthy.

TSHATSHKES. Knickknacks.

TSHOLNT. A stew-like main Shabbes dish, kept in a hot oven overnight. Those without their own ovens would bring it to the bakery Thursday and pick it up Friday night before Shabbes. The ingredients vary, but usually include some combination of meat, beans, barley, onions and potatoes.

TSIMES. A sweet vegetable stew, usually containing carrots and potatoes.

VERST. A Russian unit of measurement, approximately two-thirds of a mile.

VOV. Sixth letter of the Hebrew alphabet (see lamed vovnik).

WOBBLIES. Nickname for the members of the International Workers of the World, a revolutionary international industrial union founded in 1905 in the United States.

YARMULKE. A skullcap worn by religious Jewish men.

YENTE. A coarse, meddling, gossipy woman.

YESHIVE. Institution of higher Talmudic learning; in the United States, an Orthodox Jewish all-day school.

YESHIVE BOKHER. A yeshive student; a real scholar.

YOM KIPPUR. The last day of the High Holy Days, on which one fasts from sundown to sundown and finishes the process of repentance that began at Rosh Hashonah.

YORTSAYT. The anniversary of a death, on which a memorial candle is traditionally lit.

ZIONISM. A nationalist movement for a Jewish homeland in Palestine. Theodore Herzl formulated the theoretical basis for the Zionist movement and convened the first Zionist congress in Basel, Switzerland in 1897.